She's in love with the boss!

Acclaim for Anne Weale, Day Leclaire and Leigh Michaels

About Anne Weale

"Ms Weale's masterful character development and charming scenes create a rich reading experience."

—*Romantic Times*

Acclaim for Day Leclaire

"Day Leclaire magnificently balances a superb romance with a gripping conflict and extraordinary characters."

—*Romantic Times*

Acclaim for Leigh Michaels

"Leigh Michaels gives fans a wonderful reading experience."

—*Romantic Times*

BOARDROOM *Affairs*

SOPHIE'S SECRET
by
Anne Weale

WHO'S HOLDING THE BABY?
by
Day Leclaire

DREAMS TO KEEP
by
Leigh Michaels

MILLS & BOON®

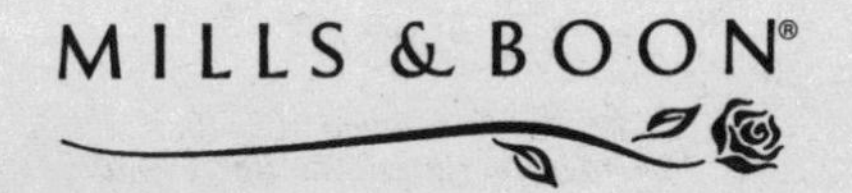

All the characters in this book have no existence outside the imagination of the author, and have no relation whatsoever to anyone bearing the same name or names. They are not even distantly inspired by any individual known or unknown to the author, and all the incidents are pure invention.

Harlequin Mills & Boon Limited,
Eton House, 18-24 Paradise Road, Richmond, Surrey, TW9 1SR

Sophie's Secret, Who's Holding the Baby? and *Dreams to Keep* were first published in Great Britain by Mills & Boon Limited in separate, single volumes.

ISBN 0 263 82412 8

05-0002

Printed and bound in Spain
by Litografia Rosés S.A., Barcelona

Anne Weale was still at school when a women's magazine published some of her stories. At twenty-five she had her first novel accepted by Mills & Boon®. Now with a grown-up son and still happily married to her first love, Anne divides her time between her winter home, a Spanish village ringed by mountains and vineyards, and a summer place in Guernsey, one of the many islands around the world she has used as a background for her books.

SOPHIE'S SECRET

by

ANNE WEALE

CHAPTER ONE

Surrounded by [illegible] Concorde passengers at New York's Kennedy Airport, Sophie Hill looked as calm and confident as the rest of the [illegible] travelers waiting to board their supersonic flight across the Atlantic to [illegible].

But her air of relaxed composure was superficial. Inwardly she was tense with excitement and uncertainty.

In her elegant suit and discreetly stylish jewellery, Sophie could easily have passed for a rising star in the legal or banking world, setting out on assignment to Europe. In fact she was a member of the utterly [illegible]-ential network of top people's personal assistants. After starting her career by temping for a [illegible] secretarial agency to gain experience, and then working in France for a time, followed by a stint with a [illegible] in Canada, for the past two years she had been PA to a New York [illegible] broker.

Now she was joining the payroll of someone much more important [illegible] [illegible] [illegible] [illegible] [illegible] [illegible] [illegible] [illegible] his name out of the papers.

Sophie had applied for the job [illegible] [illegible] [illegible] the Concorde flight [illegible] the reason behind [illegible] [illegible] in addition to [illegible] exceptionally generous salaries, her new employer treated the world[illegible]

CHAPTER ONE

SITTING in the Air France departure lounge for Concorde passengers at New York's Kennedy Airport, Sophie Hill looked as calm and confident as the rest of the cosseted travellers waiting to board their supersonic flight across the Atlantic to Paris.

But her air of relaxed composure was superficial. Inwardly she was tense with excitement and uncertainty.

In her elegant suit and discreetly stylish jewellery, Sophie could easily have passed for a rising star in the legal or banking world, setting out on assignment to Europe. In fact she was a member of the quietly influential network of top people's personal assistants. After starting her career by temping for a large secretarial agency to gain experience, and then working in France for a time, following that with a spell in London, for the past two years she had been PA to a New York insurance broker.

Now she was joining the payroll of someone even more important: the man at the summit of a vast international empire—but a man who kept a low profile and was said to maintain a press relations department to keep his name *out* of the papers.

Sophie had expected to fly business class to Italy. To find herself suddenly transferred to the Concorde flight to Paris had been unexpected, and she still didn't know the reason behind the last-minute change of plan. It seemed that, in addition to paying them exceptionally generous salaries, her new employer treated his worldwide team of personal assistants with unusual consideration.

All the same, she would have felt happier had she been able to meet him before signing the contract to work for him. The position she was taking up had some unexplained aspects that made her faintly uneasy.

She hadn't applied for the job because of its tempting salary. Its location had been the main lure. She would be working in Venice, arguably the most beautiful and romantic city in the world.

Shortly before take-off time, with most of the passengers already boarded, a latecomer entered the Concorde lounge.

Observant by nature and training, Sophie had already cast an interested eye over her fellow passengers, both those who had arrived before her and those who had followed her in. But the man who was pausing to speak to the ground stewardess by the entrance had things about him to catch the eye and the interest of even a less alert woman.

He was very tall and, despite being casually dressed, carried himself with a recognisable air of authority. Most of the men on this flight wore the uniform of chief executives: well-tailored city suits with expensive shirts and shoes, and the costly accessories appropriate to their standing.

The tall man wore cream-coloured trousers, a white shirt, open at the neck, and a single-breasted black jacket with the matt look of fine barathea. While Sophie and all the other passengers had overcoats, raincoats and various other accoutrements, he had brought nothing but a book.

As she watched him speaking to the stewardess, to her astonishment the girl nodded and indicated Sophie. With a word of thanks the tall man turned away from the desk, his stride bringing him swiftly to where she was sitting.

'Good morning, Sophie. I'm Marc Washington.'

Her job had taught her to maintain an appearance of unflappability in the face of almost any contingency. Even so, to be confronted by her new employer in these circumstances was the last thing she had anticipated and a severe test of her self-possession. She passed it, but only by a whisker.

'Good morning, Mr Washington. I wasn't expecting to meet you here.'

'Having to cope with the unexpected is one of the elements of working for me,' he replied as they shook hands. 'The flight is an opportunity for us to get acquainted. Shall we...?' The unfinished question was accompanied by a gesture in the direction of the boarding tunnel.

After stooping to pick up her bag, her book and her lightweight raincoat, she accompanied him across the lounge, her own height of five feet eight dwarfed by his much taller frame.

Although she had not had long to take in his features full face, her mind retained an impression of dark eyes under black eyebrows and a naturally olive skin still deepened by a summer tan.

But, of course, for a man of his means sunlight was available all year. Although he might have to spend much of his time in capital cities where winter brought bad weather, weekends at ski resorts or sailing from sunlit marinas would not, for him, be a rare treat. They would be frequent occurrences.

Somehow, with not much to go on, she had assumed Marc Washington would be a middle-aged workaholic, obsessed by high finance and complex power games. But he looked to be still in his thirties, with the physique of a man who kept fit in pleasurable ways—not, like her previous boss, by working out on machines in an expensive downtown gymnasium because his physician advised it.

From talking to other PAs whose bosses used Concorde regularly, Sophie knew the most coveted seats were the four at the front, often occupied by royalty. Today, two of these seats had been kept for Marc Washington and herself.

As a stewardess in a double-buttoned deep blue dress took her raincoat away Sophie couldn't help wondering if her name would have been memorised had she been travelling alone, instead of as the companion of a man whose name might not appear in the newspapers but was sure to be flagged as a VIP on the database of regular Concorde users.

Assuming he would prefer the window seat, although the window was smaller and higher than on a subsonic aircraft, she stood aside for him to precede her into their seat space. But he shook his head and gestured for her to go first.

As she sat down and fastened the seat belt across her hips, the sight of her knees reminded Sophie of one of the key qualifications required in candidates for the job she had won. Great legs.

That proviso, with its sexist implications, had almost put her off applying. But the prospect of working in Venice had overcome her disquiet that Marc Washington might expect more than secretarial services from the women he employed to smooth his working life.

Now, because he was younger than she had expected, and gave an immediate impression of powerful virility, her unease resurfaced. Was he going to expect her to be his playgirl by night as well as his PA by day?

In general Sophie took a relaxed view of the natural

hazards of being a presentable female. Perhaps she had been lucky. So far the men she had worked with had not been the kind who made unwelcome passes.

But the man settling his broad shoulders against the backrest next to hers was a totally unknown quantity. He might be a macho type who saw the entire female sex as an extended harem from which he could select whoever took his fancy and expect an amenable response.

If he thought that because he was paying her an exceptionally high salary he was entitled to everything she had to give, he could think again. In Sophie's view the duties of a PA went a long way beyond those of most employees in terms of time and support. They didn't include the kind of personal attentions he might have in mind.

Not, to be fair to him, that Marc Washington was giving the female cabin staff the once-over like the elderly lecher seated across the aisle. Her new employer seemed unaware that a great pair of legs belonging to one of the stewardesses was in close-up view while its owner spoke to another member of the cabin staff. He was arranging his own long legs.

Sophie chose to keep hers angled out of sight, apart from a few inches of black-hosed knees exposed by the hem of the black skirt which went with the black and cream plaid jacket and cream silk shirt she had chosen to travel in.

In her working life she strove to emulate the understated chic of top career women ten years her senior. The colours she loved, and which matched her large blue-green eyes, were confined to her scarf and underwear drawers and to the contents of the jewellery roll now in her capacious travelling bag.

Although it seemed unlikely that any Concorde passengers would be suffering from pre-flight nerves, they were offered champagne before take-off.

'Not for me, thank you,' she said with a smile, when the steward presented the tray to her. 'But I would like a glass of water...when you have time.'

'You don't like champagne, or you don't drink alcohol at all?' Marc Washington asked her after the steward had passed by, leaving him holding a glass of the gently fizzing wine.

'On the contrary, with pasta suppers at my New York neighbourhood trattoria I always drank my share of the carafe of house wine,' she answered. Impulsively she added, 'To be honest, I'm on a stratospheric high already...what with being on the way to Venice and the surprise of finding myself flying Concorde.'

Marc Washington's mouth didn't alter but his eyes did. Suddenly they gleamed with amusement.

'I'm glad to hear it,' he said as the supersonic aircraft rose from the ground. 'Your composure suggested otherwise. I have a powerful thirst for life, Sophie, and I like the people around me to feel the same way. My impression, when we shook hands, was of someone noticeably guarded in their responses. It didn't tally with Audrey LaRue's impression that you were exactly right for the Venetian assignment.'

'That's good to hear,' said Sophie. 'I wanted the job very much and I'm looking forward to starting it. Mrs LaRue explained that liaising with the Venetian civic authorities would be an important part of it, but beyond that I know very little.'

'That's why we're travelling together, so that I can explain it to you. Your dossier says you've been to Venice before. How long did you spend there?'

This was a question Sophie wanted to sidestep. To

answer it fully would be painful to her, and anyway the whole truth was none of his business.

She said, 'Longer than the majority of tourists who, so I read, spend an average of sixteen hours there. I know the city a little better than they do, but not as well as I'd like to.'

Fortunately her answer seemed to satisfy him. 'By the time my project is accomplished you'll know it well,' he assured her. 'I hope the problems you're going to have to deal with won't spoil the place for you.'

'I'm sure they won't. What sort of problems will they be?'

As she spoke they were handed menus.

'Before I go into that, let's decide what to eat.'

For some seconds, as he fixed his attention on the dishes listed on the card, she was able to study his face more closely than had been possible until now.

As a small child she had been taught to give close attention to the structure of people's faces, to observe how their mouths drooped or curled, to notice how features varied and to read the signs revealing a person's character.

'Faces are maps…maps of experience and temperament.' She remembered the voice and the remark as clearly as if she had heard it yesterday.

What kind of man and what kind of life was mapped in Marc Washington's face? She found it impossible to tell. She could recognise his charisma but she couldn't begin to guess what lay behind it. At this stage of their acquaintance he was a complete enigma.

Working for him would change that. The old French quote 'No man is a hero to his valet' could nowadays be updated to, No man is a mystery to his PA.

Her last boss had been a nice man with a stable marriage and no affairs on the side. At present she didn't even know if Marc Washington had a wife, an ex-wife or two, or a succession of girlfriends.

When a stewardess came to take their orders for lunch, Sophie asked for curried apricot and mint soup followed by a nest of quail's eggs with an asparagus salad and, for pudding, poached pears in red wine fruit jelly.

Marc Washington's choices were more robust. He had decided to start with oysters, followed by saddle of hare in a mustard sauce with several vegetables. He concluded his order with the three-layer chocolate mousse.

'Did your friends give you a send-off at that West Side trattoria you party at?'

As she hadn't mentioned the restaurant's location she concluded he must remember the address from her dossier. If his memory was as retentive as that, she would have to be doubly sure she never forgot any details.

She smiled at him. 'Yes, they did. I made some good friends during my time in America. I'm glad I crossed the Atlantic, but I'm glad to be going back to Europe.'

At this point their meal began. A week or two earlier Sophie's ex-boss had received a brochure about the Air France Concorde. She had read it, never expecting to travel on it. Recently the interior of the aircraft had been redesigned by the internationally famous André Putman, whose approach to design was simplicity rather than ostentatious luxury.

Sophie had already noticed that the headrest covers were of crisp white cotton piqué protecting a subdued upholstery of finely ribbed grey and beige wool. The tablecloths had hem-stitched edges, the starkly simple white china was narrowly rimmed with blue, and the cutlery was presented in a roll of corrugated paper tied with a matching cord. It was all a far cry from the garish colours and emphasis on synthetics of most airlines. Clearly Marc Washington took all this elegance for granted. Perhaps he had never experienced any other kind of in-flight meal.

As she dipped her spoon in her soup the memory of the horrible refreshments on a cut-price flight to Mexico, where she and her friend Merle had spent Christmas, made Sophie smile inwardly. Yet, even after that uncomfortable flight, perhaps they had enjoyed themselves as much as these Concorde passengers at their five-star resorts or in their luxurious houses.

As it seemed her companion preferred to enjoy his oysters in silence, she didn't speak while they ate. Out of the corner of her eye she could see the leisurely movements of his long fingers and the light catching the glass and metal of the watch protruding from the edge of his white shirt-cuff.

It wasn't an ostentatious watch, nor, although they were well kept, were his nails professionally manicured, she noticed. But in a line-up of all the expensively tailored, smoothly groomed men on this aircraft he would stand out for many reasons.

As she often did, she heard an echo from the past. 'Don't be a conformist, Sophie. Don't run with the herd. Go your own way.'

But she had conformed. With her living to earn and no special talents to take her in a different direction, there had been no option but to join the big city rat-race.

While she was admiring her next course, a pale golden hollandaise sauce coating four quail's eggs and overflowing their nest of puff pastry and puréed broccoli, her new employer broke his silence.

'One of the best eggs I ever ate was a bantam's, fried in olive oil, topping a sliver of mountain ham on a chunk of village bread,' he said reminiscently. 'It came with a glass of brandy on a very cold morning.'

'Somewhere in Italy?'

'No, in a scruffy little *pueblo* in the mountains of southern Spain. I'd been to the Sierra Nevada to see the world ski championships, but they had to be cancelled for lack of snow. So I spent a few days exploring the Alpujarra region.'

The way his tongue rolled the 'r's in the Spanish name made Sophie suspect he spoke the language. In her experience it was unusual for Americans to be linguists, unless their parents or grandparents had been immigrants. Those whose forebears had come to America a long time ago tended, like the British, to expect everyone to speak their language.

'Are you a polyglot, Mr Washington?' she asked.

'I wish I were. I have a few words of several languages but I'm only fluent in Italian...which means I can get by in Spain. What made you choose Italian as your principal language?'

'When I was small, someone in my family spoke it. I used to like listening to them...I still think it's the most musical language in Europe.' In case he should press for a fuller explanation, she said, 'You were going to tell me some of the problems I'll have to deal with.'

'First I'll explain the project. When you visited Venice, did you go to any of the other islands in the lagoon—Torcello—Burano—Murano?'

When she nodded, he went on, 'Those three are the only ones most tourists see, but there are more than thirty. The cost of saving Venice for posterity is immense. No other city in the world has so many historic buildings and no other city has its foundations in the sea. To raise more money for the preservation of Venice an auction was held for long low-rent leases on thirteen of the unused islands in the lagoon. I was one of the successful bidders. My island is called Capolavoro.'

'What are you planning to do with it?' she asked.

'It's going to become a refuge.'

'For wildlife?'

'For me. My present base in Venice is the top floor of a *palazzo* built by my mother's family. The rest of it's home to various elderly relations. I need somewhere quieter and more private.'

'I hadn't realised you were yourself a Venetian on your mother's side,' said Sophie.

Although now, looking at him with that knowledge, she wondered why she hadn't guessed that his forebears included some of the extraordinary men who had made their fortunes in Venice and spent them on the magnificent palaces along the Grand Canal.

Rogues and schemers, many of them, some cruel and ruthless in achieving their objectives, all of them had been motivated by the powerful thirst for life he had warned her he had and expected his underlings to share.

Suddenly Sophie had the feeling that she might be out of her depth, that working for Marc Washington would be unlike any previous job and, in spite of the laudatory references given her by previous employers, she might not have the skills to cope with the man beside her.

All this went through her mind in seconds, leaving only a brief pause before she went on, 'Where do you feel you belong…in Venice or America?'

Having asked, she wished she hadn't. He might think the question too inquisitive.

'I belong wherever I am,' he said. 'There aren't many parts of the global village where I haven't been or where I feel out of place.'

She had already noticed that while he talked he looked intently at her, never switching his gaze somewhere else as most people did when conversing.

'Where do you feel you belong?' he asked. 'In that little village in Devon where you were born?'

He really did have a phenomenal recall of facts, thought Sophie, switching her own gaze to the bulkhead in front of her. To remember the county of her birthplace was remarkable, and how did he know it was a village with a population of fewer than five hundred people? Perhaps Mrs LaRue had checked, adding a note to Sophie's dossier.

'No, definitely not,' she answered. 'I was there for six months as a baby and then taken somewhere else. The place where I belong is somewhere I haven't found yet.'

The meal was over and they were drinking coffee when Marc Washington said, 'Once you've been shown the ropes, I shall have to leave you to handle things on your own a great deal of the time, although you'll always be able to contact me. Your role will be to liaise with all the people involved in the restoration and development of Capolavoro. To be a mediator when they come into conflict—as they will.'

'May I ask you why you didn't engage a home-grown PA for this?'

'That was my first intention, but no one good enough applied. In Italy top-level PAs gravitate to Milan and Rome. Anyway, there are advantages in bringing in an outsider. In many ways Italy is one of the most civilised countries in the world, but getting things done quickly and efficiently has always been a problem,' he said drily. 'Americans are better at that. I was expecting all the New York applicants to be American.'

Sophie couldn't resist asking, 'What gave me the edge over the two other finalists?'

'In terms of qualifications you were very evenly matched. In that situation the choice depends on the selector's quirks. I liked the look of you best,' he added casually.

For a second or two she was flattered. Then, slightly

perplexed, she said, 'But we didn't submit photographs. When did you see us?'

'While you were in the waiting room. The Venetian mirror you noticed when you came in is also a one-way window.'

'A window!' Sophie's startled exclamation drew a glance from a passing stewardess.

'The fact that you were the only one to appreciate the nature of the frame was a minor point in your favour. I like people who take an interest in their surroundings and recognise fine things.'

'You've ruined the fineness of that mirror by replacing the proper glass with that nasty piece of one-way window glass,' Sophie informed him bluntly.

Normally she had a low boiling point, and had not lost her temper in years. But anger welled up in her now and she couldn't contain it.

'I think watching people without their knowing it is...' On the brink of saying unpardonable, she modified her word to, 'Unethical.'

'But practical,' he said coolly. 'More revealing than a face-to-face meeting when you would have been putting on a front. I saw you behaving naturally.'

'Could you hear what we were saying?'

'No, the room isn't bugged.'

His indifference to her disapproval fanned her anger. 'You surprise me,' she said sarcastically. 'If you're prepared to spy on people, why jib at listening?'

'You exaggerate. Watching people and even, in certain circumstances, listening to them, isn't the same as spying on them. It's an accepted technique which has many applications. Manufacturing companies often use it to gauge customers' reactions to their product. They set up consumer discussion groups and listen to them talking. The groups know they're being monitored but they respond more freely without the visible presence of people taking notes.'

'That's the difference...they *know*. We didn't. We thought you weren't in the building. Didn't it cross your mind that we had a right to see *you*?'

She knew she was taking a tone he wouldn't like, but she felt impelled to have this out with him. It was a matter of principle.

'If you had met me, would it have made you withdraw your application?' he asked sardonically.

The arrogance implicit in his question brought a crisp retort from Sophie. 'I already had reservations about it. I might well have withdrawn if I'd known about the mirror. I'm sure Mrs LaRue can't have liked being a party to that. I thought she looked uncomfortable when she told us you wouldn't be able to see us.'

'Audrey may not be comfortable with a lot of my methods but she knows which side her bread is buttered. If you can't accept my authority, if you're going to purse your lips every time I do something you don't like, it had better be hello and goodbye. You can fly back from Paris at my expense and I'll send for one of the other two.'

A stewardess removed their empty coffee-cups. When she was out of earshot, he said, 'Think it over. I don't want anyone working for me who can't go along with the way I do things. I'm going to read now. You have the rest of the flight to decide.'

CHAPTER TWO

FOR a while Sophie sat silently simmering, but gradually her temper cooled. She realised she had handled the whole thing very badly. When she'd found out about the mirror, she should have held her tongue until she'd had time to think it over.

This way, by speaking recklessly, she had diminished her credit with him if she did decide to stay with the job.

Now, from the window, Sophie could see the curvature of the earth and the infinity of space. It was only by courtesy of the man beside her that she was having this experience. Many people would think her crazy to put at risk the salary and the opportunities that working for him offered.

Later in the flight, while they were still in the stratosphere at their cruising altitude, he suddenly closed his book, adjusted the angle of his seat and lay back and shut his eyes. She thought he was probably thinking rather than sleeping, although there were many examples of famously dynamic men who topped up their energy with catnaps.

Either way, he looked subtly different; the angular architecture of his face was softened by the closed eyelids and unexpectedly silky black eyelashes near the downward slash of his cheekbones. When his eyes were open, the probing scrutiny of his Italian-dark irises distracted attention from his eyelashes.

She was thinking about the strange mixture of his bloodlines—old Virginian and even older Venetian—

when she had the strangest feeling that somewhere, a long time ago, she had seen him before.

Where?

Reviewing all the cities where their paths could have crossed or converged, if only for a few moments in some expensive street where she had been window-shopping and he had been buying, she failed to come up with an answer.

In one year, if you worked in a city, you saw thousands of faces, she thought. Did the brain memorise all those images, stashing them away in the back of the mind, most of them irrecoverable but a few in a special place from which they could be retrieved like the hidden files on a computer?

What she did remember, very clearly, was the evening this adventure had begun. Not that she had immediately recognised it as a turning point. Did one ever? she thought, her mind going back to the evening in question.

'So what's new in your world?' asked Merle.

After watching fifteen minutes of the news they had agreed to zap the newscast and eat their lap-suppers in peace.

Sophie shrugged. 'Nothing much.'

She was in her white terry bathrobe which, according to Merle, made her look at least ten years younger than twenty-five. Especially with her face cleansed with mousse, and her blonde hair, normally worn in a sleek, swingy bob, caught up by a tortoiseshell spring-clip from which a few silky tendrils had escaped to curl round her ears and her high cheekbones, which had emerged from the round, cheerful face captured in photographs of her schooldays.

Both her job and Merle's involved working late several nights a week. Tonight Sophie had got home in time to take a quick shower before fixing a salad to go with the fillets of salmon she had slipped under the grill when she'd heard a key in the lock of their shared West Side apartment.

'How did your day go?' she asked Merle now.

Having just filled her mouth with salad, her friend waved her fork to signal that she would reply in a moment. Like Sophie she was a PA, her boss being the founder of New York's most famous firm of headhunters.

Most of the people they hunted were senior executives required for plum positions with America's commercial giants. But sometimes they searched for people lower down the corporate scale, even recruiting secretaries when exceptional skills were asked for.

When Merle could speak, she said, 'Something came in today I wouldn't have minded trying for myself if my CV had filled the bill. Whoever lands this cushy number has to speak fluent Italian. I only have French.'

'Why is Italian a must?' asked Sophie.

'The job is in Venice, Italy.'

When Sophie had been working in London, before crossing the Atlantic, it had puzzled her that Americans always said 'Paris, France' or 'Naples, Italy'. Soon after arriving in New York she had realised that almost every town and city in Europe had a namesake, and sometimes several, in the United States.

Any mention of what, to her, was the one and only Venice always triggered her interest. She never spoke of the reasons why the Italian city was special to her, but even to see on a poster in the window of a travel agency the familiar bow-prong of a gondola, or one of the famous bridges over the network of canals, was enough to revive poignant memories.

'What is the job?' she asked.

'Same as yours,' Merle replied. 'PA to a boss who expects to have a miracle-worker in his outer office. But he's ready to pay big bucks for his wonder woman.'

Sophie's eyes widened when Merle told her the salary the job carried. 'Every PA in New York with a smattering of Italian will be lining up for an interview,' she went on. 'But, aside from being genuinely fluent, there are some other essentials that will whittle the final line-up down to single figures.'

'What are the other qualifications?' Sophie asked, aware that she was beginning to feel more than a casual interest.

For some months now she had been waking up in the morning without the sense of eagerness to see what the coming day offered that she felt people ought to experience if their life was on the right track.

New York, so exciting and stimulating when she had first come here, had begun to lose some of its charm—in the same way that London had palled after a few years of working there.

Maybe she was growing out of big cities, beginning to need a different kind of environment. But what and where was a puzzle she had yet to solve.

'For a start the successful applicant has to be free of all ties,' said Merle. 'No husband, no partner, no one she's serious about.'

'That's not going to thin out the field much,' Sophie said drily. 'This city is teeming with women who would sell their souls to have a man in their life. But the only ones they ever meet are other women's husbands or their discards. Neither of us has a guy we couldn't bear to tear ourselves away from. Will we ever?' she added, with a faint sigh.

Merle said, 'You could have plenty of dates if you

were less picky. I couldn't see too much wrong with Robert.'

'There wasn't anything wrong with him,' Sophie agreed. 'He just didn't make me feel the way people should if they're going to spend the rest of their lives together.'

'That's an ideal that doesn't work out in real life,' Merle said firmly.

Sophie knew that Merle thought her views naïve and unrealistic for a person in her mid-twenties; she had already abandoned a couple of promising relationships for reasons which didn't make sense to her friend's way of thinking.

They had argued the subject many times, and sometimes, awake in the night, Sophie wondered if Merle was right and her expectations *were* set too high.

Now, to avoid another disagreement, she recapped the qualifications Merle had already mentioned. 'Fluent Italian. No ties. What else?'

'Great legs.'

'You're kidding!'

Sophie had lived in America long enough to know what an uproar *that* requirement would cause in certain quarters. Even in Europe, where the feminist and politically correct lobbies were not yet as powerful as here, it would be considered unacceptably sexist for a male employer to insist on specific physical attributes in his female employees.

'We're not advertising that,' said Merle. 'But, although we're keeping it quiet, only the long-stemmed applicants will get through to the final interview.'

'This client must have a lot of clout to get away with that proviso. Who is he?' Sophie asked.

'No one you've ever heard of—but with as much clout, if not more, than most of the top tycoons who *are* household names,' Merle told her. 'His name is Marc Washington...the Marc spelt with a c.'

In Sophie's job it was essential to read and absorb information from all the best sources of international business news. If asked, she could have given a résumé on most of the financial and commercial top people. But her mental file didn't come up with any facts about Marc Washington.

The following day she asked her boss about him. It turned out that Washington was the heir to a fortune founded in the last century by a man with ancestral links to the Virginian family whose most famous son had been America's first president. However, although Marc Washington was known to have a finger in many successful pies, he was a mysterious figure about whose personal life little was known outside his immediate circle.

From then on, each evening, Sophie couldn't resist asking Merle how the search for someone to fill the Venetian post was progressing.

'Why are you so interested?' Merle asked, about a week later.

Sophie's answer surprised them both. Until that moment she hadn't made up her mind to take such a life-changing step.

'I'd like to apply for the job, Merle.'

Merle took a minute or two to recover from her surprise. Eventually she said, 'You fit the bill on most counts, including the great legs. But the key qualification is the fluent Italian.'

'I speak Italian as well as you speak French.'

'You do? Why didn't you tell me?'

'It never came up.'

After a pause, Merle said, 'There's quite a lot about you that's never come up, isn't there, Sophie? I've always known there were parts of your life you didn't want to talk about, and I've gone along with that, but the applicants for this job have to fill in a long questionnaire giving their entire life history. Are you prepared to do that?'

'If I want the job, I'll have to, won't I?' Sophie responded lightly.

Inwardly, she had no intention of revealing every aspect of her past to an employer whose own life was shrouded in secrecy.

On the day of the final interview Sophie already knew that only seven people had survived the preliminary sifting. Those on the short-list had then been re-interviewed by the charming but eagle-eyed woman who was Marc Washington's personal assistant in New York.

Afterwards, Sophie felt sure she wouldn't be among the finalists bidden to attend an interview with Marc Washington himself. To her surprise, she was.

After taking great care with her appearance, she arrived for the ultimate test to find she had only two rivals. Both were so poised and stylish that she didn't feel she had a hope of being the one chosen by the exacting Mr Washington.

The three of them were introduced to each other by Mrs LaRue, who had conducted the penultimate interviews. Although in her early fifties, Mrs LaRue still had 'great legs', Sophie noticed as the older woman showed them to a comfortably furnished waiting room.

'Mr Washington has been delayed. He expects to arrive very soon,' she said, before leaving them together.

Although none of the three would have been in their present jobs if they hadn't been friendly young women adept at getting along with other people, in this situation their natural warmth was under constraint.

It was Sophie who broke the ice. 'Are you both native

New Yorkers? I came here from London a couple of years ago.'

'I'm from Milwaukee,' said Amanda, a willowy brunette with designer glasses framing her long-lashed dark eyes.

Eileen, a freckled redhead, told them she came from Boston, but her colouring suggested that Ireland was where her forebears had originated.

For about fifteen minutes the three of them made somewhat forced conversation. Amanda was the most restive. She prowled the room, looking without much interest at the pictures on the walls, bending to sniff one of the roses in the arrangement of fresh flowers on a side table, and finally selecting a copy of *Vogue* from the low centre table and sitting down to glance through its glossy pages.

Of the three of them, Eileen had the best legs, Sophie considered. But she also had an irritating habit of picking at her nails. Perhaps she was only doing it because she was nervous and would control it while she was being interviewed.

'I wonder who'll go in first?' said Amanda. She had put *Vogue* back on the table and now jumped up to inspect her reflection in a large mirror with an ornate glass frame.

It had been the first thing Sophie had noticed when they'd entered the room because the ornamental frame was typically Venetian, instantly recognisable to anyone who had ever seen one before. But, while the frame was antique and very beautiful, the original glass, which would have made it worth many thousands of dollars, had been replaced by a piece of modern glass.

Mrs LaRue reappeared.

'I'm sorry, ladies. I'm afraid it won't be possible for Mr Washington to see you this afternoon after all.

Something has come up that requires his immediate attention. He's asked me to apologise to you.'

'When will he be able to see us?' Amanda asked, frowning.

'That I can't say at the moment. I'll be in touch as soon as possible.' Mrs LaRue's expression and tone were sympathetic.

Sophie had an intuitive feeling that, inwardly, she was annoyed with her employer for messing them about in this way. Perhaps he was a difficult person to work for, with little thought for other people's convenience as long as his own was never interfered with.

Going down to street-level in the elevator, the other two had some pithy comments to make.

'I'm beginning to wonder if I really want this job,' said Amanda. 'The salary is what grabbed me. I'm not crazy to spend time in Venice. I was there on honeymoon with my ex. The shops were better in Rome.'

They parted at the entrance on Sixth Avenue, the other two diving into cabs, leaving Sophie to saunter home in a mood of anticlimax. Merle was out that evening at a party given by a former colleague who was now married.

Sophie found herself pacing the apartment's living room as restlessly as Amanda had prowled the waiting room. She had hoped by this evening to know where she stood instead of being still in suspense.

She was eating her solitary supper when the telephone rang.

'Hello? Sophie Hill speaking.'

'This is Audrey LaRue, Ms Hill. Mr Washington has decided that it won't be necessary to put you to the trouble of attending a further interview.'

Sophie's heart sank with disappointment.

'After studying your CV and my report of the talk we

had last week, Mr Washington has decided you are the candidate best qualified to fill the position in Venice.'

'Oh… Oh, that's wonderful!' Sophie exclaimed, her spirits soaring. 'When does he want me to start?'

It was only after they had concluded their conversation that she realised that, while Mr Washington had Mrs LaRue's opinion of her to go on, she knew little more about him than she had at the outset.

It might be that when they did meet she would take an instant dislike to him…

Marc opened his eyes five minutes before they were due to land. Instantly alert to his surroundings and aware of his last words to her, he said, 'Made up your mind?'

Sophie took a deep breath. 'I'll come to Venice.'

'Good.' He pressed the service button and, when the steward came, asked for a glass of water. 'Would you like one, Sophie?'

'Please.'

They were both drinking iced spring water in crystal tumblers when Concorde touched down at Charles de Gaulle Airport where the time was forty-five minutes past ten in the evening. They had been in the air for less than four hours.

When Sophie had queried being re-routed via Paris when her previous Alitalia ticket had been for a flight direct to Venice, Mrs LaRue had merely said, 'Overnight accommodation in Paris has been arranged for you, and a car will take you to and from the city.'

At the time Sophie had been baffled by these arrangements. Merle's reaction had been, 'Go with the flow, honey. If they're picking up the bills, why should you worry?'

In the back of the limousine taking them from the

airport to the city centre, Marc said, 'I have an engagement this evening and two meetings tomorrow. But I'm sure you can amuse yourself. We'll fly out first thing the day after tomorrow in my plane. It was grounded with technical trouble after I flew in last week, but the problem has been fixed.'

Some years earlier Sophie had worked for some wine-shippers in Bordeaux to perfect her French. The MD had flown his own plane around south-western France but had never undertaken long flights such as crossing the Swiss Alps between Paris and Venice.

As if he could read her thoughts, Marc said, 'Don't worry, my pilot is very experienced. I have a pilot's licence myself, but I shan't be at the controls tomorrow.'

When they reached central Paris, she expected to be dropped off at a modest hotel before he drove on to one of the *grand luxe* establishments. When the car came to a halt outside an imposing entrance and a liveried doorman opened the nearside rear door, Marc stepped out first, then turned and waited for her to follow.

As they entered the building he said, 'As I'm often in Paris, I have a suite here in preference to an apartment. If you go to the desk, they'll show you to your room. We'll have dinner together tomorrow night. Tonight I suggest you have something light in your room and watch a movie on television. They're usually quite soporific. By the morning you'll have adjusted to European time.'

He turned away in the direction of the lift.

CHAPTER THREE

ALTHOUGH she rarely bought clothes on impulse, preferring to stick to a carefully thought out plan, the next day Sophie fell for a top she saw displayed in a window. It matched her eyes but, in terms of cost per wear, would take for ever to earn its keep in her wardrobe. She couldn't resist it.

Walking back to the hotel, swinging the elegant carrier bag, she knew she had bought it partly on the assumption that she would be dining with Marc in an ambience demanding something more exciting than the cream silk shirt she was wearing again today or the black silk standby in her overnight case.

When she collected her key from the desk, the hall porter handed her a message scrawled on one of the hotel's elegant note slips: 'Bring a wrap. We'll be eating out. M.W.'

She could take her silk-look raincoat. A better option would be the black cashmere shawl packed in her hold luggage. *That* had been a sensible buy, expensive but endlessly wearable. Retrieving it from her suitcase involved finding a pair of scissors to cut the band of security tape which had been on the case when it appeared on the carousel. The shawl was at the bottom of the case. As she unpacked and repacked Sophie chided herself for going to these lengths to dine with her boss.

When, later, she went downstairs and saw that the large, softly lit bar was now full of elegant people, she was glad she had taken the trouble. She remembered reading somewhere that, as well as this hotel being a home from home to the world's rich, its bar was also a fashionable early evening rendezvous for Parisians.

A man in a dinner jacket was standing just inside the bar. Evidently he was staff as he gave her a slight bow, saying in English, 'Mr Washington is waiting for you at a table in the corner, *mademoiselle*. Permit me…' He conducted her through the crowded room.

Marc rose from a velvet banquette when he saw them coming. In place of yesterday's casual clothes he was wearing a dark blue striped suit and a pale blue shirt. Its white collar emphasised his tan. His tie was plain dark blue silk. His elegance made her glad she had bought the chic top.

'Thank you.' She smiled at the man who had led her to him.

Almost before she had sat down a waiter was there to attend to them. Marc hadn't ordered yet. He had been reading a French paper.

'What would you like?'

Out of the past came a memory of a voice saying, *'Spritz al bitter, per favore,'* and of a glass filled with deep pink liquid shining in the evening light on the wide, busy waterfront of the Riva degli Schiavoni.

'May I have a Campari spritzer?'

Marc looked at the waiter. 'I'll have the same…and some *croustades*, please.' Turning to her, he asked, 'What did you do with yourself today?'

'Nothing special…just enjoyed Paris. It was too warm and sunny to be inside a museum.'

'No shopping?'

'No intentional shopping. I did buy one thing that caught my eye.'

'This?' He indicated her top.

'How did you guess?'

'It looks French. Also, women like to wear something

new as soon as possible.' Knowledge of how many women had contributed to that statement? she wondered.

'Did your meetings go well?'

'Yes, our French operation—sports equipment—goes from strength to strength. It started with a small company in which my grandfather invested before other people foresaw the masses enjoying activities that, in his day, were exclusive to the idle rich. Now we have sports supermarts in the commercial section of every large city in France.'

He was talking about the latest developments in the manufacture of indoor climbing walls when their drinks arrived, accompanied by a silver dish, its contents hidden in the folds of a white linen napkin embroidered with the hotel's monogram.

'We'll go out to eat,' said Marc. 'I don't care for the dining room here. The food's good but the atmosphere's dull. When I don't want to go out, I dine in my suite.' As he spoke he picked up his glass, removing the olive from it. 'But as you're already rather tense about working for me I won't suggest we do that this evening.'

His eyes, amused, held hers while he drank.

Sophie wondered if he was testing her, wanting to find out how she would cope with flirtation. She broke their eye contact, taking the olive on its stick out of the pink-tinted mixture of wine and soda.

'I haven't tasted Campari since I was in Italy,' she said, after sipping it. 'What time do we take off tomorrow?'

'Early. The car will be here at seven-thirty. You can breakfast at seven, if you like—room service is very efficient—or on the plane. I always run before breakfast. Tomorrow I'll have my coffee and croissants with Werner after take-off. He used to fly for Lufthansa but got tired of the same long-haul routes. Flying for me is more interesting, and often his wife, Lisa, comes with us.'

Sophie was eating her olive. After swallowing it, she asked, 'Is Lisa also German?'

'Australian. She's the daughter of one of our executives in Sydney and her parents would have preferred her to marry someone local. She's a useful person to have around. She was a nurse until Werner walked into her life. I don't know how the arrangement will work out when they have children, but she's only twenty-three so they're not in a hurry to start a family.'

This gave Sophie a cue to ask, 'Do you have children, Mr Washington?'

'No.'

For a moment she thought he was going to leave it at that and wondered if she was being snubbed because he regarded his private life as off limits.

Then he added, 'Like you, I have no "hostages to fortune"...if you know that expression.'

'"He that hath wife and children hath given hostages to fortune; for they are impediments to great enterprises, either of virtue or mischief",' Sophie quoted. 'Written by Frances Bacon in his essay *Of Marriage and Single Life*. We did his essays in my last year at school.'

'Do you agree with his view?' After unfolding the napkin, he offered her the dish of *croustades*.

Sophie had eaten them before, during her time in Bordeaux, and had sometimes made them herself when she and Merle had given a party.

'Thank you.' Taking one of the crisp golden curls of bread, spread with butter and Roquefort cheese and sprinkled with caraway seeds, she bit into it with care, trying not to scatter crumbs on her black skirt.

'We could use some napkins.' Before helping himself Marc looked around for the waiter. Having beckoned him, he said, 'Until one arrives, use this.' Taking the silk handkerchief from his breast pocket, he spread it across her lap.

She had already noticed the rich but subtle colours in the overflow of silk, wondering if it might have come from a shop in Venice where once she had feasted her eyes on wonderful ties and handkerchiefs costing hundreds of thousands of lire.

Since breakfast she had had only soft drinks and coffee in a couple of pavement cafés, sitting in the warm end-of-summer sunshine, watching the passing scene. The *croustade* tasted deliciously cheesy. She hadn't realised till then how hungry she was.

When the waiter brought two small napkins she returned Marc's handkerchief. As he stuffed it carelessly back in place she said, 'In sixteenth-century England a wife would have been an impediment to a man who wanted, for example, to explore the New World. But now that women are included in space missions and a British girl has walked the length of Africa there's no reason why a wife should be an impediment to virtuous enterprises. As for impeding mischief, she has never done that if her husband is the promiscuous type.'

Marc moved the dish closer to her side of the table. 'I have a longer reach. Help yourself. They're good, aren't they? Although not, for my taste, quite as good as Italian *crostini* hot from the oven on a cold winter morning. What time of year were you in Venice before?'

Her answer was not exactly a lie, but it came perilously close. 'This time of year.'

He said, 'I like Venice under snow, or shrouded in mist, when the only foreigners around either work there or are in love with the place. When I was small, but old enough to explore on my own, there wasn't a camera or camcorder round every damn corner between the Piazza and the Rialto. It's a vicious circle: without the hordes, Venice wouldn't survive, but their presence makes parts of the city horribly overcrowded.'

Between them they finished the *croustades*. By the time she emptied her glass, his had been empty for some minutes.

'Would you like another drink?'

'Not for me, but please go ahead if you would.'

'In that case, let's go and do some serious eating.'

Midway through dinner Sophie realised this was the best evening out she had had in a long time. They were in a neighbourhood restaurant on the Left Bank. It was not unlike her favourite West Side place. Here, as there, it was run by a family—the parents sharing the cooking, one son behind the bar and another son and daughter waiting on the dozen or so tables. The food was traditional *cuisine bourgeoise*, the helpings generous, the good but inexpensive house wine served in earthenware jugs.

'How did you discover this restaurant?' Sophie asked, following Marc's example and mopping up the last of her gravy with a piece of recently baked *pain de campagne*.

'I first came here as a student, when Maman and Papa were in their forties and Célie, their daughter, was still at school. I had a vacation job in our Paris office. For a while I had to live on my wages so I only ate here once a week. My grandfather thought it important to know how the other half live...the people who have to live on a low wage all their lives.'

Earlier, during the first course, he had given her a rundown on the many and various operations under the corporate umbrella, lacing the facts with amusing incidents and insights.

Sophie, who had sometimes found her attention wandering when her ex-boyfriend Robert had talked about his job, had found Marc's exposition riveting. She liked his quirky sense of humour, a trait it was hard to resist in anyone. But she had the feeling she was seeing only one side of him, and that there might be others she would like a lot less.

After dinner they returned to the hotel on foot. As the black calf pumps she was wearing had low heels Marc's suggestion that they should walk didn't dismay her. The exercise and fresh air should help her to sleep on a night when she had many reasons for feeling keyed up.

'One of the things you'll like about living in Venice is the freedom to walk about at night without being molested,' he told her. 'So far, we don't have that problem. I'm not saying there aren't a few areas where it would be unwise to wander with diamonds flashing or a bulging billfold on view. But from being a city where, in centuries gone by, a great many bodies were fished out of the canals with stab wounds and broken skulls it's now as safe and respectable as small-town America was when my grandfather was a young man.'

Although he made frequent references to his grandfather, there was never any mention of his parents, Sophie had noticed. Had something bad happened to them? Was he, like her, an only child? There were so many things she would like to know about him but felt precluded from asking in case he should think her presumptuous.

There was one question she could ask without giving offence.

'Have you ever been to Bordeaux?'

'Only once. Why do you ask?'

'I worked in Bordeaux. It's a beautiful city inside a hell-on-wheels ring road. I had a lovely time there.'

He looked down at her. They were strolling beside the Seine now, and a little chill wind off the river made her glad to be swathed in the soft warmth of her cashmere wrap. Marc appeared not to feel the drop in the temperature. Perhaps it was an effect of his morning run. She had noticed before that men who took a lot of exercise had better circulation than people who didn't.

'I should think you have a lovely time everywhere, don't you, Sophie? You obviously enjoyed your meal tonight, even though that place isn't in any of the good food guides.'

'It deserves to be…but let's hope it stays undiscovered. It might lose its cosy atmosphere if too many foreigners find it. As for having a lovely time everywhere, yes, I guess I do. Isn't that normal for someone my age, with no worries or problems?'

'These days it's unusual to find anyone who makes that claim. Most people seem encumbered by a raft of problems,' he said drily.

'Mmm…I suppose that's true,' she agreed thoughtfully, after a swift mental review of the people she'd known in New York. 'But a lot of people make mountains out of molehills, don't they? Or they don't look at their problems with a clear eye and tackle them.'

Her answer made Marc laugh. 'Where did you learn that attitude? On a self-improvement course? As a matter of interest, one of the islands in the lagoon, Tessera, is used by Edward de Bono, the lateral thinking guru, for courses in self-improvement. That wasn't what brought you to Venice the first time, was it?'

'I've read one of his books but I didn't know about Tessera. Is it near your island?'

'No, it's some way from Capolavoro. You haven't answered my question. Who taught you to look at life with a clear eye? Your parents? One of your teachers?'

She didn't want to tell him who had been the strongest influence on her. Maybe later, when she knew him better. For the time being it was simpler to say, 'I read a lot. I still do. Most of my ideas come from books.'

'Mine too. What are you reading at the moment?'

'A novel I bought at the airport to read on the plane. But then you turned up so I haven't started it yet.'

'Was it that hard to make up your mind?'

Although she had been careful not to drink too much wine on top of the potent Campari which, in spite of its innocuous colour, was twenty-five per cent alcohol, she was feeling sufficiently laid-back to say frankly, 'Yes, it was…and I'm still not certain I made the right decision.'

'That applies to all life's most challenging commitments,' Marc answered.

As they came to a crossing he put a hand on her shoulder to steer her past the bumpers of cars whose drivers looked set to make competitive starts the instant the lights changed.

She could see that the gesture might have been prompted by the fact that it wouldn't be easy to locate her elbow through the folds of her shawl. But the weight of his hand on the crest of her shoulder, the one farthest from him so that his arm was around her back, although not actually touching it, was a more intimate contact than the conventional hold of a man with patrician manners.

He didn't remove his hand until they had crossed the roadway and walked several yards on. When he did, she realised she had been holding her breath.

By now, ahead, she could see what Americans called the marquee of their hotel: the canopy over the carpet running from the edge of the kerb to the wide steps leading up to a revolving glass door through which passers-by could glimpse the opulence of the flower-decorated lobby.

As they approached the building a taxi drew up and the doorman saluted its passenger, a well-dressed man on his own who bent to hand some notes to the driver.

As he straightened he caught sight of Marc.

'Wash, old buddy... What are you doing in Paris?'

'Hello, Pat. I'm passing through...leaving first thing tomorrow. Sophie, this is Patrick Rivers. We were at school together. Miss Hill has just joined my team. We're on our way to Venice.'

'Delighted to meet you, Sophie.' The other man shook her hand. 'Where did this lucky guy find *you*?'

The emphasis, obviously intended to be flattering, made Sophie's hackles rise. 'In New York,' she said stiffly. 'I was with Masters and Fox.'

He was sure to have heard of them and she hoped to reinforce the fact that she was here on business.

'I bet they're sorry they lost you. I would be,' he said, smiling into her eyes. 'But you're not a New Yorker, are you? That sounds like a British accent.'

Marc answered for her, a tinge of impatience in his voice. 'It is. What are you doing here, Patrick?'

'Stopping by for a drink after a wearing day. Unlike you, I don't have someone like Sophie to soothe my savage breast when head office isn't pleased with the way things are going. What I have is a three-month-old baby who seldom stops bawling and a wife who wishes she hadn't jacked in her career. So do I,' he added, with feeling.

Sophie felt like saying that it might make his wife's life easier if he went home after work instead of stopping by bars. Instead she turned to Marc, 'If you'll excuse me, I'll say goodnight.'

'Goodnight! But the night is young,' Patrick objected.

'You must both come and have a drink with me. I haven't seen Wash in two years. We've a lot of ground to catch up.'

'Not tonight, Pat,' Marc said firmly, following her up the steps.

'Oh, come on, guys, you can't turn in this early...not in Paris,' the other man expostulated.

Then, as Sophie was waiting for someone to emerge from the revolving door before she stepped into it, she heard him add, in French, 'Or maybe you can. Who wouldn't with legs like that pair going up the stairs ahead of him? I'll bet she has splendid boobs too, you lucky...'

By now on her way through the door, Sophie was strongly tempted to turn full circle, give him a box on the ear he wouldn't forget in a hurry and tell him, in the same language, that he was the kind of man who got his sex a bad name.

Resisting the impulse, she marched to the desk for her key and, without glancing over her shoulder, stepped into an open lift and pressed the first-floor button.

CHAPTER FOUR

THE telephone woke Sophie at six-thirty. After thanking the switchboard operator for calling her, she forced herself out of bed and went to take a hot shower.

At seven, a tap on the door heralded the arrival of her breakfast tray. She had ordered fruit, yogurt and herb tea.

At twenty-five minutes past, a baggage porter came for her suitcase. As he disappeared in the direction of the service lift Sophie stepped into a guest lift. In spite of spending the night in the utmost luxury, she couldn't remember when she had last slept so badly.

As she had expected, Marc was already in the lobby, having a friendly chat with the only tailcoated hall porter on duty at that early hour.

'Good morning,' he said as she joined them.

'Good morning.' Her smile was for the porter. 'Good morning.'

'Good morning, *mademoiselle*. I hope you've been comfortable.'

'Very comfortable, thank you.'

'Ah…here is your car, Mr Washington. I hope you have a good flight and we shall look forward to your next visit.' The porter ushered them to the door.

Their baggage was already being stowed in the capacious boot as they passed the spot where Marc's schoolfriend had made his offensive remark. Minutes later they were on their way back to the airport.

At first Marc was silent, looking out of the window.

Sophie, who had no intention of initiating a conversation, did the same.

It was possible, she realised, that he had forgotten last night's incident. Men looked at life from a different perspective. Even nice men. And she wasn't even sure that, behind the civilised façade, her new employer *was* a nice man.

For all she knew his friend's comments might have amused him. While she went upstairs last night they might have gone to the bar for a drinking session, with Marc assuring the other man that it wouldn't be long before he had added her scalp to the rest of his trophies.

She didn't want to think the worst of him, but why should Patrick have made that obnoxious remark if he didn't know Marc to be a notorious womaniser?

'Werner called me at seven. The weather is clear over the Dolomites so we should have a smooth flight.'

Marc's sudden statement startled her.

'Oh...that's good.'

'Have you started your book yet?'

'I read a few pages before I went to sleep.'

She refrained from adding that, in the mood she had been in, the book had failed to grip her. Now she sensed that Marc was looking at her, but she looked at the road ahead. The car had a glass partition between the front and rear seats. The driver couldn't hear his passengers' conversation.

'Patrick didn't know you spoke French. He'd already had a few drinks or he wouldn't have made that remark.'

At that Sophie turned her head to meet the dark eyes focused on her. 'You don't have to make excuses for him. I had already decided I didn't like him before he made it. I imagine it's not at all likely I'll meet him again.' She couldn't resist adding, 'I feel sorry for his wife.'

To her vexation he smiled. 'He's not a bad guy. They're going through a difficult time. The company he works for is in trouble. On top of that the baby's birth wasn't easy and now Alice is exhausted by the baby. It's months since they had sex. Pat is a bundle of frustration, easily turned on by any attractive woman who crosses his path and envious of guys who are single and don't have the worries he has on his shoulders. I feel sorry for them both.'

'He isn't improving the situation by going home late, smelling of Scotch or whatever he drinks.'

'Vodka, which doesn't taint the breath. You're right, of course, but not everyone is as sensible as you are.'

She recognised the hint of irony.

'You think I'm being priggish?'

'Perhaps you have personal reasons for feeling strongly about people who use alcohol as a prop.'

'His drinking is his business. I only object to his rudeness.'

'In fact he was being complimentary…in an unacceptable way,' he added swiftly, forestalling her retort. 'You don't have to spell it out for me. We deal with a lot of accusations of sexual harassment, from the trivial—such as last night's example—to the serious. It's a problem for all employers of mixed-sex staff and our overall policy is to stamp on it—hard. Unless there are extenuating circumstances, as I think there are in Patrick's case.'

While he'd been talking Sophie had come round to the view that perhaps she had taken more umbrage than was justified. She was about to concede this when Marc went on, 'In fact the solution to the problem lies with women themselves. Men learn their fundamental attitudes to women from women…their mothers, their older sisters, their first-grade teachers.'

'Are you suggesting that women are responsible for sexual harassment?'

'You weren't paying attention,' he said, with more than a hint of impatience. 'I was saying that your sex have it in their power to influence masculine behaviour in its formative stages, but often they waste the opportunity and perpetuate inequalities. The mother who expects her daughters to make their beds, keep their rooms in order and help around the house but doesn't demand the same behaviour from her sons is making life difficult for her future daughters-in-law.'

She couldn't disagree with that but was faintly surprised that he understood the burden a domestically incompetent partner could be to a woman with a career. She had met them everywhere she had worked: women struggling to be superwomen because the men they loved were useless—or pretended to be—at coping with and sharing essential everyday chores.

Then, having mollified her, he went on, 'But, on the point you raised, yes, I do feel women bear some responsibility for the way they're treated. Certainly not where violence is involved. There's never any excuse for that. But if they make a habit of wearing tight skirts and revealing tops it shouldn't come as a surprise if someone makes a pass at them at the office party.'

'A lot of passes are made without any justification,' Sophie said shortly. 'The clothes I was wearing last night didn't invite your friend's offensive comments. Even his assumption that I wouldn't understand French was objectionable.'

'If it will make you happier, I gave him a sharp dressing down on your behalf.'

Her startled glance was met with quizzical gleam. The whites of his eyes, she noticed, had the slightly blueish hue of perfect health, and the irises were rimmed by a fine black line almost indistinguishable from their colour except in this bright morning light.

'I should have done it myself,' she said, looking away. 'I don't know why I didn't.'

'Your eyes said everything necessary. He had already got the message before I spelt it out for him.'

A telephone started to ring.

'Excuse me.' He opened a compartment embedded in the centre armrest to answer the call being signalled by a concealed cellphone.

His telephone conversation lasted for some time. It had to do, Sophie gathered, with a contingency being reported from the head office in Germany. Although she was only hearing one side of the conversation, she couldn't help being impressed by his quick grasp of the situation and incisive instructions for handling it.

Whatever else he might be, clearly he was no mere figurehead taking only a cursory interest in the operations which funded his jet-set lifestyle.

By the time he concluded the conversation it seemed wiser not to revive the subject they had been discussing. Probably he had already forgotten it and now had more important matters on his mind.

Most of the interior of Marc's private jet was fitted out as a comfortable sitting room, but it also had a couple of small night cabins, each with its own shower and lavatory. Sophie was shown round by Lisa, a hazel-eyed blonde with the easy friendliness Sophie had found in all the Australians she had met.

After Lisa had served coffee and microwave-heated croissants to Marc, her husband and Leif, the young Swedish co-pilot, on the flight deck, she and Sophie had their croissants together in the main cabin, which was decorated and upholstered in light grey with apricot accents. No commercial airline could compare with this for spacious comfort.

Sophie hoped that Lisa might, without being asked, fill in some of the many gaps in her mental dossier on Marc.

'You're going to love working in Venice now the hot weather's over,' she told Sophie. 'My parents live near the harbour in Sydney and there are moments when Venice reminds me of home. It's the light...the sun on the water. In most other ways they're totally different places, but the light is similar.'

'Your family must miss you,' said Sophie. 'Or do they have other children to help fill the gap?'

'Three...and five grandchildren. We're hoping to go back for Christmas. Werner's mother is dead and his father's remarried. They're not close. He's become part of my family.'

Lisa was forthcoming about her circle, but either she was too discreet to make any reference to her husband's employer or, more likely, she wasn't interested in him except as the source of their income. During the introductions it had been plain to see that she was madly in love with her blue-eyed pilot and that he felt the same way about her.

Sophie envied their happiness and hoped it would last all their lives. Their romance exemplified how much meeting the right person was a matter of luck.

Although her own early life had been shadowed by two examples of horrendously bad luck, she was by nature an optimist, but not to the extent of feeling sure that, out of the millions of wrong men she might encounter, luck would lead her to one of the few who would be an ideal partner. As was proven daily in the divorce courts, the odds were heavily against it.

* * *

Her first glimpse of Venice as they approached Marco Polo International Airport, on the edge of the mainland, was profoundly moving.

Fortunately Lisa was also intent on the aerial view of the lagoon. She didn't notice the signs of Sophie's emotion as she peered through the window, her chest heaving, her throat working, her eyes welling with tears as the plane banked and gave her a view of the place where once she had been unforgettably happy.

By the time they touched down on Italian soil she had pulled herself together. The formalities in the airport were brief. Soon her suitcases, and the cases belonging to Lisa and the two pilots, had been put aboard a sleek launch waiting for them at the quay immediately outside the airport. Marc had no luggage. He must have left the clothes he had worn last night and on Concorde in his suite in Paris.

At the stern, behind where Sophie was sitting, a blue and gold pennant fluttered as the launch moved away from the jetty. As they gathered speed she could see that the gold part was a crest, perhaps the insignia of Marc's Venetian forebears.

He was standing beside the stocky man at the wheel while the others relaxed on the side seats, Lisa sitting close to Werner.

Sophie hoped she wouldn't feel another uprush of emotion when the familiar outline of the city appeared on the horizon.

The day she had left Venice, she hadn't, like the other people leaving, had a camera to record her last sight of it. She hadn't needed one. The image had been imprinted on her memory. If she closed her eyes she could see it now. The spreading wash of the boat taking them to the airport. The glittering lagoon, the thick timber piles marking the channels. The beloved skyline, with its many churches and campaniles, gradually disappearing.

'Did you enjoy the flight?'

She opened her eyes to find Marc seating himself beside her, crossing his long legs and raising his arms to rest them on the back of the seat in the same relaxed posture as the pilots.

'Very much, thank you. We had some wonderful views of the Alps, didn't we?'

He nodded. 'I like flying over mountains on a sunny day. But the snow on the Dolomites gives a razor edge to the wind when it blows from that direction.'

'Yes, I remember,' she said.

'You had some cold weather last time?'

It was her turn to nod, hoping he wouldn't ask, wouldn't enquire into the duration of her visit. When the time was right she would explain about 'last time', but this wasn't the appropriate moment.

As Venice came into view Marc said, 'There she is... La Serenissima.'

His caressing tone and the smile at the corners of his mouth struck Sophie as being like of a man who had just seen, in the distance, the woman he loved coming towards him. She wondered if any woman had ever made him look like that, or if his deepest feelings were reserved for what the poet Byron had called a 'fairy city of the heart'.

The walled island, where Venetians were buried, and the city's northern waterfronts were as familiar to her as the streets of West Side New York. She felt her throat tightening again and was thankful she was wearing sunglasses.

Approaching the canal which would take them through the city to the wider and busier waterfront on the south side, the boatman reduced speed. As they cruised slowly past old buildings, the paint on the flaking stucco faded to the hues which made Venice a Mecca for artists, Sophie felt something close to ecstasy. She was back…and suddenly it felt as if she had never been away.

Marc said, 'Your hotel is near the Danieli, but smaller and cosier. A family-run place like the restaurant last night. I thought for the first week or two you would be more comfortable there. Later, if you wish, we can find you an apartment.'

Until he spoke she had assumed she would be housed in the *palazzo*, perhaps in the old servants' quarters. For presumably Venetian *palazzi*, like the stately homes of England, were run differently now from the days when for many people domestic service had been the only option. But perhaps, for a man of Marc's means, finding household staff was as easy as recruiting office staff, and his forebears' palace still had its full quota of minions.

On the jetty where they put in, a youth with a baggage trolley was waiting to take her suitcase from the boatman. Sophie said goodbye to the others and then turned to find that Marc was already on the jetty, waiting to take her hand as she stepped from the swaying launch to the weathered planks of the landing stage.

She had felt the strength in his fingers when they'd shaken hands the day before yesterday, and today his grip was even firmer. The wash of a *vaporetto* arriving at a nearby stop made the launch tilt more forcefully just as she was leaving it.

The water had always been boisterous along this part of the Riva, where there was a lot of traffic coming, going and passing. From lack of recent practice Sophie misjudged the manoeuvre. She sprang up with enough vigour to have made her lose her balance on landing if Marc hadn't hooked a steadying arm round her waist.

For an instant she leaned against him before pulling upright. 'I'm sorry…how clumsy. Thank you.'

'Any time.'

The amused look he slanted down at her gave a nuance to his reply which threw her into confusion. She walked quickly along the jetty in the wake of the youth with the trolley.

The hotel to which he led them had a pavement *caffè* outside it. In the shade of an awning, tourists were writing postcards and drinking coffee and beer.

The lobby was very different from the one in Paris. At present it was piled with the luggage of departing guests, some of whom were standing about waiting to pay their bills. However, when the proprietor saw Marc, he left the desk to shake hands and be introduced.

'Your room is ready for you, *signorina*,' he said, in good English. 'Forgive me for not showing it to you but, as you can see, you have come at a busy time. The boy will take you up and I will talk to you later.'

She looked up at Marc. 'When do you want me to start work? This afternoon?'

'I've been away for some time. I must attend to family matters and you need time to settle in. Spend tomorrow finding your feet and start work the next day,' he said. 'We'll begin by going to Capolavoro. Be on the same jetty at nine.'

Sophie watched him stride from the lobby, the brightness outdoors giving a sheen to his thick dark hair as he stepped into the sunlight and, a few moments later, was gone.

As she followed the baggage porter upstairs she was aware of disappointment that she wouldn't see him again till the day after tomorrow. An absurd reaction when there was nothing she wanted more than to rediscover Venice. A day and a half to explore was a bounty she hadn't expected.

CHAPTER FIVE

TOWARDS the end of the afternoon Sophie was returning to the *albergo* when she caught sight of a man she had known when he was a small boy, with untidy black curls and a mischievous grin.

Now most of his hair was hidden by the red-ribboned straw hat of a gondolier. This was not unexpected. Paolo's father and grandfather had been gondoliers and it was traditional for the skills required to steer the elegant boats around the labyrinth of canals to be handed down from father to son.

What did surprise her was that the skinny boy had grown into a strongly built man, and a handsome one too.

When she first saw him, he was trying to persuade an elderly couple to take a ride in his gondola. After they had shaken their heads and walked on Paolo turned to see if any more prospective customers were among the people coming towards the small hump-backed bridge where he was stationed.

When he spotted Sophie, his first glance was that of a man assessing a woman rather than a gondolier looking for a likely customer. He took in her small waist and her long legs—this afternoon she was wearing dark blue jeans with a checked shirt—and his smile reappeared.

'For you, *signorina*, I make a special price,' he said to her, in English.

However, although he had guessed correctly that she was English-speaking, he obviously had no idea that he was speaking to his first teacher of that language.

'How special?' Sophie asked.

'Very cheap. Only half the official price, because I enjoy showing my city to pretty ladies...especially when they have eyes like the sea in summer,' he added, with a wicked look from his own black eyes.

'You're a poet as well as a gondolier,' she said, smiling, wondering how he would have described her eyes had they been brown or grey. Later, when she had told him who she was, she would ask him.

'I am also a singer,' he told her. 'I have a very good voice. If you come with me, I will sing to you.'

The heads of passers-by turned as he suddenly burst into song, his strong baritone resounding in the narrow street bisected by the canal flowing under the bridge. Translated from the Italian, the words meant, 'Lovely lady, don't break my heart by spurning my devotion.' It sounded like a line from an opera, although Sophie didn't recognise the tune. Or perhaps he had made it up.

'When I sing, everyone listens,' Paolo told her. 'Not like the "serenades" on the Grand Canal.' He put his forefingers in his ears and contorted his face into a grimace of revulsion.

Earlier that afternoon, Sophie had returned to a secluded spot on the Grand Canal, a pleasant corner of the city which non-Venetians found only by accident. There she had perched on a sunny doorstep to watch the water traffic.

Presently three gondolas had come past in line abreast, each packed with as many tourists as they would hold as well as an accordionist and an elderly tenor, their voices long past their best. The music hadn't been quite as ear-splitting as Paolo's mime suggested, but she had to admit it hadn't compared with his short burst of song.

She said, 'I should be embarrassed by the attention you'd attract.'

'Even if I don't sing people will look at us—especially at you. When did you arrive in Venice? Where are you staying?'

'I arrived this morning. I'm staying on the Riva degli Schiavoni.' This wasn't telling him much. There were many hotels on the Riva, catering to every budget level.

'You are not with a group. And if you were here with a lover he would be with you. I think you are here with your parents, who are resting after the journey. If you live in the north of England, a long way from an airport, you had to leave home very early, perhaps before it was daylight.'

'You know a lot about tourists, but you haven't got it right this time. I'm on my own,' said Sophie, wondering if he was married now and chatting up female tourists was merely his stock-in-trade.

Paolo had been leaning against the parapet of the bridge. Now he stood up, 'It's time I took a break. I'll walk you back to the Riva and tell you about some nice places you won't find by yourself.'

'What about your gondola?' she asked, glancing down at the graceful black craft moored alongside the bridge. It was in immaculate order, the sofa upholstered in dark red velvet with matching fringed cushions on the two armchairs facing the stern.

'Nobody is going to steal it. It is not like a speedboat, which any fool can drive if he can start the motor. To steer a gondola is an art. It takes years of practice. Come—I'll show you a short-cut. If you go by the Piazza you will have to push through the crowd on the Ponte della Paglia. Every tourist who comes to Venice wants to photograph the Bridge of Sighs from what you would call the Bridge of Straw. One day it will break under the weight of so many people. At this time of day that bridge is impossible.'

'So I noticed on my way out.' Sophie didn't reveal that she already knew the short-cut he was proposing and had once known Venice as intimately as he did. For a moment she was enjoying the masquerade and looking forward to seeing his astonished stare when she revealed herself. She was also looking forward to asking him about Marc. Paolo would be sure to know something about her employer. The activities of the *palazzo* owners had always been food for gossip in the city.

She wondered how Marc would react if he could see her now, being escorted by a handsome gondolier. It was unlikely they would run into him. If he was out and about this afternoon, it would be in the smart part of Venice, where the banks and the fashionable shops were congregated.

The street they were following was too narrow for more than one person to pass someone coming the other way. Paolo had to walk close behind her until it opened out into one of the many squares called *campi*.

'If not from the north, where are you from?' he asked. 'London?'

'I've worked in London. I like it, but it's choked with traffic. It's pleasanter here, with no cars.'

'All the tourists say that. Listen, if you're alone, why don't you have dinner with me? It's not nice for a girl to have to go to a restaurant on her own in a strange city.'

'That's an old-fashioned idea. Modern women don't mind going about on their own and I'm told Venice is very safe.'

'Yes, but it's more enjoyable to have someone to talk to while you eat your dinner, don't you think?'

'Don't you have a wife to talk to you?'

'I'm not married. I'm still looking.'

Having crossed the *campo* diagonally, they entered an

even narrower street which for several yards was roofed like a tunnel by the building spanning it.

'My name is Paolo Sarto. What's yours?' he asked.

She told him without much fear that it would give the game away. Before, he had known her as Kit, a shortened form of a pet name.

'Sophie is nice. It suits you. It sounds gentle and sweet.'

'How come you speak such good English?'

'I speak all the tourists' languages, even some Japanese. It's necessary. I have to tell them about the buildings we pass, about the history of Venice.'

He did not explain his exceptional fluency in her language. Perhaps he had forgotten those early lessons. They were a long time ago.

Outside her hotel, he said he would come for her at a quarter to seven. Sophie didn't demur. She wasn't sure that she would have done even if he had been unknown to her.

She wouldn't have allowed herself to be picked up by a stranger in New York, London or even Bordeaux. But Venice was different. As a group, gondoliers were no less predatory than other men. If they sensed that female tourists were easy conquests, probably some of them made the most of their opportunities. But their ranks were unlikely to include anyone violent. She would have felt safe having dinner with one of them even if she *hadn't* already met his parents, grandparents and numerous aunts and cousins.

Paolo was wearing ordinary clothes when he came for her. Without the straw hat his hair showed thick and curly, but better cut now than when his elder sister, then an apprentice hairdresser, had been his barber.

Sophie had changed her jeans for a short black pleated

skirt, opaque black tights and a pale grey cable-patterned sweater with some mohair in it. Although it was hot during the day, after dark the temperature dropped.

'We are going to my aunt's place,' Paolo told her. 'Tourists tell me the food in Venice isn't as good as they find in the rest of Italy, but at Tia Angelita's restaurant you will eat like a princess.'

Sophie remembered his aunt and was certain Tia Angelita would quickly recognise her. Years ago, she had often remarked on the colour of Sophie's eyes.

'You don't remember me, do you, Paolo?' she said as they emerged from an alley into the *campo* dominated by the majestic church of San Zaccaria.

'Remember you?' He looked disconcerted. 'When were you here before? I thought it was your first time.'

She shook her head. 'I didn't think you would ever forget me,' she added, with an exaggerated sigh.

His look of alarm amused her. She could almost hear his brain whirring as he scanned all the girls in his memory for some recollection of her. As he searched wildly for a way to extricate himself from his embarrassing situation she let him squirm for a minute before ending his discomfiture.

'You never used my real name. You used to know me as Kit…short for Kitten. Don't you remember the Englishman who drew caricatures of the tourists? We had a pitch on the Riva. There's a bead stall there now.'

Paolo's forehead wrinkled. 'I remember the old English artist and the girl who looked like a boy… But you can't be her…can you?' He gave her a long searching look. '*Mamma mia!* How you've changed. Who could believe you would grow up to be so beautiful?'

Suddenly seizing hold of her, he gave her the kind of hearty kisses exchanged by close family members after long separations.

Sophie didn't mind being hugged. She liked it. But when Paolo went on to give her a kiss on the lips she pulled back in laughing protest at his quickness to turn the tables and take playful revenge for the trick she had played on him.

'You'll shock the old ladies...kissing in public,' she said as two smartly dressed elderly women, arm in arm on their evening stroll, came towards them.

'They aren't shocked. They are wishing they were young again,' Paolo said irrepressibly.

And indeed the two stately *signoras* taking their *passeggiata*, a ritual of Venetian life whenever the weather encouraged a leisurely promenade, were looking faintly amused by the young Italian's spontaneous display of affection.

'I still can't believe how beautifully you have grown up,' Paolo said in his own language, when, several hours later, they passed through the same square after a filling meal at his aunt's restaurant and Sophie's reunion with that branch of his family.

His father, Sophie had been sorry to hear, had died two years earlier. His mother was living with a married daughter at Mestre, the industrial town on the shore of the mainland to which many Venetians had moved for jobs in the industries there and for more modern housing.

'You've improved too,' said Sophie. 'But why aren't you married like the others?'

'There's plenty of time. For a man there is never any hurry. Why aren't *you* married?'

'I've been too busy with my career. I'm not here on holiday, Paolo. I shall be working. Have you heard of a man called Marc Washington? His mother was Venetian.'

'Everyone's heard of him. He's one of the richest men

in Venice. His father was an American millionaire who fell in love with the daughter of the old Marchese Cassiano. They were all compulsive gamblers, that family. The Palazzo Cassiano was falling to bits due to lack of money to repair it. Then the daughter bewitched this rich Yank and they had one of the grandest weddings this city has ever seen. Mamma's described it to us a thousand times. But a year later she was dead—the bride, I mean. Died in childbirth… And a few years after that her husband drank himself to death.'

'How dreadful.'

It explained why Marc's only family references were to his grandfather, thought Sophie. He hadn't known his parents. She could empathise with that. She hadn't known hers either. But what she did know was that during her parents' few years together they had been deeply happy. The transcript of the tape-recorded log of their last voyage was proof that they had been enjoying life until shortly before the storm which had capsized their boat a few hundred miles from the finish of an ocean race they had been expected to win.

'Why are you interested in Washington?' Paolo asked.

'He's my boss. I'm his personal assistant in Venice, starting the day after tomorrow. He has PAs all over the world—wherever the business empire he inherited operates. I was recruited in New York and met him for the first time the day before yesterday. We flew here together.'

'From what I hear, he's spending big money on one of the islands,' said Paolo. 'Billions of lire, so they say. They're dangerous people, the rich, Kit. You want to watch your step with him.'

She could see it was going to take time for him and his relations to adjust to calling her Sophie. 'What makes you say that? Have you heard bad things about him?'

After a pause, he said, 'Not that I can remember off-hand—except that his mother's family were a decadent lot and his father was a dipso. Not genes I'd want in me.'

'We have more than our parents' genes in us. Sometimes people are throwbacks. Marc may take after his grandparents or great-grandparents. Anyway I'm a big girl now. I can look after myself.'

'You don't look as if you can. You don't look as street-wise now as you did when you were a kid. Look, we still have a lot to catch up. If you're not working tomorrow, I'll take the day off as well and we'll spend it together.'

'Can you afford to take days off just like that?'

'Oh, sure. I'm doing well. It helps to be a good-looking fellow with a nice line in sweet talk,' he said, with a mischievous grin.

By now they had reached her hotel. Sophie said, 'It's been an exciting day. I shall sleep like a log. It's been wonderful seeing you all again. Goodnight, Paolo. Thank you for a very happy evening.'

'I'll come for you about ten. That will give you time for a lie-in, if you want one. Goodnight.' He kissed her once, on the cheek, before turning away to walk in the direction of the *piazza*.

An elderly night porter was on duty. He took her room key from a board and reached under the counter for an envelope.

'This was left for you, *signorina*,' he said, in English.

'Thank you. Goodnight.'

As Sophie walked up the staircase she looked at her name on the envelope, written in a boldly incisive hand which could only be Marc's. He must have had it sent round. She wondered why he had written to her when he could have left a telephone message.

In her room, she slit open the plain white envelope and was surprised to find the writing paper inside bore the *albergo's* letterhead. On it was written: 'Change of plan. Report for duty at Palazzo Cassiano at 0900. M.W.'

The extreme terseness of the note, unprefaced by any Dear Sophie and signed only with his initials, made her feel faintly uneasy. But why, since she hadn't been expecting him to call round this evening, should he have been annoyed at finding she had gone out?

Even if she hadn't met Paolo she wouldn't have chosen to eat in the pavement *caffè*, which was the hotel's only restaurant. It did good business by day when the sun was hot, and would be busy on summer nights, but at this time of year after sundown somewhere more sheltered was preferable. If Marc had been displeased at not finding her on the premises he was being rather unreasonable.

On impulse she went downstairs to ask the night porter if he knew when the note had been left.

'It was already here when I came in at half past seven, *signorina*.'

'Thank you. *Buena notte*.'

If she hadn't set her alarm clock Sophie would have overslept. Because her body clock was six hours behind Venetian time, she had fallen into bed with her system still geared to late afternoon in New York—not the right time to be sleeping. She had slept eventually, but not long or soundly enough to feel fresh and clear-eyed at seven.

She got up and opened her window and the dark green shutters which must have been closed by the maid who'd turned down the bed. There was no one about on the

Riva to see her in her nightdress, leaning out to adjust the clips which secured the shutters to the wall.

Out in the channel, between the deserted waterfront and the little island of San Giorgio Maggiore, a delivery barge was heading towards the Guidecca, a long strip of land most people outside Venice had heard of only because it had one of the world's most luxurious hotels on it—the Cipriani.

She had a shower and dressed, choosing a straight grey skirt with a generous kickpleat at the back, an ivory silk shirt and her navy blazer. It wasn't part of her job to make fashion statements, but rather to look acceptable wherever her working day might take her. With Marc as her boss that could cover a wide range of venues.

Downstairs, she asked the proprietor, 'How do I get to the Palazzo Cassiano?'

There was a blown-up map of the city on the wall near his desk. He put his finger on the outline representing the palace.

'To walk…about twenty minutes—if you don't lose your way,' he said, twinkling at her. 'But we make sure our visitors are never lost for long. Everywhere there are arrows pointing to the Accademia, San Marco and the Rialto. Once you know where those are…no problems.'

Outside, in the *caffè*, Sophie ordered a cheese omelette with toast and tea. By now the Riva was beginning to bustle with groups of students going to their classes. A newsvendor was selling papers to workers on their way to the *vaporetto* stops. A few souvenir-sellers were beginning to set up their stands, although it was too early for there to be organised groups of tourists about.

Her appetite stimulated by the fresh breeze from the lagoon, she would have enjoyed watching all this activity while she ate her breakfast but for an instinctive feeling of uneasiness about Marc's summons.

While drinking a second cup of tea she wrote a note to Paolo, apologising for not being able to spend the day with him.

The *palazzo's* somewhat forbidding street entrance was near the end of a cul-de-sac leading only to the edge of the wide waterway which was the city's principal thoroughfare. There was an old-fashioned iron bell-pull, but also a discreet modern push-button.

Within moments of pressing it Sophie was admitted to the courtyard by an elderly manservant. Even though it was unlikely that in past centuries the family and their equals would have used this entrance, there was an impressive doorway opening into a large hall with a wide staircase.

In the hall, a maid was deputed to show her the way. When they had climbed several flights Sophie understood why the butler had handed her over to someone younger. For ageing joints it would be a strenuous climb to the upper floors of the huge building, with its high ceilings and lavish use of space. Her mind boggled at the thought of the heating bills.

On the top floor she was shown into a large empty room. With a shy smile the maid went away. Sophie was drawn to the windows with their wide views over the city's Roman-tiled rooftops and distinctive flowerpot-shaped chimneys.

As the great bell of San Marco began to strike nine, backed by a chorus of chimes from near and far bell-towers, she sensed rather than heard Marc enter the room behind her.

'Good morning.' His tone was curt, his expression unsmiling. He was wearing freshly laundered jeans and an open-necked pale blue shirt with a navy sweater slung round his shoulders, the sleeves loosely tied on his chest. 'I hope you found your accommodation satisfactory.'

'Extremely comfortable, thank you, and the view from my window is superb.'

'Good.' He moved to an outsize desk, seating himself behind it and indicating that she should take the chair in front of it.

The desk had a sheet of glass protecting the patina of its antique mahogany surface. On one side stood a small-footprint PC, on the other a tray containing such things as a letter-opener, long-bladed scissors, pens and markers. There were no photographs, and none of the costly accessories found on most VIPs' desks.

'Did he make a pass at you?'

The blunt question rattled her. How did he know she had spent the evening with a man?

When she didn't answer immediately, he said, 'That's the usual form with susceptible tourists. I thought you had more sense than to fall for a gondolier's line of flattery.'

Sophie began to recover herself. 'Did you see us together? How did you know he was a gondolier?'

'No, I didn't see you. The owner of your hotel recognised him. There aren't many *gondolieri* left. They're a diminishing species, most of them known by sight if not by name to the older inhabitants. The one who picked you up is one of the youngest...and a well-known Casanova.'

His assumption that it must have been a pick-up made Sophie angry. For Paolo it had been that. Not for her. But if Marc was ready to jump to derogatory conclusions about her, let him.

CHAPTER SIX

SOPHIE said coldly, 'Hearsay isn't always reliable. Hardly ever, in my experience. He behaved with the utmost courtesy. We ate at a restaurant run by his aunt and uncle where the food was very much better than I might have eaten elsewhere.'

'And where he wouldn't have to pay,' Marc said drily. 'Are you seeing him again?'

'I expect so.' Common sense dictated that she explain the situation, but offended pride and resentment at his unjust assumption made her leave it at that, apart from adding, 'I'd like to master the Venetian dialect while I'm here. A gondolier and his family are useful contacts.'

His tilted eyebrow was sceptical. 'You can do as you please in your free time. But don't be surprised if there turns out to be some truth in what you dismiss as hearsay.'

Still annoyed with him, but beginning to realise that the situation had lent itself to misinterpretation, Sophie said, 'I'm sorry I wasn't there if you needed me to work on something last night. If you'd telephoned, instead of coming to the hotel, you might have caught me before I went out.'

'I came to take you out myself.'

Disconcerted, she said, 'Oh…well, that was kind of you.'

Almost echoing Paolo, he said, 'I thought you might be uncomfortable eating alone at night. Some women are.' He rose from his chair. 'Before we go over to

Capolavoro I'll show you where it is in relation to the other islands in the lagoon.

'This shows the whole lagoon,' he said moments later, when she was standing beside him in front of the large wall map.

It was as familiar to her as the layout of Manhattan Island or central London. She was watching his hand, not the map, as he said, 'All the islands in the lagoon were important once. They were only accessible by boat and each had its special function. Then Venice was linked to the mainland by railway bridge and a canal was dredged from the city to the Lido. After that the other islands weren't important any longer and gradually most were abandoned.'

Sophie was listening to what he was saying, but her visual attention was on the strong, sunburned hand pointing out the features he was telling her about.

Suddenly she found herself wondering how many women had felt those long fingers on their skin, and if he had given them pleasure as well as taking it.

Faintly embarrassed by the inappropriateness of this unbidden thought, she was slow in reacting when he said, 'And the other map shows the *valli*—the traditional fish farms.'

If her thoughts hadn't been wandering, she would have anticipated his movement towards the other map. They would have both moved sideways at the same time. As it was, her delayed response caused him to bump into her.

Although it was her fault, it was he who said, 'I'm sorry.'

Startled by the effect of the contact between his chest and her shoulder and upper arm, she said nothing. Such light, unimportant impacts were frequent on the New York subway or the London Underground at rush hour.

People might murmur 'Sorry' or they might ignore them. They certainly didn't react the way she was reacting now.

As he started explaining the locks and sluices controlling the fish ponds she felt a lingering vibration deep inside her, as if her nerves were harp-strings he had plucked and left quivering.

It was a relief when he finished his explanation. It was not that she wasn't interested in the ancient and intricate system of fish farming in the lagoon. But it was hard to concentrate when he was standing as close as he was at the moment.

Perhaps this strange over-sensitivity was an after-effect of changing time zones. He did it all the time and his system was used to it. Hers wasn't.

As they went down the stairs it struck her that she hadn't felt normal from the moment he'd entered her life. There was something intensely disturbing about him. She had never seen a tiger in reality. But sometimes, on TV, powerful zoom lenses allowed close-up shots in which the great beasts seemed to be looking directly into the eyes of the viewer.

There was a connection between the way she had felt when Marc had been looming over her, his sleeve almost brushing hers, and her response to tigers. With their beautiful markings, the formidable power concealed by the dense velvet fur and their strange, enigmatic eyes, they exuded animal magnetism. They could also be deadly dangerous, especially those who were man-eaters.

Instinct warned her that Marc had a lot in common with tigers and might be an incorrigible woman-eater.

They left the *palazzo* by the main entrance. The launch which had fetched them from the airport was waiting, with the same boatman.

'These are called *pali*,' said Marc, indicating the tall posts, painted with spiralling strips, projecting from the water on either side of the well-kept, moss-free steps. 'The colours are like the silks worn by jockeys. They tell anyone interested in such things to whom each *palazzo* belongs…or belonged originally.'

Marc had just followed her inboard when a *vaporetto* came by, some of its passengers looking with curiosity at the two people in the launch moving away from the steps of the magnificent palace.

Although it was already hot in the sun, Sophie knew there would be a cool breeze when they reached open water. She didn't take off her blazer. For seeing the island jeans would have been more appropriate. She would have to ask Marc how he felt about her wearing trousers on duty.

Last night it had seemed lucky to run into Paolo on her first day in Venice. Now she wished it hadn't happened yet. She didn't want to lose Marc's good opinion of her, but nor did she want to explain her past to him. Not until after she had been back to *her* island.

On the way to the island that Marc had leased he told her it had the remains of a fortress on it and the ruins of several small houses built by people who must have lived on what they could grow and fish from the surrounding lagoon.

He unrolled a plan he had brought with him. It showed the shape of the island and the site for the house he planned, with architect's visualisations of how it would relate to the fort, which his lease obliged him to restore.

They spent about an hour on Capolavoro. Long before they left she had grasped how important the project was to him. To anyone else the place would look a desolate spot with nothing appealing about it. But, if he could realise his vision of it, in a few years' time it would look very different.

It was nearly noon when they returned to the *palazzo*. Marc said, 'I'll show you your office. It has the basic equipment common to all the other PAs' offices, but you're free to order anything you consider necessary from the shops where I have accounts. You'll find a list of them on my PC. This week's password is Constanzia. I rotate the names of my three aunts.'

Her office was across the landing from his large room. It was small but, to her delight, it had a glass door leading onto a little roof garden with tubs of greenery and a table and chair with a furled parasol standing beside it.

'If you like, while the hot weather lasts, you can have your lunch here. Alternatively, there's a large garden at street level. You're welcome to take your coffee and lunch breaks down there. But my aunts spend a good deal of time in the garden and they're all extremely talkative. You could find them tiring. I do,' he added drily.

As he finished speaking a young female voice called in Italian, 'Marc…Marc…where are you?'

He returned to the doorway. 'I'm here. Come and meet my new assistant.'

It was difficult to guess the age of the girl who appeared seconds later, giving him a radiant smile. Her lovely skin was that of someone very young, but Sophie had never seen anyone of eighteen or nineteen who was so perfectly groomed or self-possessed.

She was wearing a very short geranium-red tunic, cinched at the waist by a wide leather belt, with tights, shoes and lipstick of the same colour and huge silver earrings and bracelets. She might have stepped straight from the cover of Italian *Vogue*.

'I've been looking everywhere for you,' she said, laying a long-fingered hand with geranium-lacquered nails on his forearm.

Marc said, 'Sophie, this is my cousin Chiara Banti…Sophie Hill.'

'Welcome to Venice, Ms Hill,' the Italian girl said warmly, offering her hand.

She spoke American English with only the faintest trace of an Italian accent, and was clearly *au fait* with modern forms of address.

'Thank you,' Sophie said admiringly. She had never seen a lovelier girl.

Barefoot, their heights would be similar. But Sophie was wearing flat-heeled tassel loafers and Chiara was perched on absurdly high heels attached to her feet by a few narrow straps. They were obviously very fashionable, but for wearing in an old house and a city of numerous bridges they seemed strikingly impractical.

'What did you want me for?' asked Marc.

'I can't decide what to wear for the party tonight. I want you to help me choose.'

'Later. Right now we're busy. Ask me again after lunch.'

She looked disappointed. 'Oh…all right.' With another smile for Sophie she left.

Marc led the way back to his room. There, with the girl out of earshot, he said, 'Don't let Chiara make a nuisance of herself. She's bored, having nothing to do but go to parties and amuse herself. She ought to be starting a career but she has a very silly, possessive mother who never trained for anything and sees no reason why Chiara should. I'm working on her to change her mind but Tia Caterina is a recent widow. Although she and her husband were often at odds while he was alive, she's behaving as if the sky had fallen in.'

'Perhaps it has,' said Sophie. 'Couples don't have to

be blissfully happy to feel bereft when one of them dies. How old is Chiara?'

'Twenty-two, but she behaves more like sixteen. She's been impossibly spoilt but has somehow managed to survive it and become a very sweet girl. You'll have to be firm with her, though. Given the smallest encouragement, she'll come up here and chatter for hours.'

For the next hour or so he gave her a thorough briefing on what was expected of her. Then he departed to lunch with his family.

'You'll meet the rest of them later. Rather than sitting through a long formal luncheon downstairs, I am sure you'd rather have a light lunch up here and get on with the process of settling in. I'll be out this afternoon, but I'll look in about four-thirty to see how you're getting on.'

After he had gone, Sophie wondered if the truth was that his aristocratic relations would not find a foreign employee an acceptable presence at their table. But he was right: she was happier eating up here.

At that moment the house telephone started ringing. When Sophie had answered it, *'Pronto, sono Sophie,'* a man's voice replied that he was the chef, and what would the *signorina* like to eat today? She had only to state her wishes and they would be fulfilled.

At the end of a delicious lunch starting with asparagus mousse followed by trout with almonds and stuffed courgettes, Sophie's final treat was a generous slice of *zuccotto*—a cake made of sponge, ice cream, chocolate and cream.

I can't eat like this every day, she thought, enjoying the last mouthful. Perhaps it's the three aunts who polish off most of the fattening dishes. Marc and Chiara don't.

It would take more than a morning run to keep him lean if *he* ate like this every day.

She had been offered wine with her meal but had asked for spring water and *camomilla* instead of coffee. Italian coffee was strong and she didn't want to drink a lot of it.

After brushing her teeth in the washroom that Marc had said was for her use only, she checked all the stationery and equipment in her office. There were several things she would need in order to work in the way she found most efficient. After making a note of them, she went to his room to check the list of shops he had mentioned.

Sophie had once read that a man's office was an indication of his character as well as his position. Here were none of the usual status symbols: the paintings by recognisably important artists, the photographs of encounters with statesmen and royalty, the antique humidor or the silver box for cigars, the trifles from Tiffany or Cartier. The most striking features of *this* room, after its views, were the wall of books and the wall of pictures and posters, even including some postcards which had obviously caught its occupant's eye.

Both walls confirmed that he was a man whose life was spent travelling, sometimes to parts of the world which had nothing to do with his commercial empire. There were books about primitive people living in remote places, and paintings by unknown artists. As she scanned the pictures her eye was arrested by one only recognisable for what it was by someone who knew every inch of this city.

It was a pen-and-wash drawing of a Venetian cat sleeping curled in the metal folds of the skirt belonging to a female figure at the base of an equestrian statue of an Italian king on the Riva near her hotel. But not many people would recognise the border on the sculpted skirt unless, like herself, they had spent long hours near that spot.

She wondered what had prompted Marc to buy that particular piece of art. Did he like cats? Or was it the contrast between the cat's soft fur and the burnished metal which had appealed to him? Later, she would ask.

The computer on his desk was, she knew, for his private use, and not linked to the one on her desk or accessible to anyone without permission. She was a little surprised he should allow her to use it.

Sophie was familiar with most of the applications in widespread use, and as Marc had written down the path to the list she needed she had no difficulty in finding it and printing a copy.

She couldn't resist finding out how well organised he was on his computer. All the other areas of his life were serviced by people like his butler, his boatman, his chef and a worldwide retinue of paid retainers who, if they weren't efficient, were replaced by people who were. But how successful would he have been if he hadn't been born into money?

It was the work of a moment to find out that he had a very large number of items stored on disk. After ten minutes' browsing, she was impressed by the way he had them organised. It was possible someone else had tailored the arrangements for him, but she didn't think so. It had all the hallmarks of a customised set-up, devised and used by a man with a brilliant mind in total command of the technology he was using.

During the afternoon various telephone calls and faxes required her attention, including a note from Audrey LaRue wishing her well in her new job.

At four o'clock, while she was typing a letter to

Merle, she heard Marc's footsteps on the staircase. When he had looked at the messages and given her some instructions for dealing with them, he said, 'But all that can wait till tomorrow. First, I'll show you some more of the house...the rooms that are only used on special occasions.'

The larger staterooms were awesome in their splendour, with chandeliers, huge paintings and ornate gilded furniture. The only room having any claim to comfort was a bedroom with papered walls and a curtained bed with some pretty porcelain displayed in the alcoves on either side of it.

'This is where, by tradition, the brides of my mother's ancestors had their first experience of the pleasures, or otherwise, of the marriage bed,' said Marc.

He turned to the wall that the bed faced. 'There's a curious story attached to this looking-glass. As you see, it's a much finer example than the one you feel has been vandalised in our New York office.' There was a hint of mockery in the glance he turned on her. 'This one has hung here for several centuries—except for one short period when it was moved to another room in which an important guest was to sleep for a few nights. During the first night she had a peculiar experience.'

He turned away to admire the artistry of the reflective glass frame surrounding the time-misted centre panel. Sophie, impatient for him to go on, watched the reflection of his face. When their eyes met in the mirror she found she couldn't look away.

'What happened?' she asked.

'The visitor didn't sleep well. She was sitting up in bed by the light of a candle when something strange happened. She was the unmarried daughter of a middle-European king who had lost his throne, and her lady-in-waiting was sleeping in the next room. The princess insisted she came and slept with her.'

'Do you mean she'd seen something frightening in the mirror?' Sophie asked.

'It frightened her. It wouldn't have frightened me. I don't know how you would have reacted.'

She suspected him of prevaricating to tease her. Perhaps the whole story was a tease.

'What *did* she see?'

'They both saw it. They left the candle alight and eventually the princess slept while the lady-in-waiting read. According to written reports of what happened—in the notes and letters people wrote before they could gossip by telephone—she was a level-headed young woman. Rather like you, probably.' Again the dark eyes reflected in the misty glass held a glimmer of mockery.

'I should have blown out the candle and gone to sleep,' said Sophie.

'Perhaps the princess snored or the book was interesting. At any rate, some time later she glanced at the mirror and saw and heard much the same as the princess had seen and heard…two people making love, in a different bed, in a different room. This room.'

'I think you're inventing this. To me it sounds pure tarradiddle,' Sophie said, using a word from her childhood.

'I promise you I'm not. Ask Chiara—ask my aunts when you meet them. Half Venice knows the story of the Palazzo Cassiano's haunted mirror.'

Not wholly convinced, she said, 'If such a thing really did happen, or they claimed it did, the princess and her attendant were either dreaming or hallucinating. It sounds about as believable as that story of the two women who claimed to have seen Queen Marie Antoinette when they were visiting Versailles.'

A thought struck her. 'I'm sure *you* don't believe it. If you did, when you were younger you'd have spent the night here to see for yourself.'

'When I was fourteen I did, and very scary it was—far away from the rest of the household in the small hours. Various people have tested the legend, including my mother when she was young. She had a group of friends to keep her company.'

'But none of you saw what the princess thought she had seen?'

'Disappointingly, no. But the legend persists.'

'As ghosts stories go, it's rather a nice one,' said Sophie.

'Actually, no,' he said drily. 'What the lady-in-waiting saw was different from what the princess saw. She, being an elderly spinster, was shocked by the erotic nature of her vision. Nowadays my aunts watch similar scenes on TV and think nothing of it. But this was in 1843 and—'

He was interrupted by a bleeping from his shirt pocket.

'Excuse me...somebody wants me. There's a house phone in the corridor. Which reminds me,' he added, leading the way, 'I must give you a bleeper. In a house this size it's as essential as a watch.'

Sophie followed him back the way they had come and stood at a polite distance while he checked with whoever had bleeped him.

Then, to her amazement, he put his hand over the mouthpiece and said, 'It's Domenico, our major-domo, with a message for you. There's a gondolier at the street door, asking what time you stop work. I gather you've set up another date with him tonight?'

CHAPTER SEVEN

'NOT to my knowledge.'

Sophie couldn't believe that Paolo could have made such a maladroit move as to call for her on her first day at the *palazzo*. She felt furious with him.

'It wasn't a "date" last night,' she added crisply. 'Please ask Domenico to tell him I can't come down now and not to wait for me.'

But what Marc said to his butler was, 'The *signorina* will be down in five minutes. We're on the first floor and she has to fetch her purse from the office.' Then he replaced the receiver. 'It's knocking-off time anyway. He may have come to take you back in his gondola. You must introduce us. I'm curious to meet this guy.'

Inwardly Sophie was fuming. But there was nothing she could do but accept the situation and make sure Paolo never repeated his *faux pas*.

She debated explaining to Marc about knowing Paolo years ago, but she knew this wasn't the right moment. Not while they were hurrying up a staircase he climbed two steps at a time while she had to run to keep pace with him.

She was breathless when they reached the top floor, and it didn't mollify her when Marc said casually, 'New York has made you decadent. By the time you've been here a month, you'll whizz up and down our stairs and think nothing of it.'

Trying not to pant and determined not to be nettled, at least not visibly, she said pleasantly, 'I'm sure I shall.

They're good exercise—which I'll need if lunch always ends with a pudding as rich as today's *zuccotto.*'

'It's not generally realised that the French learnt the art of cooking from the Italians,' said Marc. 'It was Catherine de' Medici's cooks, who took their arts to France when she married the French king Henri II, who gave French cuisine its impetus.'

'I've met Frenchmen who don't agree with that theory,' said Sophie, picking up her shoulder-bag.

'Do you want to touch up your lipstick before we go down?'

She suspected him of deliberately trying to exacerbate her embarrassment.

'No, thanks,' she said composedly.

Paolo, wearing his gondolier's clothes, was waiting for her in the courtyard inside the street door. Domenico was with him, but he went away when he saw his employer and Sophie descending the stairs from the first door.

Paolo's straw hat was on the stone table near where he was standing. 'I got your note,' he told Sophie as she came down the last steps. Then his gaze shifted to Marc.

Before she could introduce them, Marc introduced himself, by name and as her employer. At the same time he offered his hand. There was no condescension in his tone. His manner was as friendly as if socially they were equals.

In fact they were not unalike. They could have been half-brothers, Marc the son of an aristocratic marriage and Paolo born outside marriage to a girl from one of the city's poorest quarters. Their heights were different, and their features, but both looked unmistakably Venetian. Faces like theirs could be seen in paintings of La Serenissima's citizens from the centuries when it had been the gateway between Europe and the riches of the East.

'I hope I'm not interrupting anything, but I thought…er…Sophie might like to ride back with me. The *vaporetti* are crowded at this time of day,' said Paolo. She guessed it had been on the tip of his tongue to call her Kit.

'I intended to walk,' she said. 'It's not far.'

Marc said, 'I would have walked with you and shown you the stationery shop where we buy our supplies. But I expect you can find it by yourself. Enjoy your ride in a gondola. If you weren't an attractive blonde you would have to pay through the nose for it.'

For a moment he seemed about to turn away and go through the door at the foot of the stairs. Instead he gestured for her to go first through the street door and followed her.

Being called an attractive blonde made Sophie bristle. Although, on her holidays with Merle, days in the sun had bleached her hair to a much lighter shade than her present degree of fairness, she didn't think of herself as a blonde, and certainly not in the pejorative sense of being the dizzy or dumb blonde implied by his tone.

She was feeling annoyed with both of them when they reached the end of the street where the gondola was moored.

Paolo sprang lightly into the well. 'I'd better lift you down. Put your hands on my shoulders.'

As he spoke Marc took hold of her bag's strap. 'I'll take this and pass it to you.'

'Thank you.'

It wasn't the first time a gondolier had put his hands on her waist and lifted her into his craft. Paolo's father had done it. She remembered his florid face, his nicotine-stained teeth and the smell of tobacco and wine on his breath.

Paolo's face was the colour of teak, his teeth were white and he smelt of the clove-scented toothpaste called Pasta del Capitano they had used when she was a child. The faint whiff of it brought back those years with the poignancy of a grief which had never quite healed.

The Italian set her on her feet, taking hold of her hand until she was seated on the sofa. Then he took her bag from Marc, dropped it lightly on her lap and stepped past her to his place on the stern.

Marc gave them a farewell wave, his expression sardonic. She hoped he would walk away but he stayed where he was. Using his single oar, Paolo propelled them in the direction of the Santa Maria della Salute, the church like a giant wedding cake at the eastern end of the Grand Canal, and she did not look over her shoulder to see if Marc was still there.

She was thinking that if it hadn't been for the man behind her she could have been walking through the city with the other one, perhaps stopping for a drink in a street *caffè* and hearing the rest of the story he had been telling her.

Apart from agreeing that it was a beautiful evening, Sophie was a silent passenger—at first because she was angry and then because the soothing motion of the gondola and the beauty of the scene before her combined to calm her annoyance. It reminded her that where she was and what she was doing was something people trapped in the world's many ugly cities would consider a taste of paradise.

By the time the canal had widened into the glittering expanse of the *bacino* and the long line of elegant buildings along the Riva were beginning to be tinted with the rose glow of evening, her irritation had subsided.

Very near her hotel there were unadorned wooden stakes, poor relations of the painted *pali* outside the *palazzi*, driven into the bed of the lagoon as moorings for gondolas. Instead of steering towards them, Paolo kept the bow pointing parallel with the Riva.

'Where are we going?' said Sophie, turning to look at him.

From his place on one side of the stern he smiled down at her. 'I'm taking you for a drink...but not at the clip-joint prices the tourists pay.'

For a moment she thought of insisting that he drop her off on the Riva, but decided it would be better to remonstrate when he didn't have part of his mind on the water traffic.

Although it bore no relation to the rush-hour traffic snarls in New York or London, at this time of day the *bacino* was criss-crossed by the white wakes of engine-driven craft. Gondoliers had to be more watchful now than in the days when Paolo's grandfather had been plying his trade.

The broad esplanade of the Riva was cut into sections by canals crossed by small hump-backed bridges. As they glided beneath one some tourists leaning on the parapet took snaps of the good-looking gondolier. Without turning round, Sophie felt sure he was flashing his white teeth at them. He had always played to the gallery, she remembered, but not in an unpleasant way. The grown-ups had told him off, but pinched his cheek or patted his head as they did it.

In the smaller canals it was quiet, except when they came to a blind bend and Paolo's warning *'Ohé!'* would ring out.

Where two canals crossed, they gave way to another gondola carrying two portly couples.

'You can't be short of a bob, love,' one of the men called to Sophie in a broad northern accent. 'We're going to be skint after this lot. They know 'ow to charge in this town.'

Sophie smiled but said nothing, wondering if Paolo would understand what skint meant.

Evidently the other gondolier had understood his passenger's last remark. In the Venetian dialect, he said to Paolo, 'They all complain about prices. They have no values, these people. To ride through Venice in a gondola is a once-in-a-lifetime experience. When my sons are men it may no longer be possible. These stupid people should be grateful they can afford to come here. Do they think we want millions of them invading our unique city?' He looked at Sophie, his expression softening. 'She's pretty. You always get the pretty ones. I get the fat, ugly ones.'

'Would you rather work on an assembly line in a factory in Mestre?' Paolo asked him as the other gondola was disappearing from view.

'The prices here are rather steep,' Sophie remarked.

'We have to cover the months when we don't make any money. It's a vicious circle,' said Paolo. 'Without the tourists the city would fall into ruins, but now there are too many of them. In the old days they stayed longer and enjoyed themselves more. At this season it's not so bad, but in the summer…a madhouse!'

But the square where he stopped the gondola was an oasis of peace, with only a few local people enjoying the last of the sunlight at the tables outside a *caffè*.

When he had ordered their drinks, he said, 'Why did you have to work today? I thought you weren't starting till tomorrow?'

'My boss changed his mind. Paolo, you shouldn't have come to the *palazzo*. I don't have fixed working hours like other people. A PA's hours are elastic.'

'You didn't tell me your boss was a young man. I haven't seen him before. I thought he was much older. Didn't you want him to know you have a boyfriend?' he said shrewdly.

'You're a friend, not a boyfriend,' she said firmly.

'Have you grown so grand since you left us that a gondolier isn't good enough for you any more?'

'Your job has nothing to do with it. We were close as children, but now we're two grown-up people who don't really know each other. I've changed and I'm sure you have. Life is more complicated now than it was all those years ago.'

'For you, perhaps. Not for me. What are you looking for, Kit?'

'I'm Sophie now,' she reminded him. 'At the moment I'm not looking for anything. Having just landed an exceptional job, I have to concentrate on doing it well. Marc Washington is a very demanding employer. If I don't come up to scratch, he'll replace me.'

Their drinks came: a beer for him, *spritz al bitter* for her. It tasted subtly different from the one in Paris. Perhaps it was like some wines which, in wine buffs' jargon, 'didn't travel'. Maybe Campari never tasted the same outside Italy, and never quite as perfect as in the roseate twilight at the close of a day in Venice.

'Tonight we won't eat at Tia Angelita's place,' said Paolo. 'I want to have you to myself. I want to find out how you've changed...if you've really changed.'

Presently he rowed her through the twists and turns of the smaller waterways back to the Grand Canal, to a restaurant where the canal-side tables were full of well-heeled tourists. He had reserved a table by one of the windows in an upstairs room. Here the patrons were mainly Venetians eating their *antipasti*, mostly dishes of seafood. Sophie recognised *moleche*, the crabs caught in spring and autumn when they changed their shells.

Having eaten well at lunchtime, she wasn't very hungry and could only manage a bowl of fish soup and a salad. Paolo ate four courses and finished with cheese. Although he was trim and muscular at the moment, she thought that if he didn't take care he would run to fat later.

At the end of their meal, while they were drinking coffee—his accompanied by a glass of *grappa*—Sophie glanced out of the window and saw a launch flying a blue pennant cruising slowly along the canal in the direction of the Rialto Bridge.

Seated in the stern, wearing a dinner jacket, was Marc. Beside him, in a fur jacket with a rug over her legs, was his young cousin Chiara.

Something in Sophie's expression made Paolo turn his head to see what she was looking at. 'That's your boss, isn't it? Who's the chick with him?'

'A cousin…Chiara Banti. I met her today. She said she was going to a party but I didn't know he was going with her.'

'Jealous?' said Paolo, taking his eyes off the launch passing below them long enough to flash a grin at her.

'Don't be silly.' Sophie tried to speak lightly, not to betray how much his quip annoyed her. 'There's nothing I'd enjoy less than going to a fashionable party where I wouldn't know anyone.'

'If you were with him it wouldn't matter. He knows everyone. When you have his money and his background, everyone wants to know you. If there was any justice in life, he'd have a face like an ape,' said Paolo. 'She's a good-looker too, but too young for my taste.

They still giggle a lot at that age and they want to dance all night. I'm past that.' He stopped watching the launch and turned to her. 'Quiet, candlelit dinners with someone intelligent are what I prefer these days.'

Next morning, very early, Sophie went for a brisk walk along the Riva. In New York she and Merle had attended exercise classes, but here she thought she might buy some trainers and take up running.

She wondered where Marc did his running when he was in Venice. She didn't expect to meet him. It was more likely he ran along the Zattere, the waterfront on the south side of the élite Dorsoduro district, not far from his *palazzo*. But if he and Chiara had been partying half the night he might postpone today's run until later.

Paolo's chaffing remark about jealousy still rankled slightly. Paolo himself was a complication in her life. It wasn't true, as he had suggested last night, that the company of a gondolier and his family wasn't good enough for her now. It was merely that she didn't want Marc to think she had been bowled over by Paolo, like the susceptible tourists who every year lost their hearts to Italian and Spanish waiters, Greek boatmen, Swiss and Austrian ski-instructors and all the other good-looking young men who worked in the tourist industry and notched up innumerable conquests which meant nothing to them.

Yesterday, if Paolo hadn't turned up and Marc had walked her back to the Riva, she would have explained the situation to him. But it was quite a long story and needed to be told in the right circumstances, not when he had more important matters on his mind.

On the way back from her walk she stopped in the Via Giuseppe Garibaldi, a filled-in canal which was now the city's widest street but far enough from the Piazza to have a village atmosphere and for the prices in the bars and *alimentari* to be much cheaper. Sophie bought two brown rolls for breakfast and a bag of apples for her room. She ate the rolls as they were, sitting on a stone bench with the kind of view which had inspired Canaletto to paint his stupendous vistas of eighteenth-century Venice.

All the happiness she had once known in this city was beginning to seep through her veins like the rising sap in a tree. Love was no longer here: the shared laughter, the physical comfort of a strong shoulder to lean on and the warm hugs and bristly kisses. But Michael's spirit was here. She felt his presence everywhere, and heard in her mind his deep voice calling her Kitten, Sweetie and other endearments.

She arrived at the *palazzo* at a quarter to nine, reaching the top floor to find Marc already there.

'Good morning,' she said, from the threshold of his office.

'Good morning.' He rose from behind the wide desk. 'A lot has come through overnight.' He indicated the tray behind the fax machine. 'I've dealt with some of it already. We'll go through the rest together and I'll tell you what needs to be done.'

'I'll just fetch my notebook.'

In her office, Sophie hung her blazer on the hanger in the cupboard.

Freshly shaven, his dark hair still damp from the shower, Marc looked alert and well-rested. Perhaps he didn't need much sleep. It was a peculiarity of many top-level achievers that they could maintain their physical and mental energy on half the sleep required by the average person.

'Did you enjoy your evening?' she asked, when she

rejoined him. 'I saw you and Signorina Banti going past in the launch while I was having supper.'

'Chiara enjoyed herself. I was there as her chaperon. Large parties are not my personal choice for a night out. I prefer a quiet dinner *à deux*. Where did you eat?'

When she told him, he raised an eyebrow. 'Alone?'

She wished now she hadn't mentioned seeing him. 'No.'

'That restaurant's expensive,' said Marc. 'Your gondolier must be seriously enamoured. Are you seeing him again tonight?'

'No, I'm not...and it isn't—'

But Sophie's decision to explain her relationship with Paolo was frustrated by the telephone.

'Excuse me.' He reached for the receiver. *'Pronto, sono Washington.'* A moment later he was speaking Japanese and signing to her that the call would take some time.

Later she accompanied him to a meeting with his architect and representatives of the city's planning authority.

They walked to the architect's office where he was going to show them a scale model of Capolavoro's existing and proposed buildings.

On the way there many people said good morning to Marc, but not always, Sophie noticed, the kind of people who might be expected to know him. Two or three of his acquaintances were noticeably down-at-heel. Even more surprising was what happened as they mounted the wooden steps of the Accademia Bridge, where a man was crouched, begging.

There were not many beggars in Venice. So far Sophie had seen only two, and on each occasion had responded with a small donation. But most people, especially tourists, ignored them and she wouldn't have been surprised if Marc had done the same. Instead, they both put their hands in their pockets and gave the man some money.

At the top of the bridge Marc stopped, putting his palms on the edge of the sun-warmed balustrade and looking down the broad waterway with the same slightly smiling expression she had seen when they'd been approaching the city from the airport.

Standing beside him, watching a gondola going in the direction of the Rialto and a delivery barge chugging in the opposite way, she said, 'Do you always give to beggars…even when they're probably dipsos?'

Marc turned his head to look at her. 'If they've hit the rock-bottom point of asking strangers for money, the least I can do is give them the price of a drink. It's an ineffective way of addressing the problem of these people who can't cope with life, but it's better than pretending not to notice them. I thought you would be a soft touch.'

'Did you? Why?'

A light gust of breeze off the water caught and ruffled her hair, blowing a lock of it across her cheek. Before she could deal with it he reached out and did it for her, smoothing the errant strands behind her ear. The intimate, almost tender gesture astonished her.

He began to walk on. 'You strike me as someone who would always be on the side of the underdog,' he said. Then, slanting a mocking glance at her, he added, 'But perhaps not always equally sympathetic to the problems of the top dogs. Except in your professional capacity.'

After the meeting, Marc and the architect went off to have lunch together while she returned to the *palazzo* to transcribe her record of what had been said.

Although she had contributed little to the men's conversation, but had sat quietly by, taking verbatim notes while they talked, from the outset Marc had made it clear that when he was away she would be left in full charge of the island's conversion.

Whether she really had his confidence to the extent he had indicated she herself wasn't sure. But he had left the others in no doubt of it. The architect had pressed her to join them for lunch but she had thought it best to excuse herself.

A printout was on his desk when Marc returned. It had not been the kind of long, vinous lunch that made businessmen who indulged in them perform at reduced efficiency for the rest of the working day. He was back by two-fifteen, with some speedwriting notes of his own for her to type.

The late afternoon brought a stream of faxes and telexes from Canada and North America, where the working day was just beginning.

It was after six when Marc's PC played the opening bars of what Sophie recognised as a violin concerto by Vivaldi as a reminder.

'I must go,' he said.

He had shown her his engagement diaries, the desk diary duplicated on his computer. She knew that tonight he was going to a reception at the German Embassy, an attractive building, painted yellow, on the north side of the wooden bridge between the smart part of town and the Accademia, where many of the city's greatest art treasures were housed.

As he was leaving the room Marc said, 'Tomorrow we're going to Torcello. I suggest you wear a cotton frock. We'll be lunching at the Locanda Cipriani and it can be very warm in the garden there at midday.'

'Why are we going to Torcello?' She had planned to visit the island on her first free day. She didn't want anyone with her the first time she went back.

'The grandmother of one of my college friends arrived

in Venice this morning. I'm under an obligation to show her some of the sights and Torcello isn't too taxing for someone in her eighties. You can help me entertain her.'

'Wouldn't your cousin be a better choice?'

'Chiara has been to Torcello too many times to find it an interesting excursion…unless it's with a new boy-friend. She's not interested in anyone in Mrs Henderson's age group. I don't suppose you are either, but you'll make a better job of pretending to enjoy being with her. See you tomorrow.'

When he crossed the large room the way his hair flicked into half-curls just above his shirt-collar and the jut of his cheekbone rang a faint bell in her mind, like a muted and hard-to-hear version of the musical re-minder that Marc had had installed on his PC.

Then, as he disappeared, the clouded memory cleared. She knew where they had met before. How could she have forgotten? Except that the brain had a way of blot-ting out days and events too painful to recall.

CHAPTER EIGHT

IN ORDER to have some time on the island before the famous restaurant opened its doors to those who could afford to lunch there, they collected Mrs Henry Henderson from her hotel at eleven o'clock.

Marc left Sophie in the launch while he went inside the hotel. On his advice she was wearing a summer frock, but it was a conservative style with not too much bare flesh on view. The parts that were bare she had covered with a high-protection sun lotion, knowing that travelling by water increased the danger of burning. She hadn't left off her tights in case Mrs Henderson had old-fashioned, old-money ideas, and didn't approve of bare legs in elegant restaurants.

Although she had lived nearby for a long stretch of her life, Sophie had never entered the Locanda Cipriani, but Torcello received many famous visitors, both to see its church and to lunch at the *locanda*. Before Sophie's time, the Queen of England had been there and, after her time there, Prince Charles. The list of celebrities was long, including the American writer Ernest Hemingway, who had taken a room at the *locanda* to shoot duck and write a novel.

But the life Sophie had lived there with Michael had had no connection with all the comings and goings of the world's VIPs. Although, out of curiosity, she had planned to eat lunch at the *locanda* when she returned to the island, she hadn't expected to travel on a private launch, and would have preferred to be going by ferry.

When Marc reappeared with his guest, Sophie

blinked. Could this slender and upright woman in a white voile shirt and white cotton trousers, with a broad-brimmed dark green straw hat in her hand, be an eighty-year-old?

Stepping lightly into the launch, with a gracious '*Buon giorno...molto grazie*' for the boatman who gave her his hand, she said to Sophie, 'Isn't this a perfect morning? I'm Martha Henderson.'

Sophie had risen and was standing braced to keep her balance and to steady the American if, as Marc came abroad, the launch lurched under his weight.

'How do you do, Mrs Henderson?'

'Please call me Martha. I don't like to be formal,' she said, with a smile.

What a breathtaking beauty she must have been in her youth, thought Sophie. As indeed she still was, but not with the artificially preserved looks of many of her American contemporaries. There were no detectable signs that Martha had kept age at bay with surgery and long hours spent with beauticians. Her hair was white, her make-up minimal, her jewellery proclaiming her style rather than her wealth. It was her supple waist, her visible *joie de vivre* and her delicious light scent which made her seem ageless: a woman who had lived a long time but was still finding life an adventure.

That Marc was having similar thoughts was shown by the look he exchanged with Sophie while Mrs Henderson was settling herself and lifting her face to the sun with closed eyes and a wordless murmur of pleasure.

'I came here on my first honeymoon in 1936,' she told Sophie as they moved off. 'Marc tells me you arrived a few days ago. Aren't you overwhelmed by all this beauty? Don't you envy people who spend their lives here?'

'Yes, I do,' Sophie said truthfully.

'When I was here with James, my first husband, I wanted to stay. I wanted to re-plan our future. But for him that was impossible. He was a lawyer, like his father and grandfather. He had his life all mapped out and I couldn't ask him to change it. Then the war came and changed many lives, including ours.'

They were passing the Palazzo Non Finito, the unfinished building which would have been the largest palace on the canal had it been completed. Now its single white marble storey bore a sign: 'Peggy Guggenheim Collection'.

'I met her once,' Martha said. 'I envied her living in Venice for thirty years. She had one of the last privately owned gondolas, you know. But I didn't envy her private life. She must often have been very lonely. Did your grandfather know her well, Marc?'

He was sitting on the other side of her, at right angles to the two women sharing the comfortably cushioned stern seat. The breeze was ruffling his hair.

'Yes, but he disliked her collection of modern art so they were never close friends.'

'I don't like most of it either, but I do like the Marini statue of the horseman we'll see through the water-gates. When you come out of the house and walk round and see his erection, it's such a shock the first time. Was that the artist's motive, do you suppose? To shock people? I wonder if the story is true that one day, when a group of nuns were coming to visit unexpectedly, Peggy unscrewed the penis and threw it in the canal?' She turned to Sophie. 'Have you seen it?'

Marc answered for her. 'She hasn't had time to visit any galleries yet. And Sophie has too much aplomb to be shocked by anything,' he added blandly.

He must know that wasn't true, Sophie thought,

clenching her teeth. He had rocked her aplomb several times.

Martha looked closely at her. 'You do look a very calm person. What's your secret? Yoga and meditation?'

Considering how tense she was feeling about going back to Torcello, Sophie was amazed that she gave Mrs Henderson an impression of serenity, especially as she felt sure there had been nothing tongue-in-cheek about the American's comment.

'Walking and reading are my main relaxations,' she said quietly.

'Oh, mine too.' In a spontaneous gesture, Martha stretched out her hand to give Sophie's wrist a friendly squeeze. 'I haven't "measured out my life with coffee spoons". It's been a long country walk marked by a trail of books.' After a pause, she added, 'I might have that on my tombstone. What do you think, Marc?'

'I like it.' He was smiling at Martha with a look that caused curious sensations in the region of Sophie's heart. 'But if tombstones can have postscripts I think I would add, "A very short time in her company made you feel you had found a friend."'

Mrs Henderson looked delighted. As well she might, Sophie thought.

'What a charming thing to say. I feel the same.' This time it was his arm she squeezed. She was obviously a very tactile person. 'But I've heard a lot of good things about you from Hal.' She turned to Sophie. 'I had four children with my first husband and two more when I married again, after the war. Now I have a whole tribe of grandchildren. Hal is the eldest grandson. He's the same age as Marc—thirty-six. When he was eighteen, he had a terrible accident on his motorbike. It left him a paraplegic. He's married now, with two children, but at first it was very difficult for an active young man like him to adapt to life in a wheelchair. Marc helped him make that adjustment.'

'He exaggerates my contribution,' said Marc. 'It was Hal's own determination which got him through his time in hospital and the first years at Yale.'

'He says it was you who did that—cheering him up when he was low, spending your free time with him instead of having a ball with the others.'

'I liked him better than the others. Why did I never meet you before?' Marc asked.

Sophie liked the deft way he turned the conversation away from himself.

'My second husband was ill while Hal was at Yale. We were living in France and I wasn't around much then. That's a lovely hotel. That's where I stayed the second time I came here.' She gestured at the Danieli, a luxurious near-neighbour of Sophie's more modest base.

Further along the Riva, they turned down the canal which led to the Arsenale. As they glided through the lion-guarded water-gate into what had once been the largest shipyard in the world, Sophie remembered coming this way with Michael on the *vaporetto*, the only way for members of the public to see inside the walls of the Arsenale. He had wanted to paint the vast caverns of the covered docks but hadn't been able to get permission.

Marc had turned to look at something to starboard, and was showing the same quarter-profile which, yesterday afternoon, had unlocked her memory of their first encounter. If he was thirty-six now, when she'd been eleven he would have been twenty-two.

At the time he had seemed very adult, but he might still have been a student, visiting Venice on vacation. If he hadn't been there and known what to do, Michael would have died. *She* hadn't known what to do.

* * *

'The first time I came to Torcello was by gondola,' said Martha as they approached the island. The bell-tower of its ancient cathedral had been in view for some time.

'In those days you could hire a gondola, with two gondoliers to row it, for a whole day for very little. I remember we brought a picnic. It was almost dark by the time we got back to Venice. It was one of the best days of my life.'

'Aren't you nervous about coming back?' Sophie asked.

Martha gave a gentle shake of the head. 'Whatever it's like now it can't spoil that wonderful memory. They sang to us on the way back. They didn't have very good voices but even so it was lovely. There was a full moon rising and Venice looked like Camelot or Atlantis—one of those legendary places you expect to vanish as you approach it.'

'Does your gondolier sing, Sophie?' Marc enquired.

'I don't know,' she said untruthfully.

Perhaps Martha heard a nuance that alerted her curiosity. With an interested look, she said, 'Who is your gondolier?'

'He's someone Marc thinks picked me up,' Sophie told her pleasantly. 'But he happens to have an aunt who runs a very good restaurant and a large friendly family who are only too happy to let me listen in to their conversations in the Venetian dialect. Being able to speak it will be a help in dealing with local people, especially working people.'

'She omits to mention that her gondolier is too handsome for his own good and has the reputation of seducing every susceptible tourist who comes within a hundred yards of him.'

Marc was smiling as he said it, but something in his eyes reminded her of the expression on a cat's face when, with claws temporarily sheathed, it dabbed a soft paw against a terrified mouse or captured fledgling.

Controlling her indignation, she said, 'Do you have grounds for that statement?'

'One of Domenico's cousins is a gondolier. They all know each other. There are only about four hundred of them left.' He turned to Martha. 'Apparently Sophie's guy is well-known for targeting the cream of the foreign girls...with close to a hundred per cent success rate, so I'm told.'

'Well, he isn't targeting *me*,' Sophie retorted, losing some of her cool. And then, already strung up and resenting being needled, she repeated what, long ago, she had heard a Venetian girl from one of the poorer quarters say to a man who had been annoying her.

The words were no sooner spoken than she was horrified, and thankful that Mrs Henderson, even if she had some Italian, was unlikely to have understood the coarseness of her terse instruction to mind his own business and push off.

For a moment Marc's face was blank, and she had a sinking feeling he was going to dismiss her there and then. It was an enormous relief when he began to laugh.

'Is that what he's taught you to say if anyone else makes a pass at you? It would certainly have an effect. But ask yourself this: would you say the English equivalent if someone in New York or London was making a nuisance of himself? I doubt it.' He glanced at Martha. 'Don't ask me to translate Sophie's pithy mouthful. Those words aren't in your vocabulary.'

'They might not be in my personal vocabulary, but I expect I've heard them spoken or read them in books,' Martha said drily. 'I don't think I'm behind the times. I try not to be. But one thing I do dislike about contemporary manners is the way both sexes swear in front of each other.' She turned to Sophie. 'I'm sure *you* don't, my dear…except to give Marc an example of the Venetian you've learnt,' she added, with a mischievous look.

The launch was slowing down to pass the jetty where the ferry passengers disembarked. It was near the mouth of a small canal and the footpath leading to the centre of the island.

Her attention distracted by the cut and thrust with Marc, it was only now that Sophie looked at the jetty. She had so often stood there with Michael, waiting for the boat to Venice where he, with the sleeve of his missing right arm neatly folded and pinned to the side of his shirt, had earned their living drawing portraits of tourists with his left hand.

Martha gave an exclamation. 'The path has been paved with bricks. It was a dirt path last time.'

To Sophie, the other woman's voice seemed to come from a long way away. She was looking past the jetty, to the spot where *Venezia* had once been moored.

Michael had given his boat the Italian name for Venice long before he'd come to Torcello. He had loved the city all his life, but before losing his arm had been busy working in London, where he had been one of the great fashion artists of his day.

Behind the protective screen of her sunglasses, Sophie closed her eyes for a moment. When she opened them the launch had entered the canal. The painful sight of *Venezia's* empty mooring had passed out of view.

The path alongside the canal had been paved with bricks laid in a herring-bone pattern.

'That's much prettier than concrete or asphalt,' said Martha.

The pattern reminded Sophie of the paths in the walled kitchen garden of her English boarding-school—

a great country house once owned by an aristocratic family which had died out.

Shortly before his death, Michael had inherited some money—enough to send her to boarding-school and to cover her education until she was eighteen and could start supporting herself. At first she had been very unhappy away from him, but every week a letter illustrated with funny sketches had arrived to cheer her up until, gradually, she had grown to like her new environment and to throw herself into doing well and making him proud of her.

The launch glided under a bridge without any parapets. A young couple who looked as if they might be honeymooners were sitting on it. Sophie wondered if they would be a poignant reminder to Martha's of her first visit here. But everything must remind her of that long-lost happiness. It sounded as if her first husband had been killed in the war that Michael had also fought in.

'Did you come here as a child, Marc?' the older woman asked.

He nodded. 'My grandfather liked to lunch here whenever he was in Venice. He knew Guiseppe Cipriani, the founder of Harry's Bar and the Cipriani Hotel, and Guiseppe knew everyone from Winston Churchill to Charlie Chaplin and Sophia Loren. I should think the *locanda* here has welcomed more celebrated people than any other inn of its size in the world.'

Several elderly women had set up stalls selling lace and hand-embroidered linens on the path between the rustic inn and the eleventh-century church built as a shrine to a forgotten saint. The cathedral behind it was even older, its interior adorned with wonderful mosaics. Michael had often sat there, gazing at the tall black-robed Madonna, with Sophie sitting quietly beside him, trying to imagine Torcello as it had been long ago: the most important island in the lagoon, with more than ten thousand inhabitants and many churches and convents.

Today the ancient cathedral was full of visitors, and she couldn't recapture the sense of awe and mystery she had felt in this place as a child. Perhaps Martha also found the presence of other people an intrusion on her memories. They did not stay long.

A deferential young man welcomed them to the *locanda* and ushered them into a garden from which the roofs of the two churches were visible above the surrounding trees.

'Would the ladies prefer a table in the shade?' he asked Marc.

Marc looked inquiringly at them.

'I like the sun, but I have a shady hat,' said Martha. 'Is the sun too strong for you, Sophie? You're very fair-skinned.'

'I love the sun too. I shan't burn. I have lashings of sun cream on.'

'How sensible of you,' said Martha as they were shown to one of the tables in full sunlight. 'But I guess good sense is an essential qualification for your job. I often wonder how I'd have got on in the business world, but my parents were comfortably off and when I was twenty James swept into my life, so I've never had to earn my living.'

'You raised six useful members of the next generation,' said Marc, watching her put on her green hat.

Sophie listened with half an ear to their easy flow of conversation. She was looking about her, taking in the details of a place which had once seemed as inaccessible to her as a fairy-tale palace to a woodcutter's granddaughter. Not that Michael had been the modern equivalent of a woodcutter, but they had been almost as poor as the peasants in the tales he had read to her when she'd been little.

The tables had blue cloths, a paler blue than the vivid sky overhead, and the part of the garden she was facing was planted with pomegranate bushes, their bright red fruit peeping out of the foliage. Soon all the tables were taken, and the waiters, their shoes crunching on the gravel underfoot, bustled back and forth with menus, bottles of wine in buckets of ice and baskets of shell-shaped rolls.

When Marc and the two women had made their decisions about what to eat and were sipping chilled white wine, Martha said thoughtfully, 'I wonder what happened on this island to change it from the way it was in the tenth century to the way it is now? Was it struck by the plague?'

'The current theory,' said Marc, 'is that the action of two rivers caused the waters surrounding the island to become a malarial swamp. Most people don't realise how shallow the lagoon is…less than two feet in most places.'

He began to talk about the conflict between the needs of the region's human inhabitants and its wildlife, and it was clear he was a knowledgeable student of the problems involved.

Much of what he told Martha about the plant and bird life Sophie already knew, and as she listened her thoughts drifted back to the day they had met for the first time…

'I'm feeling a bit below par. I think I'll take the day off,' Michael announced after breakfast.

'Yes, why don't you?' Sophie agreed, trying not to show her concern.

For some time past she had suspected that her grandfather wasn't well. His energy had diminished. He was often tired. Sometimes he was short of breath. But when she'd suggested a check-up he'd dismissed the idea and claimed to be perfectly well and just beginning to feel his age.

He had married late, and when Sophie had come into his care, at the age of three, was already in his sixties. For most of his life he had been one of the world's top fashion artists, ranking with Eric, Bouché and Gruau, discovered by *Vogue* while he was still at art school and remaining a frequent contributor to their pages and those of other glossy magazines for several decades.

Three factors had contributed to his becoming a street artist in Venice. In the sixties drawings had lost favour with fashion editors, and then an accident had resulted in the loss of his arm. In the seventies his son and daughter-in-law had died in an Atlantic storm. He had been living in Venice at the time, with his boat in a nearby marina, and for the next few years he and his grandchild had moved from hotel to hotel, each one cheaper than the last. Eventually they had taken to living on the boat, their funds still steadily dwindling.

In competition with many local artists trying to eke a living selling picturesque views to the tourists, he augmented his income by drawing exaggerated portraits with his left hand.

Three times a week, throughout the steadily expanding tourist season, he spent all day on the Riva, taking Sophie with him. She did not go to school but was given lessons by Michael. By living abroad they escaped any intervention from what he called 'interfering busybodies', whether official or otherwise.

Michael spent the morning quietly, but soon after lunch could not hide his breathlessness. He admitted to having unpleasant sensations in his chest and went to lie down. Presently she heard him groan and went into his cabin to find him, grey-faced and sweating, with a pain shooting up his arm.

'I think I'm having a heart attack.' He began to shiver.

Sophie tucked a blanket round him and fetched the pillow from her cabin. 'I'll go and get help. Don't move. Don't exert yourself.'

Panic-stricken, but trying to keep calm, she hurried on deck and sprang ashore, scanning the channel in both directions in the hope of seeing a fast boat which could transport Michael to hospital. But there was nothing to be seen but the wide expanses of reed beds and sky-reflecting water.

The only option was to run like a hare to the *locanda* and ask them to telephone for a water ambulance. Or, with luck, there might still be a *motoscafo* there—one of the expensive water taxis which brought tourists who could afford them to visit the island.

She was only a short way along the path leading to the *locanda* when she saw a motorboat coming towards her. Waving both arms, Sophie shouted, *'Aiuto! Aiuto!'*

After her first rush of relief, she realised the boat wasn't a taxi but a private craft, with a group of good-looking young Italians on board. For a minute she feared they might ignore her and sweep past, not wanting to be bothered with someone in trouble. Even if they did stop, she wasn't hopeful that they would know how to deal with the contingency. They looked the sort Michael had once called *jeunesse dorée*, meaning literally 'gilded youth'. His tone had implied that such people were generally spoilt and selfish pleasure-seekers.

Only one of them noticed her: the young man at the wheel. He cut the throttle and brought the boat alongside. 'What's the matter, kid?'

CHAPTER NINE

'IT'S an emergency. My grandfather's having a heart attack. Please help me.'

The young man turned to the others, his sharp, 'Be quiet, you lot!' stopping their laughter and chatter as abruptly as he had cut the purr of the motor. 'Where is the old boy?' he asked her.

'In our boat...round the corner—on the far side of the ferry-stop.'

'Make room and give her a hand,' the young man said to another sitting behind him. 'She can perch on your lap for a minute.'

In other circumstances Sophie might have been shy of sitting on a stranger's lap. But now her only concern was getting back to Michael, who might already be dead.

When the motorboat reached *Venezia*'s mooring it took the young man at the wheel only seconds to make his boat fast to a mooring ring with a quick clove hitch. Sophie, who had also leapt ashore, grabbed his arm.

'You'll need help to move him to your boat. He's a big man...as tall as you are. They'll have to get out. There won't be room for him otherwise.'

'Calm down, kid. It won't help to panic.'

He headed for *Venezia*.

Michael was where she had left him. At first she thought he was dead and her own heart seemed to stop. Then the eyes in the grey face opened.

'Who the devil are you?' he asked in English, in a faint wheezing voice Sophie had never heard before.

'Take it easy, sir. We'll take care of you.'

To Sophie's surprise, the young man spoke perfect English.

To her, he said, 'You stay here and reassure him. Luckily I brought my cellphone. I'll call the nearest medic. There may be one on Burano.'

She followed him out of the cabin, saying in an urgent undertone, 'He needs more than a doctor. He needs to be taken to hospital.'

The young man whipped round to face her. He was wearing a spotless white T-shirt, jeans with bright scarlet braces and a red and white neckerchief round his long suntanned neck. He smelt nice, of soap and the stuff men put on their faces after shaving. Michael had used it once but could no longer afford it. These days he didn't shave much, or wash as often as he used to when she was smaller. He didn't smell clean any more, but always faintly musty.

The young man put both hands on her shoulders, saying quietly but with assurance, 'When someone's having a heart attack the best thing to do is *not* move them. That could do more harm than good. Let him stay where he is and we'll get a doctor to him. He'll need medication before he's taken to hospital. It's a long way from here.'

Seeing the lingering doubt in her eyes, he added, 'More than eighty per cent of the people who survive the first few hours after a heart attack get better. He'll pull through. He looks a tough old guy.'

Sophie was roused from her memories by the arrival of her first course.

'You were a long way away then,' said Marc.

Embarrassed that he had noticed, she said, 'I'm sorry...something you said took me back to my childhood.' She didn't add that, although it was far back in time, in distance the place where she had been was very near where she was now.

'I'm reaching the age when my childhood often seems clearer than what happened a few years ago,' said Martha. 'Tell me some more about *your* island, Marc. How long will it take you to make it the way you want it?'

'Probably the rest of my life. I should feel a lot happier if I'd been able to buy it, but the lease is a long one and my lawyers managed to negotiate an option to renew.'

As he summarised his plans for the island, which Sophie had already heard, she tried to analyse the difference between his face as it was now and as it had looked the first time their lives had converged.

The second and last time she had seen him had been at the hospital, late in the evening of the day Michael had been admitted. She'd been sitting on a bench in a corridor, waiting for news from the intensive care ward, when the young man had appeared, this time wearing a white dinner jacket with his dark hair tidy instead of wind-blown.

He had brought her a bag of books to help her pass the time and asked if they had fixed her up with somewhere to spend the night. She had told him about Paolo's family, who would let her sleep at their house.

At the end of their conversation the young man had said, 'Tomorrow I have to leave Venice. I'll look you up next time I'm here. You'll be back on your boat by then, I expect. I'm glad I was around to help out. *Arrivederci*.'

But perhaps by the time he'd returned he had forgotten about her as, after a while, she had succeeded in forgetting him—or at least in putting him and that day so far to the back of her mind that it hadn't been until yesterday that she had made the connection between him and the man now sitting opposite.

'Do I have a blob of sauce on my chin, Sophie?' Marc asked.

'What? Oh…was I staring? I'm sorry.'

'You're *distraite* today,' he said drily. 'First you go off in a trance, then you fix me with a stare like a cobra preparing to strike. What's on your mind?'

'Nothing…nothing at all.'

She pulled herself together and spent the rest of the meal attending to what was said and showing her appreciation of what she was eating.

'If you two feel like a stroll,' said Martha, replacing her coffee-cup in its saucer, 'I'd like to go back to the cathedral and listen to the audio-guide on one of those telephone gadgets we saw people using this morning. Such things hadn't been invented when I was here before.'

Marc signalled for the bill. 'Tomorrow, if you decide to revisit the Doge's Palace, you'll find they now have portable audio-guides that not only describe the room you're in and its paintings but allow you to backtrack or to move along faster than other people. That's a big improvement on the regular guided tour, don't you think?'

'It's a brilliant idea,' she agreed. 'I've never liked guided tours, especially not the kind where the guide holds up an umbrella so that you won't lose sight of her or tag along with another guide's group by mistake. Tomorrow I may not do any sightseeing. I may just potter around, shopping and sitting in Florian's, watching the world go by.'

Sophie knew that a stroll with Marc would offer the perfect opportunity to reveal to him that she knew

Venice better than he realised. However, now that she had remembered their previous meeting, she was curious to see if, before they left Torcello, he would suddenly slot her into place as the scruffy child he had helped.

She had changed far more than he, but not out of all recognition. Her eyes hadn't changed. Surely, when they passed the place where *Venezia* had been moored, if she lingered there he would remember her?

When Martha had disappeared inside the cathedral, they took a path Sophie knew passed by some fields and eventually wound in a loop.

She said, 'In spite of her age, I think Mrs Henderson must be one of the most glamorous people who ever lunched at the *locanda*. She looks wonderful in that green hat.'

'She has great style,' he agreed. 'You'll look that way too at her age. Women with beautiful eyes always age well.'

His tone was so matter-of-fact that it didn't seem like a compliment. She let it pass without acknowledgement. But it lit a small inner glow she doused by reminding herself that it might be something he had said to a lot of girls.

'I once stayed here overnight,' Marc told her. 'They have a few simple rooms. When the last visitors had gone home, it was unbelievably peaceful.'

I know. I've been here at dusk and at night. The words were on the tip of her tongue. For some reason, she didn't say them.

They walked on in silence, Sophie a little ahead because the path was narrow. This was the way she had always come back to *Venezia* after fetching the makings of soup from the islanders who had sold them vegetables. Soup, and bread from the bakery on Burano, the lace-makers' island, had been their staple diet, with dried beans their main source of protein.

'Have you ever imagined living in a place like this for the rest of your life?' Marc asked, from behind her.

She could have said, I don't need to imagine it. I know what it's like living here. But again she held back. 'If I didn't have to earn my living, and given the right sort of companionship and an adequate supply of books, I can imagine being very happy here.'

'What do you mean by the right sort of companionship?' he asked.

'Most people can't live like hermits. They need conversation...affection. To live here always, I'd need a husband and children.'

'Are they part of your life plan?'

'They're on my wish list. That's a different thing from a plan. A plan is achievable. For a wish to come true it is more a matter of chance.'

'A wish has a better chance of coming true if the conditions are right for it.'

They had come to a wider stretch of path where two people could walk abreast. As he came alongside her Sophie looked up at him. 'What do you mean?'

'In the context of what we're discussing, you would have to recognise that your career plan and your wish list are likely to be incompatible. For example, if I needed you to work late and your gondolier had laid on a special date, you couldn't do both. You'd have to decide whose displeasure was more important.'

Sophie halted, turning to face him. 'Let's get this straight,' she said evenly. 'Paolo isn't a boyfriend. He's a friend, period. And if I had been invited to a big family party on a night when you wanted me to work I'd send his parents my apologies. Which isn't to say that I would *always* put work first.'

'Hold still a minute. You have something in your hair.' He stepped closer to remove it.

She drew in her breath, suddenly aware that warm sunlight, vintage wine and standing as close as this to an attractive male was a volatile combination. Was he also aware of it, or was it only she who felt all her senses sharpen?

'A small spider.' He spread his hand to show her the minute insect running down his middle finger. 'It must have dropped out of that overhanging branch we passed.'

The spider stopped when it reached the dark hairs on the back of his shapely brown hand. Marc looked at it for a moment, and then he moved close to a bush and gently blew it off his hand into the foliage.

'In what circumstances would you put it second?' he asked.

For a moment the question made no sense. The feelings she had experienced while he had been extricating the spider from her hair had temporarily wiped out all memory of their conversation. With an effort, she switched off her senses and murmured, 'Well…' playing for time while she re-set her mind.

'If I had any close relations and one of them was very ill, not expected to live, then they would definitely come first.'

'Your parents are dead, I believe? Were you born late in their lives?'

'On the contrary. My mother was only nineteen, my father twenty-four. He was a dedicated yachtsman and taught her to sail. When I was three they were both drowned. My father's father brought me up. It was a great grief to him, but not for me. My childhood was very happy.'

She was going to tell him more about it, but Marc intervened, saying, 'So was I—raised by my grandfather.

He and I had everything in common, but he and his son were at loggerheads all their lives.'

'Did he disapprove of your father marrying an Italian girl?'

'Emphatically…and with reason. He suspected an ulterior motive and he was right. My mother wanted money, preferably dollars, to restore the *palazzo* and permit her to run accounts at all the best shops in Europe. When my father recognised her motives, he stepped up his drinking. It can kill you surprisingly quickly, if you work at it. But Grandfather more than made up for their deficiencies as parents. Like you, I didn't grow up with any hang-ups…or none that I recognise,' he added drily.

She was surprised he should confide these intimate details to her. She would have expected him to be impenetrably reserved about things that mattered to him, as his father's drinking must have mattered when he was very young and when he had probably had a child's tendency to assume that if anything went wrong it must somehow be his fault.

By now they were approaching *Venezia*'s mooring, but instead of being deserted, like the field path, the towpath was dotted with tourists taking a stroll while waiting for the ferry.

A woman approached them, smiling. 'Could I trouble you to take a picture of me and my husband?' In case they didn't speak English, she mimed what she wanted.

'With pleasure.'

Marc took her camera and waited until she had posed herself with the man whose legs were pale varicose stalks between his shorts and the tops of his grey city socks.

After looking through the viewfinder, Marc said, 'Where you're standing, the campanile on Burano appears to be growing out of your head, sir. Move a little to your right.'

The photograph taken, the couple were disposed to chat. Marc wasn't. He moved Sophie on with a firm hand on her arm and a pleasant but brisk goodbye to the tourists.

'Given the smallest encouragement, they would have regaled us with details of all their trips to foreign parts,' he murmured, some yards further on.

'That's a little unkind,' she answered.

'I can be very unkind. I thought you knew that.' He was still holding her arm.

'You weren't unkind to the spider.'

'Spiders are never bores. People frequently are. If I'd been by myself I should have refused to be a party to the boredom they're going to inflict on their friends when they show them their holiday snaps. But that would have embarrassed you, wouldn't it?'

'Yes,' she admitted, with a smiling upward glance. 'But I think you're teasing me. You're too...gentlemanly to inflict pain on a harmless couple like that pair.'

'You think so, do you?' His tone implied she was being naïve to credit him with any finer instincts.

Their glances locked; his dark eyes amused, hers defensive. What was it about this man which made her feel as exposed as the crabs in the lagoon at the time when they cast off their shells?

This time it was he who suddenly checked his stride, tightening his fingers so that she also had to come to a standstill. Disconcerted by the intensity of his gaze, she said, 'Why are you staring at me?'

Had he recognised her?

CHAPTER TEN

MARC said, 'Tia Clara has an aquamarine ring she doesn't often wear. Held up to the sun, it would be the same colour as your irises. They're very unusual...very beautiful.'

Unaware that he had made her heart pound as violently as it had the day when, very near here, she had begged him for help, he glanced at his watch. 'We'd better get a move on. Martha will be wondering where we've got to.'

Mrs Henderson was sitting in the shade of the *locanda's* vine-shaded veranda, talking to a white-haired man in shorts and walking boots. His arms and legs were deeply bronzed. A day-pack was slung on the back of his chair.

'Professor, these are two friends of mine—Sophie Hill and Marc Washington. Professor Grant is staying at my hotel, Marc. I've suggested he rides back with us instead of taking the ferry.'

The professor's slight accent proclaimed him to be a Scot. Marc's civil interest in him revealed he had held the chair in archaeology at more than one university.

The two men spent much of the return journey discussing thermoluminescence and other esoteric matters Marc seemed to know about.

The two women didn't contribute to this conversation. Martha looked around her at the changing views of the lagoon, and Sophie put on a show of listening to whoever was speaking while actually studying their faces. They were not unalike in the height and breadth of their foreheads and general angularity of feature. Both looked formidably intelligent.

Mark was clearly a match for the professor, in general if not specialist knowledge. It was obvious the older man found him stimulating company, and the fact that Marc made no effort to include Martha and herself in their talk made Sophie wonder if he had had enough of female society for one day and, during their walk, had begun to find himself bored.

She had not said anything scintillating, that was for sure. But then neither had he. It had been the exchange of personal background and perspective that people made when they were still in the early stages of getting to know each other.

A few minutes before they arrived back at Martha's hotel, he said, 'I have a couple of things to do downtown. I'll get off here. I'm not sure how long I'll be. I'll call you in half an hour.'

Back at the *palazzo*, Sophie checked the fax, telex and E-mail messages, played back some local messages on the answering machine and looked at the world news update on teletext. By the time Marc called she had made notes of everything he might want to know about immediately. There was nothing of crucial importance.

'Right,' he said, after hearing the summary, 'in that case you can go home, but I'd like you to be in the office by eight tomorrow. OK?'

'Of course…and thank you very much for including me in the trip to Torcello. It was a delicious lunch.'

'I'm glad you enjoyed it.' He rang off.

Walking back to the hotel, once stepping into the doorway of a shop when she saw a large tour group streaming down the narrow street ahead of her, Sophie wondered if she had only imagined a note of coolness in Marc's response to her thanks.

Usually she avoided the Piazza, with its throngs of camera-happy visitors, but today she decided to have tea at Quadri's and listen to the music for an hour before buying some fruit and a carton of yogurt for a light supper in her room to counterbalance the lavish lunch.

The afternoon shadows from the surrounding buildings with their elegant arcades of luxury shops reached the tables outside Quadri's later than at Caffè Florian, the coffee-house favoured by the Venetian élite, who had been meeting their friends there since 1720.

Florian's was also popular with artists, but on the rare occasions when he had been able to afford to drink and draw the passing throng in the Piazza Michael had preferred Quadri's.

Knowing she was going to pay through the nose for the privilege, Sophie chose a table and ordered tea. Behind her, on a canopied dais, a group of musicians led by a violinist was playing a slightly jazzed-up version of a romantic melody she had first heard on Michael's wind-up gramophone.

Mostly it had been classical music echoing across the lagoon from *Venezia*'s deck. But one or two of the records had been collections of evergreen love songs. Hearing one of them now moved her almost to tears.

In her teens she had never doubted that in a few years' time she would find her own Mr Wonderful and be as happy with him as her grandmother and mother had been with the men they'd loved.

But it hadn't happened. Twice she had started relationships which hadn't fulfilled her hopes. Now here she was, with another birthday approaching and still on her own, in a place where loneliness had an extra poignancy. Anywhere as magical as Venice needed to be shared with someone special. Where was her special person? Did he even exist, except in her mind?

'Signorina...'

As the waiter arranged her tea things—a cup and saucer, a pot of hot water, Earl Grey teabags, slices of lemon and a bill which she knew would include a hefty supplement for the music—his wedding ring glinted in the sunlight. When he finished his shift there would be someone waiting to spend the evening with him. Probably Martha and the professor would have dinner together. Everyone seemed to be in pairs. Except me, thought Sophie forlornly.

A pair of hands came from behind her and covered her eyes. She knew it had to be Paolo. This was what he had done long ago, when they'd been children.

'I don't have to guess. I know. Why aren't you working?'

He removed his hands and took the chair next to hers. 'I have to take some time off. Aren't you pleased to see me?'

'I was enjoying the music...now you'll want me to listen to you,' she said lightly.

'When I've ordered a drink, I won't say another word.' He beckoned a waiter. 'We will sit in silence, like old people who have said everything they have to say to each other.'

Somewhat to Sophie's surprise, he kept his promise. Ten minutes later they were still sitting in silence, Paolo sipping his *ombra* and watching the pigeons strut back and forth, undisturbed by the people crossing the Piazza but sometimes taking refuge in the air when a child tried to sneak up on them.

At last, taking pity on him, Sophie said, 'I should think that's the longest you've ever been quiet in your life, isn't it? Your mother would never believe me if I told her you'd kept your mouth shut for a quarter of an hour.'

'Mamma has warned me against you,' Paolo informed her. 'She's afraid you will break my heart. You think I'm joking? It's true. She wants me to settle down with a nice local girl, not waste my time with a foreign career girl like you. It's not that she doesn't like you. She does…very much. But she wants a daughter-in-law who will be happy in Venice and give her two or three grandchildren—as if she didn't have enough already.'

'Why does she think I wouldn't be happy in Venice? I grew up here…or not far away.'

'But you've been to New York, London, Paris…all those places she wanted to see before she married Babbo. She doesn't think Venice is anything special.'

'She would if she'd seen other places. The rest of the world has been ruined by cars. But she's right in seeing that we wouldn't suit each other. Even if you loved me, Paolo, you wouldn't be faithful to me. It's not your nature to want only one woman. For a while, perhaps, but not for the rest of your life.'

'Whether a man is faithful depends on his wife,' he said, with a shrug. 'Sometimes, after they're married, women lose interest in sex. They love their children more than their husbands. They wear nightgowns in bed.'

'In an old house with no central heating and snow on the roof, I'm not surprised,' she said drily. 'When I lived here, in winter we slept inside down sleeping bags.'

She remembered how cosy it had been, snuggled inside her bag, after Michael had kissed her goodnight, listening to the creaking of *Venezia*'s timbers and sometimes, according to the tide, the soft splash of water against the hull.

'Michael was old and you were a child,' said Paolo. 'If you slept with me I'd keep you warm with the heat from my body.' His look made it clear he was visualising the situation.

Sophie said briskly, 'The winters aren't long. In summer it's hot and humid. I should think most married people who can afford it have twin beds. Sharing a double can't be comfortable in August. Anyway, your mother is right. I'm a career girl, Paolo. Staying at home, having babies doesn't appeal to me.'

'I wouldn't make you stay at home. Between us we could afford to pay someone to look after the children.' He leaned towards her, seizing her hand. 'I've fallen for you, Sophie. I knew the night I took you home. Mamma saw what had happened to me.'

'Oh, Paolo—' Sophie began.

She broke off with a start as someone behind her said, *'Ciao.'*

It was Chiara, looking with undisguised curiosity at the man clasping Sophie's hand.

Paolo returned Chiara's interested smile with a scowl which made it clear that her presence was intrusive. But when, removing her hand from his, Sophie introduced them, he did stand up, albeit reluctantly and still with a far from friendly expression on his face.

Sophie's reaction to the Italian girl's arrival was mixed. She was glad to have Paolo's declaration of his feelings cut short, but thought it tactless of Chiara to butt in on what had all too clearly been a private conversation. Also, she didn't want it to get back to Marc that she had been holding hands with Paolo.

'Where did you two meet?' Chiara asked, dumping a shiny carrier bag from the Kenzo shop on the chair facing Sophie and seating herself in the one opposite Paolo.

To stop him from saying they had known each other as children—something else she didn't want Marc to learn from his cousin—Sophie said, 'Paolo is a gondolier.'

'Really?' Chiara put her elbows on the edge of the table and cupped her face in her hands. 'When I was ten I was in love with one of the gondoliers at Bacino Orseolo.' She gestured in the direction of the archway leading from the north-west corner of the Piazza to a pool which was one of the city's official gondola stations. 'Sometimes when I went past he would wink at me. He was younger than all the others and *very* handsome. But I never spoke to him. You're the first gondolier I've met.'

'That sounds like Bruno,' said Paolo. 'He had lots of schoolgirls in love with him.'

'He disappeared. What happened to him?'

'He came to a sticky end,' Paolo said, with a grimace. 'He left Venice to be a toy boy, then started drinking too much and perhaps doing drugs. Eventually he smashed himself up in the car his rich mistress had given him. He's back here now, but you wouldn't recognise him. He's an out-of-work wreck, kept by his mother. Anyone else would have left him to rot in the gutter.'

'How terrible!' Chiara looked devastated by this update on her girlhood idol.

Sophie thought it unkind of Paolo to have told her. She could imagine how shattered she would have felt on hearing a similar tale about the man with red braces who had saved Michael's life, leaving her with a memory of handsome young manhood that she had treasured for several years until, in the way of most teenage memories, it had been silted over by other experiences.

The waiter came. 'What would you like?' Paolo asked, perhaps regretting being the cause of Chiara's tragic expression.

She asked for a *cappuccino*. Sophie wondered if she would pay for it herself or expect him to.

'Who was the woman who took him away from Venice?' Chiara asked.

'Some millionaire's wife whose husband was too busy making money to worry about what she was doing. She came here to buy a gondola for a party on their private lake. She didn't realise a gondola isn't a boat anyone can row just like that.' He snapped his fingers. 'She had to hire a gondolier to go with it. Bruno wasn't the only one she approached, but he was the only one too stupid to see the job involved more than rowing her gondola for her.'

'Did she ask you?' asked Chiara.

'As a matter of fact, she did. I turned her down. She was as old as my mother, even if she didn't look it.' He put the tips of his forefingers at the sides of his eyes, tightening the skin until his lids were taut slits.

'She sounds a horrible person.'

'You girls aren't the only ones who get passes made at you,' Paolo told her. 'It happens to us all the time.' He grinned. 'I've lost count of the ladies who have lost their balance on purpose when I'm helping them out at the end of their ride.'

'I'm sure they don't do that with all the gondoliers,' said Chiara. 'Some of the ones I've noticed have been anything but handsome.' She looked him over. 'You look the way gondoliers are supposed to look.'

Paolo returned her appraisal. 'You look like a model. Are you?'

Chiara shook her head. 'It's a job I wouldn't mind, but my mother would have a fit.'

Her chair was facing the musicians' dais and the arcade between the outside part of the *caffè* and the interior of Quadri's. Suddenly she sat up straight, smiling and waving to someone Paolo and Sophie couldn't see without turning round.

'That was Marc,' she told Sophie. 'He's my cousin and Sophie's boss,' she added, for Paolo's benefit.

'I've met him.'

'Life is more fun when he's here…as long as nothing upsets him. Then he acts like a volcano.' She used her expressive hands to mime a violent eruption.

Sophie wondered how he would react to seeing his young, sheltered cousin hobnobbing with a gondolier—especially a gondolier with Paolo's reputation.

As soon as she had finished her tea, she caught the waiter's eye. 'Your coffee's on me, Chiara,' she said, taking the bill for the *cappuccino* and giving the waiter a note to cover the totals on both slips.

'No, no…I'm paying,' said Paolo. He flourished a fifty thousand lire banknote which, to Sophie's concealed indignation, the waiter took instead of hers.

'Thank you.' Chiara gave Paolo a gracious smile.

'My pleasure.' He told her the name of his gondola station and added, 'Any time you fancy a ride, for you I'll make a special price. We're not supposed to charge less than the official minimum, but sometimes I do. Why not? It's my gondola.'

'You could find yourself losing your licence if you flirt with Chiara,' Sophie informed him when, after leaving Chiara at the *caffè*, they were walking in the direction of the Riva.

'I wasn't flirting. I was being friendly,' he answered. 'Are you jealous? That's a good sign.'

'Of course I'm not jealous,' she said shortly. 'I don't want my boss annoyed—which he would be if Chiara accepted your offer of a cut-price ride.'

'Nothing naughty can happen in a gondola unless it has a cabin,' Paolo said, laughing. '"The shelter of sweet sins''. That was what your poet, Lord Byron, called the *felze*—and it was, in his time. Gondoliers had to turn a deaf ear to a lot of heavy breathing from inside *felzi* in the old days. Now we only use them during Carnival. Pity, really. There must be honeymoon couples who'd like to make love on a canal ride, if they could do it in private...and not only honeymooners. Most people would get a kick out of doing it in a gondola.'

Sophie ignored these remarks, walking as fast as was possible in an area always thronged with tourists, especially at the sunset hour. She was beginning to feel there was nowhere in the city where she was safe from Paolo's unwanted courtship. She couldn't deny that there was a strong bond between them, but from her point of view it was fraternal, not romantic.

It was symptomatic of her mood that the crowd of sightseers on the Ponte della Paglia made her clench her teeth with exasperation as she edged her way through them with Paolo behind her.

On the other side, when the jostling throng had thinned out, she said to him, 'Are you on your way to see someone?'

'No, I'm coming with you. That's a nice dress for the daytime but you'll need something warmer as soon as the sun sets. You don't have to change in a hurry. I'll sit in the *caffè* and have another *ombra*.'

'Paolo, I can't have dinner with you tonight. I have things to do. I need some time to myself.'

'You're angry with me.'

His face had the same downcast look she had seen on it when, as a boy, he'd been given a verbal lashing by his mother for some misdeed she had discovered.

'I'm not angry, but I think it's foolish to talk about being in love with me. You may fancy me, but you haven't known me long enough to love me. You only know what I was like as a child. You don't know the person I am now.'

'Don't you believe in love at first sight?'

Sophie shook her head. 'I believe in attraction at first sight. But true love is different…it grows between people…it takes time.'

'For you, perhaps. Not for me. I've had a lot of girlfriends, but none of them made me feel the way you do, Sophie. This time it's serious with me. I was sweet on you when we were kids, when you were still flat-chested and people could mistake you for a boy. Except for your mouth. You always had a pretty mouth. But my mother threatened to kill me if I ever tried to kiss you…and I was afraid of your grandfather. Although he only had one arm he was a tough old fellow and he would have murdered anyone who laid a finger on you.'

Sophie was silent, surprised that Paolo had had such thoughts about her at a time when she, although aware how babies were made, and prepared for the changes adolescence would bring, had still been a child emotionally.

Later, when, reluctantly, Paolo had gone, resigned to the fact that he would have to be patient with her, she went up to her room, before remembering she still had to shop for the makings of her solitary supper.

That done, she moved the comfortable chair close to the open French window which had its wrought-iron balustrade too close to the frame for it to be called a balcony.

By now the crowds on the Riva had dispersed, and with them her earlier irritation. It wasn't like her to be edgy. She knew it had to do with Marc's passing along the arcade and seeing the three of them together. She wondered if he would refer to it in the morning and if she would ever be the cause of one of his explosions of anger.

She recognised that she was a little afraid of him. She had never been nervous of any previous employers. Why did Marc have that effect?

He was already at his desk when she arrived the next morning.

During the night reports and memos had come through from parts of the world where, now, people were taking their lunch breaks or the working day was nearly over. Marc had already dictated several long memos he wanted her to process and transmit to various destinations.

For three hours he kept her at full stretch, and he worked equally hard. She had already had glimpses of his phenomenal memory, but this morning she had a clear view of the dauntingly intelligent mind which, like his stride, allowed him easily to outpace most other people.

Sophie knew herself to be more than ordinarily bright, but she also knew she couldn't and wouldn't wish to cope with the load on his shoulders. He was operating at a stress level which eventually, for most men, took its toll in raised blood pressure, ulcers and heart problems. But, in spite of what his cousin had said about him, Marc appeared calm and relaxed.

It was she who, when a coffee-tray was brought up by one of the maids, was glad of a breathing space. A succession of tasks requiring all her concentration had made her forget the events of yesterday afternoon and the apprehensive state of mind in which she had come to work.

It was Marc who took charge of the coffee-pot. While

filling both cups he said, 'I'm happy to see Chiara spending time with you, but her mother wouldn't have approved of the tea party *à trois* in the Piazza yesterday. All my aunts are incorrigible snobs. Chiara had a crush on a gondolier when she was at school. That was harmless. Another might not be.'

'My plan was to sit there alone, enjoying the music. Then Paolo saw me and later Chiara joined us. It was a situation there was no way to prevent. I knew you wouldn't like it,' said Sophie. 'Soon after you passed us I left, and so did he. I really don't think you need worry that he'll start a flirtation with her.'

'You know him better than I do, but perhaps I have more experience of human nature.' Marc's tone was cynical. 'Chiara could be the plainest girl in Italy and still attract men. She's that vulnerable species, an heiress. The word gets around.'

'I'm sure it hasn't reached Paolo and wouldn't excite him if it did. He could have stayed with her when I left. He passed up the opportunity,' Sophie said shortly. 'Believe it or not, there are people in the world who are content with what they have and don't want to latch onto richer people. If contentment could be measured, I wouldn't mind betting that Paolo's relations are every bit as happy as yours.'

Aware that she might have said too much, she was relieved when an incoming telephone call put an end to the conversation.

CHAPTER ELEVEN

THE day after Martha's departure, Sophie was in Marc's room, going through his schedule for the following month with him, when the man who cleaned the household's shoes and ran errands delivered a very large gift-wrapped box.

She assumed it was something Marc had ordered until the man said, 'For you, *signorina.*'

'There must be some mistake. I haven't ordered anything.'

'It's your name on the label.' He turned it over to show her.

'You're right. It's addressed to me. How odd. Well, I'll deal with it later. Would you leave it in my office, please?'

Marc intervened. 'No, leave it here, Luciano.' He smiled at Sophie. 'We aren't so busy you haven't time to open an exciting parcel.'

Wondering if it could be an extravagant gesture from Paolo, she undid the wrappings, trying not to tear the paper. The box inside was instantly recognisable. It came from Missoni, one of the shops to which Sophie had taken Martha to shop for presents for her granddaughters.

'It has to be from Martha. She shouldn't have done this.' Sophie turned back the layers of tissue, revealing a knitted garment in the distinctive and complex blend of colours which made Missoni's designs as recognisable and beautiful as a Tiepolo ceiling or a Canaletto painting.

She lifted it out; it was a hip-length jacket with a scarf collar, as warm as tweed but far more adaptable—the sort of glamorous, heirloom jacket which would go anywhere at any time of day.

'Try it on.' Marc took it from her and held it for her to slip her arms in the sleeves. 'Turn around. Yes, it's great on you…very becoming.'

'Do you realise what it would have cost?' Sophie's eyes rolled as she told him. 'It's totally over the top for a little help with her shopping.'

'She can't take it with her, Sophie,' was his dry response. 'It gives her a kick to play fairy godmother sometimes. Come here.' He drew her to him and, taking the ends of the scarf, tried tying it in different ways. 'When the wind comes slicing down from the Dolomites you'll be glad of this wrapped round your chin.'

'It's the most beautiful thing I've ever owned.' Underlying her delight in the jacket and her gratitude for Martha's generosity was the deep, secret pleasure of having him standing close and almost but not quite touching her.

He let the ends fall. 'There may be a note from Martha.' He rummaged through the tissue. 'No…not here. Feel in the pockets.'

She obeyed and produced a small envelope of the handmade marbled paper revived in Venice in the seventies. Inside was a card.

On it, the American had written, 'To keep you snug through the winter. You did so much to make my return to Venice enjoyable. Love, Martha.'

Sophie's throat closed up. She hung her head, embarrassed by the tears welling in her eyes.

'Hey…' Marc tipped up her chin. 'What did she say to make you weepy.'

'N-nothing.' Blinking hard, she gave him the card to

distract him. 'It's just such a sweet thing to do...so incredibly generous,' she said huskily. Because she was knocked off balance, she added impulsively, 'Wouldn't it be lovely if Professor Grant turned out to be the third great love of her life?'

'It would be nice for them both to find a compatible companion. Being old can be lonely, even for people who have large families like Martha's. But as for falling in love...' He shrugged.

'I don't see why not,' said Sophie. 'If people have loving hearts, what has age got to do with it? Except, perhaps, sexually, and that's not the whole of love, is it?'

She was aware, as she said it, that she was speaking more freely than was wise. Her emotions were too close to the surface. She was liable to say something she might regret later.

'I'll put this away,' she said more briskly, taking off the jacket and folding it into the box.

When she returned from her room, Marc was behind his desk, staring into space in a manner unusual for him. As she was crossing the room he returned from wherever his thoughts had taken him.

'I expect you'll be writing to Martha,' he said. 'If you like, I'll take the letter with me when I go to New York on Thursday. It will get to her sooner than if you mail it from here.'

'Thank you. I'll write tonight.'

As they resumed work she wondered if he disagreed with her unguarded remark that sex was only part of love. Perhaps he didn't believe in love in her sense of the word.

During one of Marc's frequent absences, Sophie was walking away from one of the *vaporetto* stops when someone said in English, 'Excuse me, *signorina*...'

Turning, she found a thin-faced young man smiling at her. His face seemed vaguely familiar.

'I was behind you when you bought your ticket. But you didn't have it franked by the machine. Perhaps, as a visitor to Venice, you don't realise it's necessary. There's a heavy fine for using the *vaporetti* with an unfranked ticket.'

Sophie fished in her pocket. 'Isn't the ticket dated?'

'Yes, but it still has to be franked. May I show you?'

He led her back to the walkway between the ticket office and the landing stage to show her what she should have done before boarding the *vaporetto* a few stops along the Grand Canal.

In the past Sophie had had no reason to use this form of transport, and latterly she and Paolo had walked everywhere.

'How stupid of me not to realise—'

The young man shook his head. 'Many visitors don't. Most of the ticket inspections are during the rush hour. The on-the-spot fines are high, to make it not worth the risk of travelling without a franked ticket, which, as you can see, is very easy to do.'

'How kind of you to tell me. Thank you. I feel we've met before, but I can't think where,' she said uncertainly.

'I work in my aunt's bookshop. You've been in the shop a couple of times.'

'Of course...I remember now. The last time I was there some people came in to ask the way. I thought it was very helpful of you to tell them in their own language. In your place I would have pretended not to understand. Their manner was anything but polite. They hadn't even mastered the Italian for thank you.'

'It doesn't happen often. You, I know, speak excellent

Italian, and you've been in Venice longer than most of our visitors.'

'I'm working here.'

'Then I must introduce myself. I'm Damiano Fabbro.' He offered a thin hand.

Sophie had no hesitation in telling him her name. Instinct told her this wasn't a pick-up.

The day came when Marc said, 'You've been here a month now, Sophie. I'm satisfied. Are you?'

'Very much so.'

'In that case the time has come for you to think about somewhere else to live...somewhere you'll feel more at home than a hotel room.'

'My room has a stupendous view. I'll never find a better outlook than from the middle of the Riva across the *bacino* to San Giorgio Maggiore.'

'Someone I know from Milan has a very small top-floor *pied-à-terre* in a tall house on the Zattere. The owner has gone to Rio for a couple of years and intended to put the flat in the hands of a letting agency. However, on your behalf, I have first refusal. Shall we go and look the place over?'

'Can you spare the time?'

'If I couldn't, I wouldn't have suggested it.' He was always slightly caustic when people—others as well as herself—made pointless statements or asked unnecessary questions. At first she had felt somewhat crushed, but by now she had learnt to live with it and even, sometimes, to riposte. As she did now.

'Actually that was a *politezza*.'

From cheekbone to chin, his tanned skin creased in a smile.

'Do I browbeat you?'

'You can be a little...intimidating.'

'Sometimes it's necessary…but not, I admit, in your case. You are driven by your own ambition, needing neither carrot nor stick to make you do your best. Come on; let's go.'

They went down the stairs at a run, as Marc and Chiara always did and as Sophie had learnt to.

As they left the *palazzo* and headed for the Zattere, the waterfront named after the rafts which had once been moored there, Marc said, 'My friend's flat has one major drawback as far as most people of middle age and older are concerned. To reach it one has to climb four flights of rather steep stairs. Otherwise it has every comfort—air-con for the summer heat, an excellent form of heating for the cold months ahead. It often surprises people to find it can snow here in winter. Last year one of the maids broke her arm slipping on a bridge. In icy conditions, the Three Graces don't venture out.'

It wasn't the first time he had referred in this way to his aunts. Although, whenever she had seen them together, Marc had been unfailingly courteous, she guessed that Constanzia, Caterina and Clara tried his patience. They meant well and doted on him, but they were often tactless and insatiably inquisitive. She could understand why he wanted a place of his own.

The front door of the flat was next to a *sottoportego*—the Venetian name for a covered passageway.

'In New York or London an entrance with a dark alley beside it would be considered hazardous,' said Marc as he unlocked the door. 'But here that isn't a worry.'

He went ahead up the stairs, unlocking another door at the top of the final flight. The staircase, with its drab grey walls, was an unprepossessing approach to the eyrie at the top and Sophie couldn't help wondering if she wanted to lug heavy bags of household supplies and groceries up more than sixty stairs.

But when Marc opened the door and stood back for her to enter an unusually spacious living room, at present aglow with the first flush of sunset, she forgot the long haul to reach it.

The light was filtering through the gaps in wide rattan blinds. As he began to roll these up and fasten the cords to cleats like the ones on *Venezia* and other sailing vessels, she saw that to the south was the sun-gilded skyline of the Giudecca and in the opposite direction was a vista of Roman-tiled rooftops very similar to Marc's view from his desk.

He showed her the bedroom and bathroom. The kitchen was in a corner of the living area, concealed from the rest of the room by a bank of cupboards.

'What do you think?' he asked, after showing her around.

'I love it, but what's the rent?'

When Marc told her, she raised her eyebrows. 'Surely, even with those stairs, it's worth a lot more than that?'

He shrugged. 'I wouldn't know. I'm sure the agent has advised the owner of what the market will bear.'

'It's a snip. I'll take it,' she decided.

'Would you like to move in right away? How long will it take you to pack?'

'I haven't unpacked my big case—the one with my household goods, such as they are. Packing my clothes isn't a long job…not more than half an hour.'

'Right. You go back and do that and I'll come by with the launch about seven o'clock. By eight you can be installed.'

'It's a very kind offer but—'

'That's settled,' he cut in briskly, walking back to the door. 'I think you'll be comfortable here. It's rather sparsely furnished, but from your point of view that's better than being too cluttered. There's room for some personal touches. I'll be interested to see what sort of stamp you put on it.'

Sophie had settled her account with the hotel and was sitting in the lobby with her luggage beside her when Marc arrived promptly at seven.

He had not brought his boatman, she found when the hotel porter wheeled her luggage to the launch. At the other end, it was Marc who unloaded her bags, carried them to her front door and took them upstairs, without any sign that he wasn't accustomed to such labours or found them a test of his strength.

'While you were packing I organised a few basic supplies to keep you going overnight,' he said. 'Orange juice, bread, coffee and milk for breakfast…and for tonight some wine. Let's have a glass now, shall we? Then we'll go and eat at the Locanda Montin. It's only a stone's throw from here.'

'You're being terribly kind,' she said gratefully. 'I don't think many employers would go to these lengths to be helpful.'

'Let's forget that I'm your employer for this evening, shall we?'

She wasn't sure what he meant, but hesitated to ask him to be more specific.

Marc took a bottle of white wine out of the large refrigerator and opened a cupboard near it containing a variety of glasses.

'Why has your friend gone to Rio?' Sophie asked.

'One of the world's top cosmetic surgeons has a clinic there. Trina is also a surgeon. She's going to study his techniques and use them on patients in Italy. Cosmetic surgery has scarcely begun in Europe. In America facelifts and "nips and tucks" are taken for granted. She wants to cash in on that here.'

When she made no comment, he said shrewdly, 'You don't approve?' And then, before she could answer, 'Neither do I, but when we've argued about it Trina has pointed out that *I'm* not devoting my life to a noble calling. Why should she?'

'You keep thousands of people in work. If that isn't a valuable function I don't know what is,' she said, with unintended vigour.

'Are you defending me, Sophie?' he asked, with a smile in his eyes.

'You don't need me to defend you,' she said, embarrassed.

'No...but I like it when you do.'

In the long pause that followed, Sophie was forced to acknowledge something she had been trying to deny. She was in love with him.

The walls of the Locanda Montin were hung almost frame to frame with paintings by many different artists. Most of the other diners were Italians, with only a sprinkling of foreigners at the pink-clothed tables with their homely rush-seated chairs.

As they were shown to a table by an elderly waiter with the air of a prince down on his luck, Sophie scanned the walls in search of a painting by Michael. Surely he must have come here long ago? But there was nothing she recognised.

While they ate Marc talked with unexpected seriousness about the future of the world and the best use of its resources. When he canvassed her views, Sophie found herself airing theories she had never shared with anyone before.

'You're even brighter than I thought when I took you on. How come you didn't go to college?' he asked.

Inwardly glowing with pleasure, she said, 'I needed

to earn my living sooner rather than later. Unfortunately a degree no longer guarantees a problem-free future. Some students come out of college with a massive overdraft. I played safe and opted for office skills. They've served me pretty well. There are rafts of graduates who would envy me my job here.'

When their coffee was served he asked for the bill. 'I'd better not keep you out late. You still have to unpack.'

Sophie had decided that while he was walking her home through the quiet streets of a city not noted for its night-life she would tell him her history. But Marc had more to say on the topics they had talked about at dinner, and very soon they were outside her door, which he unlocked for her. Then, handing over the key and barely giving her time to thank him for dinner, he said goodnight and strode away.

It seemed a curiously brisk ending to an agreeable evening.

An hour later, Sophie climbed into her new bed. Above it, a large skylight had been inserted in the sloping ceiling of the bedroom.

Perhaps it was having the stars overhead, evoking nights in the past when Michael had taken her sailing through the constellations, explaining their magical names to her, that made her feel his presence as if he were in the room.

'I'm in love with Marc,' she said aloud. 'Don't tell me I'm mad. I know it. The odds against him loving me are a million to one. But…I can't help myself.'

How her grandfather might have responded, had he been alive to receive this anxious confession, was something she would never know. But she did know, from what he had told her about her parents and about his own marriage to one of the beautiful models he had drawn for *Vogue* magazine, that he had believed a loving and lifelong partnership between a man and a woman to be among life's best prizes. But one not awarded to more than a fraction of the people who hoped to win it.

Although, in a way, it was a relief to have confronted the way she felt about Marc, instead of continuing to pretend she wasn't in love with him, Sophie didn't feel inclined to take Damiano into her confidence.

The bookseller was in love with an American girl spending several months working at the Peggy Guggenheim Foundation. She hadn't left a boyfriend behind and was hoping to extend her stay in Venice. But Damiano felt he had little hope of persuading her to stay there permanently. She was only twenty and seemed set on a career in the art world.

'Twenty is very young for a serious involvement,' said Sophie, during one of her chats with him.

Mostly they talked about Venice. Damiano's knowledge of the city's history was extensive, and what he told her about Marc's ancestors was not reassuring. On his mother's side, he came from a long line of powerful, ruthless men who had been notorious for their cavalier treatment of the women who had fallen in love with them.

One evening she was in the bookshop, discussing the exploits of another of the great Venetian dynasties, when Marc himself walked in.

At the sight of her perched on a high stool behind the counter his mobile left eyebrow became an inverted tick.

His greeting included them both, but then, as if she had vanished—and she wished she could—he turned to Damiano to order some books he had seen reviewed in the *New York Herald Tribune*. As she already knew, he was an extravagant book-buyer, ordering expensive art books as casually as if they were bargains from the weekend stalls in the Campo San Stefano.

As he gave Damiano the details carried in his phenomenal memory he scanned the display on the counter, opening some of the covers to read what was written on the inside flaps of the jackets.

She feasted her eyes on his face, wishing she had the skill to reproduce his features on paper—the broad forehead defined by his thick black hair and straight eyebrows, the angular cheekbones and nose, the wide mouth and strong, square chin slightly dented at its centre. Although Michael could have drawn those features with a few expert strokes of charcoal on paper, Marc's face was actually more suited to the art of the sculptor.

She was thinking this when he looked up, and before she had time to switch her gaze elsewhere he caught it fixed on him and held it.

'What are you reading at the moment, Sophie?'

She told him the name of a novel recommended and lent to her by Damiano. Knowing she would return them to the shop in immaculate condition, he often insisted on lending her books he thought she would enjoy from his stock.

'I rarely read fiction,' said Marc. 'My aunts devour it like chocolate. I prefer to read about real lives.' He placed a couple of books on top of the till. 'I'll have these as well...on my account, please.'

A few moments later he had gone, leaving her with the feeling that he disapproved of finding his personal assistant sitting in the shop as if she were Damiano's helper.

'We should miss his account if he took his custom elsewhere. He spends a lot of money with us,' said Damiano.

Sophie nodded. 'I know.' She glanced at her watch. 'I'd better be going. *Ciao*...'

Outside the shop, she looked along the street in the direction Marc had taken. He was not in sight, but even his long stride could hardly have taken him as far as the end of it yet. He must be in one of the neighbouring shops.

Knowing she was behaving like a lovesick teenager, she sauntered past them at a leisurely pace, hoping he would emerge. On and off she had spent all day in his company, yet she longed for more. The evenings seemed endless intervals between the vital hours at the *palazzo*.

Outside two of the shops she loitered, gazing at the displays, hoping to see a tall reflection joining hers in the plate glass. But it didn't happen.

She walked home with the desolate knowledge that she was making a fool of herself, and that the pain and frustration of being in love with Marc Washington was going to get worse rather than better.

CHAPTER TWELVE

ON THE morning of her twenty-sixth birthday, feeling slightly cast down by the thought that in four years' time she would be thirty, Sophie walked into her office to find it full of flowers, with several gift-wrapped parcels lying on her desk.

Three were from Marc's aunts and one from Chiara. They could only have known it was her birthday because he had told them. The largest parcel had his signature on the tag and she left it unopened while she unwrapped the others.

Chiara had given her scent and the aunts' gifts were a pair of hand-embroidered pillowcases, a silk scarf and a leather-bound photograph album. Marc's parcel contained a de luxe volume on paintings of Venice by twentieth-century artists. It was one she had seen and coveted in Damiano's aunt's shop but had felt was outside her budget. Now it was hers, the lasting pleasure of its pages immeasurably enhanced by the simple inscription on the flyleaf, 'To Sophie from Marc,' and the date.

She was unable to thank him for it immediately because he had gone to Prague and was due back that afternoon. As the aunts were not early risers, she left it until mid-morning to go down and thank them and his cousin.

They insisted she lunch with them, and the chef produced a special pudding to mark the occasion. Sophie was touched by their kindness, but it was the fact that Marc had filed her birth date in his phenomenal memory which meant the most to her.

During the afternoon she received a message from the Prague office. Marc's return flight had been put back. But he had booked a table for dinner and would collect her from her flat at eight o'clock.

In Sophie's absence, the postman had delivered a large envelope with an array of United States stamps on it: a typically funny, flamboyant American birthday card chosen by Merle, with several one-line greetings from other friends.

It was nice that they had remembered her. Inevitably, birthdays were times when she was particularly conscious of having no family ties.

Not knowing where Marc was taking her or who else might be there made it difficult to know what to wear. After reviewing her wardrobe, she decided on the outfit she had worn in Paris, but with a shorter skirt than the one she had travelled in and a new pair of sheer black tights.

She was ready long before she needed to be and spent the interval restlessly pacing the living room, annoyed with herself for being as absurdly on edge as if it were her first date. She wasn't even sure that she would have Marc to herself. He might have invited others.

When the bell rang, she ran down the stairs to find Antonio, the boatman, waiting outside the street door. For an instant she felt cold panic, fearing an accident. Then he explained that the boss was running late and would meet her at the restaurant.

After taking her most of the way by water, Antonio insisted on escorting her to the door of the restaurant and handing her over to the head waiter, who showed her to a secluded corner table laid for two.

Less than five minutes later Marc arrived. 'Many

happy returns,' he said as he joined her, only the dampness of his hair betraying that he had been rushed.

'Thank you…and thank you for your wonderful present. It's exactly what I would have chosen if I'd been offered the freedom of every shop in the city. Have you had a difficult day?'

He shrugged. 'It started badly, but—' he gave her a glinting smile '—all's well that ends well. Tell me about your day.'

The wine waiter had already brought champagne to the table and filled a glass for Sophie. So far she had only taken a couple of sips. Now he did the same for Marc who, as the bottle was returned to its bucket of ice, lifted his glass to her. 'To your twenty-seventh year. May it bring you a lot of things on your wish list.'

'Thank you.' This time she drank a mouthful of the chilled golden wine, knowing it would quickly enter her bloodstream, hoping it would give a sparkle to her conversation. She wanted to please and amuse him, but when she had told him about her other presents and the lunch party with his aunts she found herself strapped for subjects having nothing to do with their working life.

The only thing she could come up with was, 'You never finished telling me the story of the haunted mirror. I said that as ghost stories go it was rather a nice one. You said, ''Actually, no.'' What did you mean?'

As she spoke she wondered if he would remember why he hadn't finished the story and felt sure he would.

'Apparently, when the princess and her lady-in-waiting compared notes, it was clear they had seen two separate pairs of lovers,' said Marc. 'We don't know who the princess saw. Since they were in bed, naked, there were no clues to the date of the time-warp she'd entered…if you believe in such things.'

'But you don't.'

'What makes you think that?' he asked.

'You believe in realities, not fantasies.'

'On the whole, yes,' he agreed. 'But at the beginning of this century supersonic flight was a fantasy. Now millions of ordinary people are surfing the internet from their living rooms. The future is full of things which seem impossible to us. As to the past…who knows? Perhaps it's still there, like a radio station we can't reach because we don't know the waveband. Anyway, what the lady-in-waiting tuned into wasn't the same channel as the princess had seen earlier that night. There were two different people making love by the light of candles, and then suddenly a dark shape…the silhouette of a man standing at the foot of the bed.'

Sophie drew in her breath.

'We have a letter in the archives in which she described what happened next,' Marc continued. 'Briefly, the intruder moved to one side, clearing her view of the lovers. They disengaged, looking alarmed. As well they might. What happened next was a blast from some sort of blunderbuss. The results were so gruesome, the lady-in-waiting fainted.'

Sophie's face must have reflected her feelings at seeing, in her imagination, the horror he hadn't described but which she could easily visualise.

Reaching across the table to cover her hand with his, Marc said, 'I shouldn't have told you.'

The intimate gesture sent a strange frisson through her. She said, 'No, no…it's interesting. Do the archives hold any evidence that such a thing might really have happened?'

'Plenty. It happened in the eighteenth century. The *marchese* of the time returned from an evening with his mistress to find his wife in bed with a handsome young servant. He must have suspected something to enter the bedroom armed. At the time morals in Venice were notoriously lax, but he must have been a jealous man who didn't subscribe to the view that an unfaithful husband gave his wife licence to do as she pleased.'

Marc's hand still lay on hers. He seemed to have forgotten it was there. But Sophie was sharply aware of his long fingers enfolding hers, sending a current of feeling to the top of her arm. She was both relieved and sorry when the arrival of their meal caused him to break the contact.

'Let's talk about something more appropriate to a birthday celebration. How did you celebrate last year?'

'I was sharing an apartment. My flatmate, Merle, laid on a party for me.'

'Do you miss that arrangement?'

Sophie shook her head. 'I might in another big city. But Venice has a villagey atmosphere.'

'Was the man of the moment at last year's party?'

'There was no man of the moment.'

'But there have been men in your life?'

'At twenty-six it would be rather extraordinary if I'd never thought myself in love.'

'Only thought?'

'If it had ever been the real thing, I shouldn't be here now, should I?'

'I suppose not. Are you still looking for the real thing?'

'Isn't everyone?'

'Are they?' He gave a slight shrug. 'I wouldn't have thought so. Money and power seem more popular objectives. They always were among men and now they're the principal goals of many of your sex. Women like Martha Henderson don't seem to exist any more.'

'She didn't have to work, and wouldn't have been encouraged to. Chiara's the first girl I've met who doesn't have a career, or even a time-filling job. When you have to compete in the rat race you develop a protective shell.'

She had meant to leave it at that, but then, on impulse, added, 'And women see through men more. Your sex has lost its mystique. Women realise that not many men come up to their expectations of what a man should be like.'

'Speaking for yourself, what should a man be like?'

He asked with a gleam of amusement, making her feel she was about to cross a conversational quagmire and could quickly find herself floundering.

'Kind to women and children, fair in his dealings with his own sex. Not a very tall order.'

'A generalisation. Be specific. What do *you* want from a man? Surely more than kindness and fairness? If that's all you want you could find yourself saddled with dullness.'

'Naturally I want perfection,' she said, with a smile and a gesture to show she was joking. 'The brave, gentle, handsome knight of all the best fairy tales.'

'A tall order,' Marc said drily.

In response to his signal, the alert head waiter brought menus. Looking for something light for dessert, Sophie regretted her answer. Instead of sounding like a naïve teenager, she should have said something witty.

Having entered the restaurant from the street, she expected to leave the same way. Instead, as they left their table, the head waiter came forward, saying. 'If you will follow me, *signorina*...'

Somewhat baffled, she obeyed and found herself being led in a different direction, down some stairs and along a passage which, when it turned a corner, brought them to a doorway with a gondola moored outside it.

'It seemed an appropriate conclusion to your birthday,' said Marc, when she turned to look up at him.

He said a smiling good evening to the gondolier, an elderly man who had swept off his hat with a gallant flourish when he saw Sophie.

The last thing she had expected was to find herself being handed into a gondola and, when she was seated on the cushioned sofa, having a rug draped over her legs by Marc.

'Although it's not cold tonight, it's always cooler on the water, and we're taking a roundabout route,' said Marc as he tucked it round her.

When he was seated beside her, another waiter appeared carrying a small wicker hamper. He gave it to the head waiter, who placed it where Marc could reach it before bidding them goodnight.

'The basket is an heirloom,' said Marc. 'I had it sent round earlier. It was fitted out for my maternal grandfather, who liked to take the air with his current mistress beside him. He would drink and smoke a cigar and she would eat Brussels chocolates. He had a theory that chocolate made women amorous, and he liked them generously curved. Tonight...it only contains a flask of freshly made coffee and a rather special liqueur brandy I think you'll like.'

The slight pause and the hint of devilment in his smile made Sophie wonder if he was merely teasing her, or if, in his experience, a smooth but potent liqueur was more effective than chocolates in making women responsive.

A further surprise was in store for her. As the gondola glided past the junction with another canal a second gondola came into view, and in it were seated three violinists who, as it moved into place behind theirs, began to play.

'Heavens! When you organise a treat, you really go

to town,' she said, astonished that he should go to these lengths to please her.

'Why not?'

The response to that was, Why? But she didn't say it, or even allow her thoughts to linger on the reasons he might have. There were times in life when to capture the pleasure of the fleeting moment was more important than pondering the motive behind it or the possible outcome.

She leaned back against the cushions, enraptured by an experience she had often imagined but never expected to live.

By moonlight the city's waterways were at their most mysterious. She found herself seeing the Venice invisible from its bridges: tall, dark, forbidding façades relieved by elaborate windows, white marble friezes and balconies, and long-disused, barred water-gates, their steps thick with moss.

Behind them, the musicians were playing something by Vivaldi. Between them and the silver bow-prong stood a large basket filled with late-blooming roses from the *palazzo*'s sheltered garden, their sweetness wafting back like the breath of summer.

He had catered to every sense, she realised as he gave her a cup of coffee and placed a small crystal liqueur glass where she could reach it.

Every sense except touch.

Presently the lights of a restaurant, with diners sitting outside, changed the surface of the canal from silver and black to green and bronze.

'Let's not disappoint the romantics by sitting like strangers,' said Marc.

He lifted his arm and laid it along the cushions behind her shoulders. As the diners, alerted by the music, broke off their conversations to stare at the two gondolas, he took Sophie's hand and kissed it, not symbolically but with his lips touching her skin for two or three breath-stopping seconds.

From the tables behind the railing at the canal's edge came the momentary dazzle of an automatic flash as someone seized the chance to add another photo to their reel.

Someone else wanted one too. 'Do that again, would you, please?' The voice was male, the accent American.

Marc gave a smiling glance over his shoulder. 'No problem.' He repeated the gesture, this time holding her hand to his mouth rather longer.

Then the restaurant slid away behind them, the voices and laughter of its patrons lost in the sweeping strings of the violins.

Marc replaced her hand in her lap, but he didn't remove his arm from behind her. She wondered if, regardless of the gondolier, the next time they passed through a dark place he meant to kiss her properly and what she would do if he did.

Being kissed by her boss wasn't a dilemma she had had to deal with before. She had no idea how to handle it. Her common sense and her instincts were in diametric conflict. As a woman, she wanted to be kissed. As his personal assistant, she knew it could wreck their relationship and perhaps bring an end to her job here.

But Marc didn't kiss her. Gliding under the final bridge, the gondola came to the breeze-ruffled wider waterway between where she lived and the Giudecca opposite. It danced and swayed on the choppier surface and the gondolier changed his stroke with centuries-old expertise.

The music came to an end moments before they arrived at a landing not far from her door. Once ashore, Sophie thanked the violinists.

'That was beautiful...unforgettable. I'll remember it all my life,' she said in Italian.

Turning to thank Marc, she found him holding the basket of roses. 'I'll carry this upstairs for you, then walk back,' he said in English, before switching to Italian to add his thanks to the two gondoliers and the musicians.

As Sophie and he walked away, and the gondolas moved in the direction of another canal further along, the lead violinist began the opening bars of a modern love song, the other two joining in.

She stopped to wave them on their way. 'Was that prearranged?' she asked.

'Not by me. Perhaps it's their way of saying they don't often have someone as charming as you to serenade.'

Sophie received that in silence. A few yards away from her door, she said, 'I meant it when I said I would never forget their music, nor everything else about this evening. It's been a wonderful birthday. I don't know how to thank you.'

'Your company was my reward.'

Sophie fished for her key. Having found it, she said, 'I can manage the basket. Please don't bother to come up.'

'It's no bother, Sophie.'

The night he had shown her the flat he had gone up the stairs ahead of her, as mannerly men were supposed to. This time he let her go first. As they climbed the first flight she remembered the night they had spent in Paris and his schoolfriend Patrick saying to him, 'You can't turn in this early...not in Paris. Or maybe you can. Who wouldn't with legs like that pair going up the stairs ahead of him? I'll bet she has splendid boobs too...'

Did Marc also remember? Did he have it in mind to end the evening in the way Patrick had thought they were going to end it in Paris—in bed together? Had this whole lovely evening been an expensive prelude to a practised seduction?

In Paris, Patrick's assumption had filled her with indignant anger. But she hadn't known Marc then. Now she did. Now she loved and admired him. Now a night in his arms would be heaven.

But not if it were just a try-out. Or the start of a casual affair.

She went up the stairs much more slowly than she normally did, trying to stave off the moment when he would make his move and she would have to respond or rebuff him.

Would she be able to rebuff him when her senses were still alight from the expectation of being kissed in the gondola?

At the top of the staircase she unlocked the door between the landing and the living room and felt for the light switch. It was connected to a table lamp and a concealed uplighter in a corner of the little roof garden.

'How about some more coffee?' Marc suggested as he entered the room behind her.

She could have come out with the hackneyed excuse that she was tired and tomorrow was a busy day, which indeed it would be. But she put off the critical moment, knowing as she did it that she was weakening her defences.

'Of course…it won't take long. There's a very good percolator. Do the roses need a drink too? Did you have your aunts' permission to plunder their garden for me?'

He set the basket on the big table in the corner between the sitting area and the kitchen. 'They have their stems in water. The basket is metal-lined. Actually the garden is mine, although the aunts treat it as theirs. I'll be glad to have a garden I don't share with three old ladies. Are you interested in gardening, Sophie?'

His manner was reassuringly friendly. Perhaps, after all, he had nothing in mind but coffee and conversation. Perhaps kissing her hand had been merely some good-natured play-acting for the benefit of the tourists. She wished she knew where she stood with him.

'I think I could be,' she said. 'When I was at boarding-school, I made friends with an old man who worked part-time in the kitchen garden. His name was Jeremiah Jones. When he was twelve, and the house was privately owned, he started work as a garden boy. I loved listening to his stories. He died soon after I left. He—'

She broke off, not wanting to bore him with reminiscences of no interest to him. She felt she was talking too much—partly from nervous tension and partly, perhaps, from the effect of the liqueur which had tasted innocuously smooth but was probably far more potent than rougher spirits.

'How did you find out he'd died?'

'His daughter wrote to me…to stop me writing to Jem. It turned out she'd had to read my letters to him. He couldn't read or write. I think he was probably dyslexic, but in his day they didn't know about such things.'

'Were you unhappy at boarding-school?'

'A bit homesick at first. Who isn't? Later on I enjoyed it. Oh—'

Her exclamation was caused by his coming to where she was busy setting the coffee-tray and taking a carton of brown sugar crystals out of her hand.

'I don't take sugar and neither do you.' He replaced it in the cupboard above the worktops where it belonged. Then he put his arms lightly round her. 'I don't like to think of you being homesick.'

CHAPTER THIRTEEN

THEIR bodies were only inches apart. Sophie felt he must hear the violent thumping of her heart. She looked at the knot of his tie, slightly above her eye level, until by force of will Marc made her meet his eyes, before drawing her closer to kiss her.

It was eight years since her first kiss and many months since her last time in Robert's arms. Neither his nor any other kisses had prepared her for this embrace with the man she worked for, the man she loved.

After the first few moments when his lips were gentle, giving her time to resist, suddenly passion took over. He kissed her as if by right, holding her hard against his powerful body, taking confident possession of her mouth.

Sophie's response astonished her. As if it were the most natural thing in the world, she put her arms round his neck and surrendered herself without reservation.

When the telephone started ringing, the sound seemed to come from a long way away, recognisable but irrelevant. Her eyes closed, her body a turmoil of delicious sensations, she ignored it. But it wouldn't stop and leave them in peace. Eventually Marc raised his head.

'You'd better answer it,' he said huskily, putting her away from him. His dark eyes glittered with desire.

Dazed, she went to the end table where the interruption came from. Picking up the receiver, trying, reluctantly, to come down to earth, she said, *'Pronto.'*

'Is that you, Sophie? It's Merle.'

For a minute she couldn't think who Merle was. It

was on the tip of her tongue to say, You have the wrong number, ring off and hurry back to where she belonged—in Marc's arms.

Then her mind made the connection. 'Oh… Merle…hello. How are you?'

'I'm fine. How are you? Happy birthday.'

'Thank you.'

'Did you get my card?'

'Yes, I did. It's a beauty. It came today…perfect timing. Thank you.'

'I have some exciting news. I've won a trip to Europe, to Courchevel 1850…it's a swish ski resort in France.'

'That's wonderful, Merle,' said Sophie, looking in the direction of the kitchen.

Marc was where she had left him, still standing with his back to her. She couldn't signal to him until he turned round.

'It would be if I could ski, or wanted to learn,' said Merle. 'But I'm trying to get it switched to somewhere I want to vacation…preferably Venice.'

'Can you do that?'

'Maybe not, but I'm working on it.'

As Merle started going into details of how she had won the prize Marc turned slowly round. Across the room their eyes met. It made Sophie feel weak at the knees just to look at him across five metres of carpet. She knew if he kissed her again, she would be lost.

He was coming towards her when the percolator went into its final spasm. He turned back to attend to it.

Merle was still explaining. Sophie sank down on the sofa. She felt weak with longing to let events take their course from those heavenly minutes in his arms. He had brought her alive in a way she had never experienced. Her whole body ached with a yearning for those feelings to come to a natural and satisfying conclusion under the window to the stars in the other room.

Merle had started to wind up her call. 'So I'll fax you as soon as it's settled. It's nice to hear your voice. I miss you.'

'I miss you too, Merle. It will be great if you can come to Venice. I'll look forward to showing it to you.'

Merle said goodbye and rang off. Preoccupied with her prize and the hope of changing its location, she had forgotten to ask how Sophie had celebrated this year.

Marc was still behind the bank of units screening, from where she was sitting, most of the kitchen area. She debated joining him there, then decided to stay where she was, leaving the initiative with him.

Now her intelligence was coming back into play, telling her she would be mad to be swept away by her instincts.

Marc came round the end of the screen. 'Sophie, I'm going to take a rain check on the coffee. That call reminded me of a couple I have to make before I turn in. I'll say goodnight. There's no need to come down with me. Give me the key to the bottom door. I'll lock it and put the key through the letter box.'

His tone was friendly but final. For reasons she couldn't begin to guess, he had made up his mind and that was that.

Torn between disappointment and relief, Sophie went to her bag and found her keyring. As she started to detach the key he wanted he said, 'Let me do that. You may break your nails.'

The touch of his fingers as he took the keys from her sent a frisson of erotic sensation quivering through her nervous system.

Perhaps the contact had a similar effect on him. She saw his jaw muscles tense.

Detaching the key, he gave the ring back to her, but in such a way that the contact wasn't repeated. 'I'll call you tomorrow. Goodnight.'

'Goodnight...and thank you again for a wonderful evening.'

He acknowledged her thanks with a nod and headed for the door.

When he had gone, closing the door to the stairway behind him, Sophie collapsed on the sofa, taking off her shoes before drawing her legs up beside her.

A horrible feeling of rejection was beginning to come over her. Why had Marc had second thoughts? She didn't believe his excuse that he had some calls to make.

It was true he was flying out tomorrow and wouldn't be back for several days, possibly a week. But if the calls were to local numbers on personal matters he would have made them earlier, before joining her at the restaurant. Everything outstanding in his official diary had been dealt with before she'd left the *palazzo*. The calls had been a pretext to get him out of the apartment. Why? What had changed him from the man who had kissed her with such intensity to the man who had said a courteous but distant goodnight?

The question was still tormenting her when she heard various church bells strike two and rose from her rumpled bed to make herself a cup of *camomilla*, hoping it would help her to sleep.

Merle and many of the people she had known in London and New York had routinely taken sleeping pills. But it was only since coming back to Venice that Sophie had found herself tossing and turning at night. She had never lost sleep over her relationship with Robert. But he hadn't made her feel the way Marc did. She had never shivered and burned with longing for him.

She had never felt that if anything happened to him it would be the end of the world for her as well.

It was mid-afternoon the next day when Marc called her from Copenhagen, where he was attending a conference.

He sounded as if nothing had changed, yesterday had never happened and they were still on their previous footing. But she couldn't believe that their kisses had meant nothing to him. He had been as strongly aroused as she had, perhaps more so. The closeness of their embrace had given her unequivocal proof that it was not only she who had felt desire raging through her.

When she finished work, she found Paolo waiting for her outside the street door.

She hadn't seen him for some time and had concluded, with relief, that he was pursuing someone else. Perhaps he was here on his mother's behalf, the bearer of an invitation to some family celebration.

'Hello, Paolo. What brings you here?'

'I need to talk to you,' he said. 'You didn't tell me you had left the hotel.'

'I would have, if I had run into you. It was never my intention to stay there permanently, you know. It was only a temporary roost till I found a place of my own.'

'Where is your new place?'

'On the Zattere.'

He raised his eyebrows. 'Property there is expensive.'

'It's not a large place. I'm renting it while the owner is overseas.'

'Who's the owner…a friend of your boss?'

She nodded.

'That's what he told you anyway.'

'What do you mean?'

'Maybe he owns it himself. Maybe it's one of his love-nests. He has several, so I've heard.'

'Gossip!' was Sophie's succinct comment.

'Not all of it. I saw you with him last night. I thought you were going out with the guy from the bookshop?'

'We're friends. Damiano's in love with an American. I'm someone to talk to about her.'

'More fool him...and more fool you if you get involved with your boss.'

'I'm not involved,' she said, with partial truth.

'Oh, no? What were you doing in a gondola with him, then? Taking dictation? I'll bet!'

'If you must know, it was my birthday. He was merely being nice.'

'If you believe that, you'll believe anything.' Paolo retorted sarcastically. 'Or do you take me for a fool? If he didn't seduce you last night, it's only because he likes to play with his women like a cat with a mouse. Answer me this—when he left...if he left...did he shake hands or kiss you?'

'I don't think that's any of your business, Paolo.'

'He kissed you!' he said triumphantly. 'And today he's rubbing his hands because he knows he's got you right where he wants you, or as near as makes no difference. In a few hours' time he'll be ringing your bell with a big bunch of flowers in his hand, and while you're putting them in water he'll come up behind you and start to nibble your neck, and the next thing you know you'll be on your back and—'

Sophie cut short this forecast by using the book she was carrying to give him a thump in the ribs. He was too well-muscled for it to hurt him badly, but it made him yelp in surprise.

'That may be a method you've found effective, Paolo, but I don't want to hear about it. Your advice is unnecessary and your style of giving it offensive. If that's all you have to say, I'd prefer to walk home alone.'

She quickened her pace, hoping he wouldn't follow. His words had touched her on the raw because they expressed her own doubts and fears about Marc's intentions towards her.

'Sophie…don't lose your temper.' Paolo was at her heels as she ran up the steps of a small bridge.

It led to the mouth of an alley too narrow for people to pass without making room for each other. Halfway along it, silhouetted by the last of the afternoon sun, an elderly man with a stick was shuffling towards her. Politeness obliged her to wait for him, but the look she flashed Paolo was a warning not to persist.

'I'm sorry.' His tone was penitent. 'I didn't mean to offend you. I shouldn't have put it like that.'

'I accept your apology. Now let's drop it.'

Looking chastened, he stayed at her elbow while the old man came slowly towards them with short, tottering steps.

'Let me walk as far as your door with you. If Mamma finds out you've moved and I don't even know your address, she'll give me a thump to match this bruise,' Paolo said, rubbing his side.

'You've had worse,' she said unsympathetically, remembering more than one black eye acquired in his pugnacious boyhood. 'You can bring your mother to see my flat, if you like, but I won't show it to you today. I'm not in a sociable mood…but not because Marc's coming round. He's away in Denmark and from there he's flying to London.'

Paolo made no comment on this. It wasn't until they had emerged from the alley that he said, 'How's the work going on the island? Are the bureaucrats giving you a hard time?'

'No more than bureaucrats anywhere. They need the right approach.'

'And we all know what this is,' he said, with a knowing grin and a graphic twist of the wrist.

'You're too cynical. Not everyone is corrupt. I don't believe Marc would use bribes to achieve his objectives.'

There was no doubt in her mind that he was a man of integrity in his business dealings. It was only his attitude to women she wasn't sure about.

Echoing her thoughts, Paolo said, 'If he's spending a mint of his own money to improve state property, there's no reason for them to obstruct him. Listen, Sophie, don't get mad at me, but there's something I've got to tell you.'

'Something about Marc?'

He nodded, his expression troubled.

'If it's something unpleasant, I don't want to hear it, Paolo. I expect it's pure supposition.'

'No, no…this time it's fact. This is something I *know*.'

She wanted to close her ears, to refuse to listen. But curiosity won. Everything to do with Marc was of such compelling importance to her.

'Very well, then, tell me…but don't expect me to believe it.'

'I wish there was no need to tell you. When I thought he was just your boss, I kept my mouth shut. He's the father of Marina Guilio's eldest son. She used to be a housemaid at Palazzo Cassiano.'

Sophie averted her face, not wanting him to see how much this statement had hurt her. She knew Paolo wasn't malicious. As a boy he had never been spiteful or thoughtlessly cruel.

This wasn't a slanderous piece of gossip motivated by jealousy. It had to be true. And it had the same effect as the summons she'd once had to see the headmistress of her boarding-school. She had known before she'd reached Miss Wilkinson's study that there could be only one reason why she had been sent for. Michael had had another heart attack, as the doctors had warned him was likely. Now Paolo was breaking the news that another man she loved was not the wholly admirable person she wanted him to be.

'How do you know this, Paolo?'

'Maria's brother is a gondolier. I had something going with another of his sisters for a while. She told me about it. I've seen the boy. He's the spitting image of your boss.'

'Does Marc acknowledge the boy? Does he support them?' she asked in a low voice.

'I expect he's forgotten her by now. He knew she was pregnant. She told him. Most likely he told her that it was her problem. Luckily she had a nice steady fellow in love with her. By the time the baby arrived she was married to Sirio.'

'Does he know the boy isn't his?'

Paolo shrugged. 'I wouldn't know. All I do know is that your boss caused her a lot of grief, and she wasn't the only one he loved and left in the lurch. I wouldn't want to see the same thing happen to you. I expect you've got too much savvy to get yourself in the family way, but even smart girls get hurt in other ways.'

'When did this happen? How old were they?'

'Stefano, the boy, is sixteen. They live near Padova now, on the country estate of the family Sirio worked for when he lived in Venice. From what I hear, they have a good life over there. They've three other children. It's turned out well for Marina, but she might have had a bad time of it if Sirio hadn't been there to pick up the pieces.'

'If the boy is sixteen, Marc would have been nineteen

when he was conceived. How old is the boy's mother now?'

'About thirty-five, I suppose.'

'If they live near Padova, how do you know the boy is like Marc to look at?'

'They came back to Venice for a family wedding a couple of years ago. At fourteen Stefano was as tall as me and still growing. He's bright too. They say he'll get to university. I wonder if he'll ever come face to face with his natural *papa*. It would be a shock for them both...and a worse shock if your boss has a wife by then and hasn't come clean about his past.'

'You talk as if he has children all over the place,' Sophie said, with a touch of anger. 'It's not a crime to father a child, Paolo. For all you know, you may have done it yourself.'

'Not me! I made certain of that,' he assured her. 'Girls may say they're taking precautions, but you can never be sure. Besides, there are other reasons for a fellow to be careful. Anyway, now you know that your boss isn't whiter than white I hope you'll watch your step with him.'

Their conversation left Sophie very dejected. She had never closed her mind to the fact that a man of thirty-six must have what Michael's generation referred to as 'a past'. She had one herself, of sorts. They were both grown-up people living in an era when human relationships were more open, honest and, in many cases, more transient than they had ever been before.

At school she had been surprised to discover that most of the girls in her form had two sets of parents, each pair composed of a divorced natural parent and a step-parent.

Perhaps, if her father and mother had lived, their youthful marriage would have fallen apart, although somehow she didn't think so. They had both been in love with the sea as well as with each other. A bond like that was hard to break.

When Michael had talked about them he had made her believe that she, too, would one day find her true love and be happy ever after. Life on board *Venezia*, without television or newspapers, had sheltered her from the disillusionments encountered later. The ideals implanted by Michael were still deeply embedded in her psyche, and the knowledge that Marc, having seduced a housemaid, had failed to shoulder his responsibility for the outcome did not equate with her concept of chivalrous behaviour.

She wished she could hear his side of the story. Perhaps there had been extenuating circumstances. But she couldn't ask about it, and meanwhile her opinion of him had been tarnished. It made her deeply unhappy.

When Sophie went to the airport to meet Rowena Wyatt, she already knew a great deal about the English garden designer Marc had chosen to plan the grounds round the house on the island.

At Sophie's request, her opposite number in London had supplied a folder of cuttings about her, mainly from glossy magazines which had interviewed the designer and photographed gardens created by her. However, all the photographs in the file had showed the thirty-five-year-old divorcee in working gear: jeans and a blue denim shirt with a man's panama hat worn at a rakish angle, or dungarees over a heavy sweater and a knitted ski hat in the photographs taken in winter.

Expecting a country person, Sophie was unprepared for a vision of sophisticated city elegance in an aubergine suit with a short skirt and perfectly matched opaque tights showing off very good legs. The colour was wonderful with the designer's dark red hair.

After Sophie had introduced herself, she said, 'Mr Washington would have come to meet you himself, but he's in Genoa today. He'll be back this evening. Did you have a comfortable flight?'

Mrs Wyatt said that she had, except that her suitcase was missing. She had already reported this to the airline's agent and seemed confident it would turn up before she needed its contents. She was clearly an experienced traveller, and not a person who fussed if things did not go to plan.

'How long have you been with Mr Washington?' she asked on the way to the waiting launch.

'Not very long. You haven't met him yet, I believe?'

'No, this job was fixed up through friends. A few years ago the husband of a girl I was at school with bought a villa on Cap Ferrat in the south of France. I tackled the garden for them. Later Marc Washington stayed there, liked it, and contacted Delia when he needed a landscape designer. That's the way it tends to work. Where did he find you?'

'In New York, but I'm English by birth.'

'I wouldn't have guessed it, even though you speak it perfectly. You're one of those people who might come from almost anywhere.'

'Have you been to Venice before, Mrs Wyatt?'

'Call me Rowena. Yes, a couple of times. Tell me about this island. I like to know other people's impressions before seeing a place for myself.'

'I think it's lovely because I like wild, lonely places.'

'Do you? How unexpected.'

'Why unexpected?' asked Sophie.

Rowena appraised her thoughtfully. 'You look so...

urbane. Every hair in place, every detail immaculate.'

'The same could be said about you. You look rather different in your working clothes.'

Rowena laughed. 'You've been researching me, have you? I tried to do some homework on your boss, but apart from a few opinions on the social grapevine I couldn't find a thing about him. He keeps himself to himself.'

Sophie nodded. 'The garden he wants you to make for him will never be featured in any of the glossies. He dislikes publicity.'

'That doesn't matter,' said Rowena. 'The cachet of creating his garden will be enough for me. I'm told his house on Long Island is a dream of beauty. Have you been there?'

'No. I've only seen Palazzo Cassiano. By the way, there's a dinner party there tonight. If your luggage hasn't turned up, you may need to buy something suitable. Your travel insurance should cover any reasonable expenses.'

'The last time I came,' said Rowena, 'there was an irresistible shop in that street named after the uprising. They had lovely things in pleated silk and crushed panne velvet.'

'You must mean Venetia Studium in Via XXII Marzo. Their things are inspired by Fortuny's designs,' said Sophie. She knew the shop well, and admired its window displays every time she passed that way. But she doubted if the prices would be considered 'reasonable' by the people who ran insurance companies.

'That's the place,' said Rowena. 'Is it a big dinner party? Will it be very formal?'

'No—informal and only eight people. The architect and his wife and a few other people, including myself.'

She had been surprised at being included, and had assumed it was because one of the guests was an authority on the flora of the lagoon and his partner was away at the moment. If Chiara wasn't considered suitable, Sophie would have thought that Marc could have found someone other than herself to be a makeweight. But she was looking forward to it and had given a good deal of thought to what she should wear.

After seeing Rowena installed in the same hotel where Mrs Henderson had stayed, Sophie returned to her office and made a call to the flight agent to ensure that everything possible was being done to retrieve the designer's baggage.

She had been home to change, and was checking the arrangements in the smaller of the *palazzo*'s two dining rooms, when Marc appeared.

He was wearing a pale grey suit with a cream silk shirt and cream and pale blue silk tie. He smelt of bay rum and, as she caught the aroma, she had a crazy impulse to reach out and touch his jaw which sometimes, when he worked late, had darkened by this time of day.

Tonight, freshly shaved, it had the smooth sheen of bronze. He looked debonair, relaxed and compellingly attractive.

CHAPTER FOURTEEN

BEFORE inspecting the table, Marc looked at Sophie. She was wearing a black chiffon skirt over a scoop-necked black body and, over that, a long-sleeved cropped jacket of dark green silk velvet with cascades of tiny emerald-coloured beads in her ears.

'Pretty,' he said, touching one of them with a curled forefinger which didn't quite brush her cheek.

'Thank you,' she said briskly. 'Isn't the table beautiful?'

The centrepiece was an antique brass wine-cooler filled with lemons still with their dark green leaves. The golden sheen of the cooler was repeated in two large nautilus shells piled with walnuts. The wine glasses, hand-blown on Murano, had gilded rims.

While Marc was looking at the table he said, 'What do you make of Mrs Wyatt?'

'I like her. Unfortunately her suitcase went astray. It's been located but won't arrive till later. She's had to buy something to wear. She's been very calm about it.'

He gave her one of his penetrating looks. 'Would you tell me if you didn't like her?'

'Not at this stage. One has to spend more than half an hour with someone to have an opinion about them.'

'I had an opinion about you by the time we fastened our seat belts.'

'Really? What was it?'

Marc looked amused, but behind the amusement there was something else. 'That for a girl with such a kissable mouth you had a remarkably prim manner.'

Sophie leaned forward over the back of a chair to make a minute and unnecessary adjustment to one of the rat-tail forks already perfectly aligned by Domenico.

'Sometimes you make remarks some people would define as sexual harassment,' she said, in a low, tense voice.

'It's outside working hours, Sophie. Tonight you are one of my guests and I'll say what I please...within reason. I'm sure you're aware that you have an alluring mouth.'

'I've never been called prim before.'

'Perhaps you aren't...with other men. Perhaps it's only with me that you back off and put on your nun's face.'

Impulsively she said, 'It wasn't I who backed off the night you came back to my flat after my birthday dinner. It was you.'

'I can't deny that,' he agreed. 'But I wouldn't have done if the phone hadn't interrupted us. It gave me time to consider that perhaps later you might regret following things through to their natural conclusion. You'd had more to drink than usual. You were very relaxed... perhaps not in total control.'

'How fortunate for me that *you* were,' she said, in a dulcet tone edged with more than a tinge of sarcasm, before turning to leave the room.

She was forced to stay by his fingers clamping her wrist. 'When you woke up the next day, did you still regret my not staying?'

'That's an arrogant assumption,' she said angrily. 'What makes you think I regretted it at all?'

'The fact that you've brought it up now.' As she opened her mouth to protest he continued, 'I regretted it. Why shouldn't you? Are you going to deny that you enjoyed kissing me? Come off it, Sophie. You came into my arms like a homing pigeon…and would have stayed there if the phone hadn't rung.'

'Another arrogant assumption. If you hadn't forestalled me, I should have asked you to leave.'

'Why?'

'Because to have allowed you to stay would have upset our working relationship. And apart from that I don't go in for casual sex.'

'I never supposed that you did. For all I know, you may never have made love with anyone. I think it's unlikely, but it's possible. If the will is strong and the flesh weak…' His other hand closed on her waist, drawing her towards him. 'But your fleshly urges aren't weak, are they, Sophie? When I had your mouth under mine I could have been kissing Veronica Franco.'

As he spoke he shifted his grip, his fingers sliding up from her wrist to enfold her hand, his thumb pressing into her palm in a way that sent shivers through her.

'She was our most famous courtesan,' Marc said in a low voice. 'A lady who knew a lot about pleasing men…as you do…when you let yourself go.'

Sophie felt her defences melting like butter in the sun. Surely he couldn't intend to kiss her again? Not here. Not now, with his guests expected at any moment.

If it had been his intention it was frustrated by Domenico, whose footsteps on the marble floor gave Marc time to release her and step back. When the butler appeared in the doorway, his employer had masked the expression which had been in his eyes seconds earlier.

When Domenico said good evening to him, he replied with his usual affability, and Sophie was able to escape and take refuge in another room, not in use this evening, where she wouldn't be disturbed and could recover her composure.

* * *

When Rowena arrived she was wearing a long fluid tunic of deep violet velvet, another colour which set off her fiery hair. She and Marc seemed to take to each other from the moment they shook hands.

At dinner she sat on his right, with the architect's wife on his left. The table was round, with the botanist seated directly opposite Marc with Sophie on his right.

Various delicious hot appetisers had been handed round in the drawing room beforehand and the main meal began with ravioli served in a hallowed-out pumpkin.

'For a new arrival in Venice, you ask most intelligent questions,' the botanist told Sophie while they were eating the main course, roast pheasant served on a bed of red pomegranate seeds.

'Which is no reason for you to monopolise her, Lorenzo,' said the man on her other side. 'It's my turn to bore this charming young lady who speaks our language with so little trace of accent.'

Although, in deference to Rowena, who had no Italian, those near her were speaking English, the botanist wasn't fluent, and had lapsed into his own language while conversing with Sophie.

'How does that come about?' her other neighbour enquired, as a rider to his smiling compliment.

Without going into details she didn't wish to disclose until she had come clean with Marc, it was an awkward question to answer. Glancing across the table, she became aware that he, too, was waiting for her reply.

She said lightly, 'I suppose I was born with a good ear for verbal sounds, the way some people have an ear for music.'

The meal concluded with one of the chef's specialities, a spectacular tart of figs glazed with blackcurrant liqueur syrup. Sophie had had it before and found it delicious, but tonight her enjoyment was marred by her awareness of what was happening on the opposite side of the table.

Marc and Rowena were hitting it off like two people made for each other. They were the right age, their heights matched; they harmonised in every way. The snatches of their conversation she was able to catch without losing track of what her neighbours were saying made it clear their rapport was more like that of old friends than new acquaintances.

Sophie had a sinking feeling that Rowena might be the woman Marc had been waiting for.

In the days that followed, Sophie suffered agonies of jealousy, an emotion she had always despised but was helpless to control when she saw the two of them together.

What surprised her was that she didn't dislike Rowena. She found her as attractive and amusing as Marc obviously did. Whatever the reason for the breakdown of the redhead's marriage, it was hard to see how Rowena could have been at fault. The more Sophie knew of her, the more she admired her.

A few days after Rowena's return to London, she faxed Sophie to say that a favourite bracelet was missing. She thought it might have come off while she was on the island. It was possible the clasp had broken. Could someone be sent to look for it? Although not intrinsically valuable, it had sentimental associations which meant a great deal to her.

Her message included a description and sketch. Sophie remembered seeing the bracelet on Rowena's left wrist, together with an unusual watch.

The fax was still in her hand when Marc walked into her office.

'You're frowning. What's the problem?'

'Rowena has mislaid a bracelet. She thinks it might be on the island. I was wondering how soon I could go over to look for it.'

'This afternoon. We'll both go.'

The snap decision startled her. 'Oh...I don't think you should waste your time. It may not be there. She could have lost it on her way back to England.'

'Possibly, but I don't remember seeing it the day she left. We were together that morning. Two pairs of eyes are better than one. We'll leave after lunch. Be at the water-gate at two.'

He went away, making her wonder why he had come in the first place. He wasn't a man who forgot what he was doing when some other matter cropped up.

She spent the rest of the morning in a tiswas about the afternoon. When he hadn't taken Rowena to the airport, she had realised there was nothing between them. She had misinterpreted the signals, as women were apt to do when they were in love with a man.

Now that Rowena had gone, Marc might intend to resume his pursuit of Sophie. There was no denying the current of tension between them. She felt it electrifying the atmosphere whenever they were together. She didn't trust herself to resist him if he took advantage of one of the island's secluded spots to make a determined pass at her.

The bright morning didn't last. By lunchtime the sky was cloudy. She had lunch at her desk instead of outside in the usually sheltered suntrap of the roof garden.

Afterwards she thought it advisable to dash back to the flat and change into trousers, a jersey and the warm but stylish jacket given her by Martha Henderson. It could be cold on the lagoon when the wind was in its present quarter.

She was at the water-gate ahead of time, surprised to see that, instead of the launch used for the airport run and the trip to Torcello, today a small speedboat was there. Luckily she had thought to bring a scarf. It was covering her hair and tied at the back of her neck by the time Marc joined her.

'Sensible girl!' he said approvingly, noticing how she was dressed. 'It could be a chilly trip. The launch is being serviced today, so we'll have to make do with this.' He stepped aboard and offered his hand to her.

There were speed limits on the canals, but out in the lagoon Sophie had often seen motorboats smashing through the water with their bows in the air and their sterns enveloped in spray.

Perhaps Marc might have driven like that in his salad days, but today he kept the speed moderate. Even so she was glad of her headscarf and sunglasses. The lenses protected her eyes from the chilly airstream slicing past the edges of the windscreen.

'Some women are chronic losers,' said Marc, breaking their silence. 'Gloves, sunglasses, umbrellas, earrings… I hope Rowena's not one of them.'

'I shouldn't think so. Anyone can lose a bracelet.'

'You don't wear them, I notice.'

'I've never had one as a present and I wouldn't buy one for myself. I prefer earrings and clips.'

'I must remember that at Christmas.'

'Do you normally give your PAs a present at Christmas?'

He slanted a mocking glance at her. 'If they've been good girls.'

How was she supposed to take that ambiguous answer?

Sophie averted her face, torn between her pleasure in his company and her dread that the attraction between them was building up to what one of her friends called 'the proposition point'. A point from which there would be two ways forward, but never any way back to the pre-proposition situation.

A spoonbill was passing overhead, a familiar sight to her once and now a nostalgic reminder of how much she loved this region and envied the man beside her his power to make himself part of it.

'I think we'll be looking for a needle in a haystack,' he said as they neared Capolavoro. 'Even the weather's against us. A sunny afternoon would have helped. In this light the gold parts won't shine. Anyway, we'll give it a go.'

They landed at a different place from where the barges would come with all the materials needed for the building of the house next spring. Their arrival disturbed various long-legged wading birds.

For the second time in an hour Sophie felt Marc's warm, strong grip enclosing her smaller hand as he helped her ashore. But he didn't prolong the contact.

'Rowena wandered all over the place the last time I came over with her. I suggest you go in that direction and I'll go in this.' He set off by the more overgrown of the diverging tracks.

As they moved away from each other Sophie forced herself to concentrate on the search for the few inches of metal which might perhaps be a souvenir of an equally fraught relationship in Rowena's past.

She had gone back to London with six rolls of exposed film in her hand luggage. It was possible that in order to capture a view from a better angle she had sometimes moved off the track. The chances of finding the bracelet if it had fallen in grass or low-growing scrub were very small—unless Marc was prepared to have someone go over the island, metre by metre, with a metal detector.

He might go to those lengths for a woman with whom he was having an affair, but Sophie no longer felt that he was interested in Rowena for reasons apart from her professional skills. If that had been the case, he would certainly have gone to the airport with her.

As she searched she was half-consciously aware of the familiar scents carried on the wind from the surrounding *barene*, the salt flats covered with marshy vegetation only covered at high tide.

The thought of the children who would grow up on the island—Marc's children—in more luxurious conditions but with the same surroundings she had grown up with, made her ache to tell him how much she loved him.

But how could she do that when she had no idea if his feelings for her went beyond mere physical attraction? If he had been an ordinary man she would have chanced it. But he was anything but ordinary. He was clever, good-looking and rich. He could take his pick. Why should he fall for someone who was neither beautiful, brilliant nor from his own milieu?

She was probing a clump of the sea lavender which, in late summer, coloured the islets with drifts of blue and pink, when a piercing whistle made her straighten. Looking round, she saw Marc waving to her. He was beyond shouting distance but near enough for her to see him point at the sky.

Looking up, Sophie saw that while her attention had been focused on the ground dark clouds had been approaching overhead. Not far away it was already raining. In ten minutes, or less, the first drops would fall on the island.

Marc was moving now, and pointing to a stone hut where they could shelter. He reached it ahead of her.

When she joined him, he said, 'I don't think it'll last long. Rain wasn't forecast this morning.'

Sophie hadn't much faith in forecasts. Like islanders the world over, she had grown up relying on experience rather than meteorology to tell her what the weather was going to do. To her eye, the approaching downpour looked likely to last some time.

There was nothing in the hut they could sit on. Marc was wearing a lightweight showerproof blouson over his cashmere sweater. He took it off, spread if on the tamped earth floor and sat down on it, leaving room for her to sit beside him.

Feeling that to remain standing would invite some sardonic comment, Sophie joined him. They sat side by side, each with one hand clasping the other wrist and their arms looped round their knees, watching the rain begin to beat down on the land outside the hut and the lagoon beyond it.

'Sorry about this. I guess coming over today wasn't such a good idea,' Marc said. She felt him looking at her.

'Your time is more valuable than mine. If I hadn't mentioned it to you, you wouldn't be stuck here. What I should have done, in retrospect, was to track down someone with a metal detector. I think that's the only hope of finding the bracelet.'

'You're probably right, but I wouldn't think metal detecting is as popular a hobby in Venice as it is in some other places. Perhaps we should tell Rowena to bring one with her next time. She who loses an object deserves the backache of finding it, as Confucius may well have said.'

'You don't have a bad back, do you?'

He shook his head. 'Do I look as if I might?'

'No, but I've known extremely fit-looking people who have to take care of their backs because of athletic injuries.'

She spoke with her eyes on the puddles starting to form in the sandy soil outside the shed. Superimposed on that image was another: the powerful wrists and sunburned hands alongside her own.

Her shoulder was less than an inch from the top of his arm, her foot in its navy deck shoe very close to his similar shoe and bare brown masculine ankle.

Every part of his body appealed to her in a way no other man's had. She had a crazy longing to be on a spacious rug with room to lie back and run her hand down his spine and say, Make love to me, Marc.

But she hadn't the nerve to do it. She wasn't that sort of woman. Her inhibitions insisted the first move must come from him.

'I was never into athletics or organised games,' said Marc. 'I prefer sports like skiing and climbing, things one can do on one's own. I also like games two can play.' He paused. 'Chess and backgammon.'

Sophie was sure he hadn't been thinking about board games in those few seconds of silence. Or was it only her own, overheated imagination which had instantly conjured up a vision of a king-size bed and Marc sitting on the side of it, beckoning her to him?

'I can't play either of them,' she said. 'Monopoly is my level.'

'I missed out on Monopoly. Didn't have that sort of childhood. I expect I'll get the hang of it when my children are the right age.'

She found it curiously painful to think of him, years hence, holding the bank of paper money for a family game. More than anything she wanted to share that future, to be the mother of the children shaking the dice-pot and exchanging gleeful looks when Dad was sent to jail or they cleaned him out in a property deal.

By now the lagoon was invisible, hidden by the curtain of water teeming down from a sky as unrelentingly dark as those she remembered from her first winter in England. It must have rained here as well but she had no memory of it. Her childhood had seemed a time of perpetual sunlight.

The cloudburst slackened eventually, but the rain didn't let up or show any sign of doing so. They must have been talking for an hour, one subject leading to another, when Marc said, 'I need to stretch,' and the next moment was on his feet, offering his hand to her.

Long ago, in her last year at school, she had known a boy who had taught her to clasp the wrist of someone offering a pull-up. She did this now and Marc's fingers closed round her forearm and drew her upright.

Still holding her, he said, 'It looks as if we may have to spend the night here.'

'I'd rather get drenched than do that.'

She only meant that a wetting seemed preferable to staying in a hut without the makings of a fire, a pile of sacks or any makeshift comforts.

His reaction was startling. About to let go, his fingers became a vice. His brows drew into a scowl she had never seen before.

'Damn you, Sophie, when are you going to start trusting me? If all I wanted was sex, I could have had you at your flat. You know that as well as I do, but you're still tensed up like a woman marooned with a crackpot. I've had enough.'

CHAPTER FIFTEEN

MARC let go of her arm, as if dropping something repugnant, and bent to snatch up his blouson, flapping it back and forth to dislodge the dirt it had picked up. His tan was suffused with the dark red of rage as he shrugged it on and fumbled to join up the zip, his fingers made clumsy by the force of his anger.

'Goddammit!' he said, through set teeth. Then the two sides fitted together and he yanked at the tag and gave her a last furious glare before heading for the doorway.

'Marc...wait...please don't leave me.'

The apprehension in her voice seemed to abate his anger.

'I didn't intend to,' he said curtly. 'There's a phone in the launch. I'm going to call for the covered launch to come and pick us up.'

She watched him run through the downpour. She was shivering, but not from cold. It was reaction to the flare-up between them.

When he came back his hair was plastered to his head, his clothes to his body, the drenched cloth defining every muscular contour of his tall, strong-boned frame. He was carrying a waterproof kitbag.

Raking his hair off his forehead, he said, 'Fortunately all the launches are equipped with emergency packs. There'll be a towel in here and a sweatshirt and pants. I'm going to strip off, but don't panic. I merely want to get out of these wet things and into something dry.'

Sophie averted her face but could not close her mind's eye to a vision of what was happening within a few feet of her: the powerful body being stripped of the sodden clothing and given a vigorous rub-down, making the tanned skin glow.

His voice broke into her thoughts. 'How could you think I would leave you alone here?'

'I—I thought you were angry...that you wanted to punish me.'

At first he didn't reply. She could hear the friction of the towel and guessed he was drying his back.

'Your safety and comfort are very important to me, Sophie,' he said, in an oddly gruff voice. 'I was a fool to lose track of you.'

'Lose track of me...what do you mean?'

'Are you going to go on pretending you don't know we've met before?'

Her head swung round to face him, but she was too startled by what he had said to notice that he was naked. 'I didn't know *you* knew that.'

Marc wrapped the towel unhurriedly round his hips. 'I knew when you came to be interviewed that I recognised something about you, but I didn't know why. I didn't discover the reason until we had lunch on Torcello with Martha Henderson. We passed the place where your grandfather's boat had been moored and it all slotted into place. You were that funny child grown-up...grown very beautiful.' The way he said it made her heart lurch. 'Why didn't you tell me? Why did you keep it a secret?'

'I don't know,' she answered quietly. 'I suppose I kept putting it off in case it put *you* off. We weren't what you'd call respectable, Michael and I. To someone like you we must have seemed almost vagrants.'

'I did think there was a danger of you ending up on the streets if the old man died and left you unprotected. That worried him too. He told me so. There was no one else he could tell. Fortunately, having come into my inheritance, I was in a position to do something about it. The money to finance your schooling and keep the old man in comfort for the few years left to him was a drop in the ocean of my grandfather's fortune.'

'*You* paid my school fees? But Michael said it was a legacy.'

'A windfall,' Marc said drily. 'A quixotic gesture I didn't follow through because that would have been too much trouble. It didn't involve any effort to transfer some funds to a bank account in his name. To keep an eye on you afterwards was too much bother. It's a selfish age, twenty-two. Perhaps it was just as well you were only eleven. If you'd been seventeen, I might have seduced you myself. I had no morals to speak of.'

'I don't believe that,' she said. 'You saved Michael's life. You knew the right thing to do. You came to the hospital afterwards. He thought you a fine young man.'

'He didn't know me long enough to see behind the facade. I haven't deceived you, have I? You've never trusted me.' He thrust his arms through the sleeves of a scarlet sweatshirt and pulled it over his head.

With his black hair damp and dishevelled, he looked younger and somehow less formidable. Or was that because he was revealing a side of himself she had never seen before?

She decided to tell him the truth. 'It's not a trustful situation…falling in love with someone so different from yourself that there doesn't seem to be any possible future in it.'

Marc pulled the sweatshirt down over his ribs. It was stretched by the breadth of his shoulders and inches too short in the arms.

'Are you telling me you love me?'

'I've tried not to but I can't help it. If you want me,

I'm yours. I know it may end in tears, but it will be lovely while it lasts.'

'What are you proposing? That we live together?'

'That's what most people do.'

'We aren't "most people". You and I make our own rules. I want you to be my woman, my friend, my companion for the rest of my life. In my book that means being my wife—with no conditions, no safeguards, only total commitment to a lifetime of happiness.'

Sophie's eyes filled with tears. 'Oh, Marc...are you really saying this or am I dreaming?'

He came to where she was standing and put his arms lightly round her. 'I've wanted to tell you many times, but the moment was never quite right. The night of your birthday was the nearest I came to it. If it hadn't been for your friend ringing up from New York... As soon as you put the phone down I could see you were backing off—afraid I would take advantage of what your body wanted but your mind had begun to deny.'

He brought a hand up to her cheek, stroking it lightly with the back of his knuckles. 'Leaving you...saying goodnight...was the hardest thing I've ever had to do. But I knew if I went ahead it might be the first and last time for us. In the morning you'd feel I'd coerced you.'

Her feelings no longer masked, Sophie said softly, 'You coerce me every time you look at me. Something inside me melts. I'm no longer in charge of myself. It's a frightening feeling when you aren't sure the other person feels the same way.'

'I felt this way before you did...when it was still a mystery why you seemed so familiar. To love a woman before I knew her properly went against all my instincts. I'd seen too many disasters resulting from "love at first sight". The world is littered with failed relationships based on that fatal premise...'

His fingers caressed her neck, sliding upwards into her hair as he bent his head to kiss her.

The difference between this kiss and the kisses exchanged at her flat was that now her mind could surrender as eagerly as her body. She slipped her arms round his neck, delighting in the strength of the arms holding her close, the wide shoulders forming a shield between her and the world.

His ears were the first to catch the distant drone of an engine. Bringing their kisses to a reluctant conclusion, he said huskily, 'This isn't the time or the place anyway. One day this will be our home and we'll make love here many times. But tonight we'll find somewhere else...' His eyes smiled into hers. 'Somewhere a little more comfortable.'

Sophie had stopped pretending. She said, 'After you've picked up some dry clothes, you could come to my place.'

'"Two souls with but a single thought, two hearts that beat as one." Meanwhile I'd better put some pants on.'

Like the sweatshirt, the black sports pants were not a good fit, being too large at the waist and too short in the leg. But Marc had the physique and presence to carry off any clothing. It crossed her mind that when Carnival came he would look magnificent in the black tricorne hat and silk cloak, as worn by his mother's ancestors. Until now she hadn't been certain she would be here for Carnival. But now the future, this morning an unknown territory, had changed to a clearly marked map of a golden world they would journey through together.

The boatman who came for them brought an umbrella for himself and two more for them.

Marc said, 'One is enough.' And when he had opened it he drew her into its shelter with an arm round her waist. Aboard the launch, he kept her in the circle of his arm.

'What will your aunts say?' she said as the boat moved away from the landing stage. 'I'm sure they'll think me most unsuitable.'

'They'll think me far luckier than I deserve to be. They like everything about you.'

'They don't know everything about me. When they find out I'm the granddaughter of the old man who used to draw tourists on the Riva...'

'I had the impression he was someone rather special...perhaps an important artist before he lost his arm.'

Sophie explained about Michael's career in the fashion world. 'But not many people appreciate what wonderful draughtsmen the great fashion artists were.'

When they were nearly back to Venice, Marc instructed the boatman to take them to Sophie's flat rather than the *palazzo*.

'There is something I have to tell you before we announce our engagement,' he said. 'Something discreditable about me.'

'There's nothing you can tell me that would change the way I feel.'

'I hope not,' he said gravely. 'But I'm afraid it may hurt you.'

She was tempted to tell him she already knew but decided against it. Paolo's version of the story might be a long way from the truth.

In her flat, Sophie made instant coffee and asked him to pour out two brandies. When she sat down on the sofa Marc joined her there, but leaving a space between them.

'When I was eighteen,' he said, 'I thought myself in love with a beautiful girl called Marina, who worked for us as a maid. She was a little older—twenty—and she seemed to feel the same way. It wasn't difficult for us to find times and places to be alone together and the inevitable happened. We became lovers. I wanted to marry her but she felt, rightly as it turned out, that my family wouldn't consent. I couldn't touch my trust fund until I was twenty-one so we wouldn't have any money. Well, that was OK. We had all our lives ahead. We could wait a few years. Then Marina started a baby and marriage became more urgent.'

He paused, his expression withdrawn. Watching his face, Sophie knew in her bones that he had really loved the girl and hadn't been merely using her.

'When I talked to my grandfather,' said Marc, 'he wouldn't hear of our marrying. He said we were both far too young and unsuited in every way. There was a ferocious row and I told him to go to hell. But Marina wouldn't come away with me. She didn't want to leave her family and she didn't think I could earn a living for us without my family behind me. I still think she was wrong. I could have made it on my own.'

'I'm sure you could,' said Sophie.

That brought a slight smile to his face. 'Marina didn't have your adventurous spirit. She hadn't grown up on a boat under the aegis of an artist. Had I been more mature, I should have realised it was expecting too much for a girl from her close family background to run off with a guy like me. When it comes to the crunch, there aren't many women who are prepared to risk everything for love. Risk is not what your sex is about. Women are programmed to nest, not to take chances.'

Generally speaking, she agreed with him, and this wasn't the moment to say that she had different priorities.

'What happened?'

'My grandfather offered her a substantial lump sum

and a long-term income for the child providing she agreed to have nothing more to do with me.'

Sophie gave an exclamation of distress. 'That was a cruel thing to do.'

'Some people would think it was generous. He thought it fair. In retrospect, I believe it was. Being older and wiser than I, he saw that a marriage between us would have been a disaster—like my parents' marriage. The reasons would have been different, but the outcome would have been the same. If Marina had loved me she would have refused his offer and come away with me.'

'Perhaps she did love you but knew that she wasn't right for you. Perhaps her parents pressured her into agreeing.'

'I'm sure they did, but I don't think they had to press hard. If a woman loves a man, she doesn't go and marry someone else a few weeks later.'

'Surely she might if she had a baby to consider?' But even as she said it Sophie knew that, loving Marc, she could never marry anyone else. To let another man make love to her would be unthinkable.

'That premise might have held water thirty or forty years ago,' said Marc. 'It doesn't today. Italy has its quota of single mothers like everywhere else. I suspect Marina's heart healed a lot faster than mine. I already knew that my mother had taken ruthless advantage of my father's passion for her. Marina's behaviour confirmed that women were devious creatures, not to be trusted. That remained my opinion until I met you. Almost immediately I fell in love with you. In fact I was pretty far gone by the end of our first evening together, in Paris. But when I realised who you were and that, for whatever reason, you weren't being straight with me, it revived my distrust of women.'

'I was on the point of telling you lots of times. One

of the reasons I didn't was because of something that happened when I was a child. For a little while I went to school here. Only for a couple of months, and then Michael decided I wasn't being taught anything I couldn't learn from him and that I was being fed ideas he didn't approve of. The only thing I remember is being invited to another child's birthday party. I'd never been to a party so I was very excited.'

'How old were you when this happened?'

'About seven. Old enough to be worried about fitting in. I had a uniform dress to wear for school, but I didn't have any other dresses. I always wore shorts in summer and jeans in winter. So I went in clean jeans and a red jumper a lady on Burano had knitted for me. Michael had bought a red ribbon to thread through my plait. I must have looked quite nice.'

'I'm sure you looked adorable,' said Marc. 'But I suppose all the other little girls had expensive party dresses.'

'Yes, but that wasn't what hurt. The mother who was giving the party knew who I was and so did one of the other mothers. They had a whispered conversation and finally my hostess came over and led me out of the room. She said she was very sorry but I'd been invited by mistake and one of her maids would take me back to my grandfather. She gave me a big gift-wrapped parcel by way of compensation. But I never knew what was in it because Michael sent it back. I'd never seen him so angry. I was terrified he was going to go back there and storm at them.'

While Marc had been listening to this, his own expression had become increasingly thunderous. 'I'd like to know who it was who objected to you. She must have been a prize bitch,' he said. 'I don't think much of your hostess, but perhaps the other one's husband was her husband's boss—she may have been afraid to remind her whose house it was. I know there are people in Venice who worship money and status. There are people like that everywhere. But to humiliate a child...' His dark eyes were brilliant with anger.

'I don't think I felt humiliated, just baffled,' said Sophie. 'When he'd calmed down, Michael explained it to me. He said people like that didn't matter. They had different values and they were never happy. But the next day at school a lot of the girls weren't as friendly as before. One of them even parroted something said by her parents...that Michael was a down-and-out and the school shouldn't have accepted me as a pupil.'

'Surely you can't have thought I would look down on you?'

'No, but I felt your family might. I've learnt to conform to conventional society, but deep down inside I still feel I'm an outsider. Don't misunderstand me; I don't feel in any way inferior, just different. An alien being in a world where I have to survive but which often I don't like. Aliens shrink from revealing themselves,' she added, with a wry smile.

'We'll make our own world on Capolavoro,' said Marc. 'It will be even better than growing up on Torcello. I'll still have to go away sometimes, but not as often. I'm tired of jetting around from big city to big city. I want to live quietly with you and try to make up for the pain you must have felt after your grandfather died and left you alone in the world.'

'Perhaps we'll be even happier because we've both been through bad times,' Sophie said softly.

As she spoke, all over Venice bells started chiming the hour. She stood up and held out her hand to him. Marc took it and rose to his feet, his expression questioning.

'Last time you were here it was different. You thought

you might be coercing me and I didn't know where I stood with you. This time there are no obstacles. Before we go back and break the news to your aunts, could we unplug the telephone and pick up where we left off?'

He scooped her up and, cradling her in strong arms, carried her towards the bedroom.

The next time the bells chimed the hour, Sophie opened her eyes to see that the sky had cleared and the rose-gold glow of a Venetian sunset was pouring through the skylight. Turning her head a little, she looked into smiling dark eyes and gave a long sigh of happiness.

At last she had found where she belonged.

AUTHOR'S NOTE

'WHERE do you get your ideas?'

Every professional writer has been asked that question many times.

I find my ideas while travelling. One lovely October day I was on the island of Torcello, waiting for the ferry, when I noticed an old boat moored a little way along the tow-path. The sea is in my blood and I've written more than twenty books with part of the action taking place on board a schooner or some other sailing boat. On the way back to Venice I wondered why anyone would leave a boat to rot at her moorings.

Later, missing my husband, who was far away in the foothills of the world's highest mountain, I sat in a *caffè* on the Riva, with a notebook on my lap and a pre-dinner *spritz* at my elbow. As I watched the sunset I found the story you have just read beginning to form in my mind.

Of all the places I've been to since my first trip abroad, none has cast such a strong spell on me as Venice. It deserves a place on everyone's travel wish list. I shall go again, as soon as possible, knowing there are other tales of the Venetian lagoon waiting to be written.

Anne Weale

Day Leclaire is a much-loved romance author who has written more than twenty books for Mills & Boon®. She and her family live in the midst of a maritime forest on a small island off the coast of North Carolina. Despite the yearly storms that batter them and the frequent power outages, they find the beautiful climate, superb fishing and unbeatable seascape more than adequate compensation. One of their first acquisitions upon moving to Hatteras Island was a cat named Fuzzy. He has recently discovered that laps are wonderful places to curl up and nap—and that Day's son really was kidding when he named the hamster Cat Food.

WHO'S HOLDING THE BABY?

by

DAY LECLAIRE

To Frank Matthew Smith…
my one and only.
All my love—Mom.

PROLOGUE

The Great Lie
Day 1…and the games begin…

GRACE BARNES STOOD IN front of the door that read *Luciano Salvatore, President,* and took a deep breath. She could do it. Sure she could. All she had to do was knock. The man on the other side of the door would say, ''Come in.'' She'd open the door, step into the office and her deception would begin. After that, she only had to keep her job with this man for one year and she'd receive the financing necessary to start her own business. What could be easier?

She shoved her tinted glasses higher on the bridge of her nose, checked to be sure that not a single hair had escaped the prim knot at the nape of her neck and tugged at the mud brown skirt and sweater that threatened to engulf her. All right, she was ready. She lifted her fist to knock, but before she could, the door opened.

And that's when she saw him for the first time. In that instant, she realized how badly she'd misjudged Dom Salvatore and how foolish she'd been not to give him credit for knowing his son. He'd warned her. Oh, he'd definitely warned her. Every assistant Luc hired fell in love with him and ended up making a mess of the work situation. But she'd thought Dom had exaggerated. He hadn't.

Luc Salvatore was the most gorgeous man she'd ever set eyes on. High, aristocratic cheekbones and a square cleft chin complemented a striking masculine face. Thick, dark brown hair fell in careless waves across his forehead, emphasizing eyes that held her with almost hypnotic power. He filled the doorway, and unable to help herself, she took several hasty steps backward.

"Well, well..." he said, folding his arms across his broad chest and leaning against the jamb. "Who have we here?" Although he didn't have his father's Italian accent, there was a similar underlying lilt to his deep, husky voice that brought to mind exotic climes and sultry nights.

"I'm...I'm Grace Barnes," she said. To her horror, she sounded almost timorous. This would never do! What was wrong with her?

Slowly he straightened and walked toward her. She stood rigidly, not daring to speak, not daring to so much as move. For some inexplicable reason her heart pounded and it became a struggle to draw breath. *Think of Baby Dream Toys,* she told herself. *Think of Mom planning for the day we'd open our own business.*

Utilizing every ounce of control she possessed, she held out a hand. "I'm Grace Barnes," she repeated in a cool, strong voice. "Your father hired me as your new assistant." To her relief, her fingers were rock steady.

He took her hand and shook it. "It's a pleasure to meet you, Miss Barnes. Or is it Mrs.?" He released her right hand and lifted her left, studying the glittering diamond decorating her finger. "Miss Barnes. Spoken for, but not yet taken. Our loss is..." he tilted his head to one side and lifted an eyebrow "...whose gain?"

She froze, staring up at him, staring into eyes that made her think of hot, liquid gold. She prayed her tinted lenses concealed her panic. She hadn't anticipated the question and she should have. "Will…William," she replied, picking the first name to pop into her head.

His mouth curved, his expression wickedly amused. "Our loss is Will-William's gain. Come on into my office. Let's get acquainted. Would you care for a drink? Coffee, tea? I even have freshly squeezed orange juice."

She followed him, trying to gather her composure. "Nothing, thank you," she said, once again affecting a calm, collected guise.

"Sit down. I assume my father told you I was out of the country during the interview process. Explain why he chose you from all the other applicants."

She didn't dare tell him the truth. Dom had specifically asked that she not mention they'd met through Salvatore's annual young-entrepreneur contest, a contest designed to help young businesspeople start their own companies. She'd hoped to win first prize—a monetary award that would have enabled her to open Baby Dream Toys. Unfortunately, she'd placed third, a mixed blessing. Though that prize wasn't sufficient to enable Grace to open her shop, it had, fortuitously, brought her to Dom's attention and given her the opportunity to fulfill her dream…if in a rather roundabout manner.

"I gather from what your father said that you've had trouble keeping your assistants," she finally replied. Which kept Dom from fully retiring, a situation he was desperate to correct. "He felt that wouldn't be a problem with me."

Luc's eyes narrowed. "Really? And why is that?"

"Because I'm serious about my work."

And because all she needed to do was keep her job as Luc's assistant for one year—and unlike his previous assistants, maintain a strictly professional relationship—

and she'd be given the financing to start her own business. There wasn't a chance she'd fall for Luc's charms and sacrifice her dream. Not a chance.

Luc inclined his head. "Let's hope so." He leaned back in his chair. "Tell me more about yourself."

Hesitantly, she complied, outlining the résumé that rested on his desk. And all the time she spoke he watched her. He watched the way she talked and the movement of her hands as she made a point. He scanned her tightly controlled hair and her face, virtually obliterated by the huge tinted lenses. Even the prim manner in which she sat—straight-backed, ankles crossed—didn't escape his attention.

She wondered if he saw through her disguise, realized her blond hair had been tinted drab brown with a temporary rinse, that she'd dressed in oversize, unattractive clothes, that her tinted glasses had nonprescription lenses. And what about the engagement ring? It rode her finger, an unfamiliar weight as well as an uncomfortable fabrication. She stirred uneasily. For a minister's daughter, duplicity came hard.

But she wanted to attain her dream. She wanted it more than anything in the world. And this temporary deception would get it for her.

"So," she concluded her recital, "I worked there for one year before being offered this job." With nothing left to say, she fell silent.

He didn't comment, simply completed his perusal, his odd golden eyes narrowed in thought, as though analyzing something that didn't quite add up. Grace sat perfectly still, realizing that this was it—lose her cool now and she'd blow the chance of a lifetime. She regarded him steadily, knowing that if she were to be successful working for this man, she'd need to maintain a very careful facade.

At long last he nodded. ''Welcome aboard, Miss Barnes. As usual, Dad has shown excellent judgment. Let me show you to your desk.'' He stood and led the way into the outer office. ''Here's your new home. Have a seat.''

He held her chair out for her with such a natural, unconscious ease that she knew it must come from long ingrained habit. ''Thank you,'' she murmured.

''Get familiar with the setting, take some time to explore the office area, have a cup of coffee or tea and report to me in an hour. Then we'll go over office procedure, and I'll explain how we do things around here and run through your duties. Though in all honesty there's only one thing I expect you to do.''

She eyed him warily. ''Which is?''

He grinned. ''Whatever I say.''

She stared at him uncertainly. He was a difficult man to nail down. Serious one minute, teasing the next. Add to that looks and intelligence and one final trait that would be the most difficult to deal with—a wicked sense of humor—and she could understand why women fell like ninepins. Was it possible that his charm was an unconscious part of his personality, that he didn't even realize all those women had lost their hearts to him? Time would tell.

Meanwhile, she could think of only one way to deal with him. '''Whatever you say' isn't in my job description,'' she informed him in her most businesslike voice. ''You'll have to be more specific than that, Mr. Salvatore.''

His eyes glittered with laughter. ''I'll see what I can do. Oh… And one more thing.''

He circled her desk, standing directly behind her. She felt his hand brush her spine, following the row of buttons to the nape of her neck. It was as though she'd been touched with a live wire. She started out of her chair, but he pressed her gently back into her seat.

"Hold still, *cara mia,*" he murmured. "Just for a moment."

With a final glancing touch, he released her. Crossing to the front of the desk, he looked down, a crooked smile curving his mouth. She gazed up at him, once again captured by those strange golden eyes.

"What were you doing?" she demanded.

"I was doing you a favor. Your button had come unfastened." His voice lowered confidingly. "And I thought you looked like the sort of woman who isn't comfortable unless she's all buttoned up." Without another word, he returned to his office and gently closed the door.

And that, she realized with a sudden flash of intuition, would set the pattern for their relationship. She'd play the role of the stoic professional, and he'd be unable to resist pricking her composure, teasing a less-than-professional response from her.

Releasing her breath in a long sigh, Grace stared at the calendar centered on the desk. One year stretched before her in a string of endless days. Three hundred and sixty-five days, to be precise. It seemed a lifetime. Without giving herself time to consider, she opened the desk drawer and shoved through the paraphernalia cluttered inside until she found a bright red marker. With great deliberation, and even greater satisfaction, she slashed an *X* through the first day of her year-long sentence.

And in that instant Grace realized just what she'd let herself in for...and just how long and difficult the next year would be.

CHAPTER ONE

The Great Lie
Day 337 and all is well until now...

"MORNING, MISS BARNES." The security guard greeted her with a cheerful grin. "Early to work, I see. Same as always, rain or shine."

Grace leaned her dripping umbrella against his desk and stripped off her gloves. "More rain than shine, I'm afraid," she observed, offering him a warm smile in return.

"It is blustery out there. Did you have a good weekend?"

"Splendid, thank you, Edward." She tucked her gloves into the pocket of her raincoat. "And you?"

"Drove to the mountains with the wife and kids. The forecast called for snow and they don't often get the chance to see it falling. All the Thanksgiving decorations were out." He shook his head. "It was quite a sight."

An onslaught of memories from past holiday celebrations with her family brought a wistful smile to Grace's lips. The house had always been filled with friends and family and with the odors of freshly baked pies and breads. Her father would build a huge, roaring fire and her mother would festoon the mantel with gourds and Indian corn and her pilgrim candlestick holders.

Tears pricked her eyes. Lord, how she missed all that.

''The first snowfall of the season,'' she whispered longingly. ''It must have been glorious.''

''You and your fiancé ever do that? Drive to the mountains to see the snow?''

She shook her head, still lost in memories. ''Never.''

''Aw, that's a real shame.''

His expression was pitying and right away she realized she'd made a mistake, forgotten for a split second the role she had to play. ''I'll suggest a drive to the mountains for next weekend. I'm certain he'll think it's a terrific idea.''

''Yeah, sure.''

''Really. We'll go next weekend.''

She knew the security guard didn't believe her. His brow creased and she could see him fishing around for something more to add, something that would help salvage her dignity. Which was a laugh. After almost a full year of this masquerade, she had very little dignity left to salvage.

''Your fiancé is a lucky man,'' he said at last, ''having such an...an...*elegant* woman as yourself for his bride-to-be.''

She smiled wryly. He seemed intent on painting himself further and further into his corner. Grace decided it was time to put the poor man out of his misery.

''My fiancé is a fine man,'' she lied smoothly. Practice certainly did make perfect. ''I've never met anyone more eager to please. He'll be delighted to take up your suggestion of a trip to the mountains. Maybe we'll rent a cabin and stay the whole weekend.''

''What's this?'' a deep, husky voice interrupted. ''My Miss Barnes is going on a weekend assignation?''

Color mounted in Grace's cheeks and she turned to greet Luc Salvatore, struggling to hang on to the cool, calm demeanor she'd perfected these past eleven months. ''It was just a thought,'' she stated, forced to look a long way up to meet his golden gaze.

He stepped closer, trapping her against Edward's desk, an intent expression touching his handsome features. ''Not a good one, if this blush is anything to go by.'' He ran a slow finger along her cheekbone, his broad shoulders eclipsing her view of anything else. He'd cut them off from the rest of the world, and it made her nervous. Very nervous. ''No need to jump into these things if you aren't ready.''

She heard the concern in his voice and her brows drew together. She felt like a heel, worrying Edward and Luc with a conversation about an imaginary romantic interlude with an equally imaginary fiancé. ''Thanks for your advice,'' she said discouragingly, hoping to end this particular discussion before she got in any deeper.

''You're welcome.'' Cupping her elbow, Luc escorted her toward the elevators. ''Why all this sudden talk about a weekend trip with what's-his-name?''

She shot him a look of annoyance. ''His name is Will…William, as you know full well.''

''And Will-William is dragging you off to his mountain lair to have his wicked way with you? Is that what you were telling Edward?''

''That's none of your business.'' She studiously faced the elevator doors, refusing to so much as glance his way. Not that it helped. The shiny gold doors acted as a mirror, reflecting the determination in his gaze. ''And don't think I didn't see that look you and Edward exchanged,'' she added for good measure.

''It's my business if I choose to make it my business.'' He positioned himself in front of her, blocking the doors. ''And what look are you referring to?''

She deliberately kept her attention fixed on the red silk tie knotted at his throat. As usual, it was slightly askew. And as usual, she valiantly resisted the temptation to straighten it. With each passing day, however, the temptation grew stronger.... One of these days she'd give in. If she was lucky, that would also be day three hundred and sixty-five on the job. "You know the look I mean. That significant man-to-man, women-are-such-fools one."

"Ah... You mean our look of mutual concern."

Her gaze flashed upward, locking with his. It was a mistake. He could melt ice with those eyes. Her annoyance didn't stand a chance—it evaporated like mist beneath a hot sun. "My personal life is none of your business," she managed to say. Finally succeeding in breaking eye contact, she addressed his tie once again. "And it is most certainly none of Edward's."

"On the contrary. You elected to share your personal life with Edward, so you have no one to blame but yourself if he offers an opinion." His long, lean fingers brushed her jaw, making her face him. "And whether you believe it or not, everything about you is my affair." He made the sweeping statement with such utter sincerity that it left no room for doubt.

Her breathing stopped. "Why would you care if Will...William and I went away for the weekend?" She still choked every time she uttered her fictitious fiancé's name. And Luc—darn him—took due note.

The elevator doors slid open and he stepped aside so they could enter. He keyed the lock for the top floor before responding. "Is he pressuring you?" Luc asked.

She knew exactly what he meant, but she lifted her chin and gave him a bland smile anyway. "Pressuring me? Whatever do you mean?"

He turned on her, disapproval carving his features into a stony mask. "To have sex, as you well know. And don't bother with that innocent expression and the coy lies. You're not good at it, Grace."

She fought to keep a straight face. Little did he know. Over the past year she'd become unbelievably adept at lying. And if her father ever found out, it would break his heart. "I refuse to discuss this matter further," she announced in no uncertain terms. "I repeat. It's none of your business."

He stabbed a button on the elevator and the car jerked to a stop. "Don't do it, Gracie," he urged in a husky voice. "Don't go away with him on a whim. You deserve better than that."

She glared at Luc, sick of her deception, wishing she could be herself instead of guarding every word she uttered. But she couldn't, and she forced herself to demand, "What could be better than a snow-covered mountain chalet buried deep in a redwood forest?"

His hands snagged the collar of her coat, rubbing the butter-soft wool along the length of her jaw. "For your first time...I think a second-floor suite at the Ritz in Paris overlooking the *Place Vendôme* would suit you best."

She stared at him in alarm. He'd never made such personal remarks before, never touched her like this or gazed down at her with such a smoldering expression. This sudden change in their relationship unsettled her. "Who said it would be my first time?" she asked weakly, an odd tension gathering in the pit of her stomach.

"I say," he replied.

She didn't dare argue the point. Not when he was right. Instead she maintained, "I happen to think snuggling with my fiancé in front of a roaring fire with nothing between me and a bearskin rug but a scrap of lace sounds perfect.'' She could hear the tension in her voice now, but for some reason she couldn't bring herself to end this strange and intimate conversation.

His eyes half closed and he bent closer, murmuring, ''Making love on top of dead animals doesn't appeal to me. And with your skin, nothing but silk will do. Something low cut and simple.'' He released her collar, the back of his hand stroking a leisurely path across her cheek and jaw. ''Better yet, why don't we try a feather mattress and nothing between us at all. What do you say to that?''

She shivered beneath his touch, horrified by the magnitude of her reaction to him. Where was her control? Where was her detachment? ''Luc...'' His name escaped on a breathless sigh.

His mouth curved upward. ''Is that a yes?''

Her eyes widened in panic and she inhaled sharply, fighting the desire that swept through her veins like wildfire. ''No!''

''Just checking,'' he said with an easy shrug. ''So good old Will-William the accountant from San Jose—''

''San Mateo!''

''—wants sex beside a roaring fire and is offering a chalet, champagne and dead animals to get his way. Is that about it?''

He hadn't been serious about making love to her, she realized then. He'd merely been teasing again. He didn't really care—not on a personal basis. The knowledge bit deep. It didn't matter what he thought of her, she tried to convince herself. It didn't. *It didn't!*

''Maybe,'' she said in a hard, tight voice, ''that isn't what he's offering, but what *I'm* offering.''

She pulled free and jabbed the button to resume the ride, but not before she saw anger flash across Luc's face. Good. Let him be on the losing side of a disagreement for once. She faced the elevator doors again, seeing her metallic reflection as he saw it.

She'd kept her hair rinsed to a nondescript shade of brown and still pinned it into a tight knot at the nape of her neck. The tinted glasses she wore had proved most effective, swamping her delicate features, concealing her leaf green eyes and high-boned cheeks. Her experiments with makeup only added insult to injury. The foundation she'd chosen gave her face a pallid, sallow appearance. And completing her disguise were her clothes, the businesslike suits a size too large and ranging in tone from a dirt brown to navy and black.

It was absolutely perfect.

It also made her want to cry.

This past year had given her an acute awareness of how cruel the world could be toward unattractive people. All her father's little sermons about vanity, about it being a person's inner beauty that counted most, came home to roost. Never again would she ever judge by appearances alone.

"I didn't mean to upset you," Luc said at last. "I'm sorry."

"That's quite all right," she replied in a stilted voice. And though she'd just vowed to never again judge by appearances, she couldn't help wishing—wishing with a passion that shocked her—that he could see her as she really was.

The elevator slowed and the doors opened. Blocking her avenue of escape, he said, "But you still shouldn't sleep with him unless you're sure. Very sure."

He stepped off the elevator, leaving her openmouthed

and fuming. Before she could dart between the doors, they closed with a snap, forcing her to endure a return trip to the lobby. Just as well, she decided with stoic resolve, since she'd left her umbrella leaning against Edward's desk.

Five minutes later, she arrived back on the executive floor and hurried to the reception area outside Luc's office. She disposed of her coat and umbrella in the office closet and sat at her desk. Removing a bright red marker from her drawer, she took even more than her usual delight in crossing one more day off her year-long sentence.

She looked up to see Luc standing at his door, watching.

''You do that every morning,'' he observed. ''It's almost as though you were counting the days until...'' He shrugged. ''Something.''

She stared at him, stricken. ''Nonsense.''

His eyes narrowed. ''It's not nonsense. What are you counting down to?''

''Nothing!'' Had she somehow given herself away? She couldn't have!

''That's twice today,'' he stated ominously.

She swallowed. ''Twice?''

''Twice today you've lied to me.''

He frowned and she froze. His frowns, rare though they were, worried her. A lot. They invariably preceded an explosion. Only once had that explosion been directed her way, and she'd decided then and there it would be the last time she'd give him cause to exercise that infamous temper of his.

''I don't like it, Grace,'' he said softly, a certain menace marking his voice. ''Don't lie to me again.''

She didn't dare respond, didn't dare dwell on what

would happen should he discover the deception she and Dom had instigated—especially considering it was aimed directly at Luc. She could only pray he didn't find out. Because if he ever did… She shuddered.

So, what had tipped him off about her latest fibs? And why weren't they working today? She thought she'd gotten rather good at evading the truth, but perhaps months and months of practicing such a bad habit had caused a sort of short circuit and she was all lied out. Or perhaps Luc's dislike of them had finally rubbed off on her.

Her father would be delighted, were he to know. Grace was horrified.

Luc didn't wait for an answer, which was a relief since she had none to offer. Instead, he returned to his office and closed the door with gentle emphasis. She stared blindly at her calendar. Four more weeks. That's all she had to get through. Just four more weeks.

In just under three of those weeks Dom Salvatore would return from his year-long sojourn to Italy and appoint a relative to take over as Luc's assistant. One quick week of training and Grace would be free to open Baby Dream Toys. Her dearest wish—her mother's dearest wish—would finally be realized.

She focused on the calendar. She could do it. Just four more weeks of lies and half-truths, disguises and evasions. What could be easier? The problem was, would she still think it worthwhile once she had her shop? She'd worried about this at length. When she'd first agreed to Dom's plan, she'd wanted her own business so badly that she hadn't paused to weigh the consequences. She'd had plenty of time since to reconsider her hasty and ill-planned decision. And now she wasn't so sure she'd made the right choice. Using deceit to attain her goal, even when it was a lifelong dream, went against the grain.

She was living a lie. And she'd never been more uncomfortable in her life. Worse, she liked working for Luc. He was a fantastic employer—generous, intelligent, creative. She'd even found their frequent battle of wills challenging. If not for the lies, it would be the perfect job.

A small sound caught her attention, and looking up, Grace noticed a beautiful young woman standing in the doorway of the reception area. She carried a huge diaper bag over one arm; in the other she clutched a baby.

"May I help you?" Grace asked, shoving her glasses higher on her nose.

The young woman shot Grace a suspicious glance, then shook her head. She peered around rather frantically. When her gaze landed on Luc's door and the plaque that read *Luciano Salvatore,* she let out an exclamation of relief. Eyeing Grace with a measure of defiance, she sidled toward Luc's door.

Grace stood. This did not look too encouraging. A young woman, infant in arms, acting as though Luc's door held the answer to all her prayers... "Excuse me, but do you have an appointment?" she asked, though she could guess the answer to that one. This little entrance had "surprise visit" written all over it. Her hands closed into fists. How would Luc take to his newly discovered papahood? she wondered in despair. She already knew how *she* felt about it, the sick, sinking feeling in the pit of her stomach all too clear an indication.

More to the point...when had her feelings for Luc changed? When had she begun to care?

There was no mistaking the young woman's resolve. She glanced from Grace to the door as though judging her chances of winning a footrace. As Grace came around the desk, determination glittered in the woman's huge sloe eyes and she literally threw herself at Luc's door. Yanking it open, she launched into a spate of very loud Italian and slammed the door in Grace's face.

Grace's mouth fell open.

"Miss Barnes!" Luc's roar rattled the rafters an instant later. "Get in here!"

It took her a split second to gather her wits sufficiently to obey. Then she, too, charged the door and threw it open. Mother and infant had found sanctuary in Luc's arms, and between sobs the woman poured out what appeared to be a most heartrending story. Luc fired a quick question and the woman stepped back, her Italian loud and furious. Startled from a sound sleep, the baby burst into tears, his wails competing with his mother's.

"You bellowed?" Grace asked.

He stabbed a finger at her. "Don't start. Go down the hall and drag my brother Pietro out of his office. I want him in here. Now."

She turned to leave, only to discover Pietro standing behind her. "What's all the shouting?" he asked, then took one look at the woman at Luc's side and cried, "Carina!"

The sudden realization that the child was, in all probability, Pietro's and not Luc's, grabbed Grace's full attention. Fighting to ignore an overwhelming sense of relief, she slipped farther into the room, watching this latest development with intense interest.

Pietro crossed to Carina's side and started to take her into his arms. Grace could tell the instant he noticed the baby. It took precisely two seconds for the significance to sink in. "What the hell is this?" he shouted.

"What does it look like?" Carina shouted back. "It is a baby."

The infant in question started crying again. Grace, realizing the door to Luc's office stood open, turned to close it. A gaggle of secretaries had gathered in a loose semicircle, listening with open mouths. "I'll get security," one of them offered, and darted down the hallway before Grace could stop her. With a sigh, she shut the door. One problem at a time.

"Enough!" Luc thundered. "I want quiet and I want it now!" To Grace's astonishment, all obeyed, even the baby. "Excellent. Now. Do you think we could get to the bottom of this mess?"

"Fine. Your brother, he is a pig!" Carina condemned, then broke into a long litany of passionate Italian.

"English, please," Luc requested.

"My English, it is not so good."

"Really? Pietro's Italian is even worse." He eyed the baby grimly. "I see you managed to overcome the language barrier despite that small obstacle. I think introductions are in order. Don't you?"

"Luc," Pietro spoke up. "This is Carina Donati. Carina, my brother Luciano and his assistant, Miss Barnes."

"*Buon giorno,*" Carina acknowledged them with an abrupt nod.

"Carina and I... Well, we met at UC Berkeley," Pietro confessed. "She's a foreign-exchange student."

"Not any more," she interrupted, hugging the baby to her breast. "Now I am statistic. Unwed mother."

Pietro turned on her. "And whose fault is that?"

"Yours!" She offered him the baby. "You do not believe you are the papa?"

His hands balled into fists. "I damn well better be!"

"Children..." Luc inserted softly.

Grace crossed the room and held out her arms. "Why don't I take the baby?" she suggested, hoping to remove the poor infant from the field of battle. To her relief, Carina handed over her bundle without a single protest, and Grace retreated to the far side of the room.

Pietro addressed Carina, speaking at a more moderate level. "I phoned. You wouldn't answer any of my calls. I came over to the house. They said you'd moved out and hadn't left a forwarding address. I went everywhere I could think of to find you. It was like you'd vanished off the face of the earth."

Carina planted her hands on her curvaceous hips, scorn flashing in her magnificent eyes. "Of course I vanished. You lied to me!"

"I never!"

"What about Giovanna Carducci?"

"You left me because of Giovanna Carducci?"

Pathetic tears filled her eyes and she pointed a trembling finger. "See! He admits it."

"I'm not admitting anything!"

"That's enough," Luc interrupted once again. "Let me see if I have this straight. You and Carina met, fell in love, had a falling out over someone named Giovanna Carducci—"

"No!" Pietro denied.

"*Sí!*" Carina insisted.

"*And,*" Luc seized control of the conversation once more, "unbeknownst to Pietro, Carina conceived..." He gestured toward Grace and the baby.

"Tony," Carina supplied.

"Tony. Does that about cover it?"

"*Sí,*" Carina agreed. "In a nut case."

"Nutshell," Pietro corrected.

She tossed her hair over her shoulder. "Whatever it is, I don't care. The big man, he is right."

The "big man" sighed. "I hesitate to ask this, Carina, but you now want…what?"

As though on cue, the tears reappeared. Pietro took one look and pulled her into his arms. "Darling, what is it? What's happened?"

"My mother in Italy, she is very sick," Carina confessed, her voice breaking. "I must go to her. But I cannot."

Pietro stared at her in bewilderment. "Why not?"

She pulled free, glaring at him. "Why not? You look at my sweet, little Tony and ask, why not? I come from a very small village. My relatives are old-fashioned. If they ever find out I have a baby with no husband, I would be disowned. So I come up with solution."

"Which is?" Luc asked.

The tears finally escaped, sliding down her cheeks. With a cry of distress, she snatched Tony from Grace and repeatedly kissed the tuft of black hair peeking out of the blanket. Then Carina thrust the tiny bundle at Pietro. "Tony is also yours," she said, choking on a sob. "You take care of our baby while I am in Italy. When my mama is better, I will return and be an unwed, deserted mother once more." Dropping the diaper bag to the ground, she pushed past Grace and fled the room.

"Wait!" Pietro called. He started to follow, then realized he was somewhat encumbered.

"We need to discuss this," Luc began.

"Later." Pietro fumbled awkwardly with his armload and shot his brother a look of anguished pleading. "I have to stop her!"

"Mr. Salvatore?" Edward filled the doorway. "Is there a problem?"

"Yes, there is," Luc said. "Call down to the front desk. There's a young woman, petite, long dark hair, and probably crying. I want her detained. She's..." He glanced at the baby. "She's left behind a rather important package."

"Right away, sir," Edward agreed, and disappeared.

Luc turned back to his brother. "Pietro—"

"No! There isn't time." Without further ado, Pietro dumped the baby into Luc's arms. "You watch Tony. I'll go get Carina."

"Wait a minute! Come back here!" But it was too late. Pietro was gone. Luc stared in dismay at the baby, then glanced at Grace. A suspicious gleam appeared in his eyes. "Why, Miss Barnes," he practically purred, advancing toward her with his most charming—and determined—smile. He held out the baby. "Look what I have for you."

CHAPTER TWO

The Great Lie
Still Day 337 and all is not so well...

GRACE HELD UP HER HANDS and backed away. ''Oh, no,'' she protested. ''This is your problem.''

Luc stopped dead in his tracks, staring in astonishment. ''You'd desert me in my hour of need?''

''Yes.''

''You'd leave Pietro and Carina in the lurch?'' he demanded in disbelief.

''Without question.''

His brows drew sharply together. ''You'd turn your back on a poor, helpless baby?''

She stared at him, stricken. He'd gotten her with that one. She adored children. She always had. Throughout her teen years, when anyone had needed a baby-sitter, they'd called her. When the church needed someone to supervise the nursery on Sundays, her name was the first one mentioned. And though she wasn't terribly experienced with babies, she was still an easy touch when it came to their welfare.

''That's not fair,'' she complained. But he had her. And if he didn't know it, he undoubtedly sensed it.

''Come, *cara mia.*'' He held out Tony and offered a helpless smile. ''I know nothing of babies. Besides, it won't be for long. Only until Pietro returns with Carina and they sort out their little problem.''

Unable to resist, she took the ''little problem'' and peered into his sweet, sleeping face. Luc leaned over, running a long finger across the baby's flushed cheek.

''He's a Salvatore, all right,'' Luc pronounced. ''He's the image of my brother.''

''What's going to happen with Pietro and Carina?'' she asked in concern.

''They'll marry.'' His golden eyes reflected his amusement. ''It promises to be a rather volatile relationship, wouldn't you agree?''

She shuddered. ''Too volatile.'' A far more serious question troubled her, and she gathered her nerve to voice it. ''How will your father take the news?''

''Not well,'' Luc admitted. ''He's as old-fashioned as Carina's parents.'' He smoothed the tiny line forming on Grace's brow, his touch easing her distress and yet fermenting a strange agitation. ''Don't worry. I'll handle him. The first order of business is to get them married. That should go a long way toward placating my father.''

''Perhaps you could be a little vague about the exact wedding date,'' Grace suggested. ''Not lie, of course.''

His lips curved. ''No, we'd never lie, would we?''

She ducked her head. ''Never,'' she agreed in a muffled voice. ''But if we were to omit one or two minor details...?'' She peeked up to see how he took to the suggestion.

He shrugged, his expression unreadable. ''We'll play it by ear. Let's hope that seeing his very first grandchild will temper my father's reaction.''

She gnawed at her lower lip. ''He...he wouldn't throw Pietro out of the family, would he?'' She'd known parents who'd done that over far less serious infractions.

But not Dom. He was the sweetest, most benevolent man she'd ever met. Surely he wouldn't overreact to such an extent. He had to realize it could tear his entire family apart if he were to disown Pietro. And she knew for a fact that family meant everything to him.

''He might,'' Luc acknowledged grimly, confirming her worst fears. ''He has very strong opinions about this sort of thing. And his opinion is...it doesn't happen. Period.''

She stared at Luc in alarm. ''But—''

He dropped a casual arm around Grace's shoulders and gave her a reassuring hug. ''Relax,'' he said, his touch once again arousing a strange, disturbing flutter deep in her stomach. ''You're not to worry. I'll take care of everything. Trust me.''

Grace nodded, believing him. If there was one thing she'd learned about Luc, it was that he did precisely what he promised. If he said he'd take care of Dom, then he'd take care of Dom. As far as trusting him... She stared at Luc, stared at the lean, chiseled features that reflected his strength and power, and at the direct, golden eyes, so full of confidence and determination. Slowly, she relaxed.

She'd trust him with her life.

He released her, crossing to the large built-in cabinet on the far side of the room. ''Let's see what's happening downstairs,'' he said, folding back the cabinet doors and revealing a bank of monitors inside. Switching them on, he called up a view from the security camera in the lobby and put it on the large center screen. ''There's Pietro and Carina. I don't see Edward, yet. I wonder what's taking him so long?''

''He must have gotten delayed in the elevator,'' Grace

murmured, crossing to stand beside him. ''Oh, dear. They're arguing again.''

''That's not arguing. That's shrieking.''

She frowned, cuddling the baby. ''Maybe you should go down there and mediate.''

After a momentary hesitation, he shook his head. ''Pietro wouldn't thank me if I butted in. He's made it clear over the past year that he prefers taking care of his own problems without big brother's interference. He'll call if he needs help.''

''You're sure?''

''No.''

''No!'' She spun to stare at him. ''Did you say no?''

''I said no.''

''That doesn't exactly make me feel any better,'' she pointed out.

He shrugged. ''Considering how stubborn Pietro can be, it's the best I can offer.''

''It would seem stubbornness is a Salvatore trait.'' She switched her attention back to the monitor. ''I wish we could hear what's going on. I don't suppose you read lips.''

He gave a short laugh. ''I don't need to. It's obvious what they're saying. Pietro's yelling, 'Why didn't you tell me about Tony?'''

Grace allowed herself a brief smile, despite her concern. ''And Carina is shouting back, 'Why should I have?'''

He slanted her a quick look, a spark of humor glittering in his eyes. ''Because I'm the father of your baby.''

Her smile widened. ''So?''

''So, you shouldn't have hidden my son from me.'' He shifted closer. ''I had a right to know about him.''

Getting into the role, she replied, ''You have no rights

as far as I'm concerned. You betrayed me. You had an affair with...*her.*"

Luc slipped an arm around Grace's waist. "That other woman means nothing to me, *mia amorata,*" he murmured, his mouth practically brushing her cheek.

She shivered, fighting the urge to return his embrace, fighting the sharp desire that intensified with every passing moment. How had this happened? How had this attraction managed to slip past her guard with such stunning ease. And why now, when she was so close to attaining her dream? She struggled to remember the role she played. "The...the other woman..."

"You're the only woman I care about, the only woman I—"

"Don't say it," she cut in sharply, tumbling out of her role with a vengeance. "Not unless you mean it. Because I know you don't care. Not really."

"I do."

She shook her head. "No. You love all women. I'm just one of many."

"You're right. I admit it. I do love women." He, too, had dropped the playacting, she realized, his eyes darkening, losing their glint and turning serious. Deadly serious. "I love all women, young and old, short and tall, with dark hair scraped back in a bun or with long blond hair left loose around the shoulders. They are all beautiful to me."

She gazed up at him in alarm, resisting the urge to touch her hair. Nervously, she licked her lips and whispered, "Then you admit it?"

His index finger brushed her lower lip, the caress fleeting yet potent. "I admit only that I love all women. I love the diversity of their appearance. I love the unique scent of a woman—musky or flowery or as fresh as the first breath of spring. I love to listen to them speak, how one will sound rough and smoky and another as smooth as thick maple syrup. I love to watch them move, all long limbed and coltish or tiny dynamos bustling with energy. But my favorites are those who dance to some inner music only they can hear, supple and graceful and filled with the joy of living...like you.''

She shook her head. ''No... Don't say any more.''

But he didn't stop. Instead his hands cupped her shoulders, his thumbs stroking the sensitive hollow of her throat. ''Did you know that touching a woman is one of life's greatest joys? To explore each silken curve and feel the hot rush of her passion, to hold her in your arms and know that your touch brings her to life.''

She wanted to jerk away, but she couldn't. Not while hampered by the baby...hampered by her reaction to his words, his touch. ''Luc, you shouldn't be saying these things to me,'' she insisted weakly.

''But I haven't told you the best part about women. Do you know what it is?'' He didn't wait for her answer. ''It's their taste. The taste of a woman is a gift from the gods. It's headier than the finest wine and more intoxicating than the strongest rum. And it only improves with age...and with experience.''

She shut her eyes, afraid to look at him, afraid of the passion she read in his face. ''You're forgetting about Pietro and Carina,'' she whispered, knowing she should be watching the monitor but unable to tear her gaze from Luc's.

''I haven't forgotten them,'' he murmured. ''You accuse me of loving women. And I admit my guilt. You're right. I do love women. But how I feel about them is nothing—absolutely nothing—compared with how I feel about you.''

She shook her head, holding Tony tight to her breast. "You tell such sweet lies, beautiful lies. But that's all they are—lies. Women fascinate you. You find them irresistible. Too irresistible to ever settle on just one."

"You're wrong." His voice was deep and husky, the underlying lilt more pronounced than ever. "Once a Salvatore falls in love, it's for ever. He never strays."

She forced herself to look at him again, to try and judge the degree of honesty in his expression. "I—I don't believe you."

"Yes, you do, because it's the truth. Salvatores never stray. Never." Then he released her and stepped back. "And that, *cara mia,* is what Pietro is saying to Carina. It's what I'd say in his place to the woman I loved."

Grace blinked, the spell of words he'd cast slowly fading. She didn't know what to think, what to say...what to feel. Her gaze fell from his, and out of desperation she focused on the monitor. "Luc, look!"

Carina and Pietro were no longer arguing. Action seemed to be the order of the day. Gesturing wildly, Carina grabbed a huge porcelain vase from off a pedestal beside the front door and dumped the contents over the top of Pietro's head. Water, gladioli and bits of fern dripped from his shoulders and puddled on the floor.

Grace winced. "I guess his explanation wasn't as smooth as yours," she murmured.

"I guess not. But she shouldn't have done that," Luc said with a sigh. "He's not going to take it at all well."

Sure enough, Pietro exploded, gesturing wildly. Just then, Edward appeared on the scene. Eyes practically popping out of his head, he attempted to brush the flower petals and pieces of greenery from Pietro's suit.

"I wish Carina would put that vase down," Grace said, shifting Tony to her shoulder.

"It's *where* she'll put it down that worries me."

No sooner had he said that, than Edward endeavored to wrest the vase from Carina's hands. For a few tense seconds they tussled. Jerking it free, it flew from Edward's hands and crashed against the side of Pietro's head. He went down like a ton of bricks.

Luc raced for a phone and called down to the security desk. "Call the staff doctor to help Pietro. Fast! I'll be right there."

"Luc, wait! You better check this out first," Grace called in a panic. "It doesn't look good."

They could no longer see Pietro. A huge crowd had gathered around him, blocking the view. Off to one side, security men were converging on Carina, who wept copiously. Far worse, two police officers came bursting through the front doors. Carina looked from the security men to the police, and apparently decided the law was a safer bet than the furious employees of a stricken Salvatore. She darted to their side.

"I don't know what tale of woe she's spinning, but it's making quite an impression," Luc observed in disgust. "She'll be gone before I even reach the elevators. Yep. There she goes. Out the door, into the first cab that passes by and on her way to the airport."

"What about Pietro?" Grace asked in concern.

"Wait a sec. He's up." Luc relaxed slightly. "Thank heavens."

"He seems to be all right, but he could still have a concussion. I wish the doctor was there," Grace fussed. "Oh, no. Now he's yelling at the police."

"Probably for letting Carina go."

"Why does that policewoman have her handcuffs out? They're not going to arrest him, are they?" she questioned in alarm. "He hasn't done anything wrong."

"Except give the police a hard time, knowing Pietro. They tend to frown on that." He watched the screen, an intent expression on his face. "Good. They're releasing him."

"Great, except where's he going?" She pointed at the screen. "Now he's leaving the building, too."

"Damn!" Luc thrust a hand through his hair. "He's going after Carina. I should have guessed he'd pull something like that."

"But what about Tony? He can't expect us..." Her eyes widened in disbelief.

He smiled grimly and nodded. "Looks like we have baby-sitting duties until Pietro catches up with Carina."

"Oh, no. No way. Not a chance."

Before he could respond, the phone rang. Luc snatched it up. "Edward? How's Pietro? Yes, yes. I know he left. Where's he headed?" He covered the mouthpiece and spoke to Grace, "I was right. He's on his way to the airport. Hang on, Edward. I'm putting you on the speakerphone." He punched a button.

"Er...Mr. Salvatore? Can you hear me? This is Edward Rumple speaking. Over."

"We hear you," Grace said quickly. "Is Pietro all right? He isn't hurt too badly?"

"Just a goose egg, Miss Barnes. Hardly any blood at all." He cleared his throat. "But there is just one little problem."

"What is it, Edward?" Luc asked.

"Well, ah, you aren't going to like this, but..."

"Spit it out."

"Yes, sir, Mr. Salvatore. See, Mr. Pietro happened to mention the baby the young lady left behind and, ah, well, the truth is... To be perfectly honest..."

"Edward!"

"I thought I'd better warn you that—"

A loud pounding sounded on the outer door. "Police. Open up, please."

"—the police are on their way up," Edward finished lamely.

For an instant Luc didn't move. Then in a calm, collected voice, he said, "Thank you, Edward. Keep everything under control down there and notify me the instant Pietro returns. I'll deal with the police." Hanging up the phone, he crossed to the door.

"Luc?" Grace said uncertainly.

He spared her a brief glance. "It'll be okay. Just try not to look worried and let me do the talking." At her nod, he opened the door and held out his hand. "Hello. I'm Luc Salvatore, president of Salvatore Enterprises. What can I do for you—" he checked their name tags "—Officers Cable and Hatcher?"

"We're responding to a report of an abandoned infant," said Officer Cable. She glanced at the baby Grace held. "Is that the child?"

"This baby isn't abandoned," Luc stated firmly, moving to stand between Grace and the policewoman.

"No?" Officer Hatcher, a tall, sturdy man, stepped forward. "Is he yours?"

"He's my nephew."

The two officers exchanged quick glances. "I'm afraid we'll have to see some identification," Cable requested.

Grace could tell from their attitudes that they were taking this situation very, very seriously. Luc removed his driver's license from his wallet and handed it to the policewoman. "Perhaps an explanation is in order?" he suggested with a quick smile.

Grace waited for Officer Cable's reaction to that

smile. It wasn't long coming. She fumbled for his license, effected a swift recovery, then made a production of recording the information on her clipboard. A spot of color appeared high on each cheekbone. Luc didn't even notice.

Grace sighed. But then, he never did. He'd bowl them over like ninepins and never realize they'd fallen. To his credit, it wasn't calculated. As Luc had admitted, he simply loved women and treated every last one with a devastating courtesy and warmth. It was, without question, his greatest charm.

"I think an explanation would be very helpful," Hatcher interrupted, keenly attuned to his partner's reaction. He strode across the room, firing a quelling glance at Cable. Somewhat chagrined, she reverted to a more professional demeanor.

"I believe you met my brother Pietro Salvatore downstairs," Luc began.

"He was the one involved in the altercation with the young woman?"

"A small family squabble," Luc said dismissively. "We're a very...emotional household."

"The young woman is...?"

"His wife."

Grace's mouth fell open at the blatant lie—the first she'd ever heard him utter—and a tiny gasp escaped before she could prevent it. She stared at Luc in disbelief; he never blinked an eye. Nor did he look at her. But Officer Hatcher did. Grace quickly shut her mouth and focused her attention on the baby, but she suspected it was too little, too late. Sure enough, he approached.

"You have something to add, Miss..."

"Barnes. Grace Barnes. And yes, I do. Could...could

you hand me that diaper bag? I believe we've had a little accident here,'' she murmured weakly.

The officer's eyes narrowed but he didn't call her a liar to her face, which came as a relief. He bent down and picked up the bag. She took it with a grateful smile and gently deposited the baby on top of Luc's desk, smack-dab in the center of his leather blotter. Serve him right if it was ruined, she decided. He shouldn't have lied to the police. She unwrapped the blanket around Tony and made a production of unsnapping the bottom of his jumper.

''To get back to the matter at hand,'' Officer Hatcher continued. ''The young lady we questioned, her name is...?''

''Carina Donati...Salvatore,'' Luc replied.

''And she left to go to the airport?''

''Yes, her mother in Italy is very ill. My brother asked her to wait until they could all fly together, but she wanted to get home as soon as possible. I'm sorry you had to be involved.'' He shrugged. ''It really wasn't necessary.''

''About the baby,'' Officer Cable interrupted. ''You've been left with the infant until your brother returns?''

''It's only for a few hours.''

Grace kept her head down and removed a fresh diaper, wipes and powder from the bag. Sliding the rubber pants off Tony's plump, churning legs, she discovered to her relief that he was, indeed, wet. She unpinned the soggy diaper.

The officers conferred in low voices and she could tell they weren't comfortable with the situation. So could Luc, for he sighed. ''Look. I'm a responsible man, respected in the community. I'm baby-sitting my nephew for a few hours. Why is that a problem?''

Grace slipped off the diaper, then glanced, wide-eyed, from the baby to Luc. Uh-oh. If she didn't move fast, something very nasty would hit the fan. Tossing the dirty diaper toward the trash can with one hand, she fumbled for a clean one with the other. To her horror, it slid to the floor.

''Would it help if I provided references?'' Luc offered.

''You have someone who can vouch for your baby-sitting abilities?'' Hatcher retorted. Clearly, he resented Cable's less-than-professional reaction to Luc and intended to make matters as difficult as possible. ''You look like a busy man,'' he added, his gaze suspicious. ''Are you sure you can provide adequate care?''

Grace saw the fierce expression on Luc's face and froze. That look did not bode well for any of them. He glanced at her with grim intent, then at her left hand and she knew, before he even moved, what he planned to do.

Without a moment to lose, she whipped a new diaper from the bag, dropping it across Tony's lower extremities the exact same instant Luc dropped a possessive arm around her shoulders. Fighting his embrace, she struggled to position the diaper and pin it.

''*Cara,*'' he muttered. ''Let me show them.''

''Not now!'' she whispered frantically.

''Yes, now.'' He grabbed her left hand and held it out toward the police officers. ''Perhaps I should have said my *fiancée* and I will be baby-sitting little Tony.''

''Luc, the baby,'' Grace whispered. He frowned at her, and she snatched her hand from his grasp. ''I have to finish changing…him.''

Not daring to give the police time to come closer, she gave up on the pins. Yanking the rubber pants up the tiny, kicking legs and praying the diaper would stay in place for the next two minutes, she wrapped the blanket around the baby. Then she collapsed into Luc's chair, lifted Tony to her shoulder and began to pat the baby's back, as if a brisk burping commonly followed a diaper change.

"You're engaged?" Officer Cable asked, not hiding her disappointment. Hatcher shoved his hat to the back of his head and grinned.

Grace shot Luc a fulminating glare. "Yes," she admitted, forcing out the lie. "I am." Fortunately they didn't ask if she was engaged to Luc. Lying to the police came low on her list of ambitions in life—not that she hadn't lied anyway, considering she wasn't really engaged at all.

Officer Cable gave a philosophical shrug. "I guess it's a false alarm," she said to her partner.

Officer Hatcher wasn't so accommodating. "We'll be writing this up," he informed them, without question suspecting that several vital details had been omitted from their story. "Next time I come here—and I will be back—I'll be having words with the baby's parents."

"Of course," Luc agreed.

He escorted the police officers to the elevators, leaving Grace and Tony behind. The minute they were gone, Grace returned the baby to the desk and quickly and efficiently repaired the droopy diaper. Tony fussed through the entire procedure, undoubtedly annoyed at having to suffer the same fate twice in less than five minutes.

Luc appeared in the doorway. "What are you doing?" he asked.

"Changing the baby."

"Again?"

"Yes, again. I was in such a hurry the first time, I didn't get it right."

"Why—"

She turned on him. "Do you realize what would have happened if Officer Cable had come over while I was changing the baby?"

Amusement sparked in his eyes. "She would have seen how a baby gets changed?"

"She would have seen that Tony is actually Toni."

"Come again?"

"I mean...Toni isn't your nephew but your niece!" Grace snapped. She picked up the baby and carried her to the couch, nestling her safely among the cushions.

"What?"

Grace folded her arms across her chest. "Toni apparently stands for Antonia, not Antonio."

"You're kidding!" Luc grinned in amazement. "That's wonderful. She's the first female Salvatore in...in four generations. Or is it five?"

Grace struggled to control her temper. "You're missing the point. If the police had discovered that you didn't even know the sex of your brother's child, the whole game would have been up. They'd have thrown us both in jail and taken the baby into custody."

He shook his head. "I wouldn't have let them."

"You couldn't have prevented it!" She didn't remember when she'd last been so angry. "How dare you!"

He stood, leaning against the doorframe, watching her intently. "How dare I what?"

"How dare you lie to them! I mean, when you finally cut loose with a fib, it's a whopper. But did you *have* to start with the police?"

He shrugged. ''It seemed...appropriate at the time.''

''Great,'' she grumbled. ''So why involve me in your family problems?''

He grabbed her shoulders, hauling her close. ''*Our* problems,'' he reminded in a soft, deliberate voice. ''We're engaged. You even told the police that, remember?''

She shook her head frantically. ''No. I...I didn't. I just agreed that I was engaged, not that I was engaged to—''

He cut her off. ''That isn't how they'll recall the conversation.''

''But, it's all a lie,'' she protested. ''Every bit of it. I'm not engaged to you. Pietro and Carina are not married. Darn it, Luc, the baby's not even a him.''

She saw the storm gathering in his eyes, saw the fury and determination lock his expression into a cold, taut mask. ''Let me explain something to you. I will not allow the police or anyone else to take Toni from me. I will do anything, *anything,* to protect her.''

She didn't doubt him for a minute. And she could even sympathize with his feelings. The Salvatores were a close, unified family—all for one and one for all had long been their credo. And if truth be known, she did feel a certain obligation to Luc. After all, hadn't she spent the past year lying to him? She...she *owed* him a lie. But only a small short-term one. After that, she'd consider them even.

''What do you want from me?'' she asked warily.

He had her and he knew it. He relaxed, the fire in his eyes dying until the gold gleamed like banked embers. His grip relaxed into a caress. ''Not much. I just want you to stay with me—posing as my fiancée should the need arise—until Carina or Pietro return.''

"Two hours. That's all you get," she bargained.

"Not good enough. I need you until my brother picks up Toni."

"No."

He gave her a wounded look. "You'd desert me in my hour of need?"

"Yes."

"You'd leave Pietro and Carina in the lurch?"

"Without question. We've been through this before. Remember?"

"So we have," he agreed softly, releasing her. "I believe this is where I ask if you'd turn your back on a helpless baby. As I recall that seemed to make a difference last time."

She really, truly tried to refuse. But she couldn't. She couldn't desert Toni, no matter how mad she was at Luc. "You don't play fair," she complained.

"No," he agreed. He caught her hand in his and raised it to his lips in a graceful gesture. Then he smiled, a most charming, dangerous smile. "I play to win."

CHAPTER THREE

The Great Lie
Day 337 continues to worsen...

"NO, NO! THAT'S TOO MUCH. It says here three scoops of formula to *six* ounces of water. Dammit, Grace, now look what you've done. You've spilled it!"

"*I* spilled it?" Grace shoved a tumble of curls out of her eyes and glared at Luc. "*You* jostled my arm."

"Well, your arm was in my way. This time watch what you're doing or you'll knock it to the..." The bottle clattered to the ground, milk soaking into the rug.

"Floor?" she inserted with a long-suffering sigh.

"Get another bottle. This one's contaminated. We'll have to start over."

"We can't."

He planted his hands on his hips. "And why not?" he demanded aggressively.

"Simple," she retorted, struggling to remain cool, calm and collected in the face of staggering odds—namely one Luc Salvatore. "We're out of bottles."

"Not for long." He marched to the phone, snatched it from the cradle and punched some buttons. "Edward? We're out of bottles. Order up another batch. And send out for more formula, too. Grace has gone clumsy on me."

"How could I have ever thought he was charming?"

she muttered, struggling to repin her hair in its customary knot. "Charming, in a pig's eye. I must have been out of my mind."

He slapped his hand over the receiver. "What's that? Did you say something?"

"I said, make sure he gets the right kind."

"Edward. Make sure you get the right kind of formula. Grace is afraid you'll screw up again."

She raced to the phone and yanked it from his hand. "Edward? It's Grace. I did *not* say that. I didn't even think it. Hello? Hello?"

Luc lifted his finger off the plunger. "Hang up on you, did he?"

She returned the phone to its cradle and confronted him, poking her glasses higher up the bridge of her nose. "That was really low, even for you. And considering how much you need my help, I suggest—"

"Shh. The baby, remember?" As though in response, a tiny squawk drifted from across the room. "Uh-oh. Too late." He folded his arms across his chest and regarded her accusingly. "*You* made her cry."

"Ohh. I ought to—"

"Temper, temper." He grabbed for the phone again, raking a hand through his hair as he dialed. "Edward! Edward, she's crying.... What? How do I know? I haven't been a baby for years. Oh, really? No, kidding. Diapers or bottles, you say?"

Grace winced at the sarcasm. Time to take matters into her own hands. She headed out of Luc's office and into the reception area. Luc's voice drifted to her through the open door.

"That might prove a little difficult since you haven't sent any up! And another thing—"

She settled a hip on the edge of her desk and lifted

the extension phone. "Edward? It's Grace. Just so you know, I did not say I thought you might screw anything up. I want that clearly on the record."

"Yes, Miss Barnes," Edward said with a deep sigh.

She opened her steno pad. "Now. You've ordered the correct formula? It has to be exactly like the can Carina left. The one with extra iron."

"Yes, Miss Barnes."

"He's not an idiot, Grace. He's not going to make the same mistake twice," Luc informed her. "Are you, Edward?"

"No, Mr. Salvatore."

"Luc, hang up. I can handle this."

"Like you handled the bottle and formula?"

"That wasn't my fault! Hello? Hello?"

"He hung up, Miss Barnes."

"Oh. Well, good. Let's see... What else do we need? Here it is. We must have those sterilized bottles as soon as you can get them." She made a quick notation, then asked, "And what about diapers? We're almost out. Perhaps disposable would be a good bet."

"What size?"

That stopped her. "Small?"

"They go by weight."

Grace nibbled on her lip. "I'll have to get back to you on that."

"Yes, Miss Barnes."

"Damnation!" The shout came from Luc's office. "Grace? Grace! Get in here, quick!"

"Gotta go, Edward."

"I couldn't be that lucky."

"Grace!"

She frowned. "What was that, Edward?"

"I said, er, that would be just ducky."

Luc appeared in the doorway. ''Get off that phone. Now. And get in here. There's something wrong with Toni.''

Without another word, she hung up and hurried after him. He crossed to the makeshift crib they'd constructed out of couch cushions and winter coats. ''What is it?'' she asked, standing beside him and peering down at the baby. ''What's wrong?''

''Look at her,'' he ordered. ''She's foaming at the mouth. That's bad, right? Don't they shoot you when you do that?''

''She's blowing bubbles,'' Grace explained. ''At three months, we say it's cute. We frown on it when a child turns six. At thirteen, a stern reprimand is in order. It's only bubble-blowing adults we shoot.''

''You're certain?''

''Absolutely. Now for the next problem.''

He relaxed. ''You mean the problem of getting any work done today?''

''No. The problem of diapers.''

''I'll call Edward—''

''No, you won't. I've already spoken to him about it and we need to know what size to order.''

''Small. Very small,'' Luc decided promptly.

She flashed him a superior look. ''It goes by weight.''

''Light. Very light.''

Her lips twitched, and an instant later Luc laughed, a low, rumbling sound that drew her in and before she knew it, forged yet another bond of intimacy between them. Unable to resist, she laughed, too. ''This is crazy, isn't it?'' she asked with a wide, open smile.

''But fun. I have a niece. That's a nice feeling.''

He slid an arm around Grace's shoulders, tucking her close, and together they stared down at Toni. It was a comfortable fit. Too comfortable. She should move away. But she didn't want to. With a tiny sigh, Grace gave in to the companionable mood and accepted his embrace. Hardly aware of what she did, she snuggled her head into the crook of his arm and relaxed her curves into his angles.

Just for this moment, she'd let down her guard and enjoy what the gods offered. It didn't mean anything. She knew better than to take it seriously. But right now, after all she'd been through, she needed his touch as much as she needed food and drink. Maybe even more.

"Listen..." His head bent closer to hers. "What's she doing now?" he whispered.

"She's cooing," Grace whispered back, shivering at the warm brush of his breath across her face.

"What does cooing mean? Is she hungry or is she wet?"

"I think it means she's happy," she murmured.

"Ah... Happy. That's good."

"Yes. Yes, it's very good. Happy is excellent." She turned into his arms and looked up at him, the strangely intense expression on his face catching her by surprise. Her hands clenched. "Luc..."

"Yes, Grace?"

"We need diapers." Somehow she'd managed to gather a fistful of his shirt, clinging to him as though her life depended on it. Self-consciously, she splayed her hands across his chest, smoothing out the wrinkles she'd created, her fingers lingering on the hard ridge of muscle beneath.

He shook his head. "I don't need diapers. I do need something—and I need it very badly. But let me assure you, it's not diapers."

Hot color flooded her face. "I mean, the baby needs

diapers. Toni. She needs them. Not you. I know that you don't."

"Very observant. Though if you keep rubbing my chest like that, you'll find out precisely what it is I *do* need."

She jumped back as though scalded. "I didn't mean to—it was an accident."

"Let me guess. You confused me with Will-William."

Horror filled her. How could she have been so foolish? How could she have let her defenses down for even one tiny second? She knew what Luc was like. She knew how dangerous he could be. And yet she'd allowed him to touch her. Worse, she'd touched him back.

"It won't happen again," she said stiltedly.

He stepped closer. "What won't? Your confusing me with Will-William or your rubbing my chest?"

"Neither. I didn't mean to—to," she gestured wildly, "you know."

He smiled. "To what?"

She hated him. She absolutely loathed him for putting her in such an awkward position. "*Touch* you, all right? I didn't mean to touch you. And I'm perfectly well aware that you're not Will...William."

A grim smile flickered across his mouth. "You can't even say his name without stumbling over it, can you? What sort of relationship is that?"

"William. William. William. There. Are you satisfied now?" She took a deep breath, struggling to curb her sudden spurt of anger. It wouldn't do to lose her temper around Luc. She'd never keep everything under control that way. Lifting her chin as though daring him to say anything further, she asked, "Could we please get back to the issue at hand? Diapers for Toni, remember?"

For a minute she thought he'd argue the point. In the past few months he'd become very concerned about her relationship with the nonexistent William. She could tell, just from his tense, combative stance, that he wanted to push the discussion back onto a personal note. And she'd do just about anything to avoid that.

"It's been a rather stressful day," she said. "We're both worried."

"And we don't want to say anything we might regret, is that what you're suggesting?"

"Yes. That's what I'm suggesting."

"In that case—" he reached down and scooped Toni into his arms "—let's get the diaper situation taken care of. Follow me."

He strode from the office and headed for the elevators. After a momentary hesitation, she followed. Within five seconds, he'd collected a swarm of oohing and ahhing secretaries. To Grace's disgust, they darted around him like bees desperate for pollen. He took it as his due, beaming proudly, as if he and he alone were responsible for Toni's adorable perfection. The elevator arrived and he excused himself from the chattering horde. Snagging Grace's elbow, he ushered her into the car and pushed the button for the basement.

"Where are we going?" she asked, her tone sharper than she'd intended. Great. Just great. Give him something more to comment on. Just what she needed.

"We're going to the mail room," he answered in a suspiciously bland tone of voice.

"Why are we going to the mail room?"

"Wait and see. But be prepared to be impressed."

"I can hardly contain myself."

"Try," he suggested dryly.

Exiting the elevator, he led the way through the carpeted hallways to the enormous mail room. All work ceased the moment he walked into the place, but Luc didn't even seem to notice. He crossed to one of the desks and gently placed his precious bundle in the middle of a postage scale.

"Twelve pounds, eleven and one half ounces," he announced with satisfaction. "Grace, order the diapers."

"Okay. I admit it," she said with a sigh. "I'm impressed."

His expression serious, he leveled an intense, dark gaze at her. "Not yet, you aren't. But give it time. Because before long I intend to impress the hell out of you."

She could only stare at him, her breath fast and furious, her eyes huge. "What are you talking about?" she finally managed to ask.

His gaze turned enigmatic. But "Time will tell," was all he'd say.

With no comeback to offer, she went to the nearest phone and put a call through to Edward. Then they returned upstairs. Within thirty minutes sterilized bottles, formula and disposable diapers filled the reception area. Fifteen minutes after that, Grace settled into Luc's leather couch with a fresh and sweet-smelling Toni and popped a bottle into the baby's tiny puckered mouth. Snuggling into the deep, soft cushions, Grace kicked off her shoes and put up her feet.

Luc looked over at her. "Comfortable?" he asked.

"Very."

"Good. Sit there and relax. I'm going to try and clear up some of this backlog." He reached for the first file off the stack of work piled on his desk.

"Great idea," she said sleepily. "You know something?"

He spared her a brief glance. "What?"

"As exhausting as it is playing mommy, I've decided that there's nothing more special in all the world than cradling this little piece of heaven in my arms." She yawned.

He leaned back in his chair, tapping his pen against his blotter, his expression hooded. "I can think of one other thing just as special," he replied.

"Can you?" She considered.

Maybe being held in a pair of strong, protective arms by the man you loved could match it. But she wasn't about to admit that to Luc. Even imagining such a thing was dangerous. And yet... Too tired to fight the wayward thought, she allowed her imagination free rein. Beautiful, delicious and utterly impossible images filled her head, and with a tiny, secretive smile, she drifted off to sleep.

"GRACE, WAKE UP."

"Go away," she protested in a muffled voice.

"Wake up, *cara mia.* It's time to go home."

"Home?" That penetrated. With a groan, she sat up, then gasped in horror. "The baby! I fell asleep—"

"Take it easy, sweetheart. Toni's fine. I slipped her out of your arms the minute you nodded off."

She sat up, the image of Luc watching her sleep an uncomfortable one. "What time is it?"

"Six."

"Six! Is Pietro back?"

"No."

"What about Carina?"

He shook his head. "Afraid not."

She shoved her hair out of her eyes and twitched her skirt hem down over her knees. Her disguise was rapidly falling apart. If she weren't careful, all of Dom's fine plans would soon come undone. Had Luc noticed anything unusual? She searched his face. Responding to her scrutiny, he lifted an eyebrow in question.

"Something must have happened to them," she said. "It doesn't take this long to get to and from the airport. They should be back by now."

"They had a lot to discuss." He shrugged. "Pietro knows Toni's safe with us. We'll hear from them soon."

Right on cue, the phone rang and Luc glanced over his shoulder. "My private line."

"Thank heavens," she whispered, knowing that only family used that number.

He crossed to his desk and snatched up the phone. "Pietro? Where the *hell* are you?" He listened for several minutes, then switched to Italian. Not that it mattered. From the anger in his voice, Grace knew this discussion didn't bode well for her future. "I want an update tomorrow, you understand?" he finally said. "Or I go to Father with this." He slammed down the phone.

Night had fallen and only a small desk lamp illuminated the room. Luc thrust his chair away from his desk and stood, crossing to the window behind him. San Francisco lay sprawled below, the city lights glittering through the misty rain.

"Good news?" she joked uneasily.

He wasn't amused. "Pietro missed Carina at the airport, as I'm sure you've surmised."

"When is he coming for Toni?"

"Not tonight." He turned to face her, deep shadows cutting across his face and concealing his expression. "And not tomorrow night."

"What—what does that mean?"

"It means we're in for a longer haul than I anticipated.'' He moved into the light and she caught her breath as she discerned the full extent of his displeasure. ''Pietro was calling from a plane phone. He's followed Carina to Italy.''

From across the room, the baby let out a loud wail.

Grace hurried to Toni's side and picked her up. ''You said it, sweet pea,'' she muttered, hugging the baby. Uneasily she recalled her promise—to stay until Carina or Pietro returned for Toni. She peeked nervously at Luc. From his cold, calculating look, he hadn't forgotten, either.

She closed her eyes and shivered. Oh, Lord. What had she let herself in for?

''GRACE. THE DOOR. NOW.''

''If you'd move out of my light, I'd get it open a lot faster. For such a ritzy apartment complex, they sure don't light the hallways very well.''

''Grace...'' His tone held an implacable warning. ''If you don't hurry up, I'm going to drop the strained spinach and squash surprise all over our feet.''

Grace blew a loose curl of hair out of her eyes and focused on the door to his apartment—and the stubborn lock that kept her on the wrong side of that door. ''I told you when we were at the grocery store not to get the strained spinach and squash surprise. Babies this young don't eat strained spinach and squash surprise. They drink milk, and some eat flaked cereal.''

''I wanted to be prepared, just in case.''

She gave up on trying to work the key while holding a squirming baby. ''In case, what? In case Toni gets a sudden craving for big-boy beans and peachy peaches?''

''Dammit, Grace!'' Luc peered into the bags. ''I think I forgot the peaches.''

''Oh, dear. I'm crushed. And look at Toni. She's crushed, too.''

''The only one in danger of being crushed is me. You'd better get that door open fast or—'' The bottom of one of the bags ripped and jars tumbled to the floor. Luc let fly with a very nasty word.

''Is that any way to speak in front of an innocent baby?'' Grace demanded in disgust.

''Yes!'' he snarled. ''That's exactly how I speak in front of an innocent baby, when fifty pounds' worth of baby food jars have just nailed my big toe.''

''I told you—''

''I know. I know. Not to get any baby food. And I told you, I wanted to be prepared. I don't know how long we'll have to take care of Toni.''

''She won't be ready to eat that stuff for months,'' Grace snapped. ''Are you planning on keeping her hidden away in here for that long? I think the police will have a thing or two to say about that.''

A door across the hall opened. ''Mr. Salvatore? What's going on out there? Who's using profanity?''

''Mrs. Bumgartle,'' Luc said, his smile less captivating than usual. He climbed over the spilled baby food jars. ''Did we wake you? I'm so sorry.''

To Grace's astonishment, Luc's unfailing charm failed. Utterly. It was, without question, a first. The old woman adjusted her glasses on the tip of her long, narrow nose and scowled. ''Is that a baby?''

''Where?'' He glanced over his shoulder. ''Oh, that? Why, yes. That is a baby, isn't it?''

Mrs. Bumgartle's eyes narrowed. ''I'm delighted we agree that it's a baby. The question is, whose baby is it?''

''Whose baby…?''

''Yes, Mr. Salvatore.'' She yanked the belt of her thick woolen robe tight about her ample middle. ''Whose baby do you have there?''

''It's my brother's baby,'' Luc explained. ''This is my niece. We're baby-sitting her for a short time.''

''Just baby-sitting,'' Grace confirmed. ''That's all we're doing.''

Mrs. Bumgartle looked from Luc to Grace, her gaze finally settling with needlepoint sharpness on Luc. ''You, Mr. Salvatore, are up to something,'' she said in clear, carrying tones. ''And I suspect it's nothing good.'' With that she disappeared back into her apartment.

Luc sighed in exasperation. ''Great. Just great. Open the door, Grace, and let's get out of the hallway before we wake up the entire apartment complex.''

''Here.'' Passing him the baby, Grace applied herself to the unyielding lock with due diligence. A moment later the door swung inward.

Grace held out her arms for Toni and stepped into Luc's apartment, fumbling for the light. Luc picked up the numerous bags of groceries and baby paraphernalia, kicked the spilled jars of baby food in the general direction of the entranceway and followed her in. He fought to close the door.

''You've left half the jars outside,'' she informed him.

''Since you're so certain we don't need any baby food, they can stay out there until I'm good and ready to go after them.'' His jaw inched out and he leaned down until his nose almost touched hers. ''You have a problem with that?''

''Not I,'' she was quick to assure him. ''Mrs. Bumgartle might, however.''

''You leave Mrs. Bumgartle to me,'' he said, dropping

his armload to the floor of the front hall. ''I'll talk to her.''

A tiny, unladylike snort escaped. ''Charm her you mean, like you do every other woman in the world? Or perhaps the operative word is *lie.*''

Luc merely glanced at her, then dug through their purchases until he uncovered the portable crib. It took him less than a minute to open it and settle Toni inside. He carried the baby into the living room, and there faced Grace. ''For your information, Miss Barnes, I never lie.''

''Oh, really? What do you call that story you told the police?''

''A truth-to-be,'' came the prompt reply. ''Because the truth is we are baby-sitting my niece. And the truth is Pietro and Carina will return for Toni. And the truth is they will soon be married or suffer the consequences.''

''What about our so-called engagement?''

He shook his head. ''I think we'll save that particular truth for a future discussion. I'm not proud of what I did today. But I considered it imperative. I hate lying and I hate liars....'' He seemed to watch her closely. ''Which is why I get along so well with you, Grace.''

A blush lit her face and she prayed he would attribute it to embarrassment rather than sudden, intense guilt. Because if he ever found out about her conspiracy with Dom, Luc would be very angry. It would also change everything between them, and she realized for the first time how much she'd hate that change. ''Luc—''

''As far as charming women,'' he interrupted ruthlessly, ''of course I'm charming to women. I told you. I love women. I adore women. They're easy to be charming to. What's wrong with that?''

She took a hasty step back. ''Noth-nothing.''

He swallowed the distance between them in one

stride. "If," he continued, his voice dipping low and taking on a raspy edge, "you weren't so cold and remote, I'd have been more charming to you, too. Only that and one other thing has held me back these past eleven months."

Grace swallowed nervously. "What's the one other thing?" she dared to ask.

"Your engagement," he responded promptly. "And do you know why?"

"No," she whispered.

He leaned forward, his eyes gleaming gold in the subdued lighting. "Because I don't poach." He took another step toward her and smiled, a predatory sort of smile. "Until now." And then he reached for her.

"No!" Grace shook her head frantically, pushing her hands against his chest. "You're only saying that to… to…"

Luc tilted his head to one side. "To what?"

To drive me crazy. To tempt me beyond endurance. "To…to give me a hard time," she insisted, leaping at the only safe excuse she could think of. "But it's not true. Maybe if I were beautiful like your other women—"

He cut through her words without hesitation. "All women are beautiful. Even women who hide behind these." He slipped off her glasses, dangling them carelessly from one finger.

"I need those!" She made a grab for the glasses, but he tossed them aside with casual disregard. They hit the soft cushions of the couch, bounced once and settled in the middle of the cushions, the lenses winking in the subdued lighting.

"You need them?" he asked and she couldn't mistake the irony in his voice.

Did he know? Did he suspect the glasses were part of her disguise? She didn't dare lie. Not when he watched her so closely. Not when she felt so vulnerable, stripped of the defenses she'd worked so long and hard to maintain between them. Instead, she fought his hold. "Luc, stop it!"

He didn't listen. Nor did he release her. "What I don't understand is why." His fingers slid into her hair, scattering the pins, the heavy curls tumbling free. "Why would a woman as beautiful as you..."

"No, don't!" She tried to step back, but he cupped her shoulders and refused to let go. To her horror, his hands drifted downward, gently tracing the curves hidden by her voluminous blouse and thick woolen skirt, before settling on her hips.

"...want to hide her light beneath a bushel?" he finished in satisfaction. "And you have been hiding your light, haven't you, my sweet? Is that Will-William's doing, I wonder?"

"Luc, please," she moaned, struggling to slip free.

He tightened his hold on her hips, yanking her closer. "You, *cara mia*, are stunning," he whispered, his mouth a hairbreadth away. "And for just this once, good old Will-William can go to hell."

CHAPTER FOUR

The Great Lie
Day 337 at 23 hours, 29 minutes...

LUC DIDN'T TRY to force a kiss on her as Grace half expected...half hoped. Instead his fingers combed through her loosened hair and he cupped her head, the rough edges of his thumb stroking a line of fire along her jaw. He bent closer, his rich golden eyes glowing with a fire and passion that trapped her, entangled her in a web of long-suppressed need and desire.

A small, still rational part of her knew she shouldn't be allowing this to happen. She should be resisting, fighting his touch...his hold...his charm. She was supposed to be an engaged woman, for heaven's sake. She couldn't allow Luc to believe she could be so easily seduced by a man other than her fiancé.

As though reading her mind, he brushed a swift, gentle kiss across her lips. ''Forget William. This has nothing to do with him. This is between the two of us, something that we've both been curious about for a long time.''

She shook her head. ''That's not true,'' she instantly denied.

''No?'' His expression mocked her. ''You've never thought about how it would feel to be held in my arms?''

''Never,'' she affirmed.

"You've never wondered how my kisses compare to William's?"

"I'm perfectly satisfied with my fiancé," she insisted, adding for good measure, "in every way."

He continued to hold her, his hands tangled in her hair, his thumb teasing along her jaw to the tiny pearl stud centered in her earlobe. "You're trembling."

"I'm cold."

"No, you're warm. And soft. And your cheeks..." He stroked the ridge of her cheekbone with his fingertip. "They're flushed with desire."

"That's makeup, not desire."

"You aren't wearing any makeup. At least, not blush." His voice dropped, seducing her with its deep, lilting timbre. "And what about your eyes? They're the most beautiful shade of green I've ever seen. But they give you away. They're glowing."

"They aren't glowing. They're glazed because I can't see without my glasses."

He laughed in genuine amusement, his smile a gleaming flash in his bronzed face. "You, Grace Barnes, are having a serious problem with fibs today. That'll have to stop—and I know just how to make sure it does."

She knew what he intended. He was going to kiss her. And when he did, she wouldn't have the strength to resist. "Luc, don't," she pleaded, attempting one last time to prevent the inevitable. "You'll regret it. We'll both regret it."

He shrugged, his smile fading, his expression turning serious. "You may be right, but at least let me give us something worthy of regret." His thumb drifted across her lower lip, teasing the fullness of her mouth for an instant before he lowered his head and finally kissed her.

It was magic. The instant his lips touched hers, her

heartbeat doubled. She couldn't get enough, every sense throbbing to life, the blood singing through her veins. She could smell his distinctive spicy scent, feel the hard planes and angles of his body beneath her hands, hear the sound of his harsh breathing whispering in her ears. Even the taste of him intoxicated her, the sweet, delicious flavor driving all reason from her mind and leaving in its place pure sensation.

His hand slid down her spine, his arm wrapping around her waist and pulling her up against him. She fit perfectly. But somehow she'd always suspected she would. Unable to help herself, she wound her arms around his neck and returned his kiss.

It had been a long time since she'd last been in a man's arms. Too long. She'd forgotten how wonderful it could be. Yet this was different…and the difference unsettled her. There was a peculiar combination of finding both sanctuary and jeopardy within Luc's arms, of knowing both security and vulnerability. He was at once a delight and a threat. Worst of all, he was a temptation—a temptation she couldn't afford to indulge in.

As though sensing her alarm, Toni began to cry. It was a timely interruption. Grace pulled free of Luc's arms and knelt beside the portable crib. Scooping up the baby, she turned to face the picture windows, her back to Luc.

She could see his image mirrored in the plate glass. His hands balled into fists, his chest rising and falling with each ragged breath. So…she hadn't been the only one affected. That knowledge didn't bring her any relief. Instead, her alarm grew. The path they walked led to disaster, and she had too much at stake to follow blindly along. She had to end this before it went any further.

"I'll change Toni and then it's time I went home," she announced in a calm, unemotional voice.

"Feel free to change her," Luc agreed, coming up behind and dropping his hands to her shoulders. "But you aren't going anywhere. Not tonight and not tomorrow night, either."

She didn't dare turn around. She knew from long experience what that tone meant, heard the determination and the intensity that roughened his voice. She'd never yet won an argument when he spoke like that. Still, she had to try.

"You can handle Toni on your own. You don't need me. I'll return first thing in the morning—"

His hands tightened and he forced her to face him. "No. You promised to stay until Pietro or Carina returned, and I intend to hold you to that promise."

She'd also promised his father she wouldn't become personally involved with Luc. Seemed her promises weren't worth a plugged nickel these days. "Luc... It isn't right that I stay. It's not—"

"Proper?" He laughed, the sound harsh and empty of humor. "Do you think I give a damn about what's proper? I care about that baby you're holding. I care about doing what's best for her. What I know about infants can be summed up in one word. *Niente.* Nothing."

She frowned. "I don't know much more than you. Besides, you've learned the essentials today. You know how to change her, how to feed her. Surely you can get through one night without me."

A strange look glittered in his eyes. "I might. But why should I? I want you here, right beside me, helping to make sensible decisions."

"Hire a professional nanny," she suggested in desperation.

He shook his head. "Too risky. I don't want to chance the police becoming involved again. It's only for another day or two. Soon Pietro and Carina will return for Toni and everything will be back to normal."

Grace cuddled Toni close, inhaling the sweet aroma of powder and formula and baby. Things would never return to normal. Her life had been irreversibly altered. She could only hope it would all work out in the end. That Pietro and Carina would return. That Toni would be reunited with her parents. That Luc could be held at a safe distance. And that Dom would never learn of her brief indiscretion.

But most of all she hoped she could escape with a whole heart, that her brush with insanity wouldn't have any lasting repercussions. Because she knew that when it came to women, Luc couldn't be trusted. Besides, she had a dream to fulfill, a promise to keep. She wouldn't allow Luc or anyone else to distract her from her goal.

"I won't touch you again tonight," Luc said unexpectedly. "You'll be safe here with me. I swear it."

Safe? Not likely. She glanced down at Toni and her shoulders sagged. She really didn't have any choice, she realized. If she hadn't been able to abandon the baby earlier, she certainly couldn't do it now. What she could do was make sure that she didn't share any further intimacies with Luc. She'd hold him at a distance. She could do it. She'd had more than eleven months of practice accomplishing precisely that. The few weeks left would be a cinch.

"All right, I'll stay," she agreed.

Satisfaction glittered in his eyes. "You can sleep in one of my shirts. And I'll bring you a spare robe and a toothbrush. There are only two bedrooms. Do you want the baby tonight or should I take her in with me?"

"I'll care for her tonight, and you can have tomorrow," she said, her reply conceding that there would be a tomorrow night.

He nodded. "Fine. There's a bathroom that adjoins the guest bedroom. If you'd like to grab a shower, I'll watch the little stinker."

"Stinker?" A tiny smile escaped before she could prevent it. "Diapers are in the hall."

With that, she headed for the bathroom. In minutes she stood beneath a hot, relaxing deluge, rinsing away the tension of an unbelievably stressful day. Wishing she could stand there forever, she squared her shoulders, took a deep breath and reluctantly turned the shower off. Returning to the bedroom, she found a silk shirt and robe spread out on the bed.

Dressing quickly, she brushed her wet hair. She'd have to get another bottle of color rinse and soon. Already she could see the natural gold gleaming through the muddy brown dye. Another shampoo or two and this part of her disguise would be uncovered, as well. And what would Luc say then?

She shuddered. It didn't bear contemplation.

A soft knock sounded on the door. "You decent?" Luc called. At her affirmative response, he came in carrying Toni. "I've changed her and offered a bottle. She didn't seem very interested. If you'll take her, I'll bring in the portable crib."

In short order, he had them settled for the night. Grace stood in the middle of the room, uncomfortable beneath Luc's watchful eye. From the expression on his face she was fairly certain her disguise was shot to pieces. Not that it hadn't been when he kissed her…touched her. He had to have realized that she wore clothing several sizes too big. Standing before him now, wearing nothing but a clingy shirt and a silk paisley robe, there must be no doubt in his mind.

"Is there anything else you need?" he asked softly.

She shook her head, the damp curls swirling about her neck and shoulders. "Nothing, thanks. I'll...I'll see you in the morning."

"No question about it. But if you do need anything—" He grinned. "Anything at all, don't hesitate to come and get me."

She lifted her chin and gave him a cool look. "I can cope."

"Goodnight, then." He started to close the door, then stuck his head back in. "Oh, and Grace?"

She stared at him warily. "Yes?"

"I notice you seem to see just fine without those glasses. A miracle cure, perhaps?"

The door banged closed behind him and Grace let out a small groan of despair. How could she have been so foolish? And what must he be thinking? Perhaps she could tell him her eyes were sensitive to light. Perhaps she could say that the doctor prescribed tinted glasses to prevent eyestrain.

She sighed. Perhaps she should dispense with all the lies and hope something could be salvaged from this mess. She glanced over at Toni. The baby slept soundly, her rounded bottom thrust high in the air, a chubby fist pressed against her puckered mouth. Tucking the blanket securely around her tiny form, Grace crossed to her own bed, slipped beneath the covers and turned off the bedside lamp.

Moonlight brightened the room and she folded her arms behind her head, studying the ceiling. Here she was, bedding down for the night in Luc's apartment. If

Dom ever found out, he'd have a coronary. She yawned. She'd just have to make sure that he never did.

More important, she'd have to make sure that Luc never found out she wasn't really engaged. Somehow, she suspected that if he did she'd find herself in deep, deep trouble. And not just for having lied to him. That kiss had been a mistake. A big mistake. A mistake she had no intention of ever repeating.

Four more weeks to get through.

All of a sudden, it seemed a lifetime.

A THUMP SOUNDED SOMEWHERE deep in the apartment and Grace rolled over, glaring at the clock on the nightstand. It couldn't be three in the morning. It couldn't be. She hadn't slept a wink. This was all Luc's fault. He had to have the noisiest apartment in the entire complex. Every little sound made her jump. Worse, it made Toni jump. Whenever the baby had been on the verge of drifting off, some tiny noise would wake her and she'd start to fuss.

Right on cue, a pitiful wail rose from the far side of the room and Grace groaned. Struggling out of bed, she shoved a tumble of curls from her eyes and approached the crib.

''I'm coming, munchkin,'' she muttered. ''Keep your diapers on.'' Toni lay on her back, her covers kicked off, her feet pumping like a crazed locomotive. Two chubby fists pinwheeled the air. Grace eyed the activity with deep suspicion. ''You do that to help suck in more air, don't you?'' she asked the red-faced infant. ''And once you're finished inhaling, out it all comes in one huge bellow. Right?''

Not giving Toni time to vent her agreement, Grace picked up the baby and slipped from the room. Where had Luc left the diapers and bottles? To her relief, the diapers were in plain sight in the living room. She found bottles of formula already mixed in the refrigerator. A short spin in the microwave warmed the milk to the perfect temperature.

Returning to the living room, Grace drew a chair over to the picture window and settled into it, Toni nestled in the crook of her arm. San Francisco glittered before her. Even at three in the morning, the city seemed alive with lights and movement.

A nearly full moon hung in the sky, the light spilling through the window, bathing the room in its silver glow. Grace stared down at Toni. With her flushed olive skin and huge dark eyes, she was the most adorable creature Grace had ever seen. How could Carina bear to be separated from this precious bundle for even one tiny moment? It must have been pure agony for her to make such a decision.

And what about being twenty, a foreign-exchange student and an unwed mother? In all likelihood, poor Carina hadn't dared go home to face her parents with the results of her indiscretion. She'd apparently been just as reluctant to turn to Pietro for help, though the reason for that wasn't quite as clear. Of course, if Pietro was half the womanizer Luc was, Grace could understand Carina's reluctance. And yet…

Grace frowned. Somehow, she couldn't see Luc abandoning his lover in her time of need, let alone his child. Nor could she imagine him leaving any woman in the lurch—he cared about them too deeply. Unfortunately, he cared too deeply about all women to ever settle on any one. Still…

She knew Luc. He would have done everything in his power to prevent an accident like Pietro and Carina's from occurring in the first place. But if it had, he would have taken on the responsibility of both mother and child. She didn't doubt that for one minute. And wasn't that just what Pietro was attempting to do? Perhaps it was a Salvatore trait.

Grace gazed down at the baby in her arms, filled with an overwhelming desire to protect this child. She could fully understand Luc's determination to keep Toni safe. In less than twenty-four hours, she'd grown impossibly attached to Toni, herself. She could even imagine having a baby like this one. She could imagine the father, too.

There was just one catch. She wanted a man who would love her exclusively, who'd choose her above all other women and never once look back. She bit down on her lip, tears stinging her eyes. That man wouldn't be Luc. Not a chance. She stared out the window, and suddenly her reflection was joined by another and Luc crossed to her side.

"Everything all right?" he asked in a soft voice, stooping beside the chair.

"Everything's fine." She bowed her head, embarrassed to be caught with tears in her eyes. She hadn't realized how much she depended on her tinted glasses to conceal her thoughts and emotions from him. Come morning, those glasses would once again be perched on the end of her nose. "Toni woke up hungry and wet."

Luc's mouth curved into a wry smile. "Even with only a single day's experience of baby care, I've discovered they have a nasty tendency to do that." He eyed Grace closely. "You look tired. Want me to take over for a while?"

Her throat tightened and she shook her head. "I'm fine," she managed to say. He reached out and tucked a curl behind her ear, his touch unexpectedly gentle and soothing.

"You don't sound fine. You sound exhausted." His hand moved from her hair to her shoulder, massaging the tense muscles along the back of her neck. "It's going to work out, Grace. I know everything looks a bit bleak now—"

"What if she doesn't come back?" The question practically burst from Grace. "What if she abandons Toni?"

He didn't hesitate for an instant. "Then Pietro will take care of his daughter. And we'll work it out somehow." He seemed so strong, so resolute. "This baby's a Salvatore. And I'll do everything within my power to protect her."

She didn't doubt him. "Your family's lucky to have you to watch out for them," she told Luc quietly.

"And your fiancé's lucky to have you. Not many women would have done what you did today."

A tiny smile touched her mouth and she glanced at him. "Was there a choice?"

He didn't return her smile. Instead his gaze was filled with an intensity that unnerved her. "Yes. You had a choice. You could have walked. You could have told me to go to hell. But you didn't. You stuck by me, Grace. That means a lot."

His thick, dark hair tumbled across his brow and a shadow of stubble clung to his jaw. He'd thrown on a robe not unlike the one he'd loaned her, and she suspected he wore little or nothing beneath it. The robe veed deeply and she could see the crisp, dark hair covering his chest. For a crazy instant she almost reached out and touched him.

She closed her eyes. It was late. She was tired. And

he attracted her more than any man she'd ever known. "Luc, you have to leave now," she whispered.

Turning to him, she saw the passion spark to life in his eyes, saw the hint of a flush mount his angled cheekbones. "You look very beautiful sitting in the moonlight," he murmured. "It streaks your hair with shiny gold threads."

She froze. "A trick of the light," she insisted. "Go to bed, Luc. Please. You promised."

"I promised I wouldn't kiss you again last night. But I didn't make any promises about today. And in case you hadn't noticed, this is a brand-new day. Nor did I promise I wouldn't sit in the moonlight with you. That I wouldn't talk to you. That I wouldn't watch you hold Toni as if she were your own."

His every word seduced her. She turned her head away, turned from near overwhelming temptation. "You're forgetting about my fiancé."

"No, I'm not. But perhaps you should forget about him. He isn't good enough for you. Not if he encourages you to wear those ridiculous outfits and scrape your hair back instead of leaving it loose around your face. You're so beautiful, Grace. And hiding that beauty is a sin."

The bottle empty, Grace lifted Toni to her shoulder and patted the infant's back, using this moment to gather the remaining shreds of her composure. At last she forced herself to say, "Luc, I'm your assistant. I'm engaged to be married. You asked for my help and I'm helping you. Don't make this more difficult than necessary. I'm not interested in having a...a relationship with you. I have William." For the first time she got that name out without stammering. "He's all I need. All I'll ever need."

She might as well have struck Luc. He reared back,

and without another word he stood and walked away. For an insane instant, Grace considered following him, confessing the truth. But she knew she couldn't. She couldn't afford to become emotionally involved with Luc. Not if she wanted her own business. And not if she wanted to come out of this situation with her heart intact.

"RISE AND SHINE!" Grace rolled over and groaned, flinging an arm across her face to block out the blinding sunlight. "Go away," she snarled.

Luc chuckled. "I have coffee," he tempted.

She peeked out from beneath her elbow. "Coffee?"

"A cup for now and a whole fresh-brewed pot waiting in the kitchen."

She sat up and looked over at the crib. It was empty. "Where's Toni?"

"On a blanket in the living room shaking her fist at dust motes." He headed for the door. "We have a lot to do today, so hurry up and get dressed."

Drawing her knees to her chest, she said, "I don't have anything clean to wear."

"We'll stop by your apartment on the way to the stores. You can change and pack a few days' worth of clothes."

She eyed him suspiciously. "A few days?"

"A few days," he confirmed. "Pietro called." And with that he breezed from the room.

It took ten minutes to pull herself together. The coffee helped substantially. After locating her glasses on the living room couch and popping them on the end of her nose, she swept the carpet for her scattered hairpins and pocketed them. Reluctant to face reality—even more reluctant to hear what Pietro had to say when he'd called, she played with Toni for a while. Eventually, hunger forced her to track Luc down in the kitchen. Open confrontation seemed the best course of action.

"What do you mean a few days?" she demanded, jumping right in. "What did Pietro say?"

"He missed connecting with Carina in Italy. Her mother is being seen by a specialist in Switzerland, and Carina went there. Pietro's following."

"Did you tell him about the police? Did you tell him we haven't a clue how to take care of a baby? When's he coming back?"

"Yes. Yes. And as soon as possible." Luc ran a hand through his hair, an edge of impatience creeping into his voice. "You're upset about this, and so am I. But there isn't anything I can do about it. Not yet. So let's make the best of things."

Right. Until the police showed up. Or worse, Dom. And then Luc's clever, little scheme would come crashing down around both their ears. And so would Dom's... She tried to stay calm. Shrieking wouldn't accomplish a thing. Except make her feel a whole heck of a lot better. She took a deep breath, wavering between anger and capitulation. "What's your plan of action?" she finally asked, giving in to the inevitable. At least, with Luc, it was the inevitable.

"First we go to your apartment. Then we go shopping for Toni. I've called in at the office and had everything postponed for a few days. In the meantime..." He brandished the coffeepot. "Let me pour you more coffee. There's cereal for breakfast or I can scramble you some eggs."

"Cereal," she informed him coolly. "I can't face anything yellow first thing in the morning."

Once they'd eaten, they began to prepare for their outing. Getting ready to leave took longer than Grace ever could have thought possible. Packing the diaper bag alone was a major undertaking. "Diapers. Check. Wipes. Check. Powder. Check. Spare clothes. Check. More diapers. Double check."

"You forgot the bottles and formula."

She glared at Luc in exasperation. "Then you better get a second diaper bag, because nothing else will fit in here."

"How about a cooler for the formula?"

"Terrific. One more thing to carry. And how are we supposed to heat the bottles?"

"In a microwave, of course."

Keeping her temper while working for Luc, day after day, had proved a challenge. Keeping her temper while stuck with him day in and day out was an impossibility. She planted her hands on her hips. "A microwave? Were you planning on bringing that along with us, too?"

"That won't be necessary. Everyone has microwaves. We'll just ask to borrow somebody's." He slung the diaper bag over one shoulder, picked up the cooler and his jacket and headed for the door. "Come on, Grace. It's getting late and we have a lot to do today."

She folded her arms across her chest. "Aren't you forgetting something?"

He glanced around. "Diaper bag, cooler, jacket, changing pad and a garbage bag for dirty diapers. Nope. Got it all."

Grace sighed. "Everything except the baby. Why don't I take care of that?"

Thirty minutes later, they'd crossed the Bay Bridge out of San Francisco and reached the small apartment Grace rented on the Oakland-Berkeley line. A short walk from BART, the electric railway, it was an easy commute to work each day and much less expensive than living in the city.

"I'll just run upstairs and pack a bag," she suggested. "Why don't you wait here with Toni."

To her dismay Luc released his seat belt, climbed out of the car and calmly unfastened the baby from her car seat. "Toni would like to see your apartment and so would I. Besides, I want to make sure you don't pack any of William's clothes."

She stared at him in confusion. "William's clothes?"

"Two sizes too large and three decades too old."

Having no choice, she led the way to her door. "Make yourself at home," she said with more than a hint of irony. "I'll go pack."

In the bedroom, she yanked a small cloth suitcase down from the shelf in her closet and began tossing in the essentials. A minute later, Luc and Toni appeared at the door.

And in Luc's hand was her third-place award for Salvatore's young-entrepreneur contest.

He held it up, his eyes cool and watchful. "What's this, Grace?"

CHAPTER FIVE

The Great Lie
Day 338 and Grace's disguise is slipping…

CROSSING TO LUC'S side, Grace took the award from him and placed it on her bureau. "You know what it is."

"You're right, I do. I guess my question is, what are you doing with it?"

Returning to her packing, she carefully folded a blouse and tucked it into the suitcase. "I think that's obvious, too. I won it."

"In this past year's contest?"

"Why the questions, Luc?" she snapped. "What's the problem? Yes. I won third place in this past year's contest. As a result, I met Dom."

"And?"

"And," she finished impatiently, "he thought highly enough of me to recommend me for the job as your assistant. I thought you knew all that."

"No. I didn't."

He frowned, his gaze searching, and she glanced hastily away. But it was too late. He suspected she was hiding something, and knowing Luc he wouldn't leave it alone until he'd settled the issue to his satisfaction. She could practically see the wheels turning as he mulled over what he perceived to be a puzzle.

"Let's try this tack and see if it gets us anywhere..." he began. "*Why* did you take the job as my assistant?"

"This is ridiculous. I took the job for the same reason millions of people all over the world take jobs." Using less than her usual care, she balled up another blouse and thrust it into the suitcase. She just wanted to end this conversation and get out of here before she did something...said something...incriminating. "I needed to earn money."

"Yes, but contestants who enter the young-entrepreneur contest are interested in starting their own business, not working for someone else."

"What's your point, Luc?" There was an edge to her voice.

His eyes narrowed. "Are you? Interested in starting your own business?"

She couldn't lie. She'd told him enough of those already without making it any worse. Looking directly at him, she said, "Yes. I'm interested in *someday* starting my own business. In the meantime, working for you should be good experience."

He settled Toni in the crook of his arm and propped a shoulder against the doorjamb. "And has it been? Has working for me been good?"

She turned back to her packing. They continued to tread on dangerous ground—different ground, perhaps, but dangerous, nonetheless. "Yes. It's been good," she agreed shortly. In fact, it had been more than good. Working for Luc had been surprisingly enjoyable. She'd thrived on the challenges, appreciated the fast pace. She'd even relished their heated arguments. She frowned. She'd miss all that when she left.

"What sort of business do you plan to open?" he asked.

She glanced hesitantly at him. Would he laugh when she told him? ''It'll be a toy store. One that specializes in babies. All the toys will be unique—handcrafted by local artisans, educational and safe.'' Her mother had always insisted on that.

He glanced down at Toni, a smile curving the corner of his mouth. ''Seems we picked the perfect woman to help us, after all.'' He approached, his movements lithe and graceful. ''Here. Take the kid.''

She obeyed without thought. Not until he turned and began to rummage through her suitcase, did she realize his motives for handing her the baby. ''Cut that out, Luc! You have no right going through my things.''

''I just want to make sure what you pack is practical.'' He yanked out the skirt and blouse she'd just shoved in. ''Which this is not,'' he decided, and reached for the next garment. ''Nor is this.''

''Stop that! Those are eminently practical and you know it.''

''Practical for the office, not for taking care of a baby.'' He glanced at a skirt label. ''This has to be dry-cleaned. One good burp and it's history.''

''Luc!'' Toni's little face screwed into a frown and Grace quickly moderated her tone to reflect sweetness and light. ''Let me put it this way. You take one more item out of my suitcase, and I'll kill you.'' Too bad her glasses hid the glare she shot in his direction—not that he was looking anyway.

''As long as we're dispensing with the impractical, I think we'll dispense with the ugly, as well,'' he said, ignoring her threat. Clothes flew through the air and landed on the bed. ''Ugly. Impractical. Ugly. Ugly. And very ugly. Don't you get depressed wearing this stuff?''

''No, I don't.'' At least, not often. Dom's promised

reward offered more than adequate compensation. She scowled in impotent fury. "And what difference does it make if they're ugly? They don't belong to you."

He glanced up, a dangerous glitter in his golden eyes. "They may not belong to me, but I have to look at them. And so does Toni. I won't have you around my niece day and night, displaying such a lack of fashion taste. It'll warp her. Hell, it's already warped me."

"That's ridiculous!"

"Want to bet?" he asked derisively. "It's gotten so bad, I've begun to think brown is pretty. At least on you." Finished with the suitcase, he headed for her closet.

She looked about, desperate for a safe place to deposit the baby so she could stop him—physically, if necessary. "What are you doing now? Get out of there!"

"Hello. What's this?" He yanked free a mint green dress. "Ah, much better. Do you save this for when William's here...?" He lifted an eyebrow, his expression turning wicked. "Or perhaps it's to wear when William isn't around."

"William loves that dress!" she protested, then blinked. What the dickens was she saying?

"Sure he does. That's why he has you running about looking like a bag lady most of the time. That's one sick relationship you have going there."

"My relationship with Will...William is none of your concern." How she wished she could get that name past her lips without stammering. Unfortunately, nine times out of ten it wouldn't come.

"Your relationship with him isn't my concern...yet. But, give it time."

Grace stared in alarm. What did he mean? That at some point her relationship with William would become his concern? And precisely what did he have in mind, once it did? Confronting the nonexistent William? A tightness settled in her chest. Matters grew more complicated by the minute.

Rummaging through what she privately referred to as her off-duty clothing, he stripped a pair of soft rose-colored slacks, black stretch pants and several brightly patterned pullover sweaters from their hangers and dropped them into her suitcase. After a moment's consideration, he added a totally impractical white slip dress with a bolero jacket to the pile.

"What's that for?" she demanded.

"For the hell of it."

Clearly, nothing she could say would stop him. She hugged Toni to her breast. "Are you quite through?"

"No. Where are your cosmetics?" He crossed to her dresser. "Never mind. I've found them."

"I can do that," she insisted.

His response sounded suspiciously like a snort. He rifled through the bottles and tubes cluttering the tabletop with a knowledge and decisiveness that could only have come from long experience—a fact that didn't escape her. Clearly, he was familiar with women. With everything about women. But then, she'd long suspected that when it came to the fairer sex, Luc was an expert.

"Fascinating colors here," he said in disgust. "Not one of them suits you. Except… Here we go." He swept foundation, blush, eye shadow, mascara and lipstick into a cosmetic bag and tossed it into her suitcase. Then he turned and folded his arms across his chest. "What's going on, Grace?"

She shoved her glasses high up on the bridge of her nose and cuddled Toni close, as if for protection. "I don't know what you're talking about,'' she claimed. But they both knew she lied.

He lifted an eyebrow, his expression sardonic. ''Oh, no? Two separate wardrobes. Two distinct sets of cosmetics. And you have no comment?''

''Right. I have no comment.''

The dangerous light reappeared in his eyes. ''You have no comment…yet.''

She swallowed. There was that word again. ''Yet?''

He crossed to stand directly in front of her. ''Yet. It implies a temporary situation.'' He leaned down until they were almost nose to nose. ''One that *will* change in the near future. Are we clear on that?''

She took a hasty step backward. ''Crystal.''

''Fine.'' He turned to her suitcase and zipped the bag closed. ''Just so you know, I'm taking this new Grace home with me. I've had the other at the office for quite long enough.'' He lifted the suitcase off the bed and eased Toni from her arms. ''Get changed and meet me down at the car. Next stop—Toys-a-Trillion.''

She didn't dare say another word. He was letting her off easy and she knew it. She also didn't doubt for one little minute that he'd eventually ask some pointed questions. She nibbled her lower lip. What would she say when he demanded answers? The thought of telling him the truth about her ''deal'' with Dom appalled her.

It had all seemed so simple and harmless when the idea had first been proposed. But now… Luc would not react well if he found out. And the chances of his uncovering the truth were becoming more and more likely. Which made her dream of starting her own business more and more *un*likely.

She didn't waste any time. Stripping off her dirty clothes, she rushed through her shower. Next came a hasty debate over whether to wear off-duty clothes or office clothing. Wrapped in a wet towel, she stood shivering in front of her closet considering her choices—not that her decision took a lot of thought. Office won, hands down. Whether it was a perverse gesture on her part or a desperate need to cling to what camouflage she could, Grace couldn't say. But the bulky wool suit in a nondescript shade of gray gave her back a sense of security she hadn't experienced since Toni had fallen into their lives. Gathering up a fistful of pins, she slicked back her damp hair and skewered the wayward curls into a tight, forbidding knot at the nape of her neck. She still hadn't acquired any more dye, nor did she have any extra bottles stashed at the apartment. Already bright gold streaks could be detected beneath the mousy brown rinse. How long would it be before Luc noticed—assuming he hadn't already?

Disguise somewhat in place, she left her apartment. Joining Luc in the car, she glanced anxiously at him to see how he reacted to her costume. Aside from sparing her a quick glance of amusement, he didn't say a word. Instead, he put the car in motion.

It took them another half hour to drive to the toy store. Located in the East Bay near a mall, the huge barn of a building contained every imaginable toy ever invented. Grace looked around in bewilderment. She'd never seen so many toys. And the setup! Some insane person had stacked the inventory from the floor to the thirty-foot ceiling. How in the world could anyone possibly obtain, let alone purchase the higher-altitude items? Crazed kids raced up and down the aisles scrambling through the displays, harried mothers in hot pursuit. One ambitious youngster busily climbed the shelving above her head.

She turned to Luc. ''Get the manager before that child kills himself,'' she ordered.

Luc simply grinned. ''Be glad it isn't closer to Christmas. This place turns into a real zoo, then.''

''You've been here before?'' she asked in astonishment.

''Of course. Haven't you?''

''No,'' she admitted, eyeing the determined climber. ''And if I'm very lucky, I never will again.''

''Don't be such a spoilsport.'' He reached above her, plucked the squirming youngster off the shelf and set him on the floor. Hollering in protest, the boy rounded a corner and disappeared from view. ''I do all my Christmas shopping here. My brothers count on it.''

''Your brothers are grown men,'' she informed him.

''Yes, but they're kids at heart. And they like toys.'' He grabbed a cart. ''Let's get down to business. Follow me.''

''Where are you going?'' Without answering, he headed toward the middle of the store. Grace scurried behind. She'd be lost in here for the next five months, if she didn't keep up with him.

Presently he stopped in the infant department. ''Take a look at these. Baby pouches.'' Without further ado, he ripped a carton apart, removed the pouch and tossed the empty box in the shopping basket. ''Let's try it on for size.''

''Luc!'' she exclaimed, appalled. ''You can't do that. They'll arrest you for shoplifting or something.''

He shot her a look of disapproval. ''Shoplifting implies leaving without paying for something. I would never do such a thing. The box is in my cart, plain as day. And I have an eager little plastic gold card revving in my pocket.''

"But—"

"Relax, Gracie. They know me here." He frowned at the sling, examining it from various angles. "How the hell does this thing work?"

"Maybe if we read the directions?" she suggested.

"Directions are for amateurs."

"We *are* amateurs," she reminded gently. She picked up the box. "It looks like you fasten the two top straps around your neck and the bottom two around your waist."

"I know that! But it doesn't show which is the top and which is the bottom. Wait a sec… Got it." He fastened the belts and snaps and grinned, spreading his arms wide. "What do you think? Is Toni ready for her first ride?"

Grace bit her lip to keep from smiling. "No."

He frowned. "No?"

"You put her in there the way it is now and you'll dump your precious niece right on her cute little head."

He peered down at the pouch. Sure enough, the opening for the head pointed south, the leg holes pointed north. "Well, shoot," he muttered, nonplussed.

A salesgirl appeared at his elbow, white teeth flashing, lashes fluttering. She flipped her long bleached hair over one shoulder and planted a hand on her trim hip. Her name tag read, "Hi! Debbi can't wait to assist you!"

"Why, Mr. Salvatore," Debbi-who-couldn't-wait-to-assist squealed. At least it sounded like a squeal to Grace…a squeal reminiscent of those emitted by the porcine family. "You haven't visited for ages. Is there something I can help you with?"

He gestured at the baby sling strapped to his chest. "What am I doing wrong?" he asked with a helpless, men-are-all-thumbs-when-it-comes-to-baby-contraptions grin.

"You put it on upside down," Grace pointed out acerbically.

Debbi pursed her lips. "I think you put it on upside down," she proclaimed, as if she'd just invented the thought.

Removing the sling, she flipped it around and then refastened it. In the process her hands managed to investigate every square inch of Luc's torso. Clearly satisfied with the results of her investigation and with the position of the sling, she gave the pouch a final pat.

Unable…or unwilling…to explain her reaction to dear Debbi, Grace stepped forward the second the salesgirl stepped back. But helping Luc slip Toni into the sling while at the same time doing her level best to flash her engagement ring under Debbi's nose proved to be a challenge she couldn't resist. "That's perfect," she announced and even managed a friendly smile in the salesgirl's direction. "Antonia's the first Salvatore girl in…how many generations, Luc?"

"A lot."

"The family's thrilled. Absolutely thrilled. Aren't they, Luc?"

He lifted a quizzical eyebrow. "Oh, they're thrilled, all right."

The salesgirl looked from Luc to Antonia to Grace to Grace's ring and sighed. "How…how thrilling. Well, if I can help you with anything else, don't hesitate to call."

"Oh, we will," Grace assured her. Yes, they'd definitely hesitate before calling. "Bye."

With a final, wistful glance in Luc's direction, Debbi trotted down the aisle.

"Grace…Grace…Grace," Luc murmured, shaking

his head, his golden eyes glittering with laughter. ''What has happened to my cool, aloof assistant?''

She lifted her chin. ''I haven't a clue what you're talking about.'' A long moment of silence stretched between them, and she could feel the hot color mount her cheeks. Desperate to escape his probing gaze, she made a pretence of checking to be sure Toni rested comfortably in the sling. Not that she fooled anyone. The baby, tucked close to Luc's heart, slept peacefully in her little pouch.

''What's next on the list?'' Grace asked, unable to stand the strained silence for another instant.

''You.''

Her eyes widened and she took a hasty step back. ''Wh-what?''

He cupped her elbow in one hand and pushed the cart with his other. ''All good temporary mothers need a stroller. So next we get you a stroller.'' He eyed her, a wicked grin curving his mouth. ''What did you think I meant?''

She cleared her throat. ''Why, precisely that, of course.''

He released a gusty sigh. ''I see you haven't used them all up.''

She gave him a suspicious look. ''Used up what?''

''Your quota of fibs.''

With that, he headed toward the center of the store, where racks of strollers were displayed. He tried several models, pushing them about, cornering sharply to see if they tipped. He even pulled down a double stroller for inspection.

''We only have one baby,'' Grace pointed out.

''With all the junk she needs, we could use the other side for storage.''

Actually, he had a point. "What about the one over here? It's dual purpose. You can hook the two strollers together to form a double or separate them into individual units."

"Sold." He removed a large box from the shelves and fitted it into the cart. "Now for the serious stuff." He grinned down at her. "Toys."

Two hours...and three carts later, Grace decided to call a halt to his shopping binge. "This is ridiculous, Luc. The baby can't use a tenth of what you're buying. It'll go to waste."

"Don't fuss," Luc replied, swooping up a dozen rattles. "Anything Carina and the baby can't use, I'll donate to charity. Relax and enjoy yourself. Spend some of my money. Better yet, spend a lot of my money. I'm having fun. Aren't you having fun?"

"Yes, but..."

"Then, not another word of argument." He leaned closer, his eyes dark and intent. "I'm tired of the 'office Grace,'" he murmured. "Send her home and let the other Grace come out and play. The one who wears pale green dresses that match her eyes and tight stretch pants with soft wool sweaters. I want to get to know that Grace."

She shook her head, suddenly afraid. She was out of her depth and knew it. All her lies were steadily unraveling and soon she'd be exposed and vulnerable. She didn't dare consider what might happen then....

To her relief, Toni chose that moment to put an end to both their conversation and the shopping spree. Finished with her nap, she began to complain bitterly and at great volume at being trapped for so long in the baby sling.

"Time for a bottle, young lady," Grace decreed, lifting her off Luc's chest. ''If you'll let me have the diaper bag, Luc, I'll go feed and change Toni while you give your credit card a workout.''

''I checked and there's a microwave in the employee lounge. They won't mind you heating up Toni's bottle there. I'll come and get you once I've loaded the car.''

Grace glanced at the overflowing carts and grimaced. ''Now I know why families buy those huge vans when they start having kids.''

Luc snapped his fingers. ''Vans. That's what I forgot to buy. Let's see... I think they're over on aisle eight next to the Lear jets.''

''Very funny.'' Grace rocked the tearful Toni, gently patting her back. ''We girls will be in the lounge with our feet up enjoying a warm mug of formula. See you in a while.''

To her surprise, Luc joined them a few minutes later. Though why it should surprise her, she didn't know. She suspected the powers-that-be at Toys-a-Trillion tended to jump through hoops when Luc Salvatore walked into their store—especially if he was in the habit of spending as much as he had today. By the time she'd finished with Toni, the most important of their selections were paid for and loaded in the car, the rest to be delivered the next day. It amazed her what charm and money could accomplish.

Having fastened Toni into her car seat, Grace buckled her own seat belt and sighed. ''I need to get back to work so I can rest,'' she joked.

''You can rest tonight. I've invited my brothers over for dinner, and you can relax while they entertain Toni.''

She glanced over at him. ''Do they know about her?''

He started the engine and pulled out of the parking space. ''I thought I'd surprise them. That way I can impress on them the importance of keeping this information quiet until Pietro and Carina return.''

''And do your brothers always fall in with your demands?''

He inclined his head. ''They tend to find it in their best interest to do things my way.''

''Because you're the oldest?''

He grinned. ''That, and the fact that I'm their boss. He who controls the purse strings...''

''Calls the tune?''

''The metaphor may be mixed, but the meaning's accurate enough.''

Accurate, indeed. She nibbled her lip. If she were smart, she'd do well to remember who called the tune she danced to...and who controlled the future purse strings for Baby Dream Toys.

''GRACE! That's the doorbell. Could you get it? I'm up to my elbows in...in...in real nasty stuff.''

Crossing to the front hall, she opened the door. All four of Luc and Pietro's brothers stood grouped in the hallway arguing volubly. ''Ten bucks, it's good news.''

''Fifteen, it's bad.''

''Twenty to one, he's gone and got himself engaged.''

''Not Luc. Not a chance. I'll bet twenty-five dollars you're all wrong.''

The door across the hall opened and Mrs. Bumgartle peered out. ''What's going on there? Who's gambling?''

''Hello, Mrs. Bumgartle,'' the four chorused a greeting.

''Don't give me any of your lip,'' she retorted. ''Gambling's illegal in this state, you know.''

''It's just a friendly wager,'' Alessandro assured her. ''Just trying to figure out what Luc's up to.''

''He's up to no good. No good a'tall,'' she snapped. ''Now, stop cluttering the hall, or I'll call the building manager.'' With that, the door banged closed.

Grace cleared her throat. ''Would you gentlemen care to come in?''

''Oh, hello, Grace,'' Alessandro said, leading the way into the apartment. ''Something special going on?''

''No cheating!'' the twins, Marc and Stef, exclaimed in unison.

''And no fair pumping Grace,'' Rocco added with a wink, giving her a brotherly peck on the cheek. ''Anyone else here?'' he whispered in her ear.

''Just Antonia,'' she whispered back.

He lifted a speculative eyebrow. ''Antonia, huh? Pretty?''

''Gorgeous. Short dark hair, huge brown eyes, a smile that could melt a snowman's heart and...''

''And?'' Alessandro prompted, coming up behind them.

''And little bitty dimples on all four cheeks.'' They stared at her in shock, and barely able to suppress a smile, she led the way to the living room. ''Can I get you anything to drink?''

''Come on, Grace,'' Stef pleaded. ''Give. What's going on?''

She shook her head. ''I can't tell. Besides, it's Luc's story.''

''Pietro's story, to be exact,'' Luc corrected from the doorway.

The expressions on the four younger Salvatore brothers were all she could have hoped for. Ranging from bemusement to shock, they stared in absolute silence at the baby in Luc's arms. Alessandro was the first to recover.

"This is Antonia of the four dimples, I assume."

"Is she...*yours?*" Rocco asked in disbelief.

"Pietro's," Luc repeated.

Marc snapped his fingers. "Pietro and—what was her name...? The little foreign-exchange student he was so crazy about. Carina! Is it hers?" He shook his head, not bothering to wait for confirmation. "I'll bet her parents had a thing or two to say when they heard about this little incident."

"You've met Carina?" Grace questioned in surprise.

"Once," he confirmed. "Briefly. Pietro was very protective. He didn't encourage me to stick around for long."

Stef nudged his twin in the ribs. "Afraid big brother would steal his love away?"

Marc grinned. "I would have, given half the chance. She's quite something."

"Why don't we get dinner started and I'll bring you up-to-date," Luc ordered.

Within minutes all five Salvatores were gathered in the kitchen, working as a well-orchestrated team to prepare dinner. Grace watched in amusement. They'd obviously done this before. Each took a different duty, occasionally asking Grace to pass a pot or a measuring cup or utensil. Toni, delighted to be the center of so much masculine attention, was passed from one set of arms to the next.

"Dinner will be in twenty minutes," Luc announced. "Marc, set the table." He turned to Grace. "And you, my fine beauty, may go change out of your office clothes and into something more festive. Tonight, I feel in the mood to celebrate."

Four pairs of eyes, wide with astonishment, turned in Grace's direction. She could feel an intense blush blossom across her cheeks. Apparently, her masquerade was still a success with four of the five Salvatores present. She didn't know whether to be pleased or insulted.

Noticing his brothers' reactions, Luc explained, "Will-William, her fiancé, has her in disguise. For some reason, he wants her to look like a bag lady. I haven't quite figured out why. I will, though. I will."

"A disguise?" Stef asked, intrigued. "Like in the movies?"

Rocco approached. "You mean all I have to do is..."

Before she could protest, he whipped off her glasses. From behind, Alessandro slipped the pins from her hair, fluffing the wayward curls around her face and shoulders. "This isn't fair," she protested. "Stop it!" Marc advanced next, and she knew from his mischievous grin that he intended to investigate what lay beneath her bulky wool suit.

Apparently, so did Luc. Sweeping her clear of his brothers' clutches, he gave her a gentle push toward the door. "Put on the green dress," he said.

And by the remorseless gleam in his golden eyes, she knew it wasn't a request.

CHAPTER SIX

The Great Lie
Still Day 338 and Grace's deception is fast unraveling…

GRACE SPENT FIFTEEN of the next twenty minutes debating whether or not to wear the green dress. Uppermost in her mind was Dom and his reaction should he find out about her stay at Luc's. Did Luc's brothers know she'd spent the previous night in this apartment—or that she'd also be spending tonight here? If so, Dom would learn the truth eventually from them. She couldn't very well ask them not to mention it. What excuse could she give?

She sank onto the edge of the bed. This was getting too complicated. Perhaps she should give up her disguise. Or what was left of her disguise. If Dom found out, she'd be frank. She'd explain the situation to him and pray he'd understand. After all, she'd only been trying to help his family.

Despite that one rather tumultuous kiss, her relationship with Luc hadn't gotten too far out of hand—until Toni's advent into their lives, they'd had no real personal involvement at all. Nor could she be blamed because Carina and Pietro had chosen to dump Toni in Luc's lap and take off for parts unknown. What was she supposed to have done? Refuse her aid? Leave Luc and Toni to fend for themselves? It wasn't in her nature to be so cold and uncaring. Surely Dom wouldn't hold that against her.

Would he?

Giving up on such a fruitless debate, Grace reluctantly pulled the green dress from the closet. She'd bought it a month ago to wear home for Christmas. The trip was a gift to herself for having completed her year's sojourn at Salvatore's, and she'd wanted to treat herself to something special...something spectacular. And the silk dress was certainly that. Even shopping for it had been fun.

Without giving herself time to reconsider, she stripped off her suit and slipped on the dress. It was sheer perfection. Long-sleeved, with a fitted bodice and V neckline, the belled skirt floated to her knees. A string of pearls and earrings her parents had given her for her twenty-first birthday lent a final glamorous touch.

Crossing to the adjoining bathroom, she opened her cosmetic bag and applied a touch of makeup. It was always a pleasure slipping back into clothes that fit and wearing colors that flattered rather than detracted from her appearance. Stepping back from the mirror, she eyed the results with approval. Suddenly, she felt like herself again.

Next, she brushed out her hair. She assumed Alessandro still had her pins, so she'd have to leave it down. She tilted her head to one side. Swept back from a deep widow's peak, her hair framed her face and fell in soft curls to her shoulders. A good portion of the rinse had washed out, leaving interesting streaks of gold mixed in with the brown, as though her hair had been partially bleached by the sun. It actually looked quite attractive.

Slipping on a pair of heels, she left the bedroom and followed the sound of masculine voices to the dining room. Dinner had just been put on the table, the assorted bowls and platters steaming, a variety of delicious odors wafting in her direction.

Luc noticed her first. To her dismay, he didn't seem the least surprised by her altered appearance. With an annoying calm, he settled Toni more comfortably on his lap. But then a slow smile of satisfaction slid across his face and his eyes took on a gleam of hot intensity that shook her to the core. Had he known she'd look like this? she wondered uneasily. But how? Was it possible…? Had he seen through her disguise from the beginning? It was a frightening thought.

Rocco noticed her next, stumbling to a halt in mid-sentence. His mouth opened and closed, but he couldn't seem to get any words out. At that, all conversation stopped. If the varied reactions to Toni had been amusing, the reactions to Grace's transformation were even more so. Luc's brothers scrambled to their feet, tripping over themselves as they fought their way to her side. An instant later four large, gorgeous men had her completely surrounded.

It felt wonderful.

"Grace!"

"What the hell have you done to yourself?"

"Never mind that! What the hell were you doing running around looking like you did when you could have looked like… Damn!"

With a teasing grin, Marc threw himself at her feet. "Marry me, Grace!"

Alessandro turned to confront Luc. "You kept her all covered up on purpose. That's not fair."

Luc shrugged. "I told you. It wasn't my idea. Blame Will-William."

Marc gained his feet, a frown darkening his handsome

face. "Your fiancé makes you dress like that? Like... like..."

"Like a bag lady," Luc supplied helpfully.

"He makes you dress like a bag lady?" Marc's frown grew darker. "What the hell for?"

"Yeah," Stef echoed, an identical frown lining his brow. "What the hell for?"

For the first time, Grace managed to get a word in edgewise. "To protect me from my boss," she deadpanned, trying to relieve the mounting tension. It hadn't occurred to her that they'd see her disguise in such an ominous light.

"To protect you?" Rocco questioned in astonishment. "From Luc?"

"It worked, didn't it?" she said with an impish grin.

Her jest broke the mood, the four brothers bursting into laughter. Crossing to the table, she caught a brief glimpse of Luc's narrowed, thoughtful gaze. That one look was sufficient. She didn't dare glance his way again. It was as though a light bulb had just gone on in his head. She suspected that she'd given a little too much away with that last crack, and Luc had caught her slip.

Anxious to change the subject, she scooped Toni out of Luc's arms. "So, what do you think of your niece?" she asked the room at large.

Her question brought a slew of responses, each proud uncle attempting to outflatter the others. It was clear they adored the newest member of the family. Within minutes, she'd been snatched away from Grace, and even as they enjoyed their meal, Toni continued to be ensconced on one or the other of her uncles' laps. On the receiving end of so much adoration, she kicked her little legs and waved her hands, blinking adoringly into each handsome face.

"Flirt," Rocco announced in proud disgust. "It's a good thing you have so many uncles. You'll need them to beat off the boyfriends."

"So, when does Pietro return?" Alessandro asked.

"Soon, I hope," Luc responded. "Until he does, Grace has agreed to help me with Toni."

"You're staying here?" Marc questioned with an impudent grin.

Throwing a troubled glance Luc's way, she nodded. So much for keeping this episode from Dom. She could only hope he'd be reasonable. If she could continue to hold Luc at a distance, she didn't think there would be a problem. The only question being, could she do it? She hadn't realized how much she'd come to depend on her disguise for protection. With that blown, she'd just have to cling even tighter to the imaginary William.

"Yes," she said. "I'm using Luc's guest room until Pietro or Carina returns. Which reminds me..." She slipped from her chair and addressed Luc. "I need to call my fiancé and give him an update. Do you mind if I use the phone in your study?"

"Feel free." She couldn't read his expression, but somehow she suspected it held amusement. "Oh, and Grace..."

She glanced back over her shoulder. "Yes?"

This time she couldn't mistake his amusement. "Be sure and give him my regards."

The buzz of questions began the moment she stepped from the room. She didn't doubt for a minute they were about her and William. And from their tone, she also didn't doubt they were critical. Not that it mattered. A few more weeks and she could dispense with her engagement ring and be finished forever with lies and pretend engagements and futile disguises.

Sitting in Luc's study, she punched in her home phone number and spoke sheer drivel to her answering machine for the next ten minutes. Luc appeared in the doorway just as she'd cradled the receiver.

"How's Will-William?" he asked.

"Anxious for Carina and Pietro to return so our lives can get back to normal," she lied with composure.

He continued to stand in the doorway, blocking her only avenue of escape. "He's not concerned about your staying here?"

She lifted her chin. "Should he be?"

"I would, if I were your fiancé." He left the doorway and approached, standing directly in front of her chair. "In fact, I wouldn't allow you to spend five minutes in another man's apartment without me, let alone the entire night."

Anger sparked in her eyes. "But then, you're not my fiancé. And for the record, no man *allows* me to do anything. I do what I choose."

He smiled with a complacency that made her very, very nervous. "And you've chosen to stay with me."

"With Toni," she amended.

He let her correction slide without comment. Folding his arms across his chest, he tilted his head to one side. "Have I told you how beautiful you look tonight?"

"Thank you." She practically leapt from the chair, anxious to end this conversation and put some extra bodies between them. Nice, tall, protective bodies in the form of four Salvatore brothers. "Shall we join the others?" she suggested. He didn't move and to her distress, now that she was standing, they almost touched. Perhaps leaving the safety of the chair had been a mistake.

He lowered his head, asking softly, "Nervous, *cara?*"

She froze. "Not at all," she managed to say, wondering if she could edge around him and escape out the door. "But as you've just pointed out, I am engaged, and this conversation isn't appropriate."

He lifted an eyebrow. "No? What's inappropriate about it? The fact that I called you beautiful? Or the fact that we're here...alone...together?" A smile edged across his mouth. "We'll be alone tonight, and yet you just said that wasn't a problem."

"It's not!"

"Then perhaps it's that we're standing so close."

"Luc—"

"But that can't be it. We stand this close to each other at work all the time." His gaze dropped to the rapid rise and fall of her breasts. "Though I don't remember it having quite this effect on you." He captured her chin in his hand, his golden eyes once again on her face, watchful and dangerous. "Did it?"

"No!" she denied instantly. "It didn't. It still doesn't."

He tilted his head to one side. "You're lying," he told her bluntly. "You know how I can tell? Your eyes. Those clear, bright green eyes cloud over like a stormy sky when you aren't being honest. Is that why you wore those glasses? How many other lies have you told me while hiding behind a pair of tinted lenses, I wonder?"

"Luc, please..." she whispered.

"I want to please you." His voice was husky, deepening with an emotion she didn't dare try to identify. "You don't know how much I want to please you."

She bit her lip. "Our lives are complicated enough. Don't make it any worse."

"Worse? I'll make it better. Much, much better. Give it a chance, Grace. Give me a chance."

She was so very, very tempted. She shut her eyes and

instantly a picture leapt to life. A picture of her mother sewing bits of lace and ribbon to the clever little stuffed animals she so lovingly created. "Baby dreams," she'd called them. And from that the idea for Baby Dream Toys had been born, a business they'd plotted and planned to someday open together. She shook her head. She couldn't do it. She couldn't sacrifice something so precious for a fleeting moment of pleasure. "No," she whispered, opening her eyes. "I can't. Let go of me, Luc. Please."

For a long minute he stood without speaking, his thoughtful gaze narrowed on her, as if trying to analyze something that defied analysis. His attention dropped briefly to her engagement ring and a small smile touched his mouth before he released her. "By all means. Join my brothers. They're about to leave, anyway." He moved toward the phone. "I want to make a quick call. I'll join you in a minute."

"All right." She hesitated, something in his face setting off warning bells. But she couldn't figure out why.

He picked up the receiver and raised an eyebrow in question. "Anything else?" he asked.

She shook her head, and without another word went in search of Luc's brothers. She found them grouped in the living room, slipping on coats and giving Toni goodbye hugs and kisses. Grace smiled. That little girl was going to grow up being very spoiled...and very much loved.

"Time to move out," Alessandro announced, throwing open the front door and handing Grace the baby.

"Look!" Marc exclaimed. "She smiled at me."

"So what?" his twin scoffed. "She's been doing that to me all evening."

"Only because she got the two of us mixed up."

Luc suddenly appeared, bringing up the rear. "Quiet down," he ordered. "And don't forget. No one is to know Toni's here. One run-in with the police was enough. We can't risk another."

"You got it."

"Mum's the word."

"Not a problem," Alessandro assured. "Oh, hello, Mrs. Bumgartle. Were we being too noisy again?"

A long, sharp nose poked around the doorway opposite. "This time I'm calling the manager. He'll take care of you hooligans. See if he doesn't!"

"I'm sorry, Mrs. Bumgartle," Luc said, crossing the hall to speak to her. "My brothers were just leaving. You won't hear another sound out of them." He threw a stern glance over his shoulder. "Right, boys?"

She peered at Luc, then at his brothers, her eyes narrow with dislike. "Hooligans, the lot of you!" And with that she slammed the door.

"Whoo-hoo," Marc said with a chuckle. "I do love seeing Mrs. Bumgartle. It reminds me there's one woman on this planet you can't charm."

"Two women," Stef corrected. "You're forgetting about Cynthia. Remember? The tall, gorgeous brunette? Totally immune. She could freeze Luc dead in his tracks with one look."

Rocco slapped Luc on the back. "Don't worry, big brother. Two out of millions. We won't hold it against you."

Luc grinned. "Get out of here, before I knock some heads together. I'll let you know when I hear from Pietro."

The four trooped toward the elevator and Grace lifted the baby to her shoulder. "I think that's enough excitement for one day. Time for bed, young lady,'' she announced and slipped back into Luc's apartment.

Across the hall, the door opened again. ''Good night, Mrs. Bumgartle,'' Luc called cheerfully. The door crashed shut and with a shrug he followed Grace into the apartment.

''Did you speak to her about yesterday?'' she asked, moving over to the picture windows in the living room. ''I don't want her to put the wrong connotation on anything she might have overheard.''

He shook his head. ''I never got the chance. It doesn't matter. She makes empty threats all the time.''

Grace frowned. ''Still...''

''Forget about Mrs. Bumgartle.'' He came to stand next to her, dropping an arm around her shoulders, wrapping her and the baby in a protective embrace.

She gazed at the window, fascinated by the image reflected there. They might have been a real family. Luc towered above her, elegant and broad shouldered in black trousers and a pullover sweater. Her soft green skirt seemed to cling to his legs with a life of its own. And Toni gurgled, her arms pumping the air as though trying to catch hold of him.

''Tell me, Grace.'' His hand slipped along the nape of her neck and he caught a fistful of streaked curls in his hand. ''Is it my imagination, or is your hair lighter?''

She stiffened against him, hastily ducking to press a kiss to the top of Toni's head. ''Does it seem lighter?'' she asked in a muffled voice, tufts of soft black hair tickling her lips. ''I hadn't noticed.''

''Don't play games with me, Grace.'' His voice acquired a rough, impatient edge. ''You've been coloring it. Why?''

She shrugged. ''It's a woman's prerogative, isn't it?''

"To go from gold to mud brown?" he asked derisively. "Of course. It makes perfect sense."

She attempted to step free of his arms, but he still held her hair clenched in his fist and for a moment she didn't think he'd let go. "I'd like to put Toni down," she said quietly.

He opened his hand, releasing her. "I'll help."

She knew better than to argue when he used that tone. She inclined her head in agreement and led the way to the guest room, which was rapidly being converted into a dream nursery. A changing table now stood near the gleaming white crib—both special deliveries from a nearby furniture store. Next to the changing table hung a Toys-a-Trillion pet net, a triangular hammock that attached to the wall and held every conceivable stuffed animal.

Laying Toni on the changing table, Grace wound up a music box to keep the baby entertained while she took care of the lengthy process of putting on dry diapers and slipping a wiggly baby into pajamas.

"Why don't you sleep in my bed tonight."

Grace started, jabbing herself with the diaper pin. "Ouch!" She glared at Luc, holding up a wounded finger. "Look what you made me do."

A lazy grin drifted across his mouth. "You want me to kiss it better?"

"Not a chance." She snatched a damp baby wipe from its plastic box and wrapped it around her finger. "And just to clarify... That 'not a chance' is in response to both of your requests. You know I won't sleep with you. I'm engaged."

"So you keep reminding me. But, I don't recall asking you to sleep with me, though if you're offering..."

"I'm not," she snapped, carrying Toni from the

changing table to the crib. ''Then what were you asking?''

''Offering, not asking. I'm offering my bed. It's my turn to get up with Toni for the middle-of-the-night feeding and diaper change. So either we push the crib into my room or I sleep in here.''

''Don't worry about it,'' she said, dismissing his concerns. ''I'll take care of Toni. You stay right where you are.''

He shook his head, a crooked smile drifting across his mouth. ''Sorry. I can't do that.'' He switched off the lamp on the nightstand. A silly clown face night-light glowed near the crib, holding the darkness at bay. He moved toward her, his shadow leaping across the wall, joining with hers. ''It wouldn't be fair.''

''I don't mind,'' she insisted.

''I do.'' He caught her hand and tugged her out of the room. ''Come on. We'll go back to the living room and argue about it there.''

''Luc...''

''You don't want to argue about who takes care of Toni tonight?''

''Not really.''

Refusing to let go of her hand, he crossed to the couch, pulling her down next to him. ''Then we'll argue about the real reason for the disguise you've been hiding behind for almost a year.''

''Why don't we talk about the weather,'' she suggested dryly, moving to the far side of the couch. ''That's always a nice, safe topic.''

''The weather? Fine.'' He closed the distance between them, crowding her against the cushions. ''I sense a sudden heat wave. How about you?''

She pressed her hands to his chest, aware that she'd

just as soon wrap her arms around him as push him away. "Luc, cut it out. This isn't a scene out of some 1940s romantic comedy, you know."

"You're right." He reached past her and turned off the lamp on the table behind them. Instantly, the room plunged into darkness. "Now it's a scene out of a 1940s romantic comedy," he murmured, his mouth nuzzling her ear. Moonlight filtered in through the picture windows and bathed them in a silvery glow. "The seduction scene to be exact."

Her breath stopped in her throat. He was so close, practically lying on top of her. "And I thought talking about the weather would be safe. I'm beginning to think there aren't any safe topics with you," Grace said.

"Then let's not talk."

"Don't, Luc. I don't want this."

"I think you do. Shall I tell you what else I think?" He didn't wait for her answer. His hand tangled in her hair, the streaked curls spilling from between his fingers. "I think you dyed your hair and wore suits three sizes too large for a reason."

"What reason?" she asked, feeling alarmed.

"For the same reason behind this." He lifted her left hand and touched her engagement ring. "For protection."

She stared at him in shock. Did he know? Had she given herself away? She fought his hold. "You're crazy."

"Am I?" His arms moved around her, pulling her tight. "You could be right about that. Let's be crazy together."

He didn't say any more. He simply lowered his head and kissed her. In that instant, she realized that her reaction to their first kiss hadn't been a fluke. It was as if someone had thrown on a main power switch. Her senses came on-line, leaping to life with a jarring force that swept away all resistance, all thought, leaving only a desperate need behind, raw and undeniable.

His kiss stole her breath, stole her will, and she almost groaned aloud. He tasted wonderful, as heady as fine champagne. One sip and her palate was forever jaded, never again to be satisfied with anything but the best. And he was the best.

He broke off the kiss and shifted closer, his weight pressing her deep into the cushions, his body hard and taut against hers. She gazed up at him, wanting him to kiss her again but unable to ask, afraid of the words—afraid of the desire such words would express. His thick hair tumbled across his brow and he stared at her, his eyes no longer golden but two glittering shards of jet.

''You're safe with me,'' he murmured, and she knew he'd sensed her fears as well as her desire. ''I won't hurt you, Grace, I swear it.''

He kissed her again and she tilted her head, exposing the long line of her neck. His mouth drifted downward, following the deep V of her dress. Tenderly, he cupped her breast, caressing, stoking the fires that raged within her, driving her toward a sweet ecstasy she'd never before experienced.

''Come to my bed, Grace,'' he urged. ''Let me show you how good it can be between us.''

She wanted to. Oh, how she wanted to. But it would be wrong, for so many reasons. His mouth found hers again, tantalizing her with teasing little kisses, until all she could think or feel was a desperate craving for more. Lord, he was good at this. Unfortunately, that indicated he'd had plenty of practice. Which meant…

''Luc...'' she forced herself to say. ''This isn't smart. We can't do this.''

He laughed with genuine humor, the sound warm and beguiling. ''Of course we can. I've wanted to do this for ages. Haven't you?''

She shied away from his question, asking one of her own instead. ''If you wanted to do this for so long, then why haven't you?''

He hesitated, then shrugged. ''There were... roadblocks.''

As far as she knew, most of the roadblocks remained. He might suspect her engagement to William was an invention. But he had no real proof. And though he wasn't aware that her agreement with Dom prevented a personal relationship with him, their business association should be more than enough to give him pause before starting a...a *fling*.

''And now there aren't any roadblocks?'' she questioned.

He eyed her closely. ''You tell me.''

She didn't dare mention William or Dom. ''What about my job?'' she asked instead, seizing on the one obstacle they could openly discuss.

''What about it? It's not going anywhere.''

''What about after we...? What happens to my job, then?''

He pulled back and frowned. ''What the hell does that mean?''

She shook her head. ''You think I haven't heard about my predecessors? There must be a regular army of women who've left your employment because they fell in love with you.''

''For your information, I have never had an affair with anyone who worked for me.''

"Until now?"

The question seemed to hang between them. For a minute she didn't think he'd respond. Then he nodded. "Until now," he conceded roughly. He cupped her face and kissed her with a desperate urgency, as though he wanted to drive all thought, all resistance, from her mind. She almost allowed herself to give in to desire, to allow him to sweep aside all concerns but a selfish need to be loved.

In that instant, she saw her choices more clearly than she ever had before. She could break all the rules she held dear and have a few brief, stolen moments with Luc—and they'd be wonderful memories, memories she'd retain for the rest of her life. But then his interest would move on to the next woman and he'd break her heart. Or she could stop the relationship now, before it went any further.

In a few weeks, Dom would return and she'd leave Luc's employment. Maybe she'd experience a few regrets—maybe more than a few. But she'd have Baby Dream Toys. More important, there was still a slim chance she could emerge from this with her heart intact. Which left her only one option.

Now all she had to do was find a way to distance Luc.

Not giving him time to realize what she intended, she ripped free of his embrace and stood. "Why are you doing this?" she demanded, driven by sheer self-preservation to take the offensive. "I'm your employee, trying to help you out of an awkward situation. And you're—you're attacking me."

He lifted an eyebrow, his expression amused. "What a vivid imagination you have. Do you really consider what I did attacking you?"

"Yes! No!" She'd never succeed at putting him off

if she couldn't do better than that. There was only one out available, and she'd darned well better take it. She lifted her chin and folded her arms across her chest. Using her most businesslike voice, she said, "If you want to continue having my help, you'll keep our relationship professional. I don't want you to make suggestive remarks or—or touch me. If you do, I'll leave. Is that clear?"

She held her breath, praying that this time he'd believe her, believe what was fast becoming more and more of a lie. To her distress she realized that, despite the choice she'd made, she didn't want just a professional relationship with Luc. And far from finding his remarks suggestive, she found them romantic and all too appealing. She shied away from thinking about his touch, and the fact that she'd begun to crave each casual caress with a passion that frightened her. She had to remember Baby Dream Toys and her mother. She *had* to.

He sat up, his expression unreadable. "It's clear." He studied her for several minutes, as though trying to understand what had gone wrong, and then his voice softened. "There's no need to be afraid, you know. We can take this slow. If I'm rushing you, you set the pace."

With a quick shake of her head, she said, "I'm not interested in setting any pace."

"Except a full retreat?" Irony colored his words.

"Shall I go pack?"

He held up his hands. "You win. If you don't want to see where this might lead, I won't push it."

"Thank you." There wasn't anything left to be said. Without another word, she headed from the room.

"Grace?"

She hesitated, but didn't turn around, waiting for him

to say what he had to so she could finally escape. ''What is it, Luc?''

''I don't want to lose you. So I won't touch you again, if that's your preference.''

''Thank you,'' she said again.

''Don't thank me. It's not what I'd do if the choice were mine. If you were honest with yourself, you'd admit it isn't really what you want, either.'' His voice held a grating quality she'd never heard before. ''And one more thing.''

''Yes?'' she whispered.

''Take my bed.''

She turned around at that. ''No! That's—that's not necessary.''

Slowly he rose from the couch and she realized to her dismay that a very large, frustrated man stood before her. ''Take my bed,'' he repeated.

''Fine.'' She swallowed nervously, backing from the room. ''I'll take your bed.''

He stalked after her. ''And for your information, *bellissima mia,* just so there isn't any doubt in your mind... All through that passionate little speech your eyes were as cloudy as I've ever seen them. Run away for now, but don't leave thinking I believed a word you said. You do want me. And soon, very soon, you'll admit it to yourself...and to me.''

She didn't dare say another word. Instead, she turned on her heels and ran.

CHAPTER SEVEN

The Great Lie
Day 339 and trouble is at the door…

LOCKING HERSELF IN Luc's room did nothing to make Grace feel safe. Standing by the bed, she wondered how in the world she could be expected to sleep here. She didn't even have her pajamas. Darn him! She didn't even have a toothbrush. Nor did she have any intention of going after the forgotten items.

As though in answer to her silent raging, a brief knock sounded at the door. It could only be Luc. As she stood motionless, debating whether or not to open it, the knob turned. She heard his muffled laugh as he realized she'd locked him out.

''If you want your nightgown, it's here,'' he informed her through the wooden panel. ''Feel free to use my toothbrush. Good night, Grace. Pleasant dreams.''

She waited several minutes before opening the door. Sure enough, her gown and robe lay neatly folded on the rug. Luc was nowhere in sight. She crossed to his dresser and rummaged through drawers until she found a pair of pajamas. Returning to the hallway, she swapped nightclothes and slammed the door shut, locking it once again. As far as a toothbrush was concerned…use his? Not likely. It was bad enough that she had to use his bed.

Stripping off her dress, she tossed it across a chair and glared at the pool of soft green silk. In her mind's eye she saw Luc's hand against the pale dress as he cupped her breast, his dark hair contrasting with her white skin as he bent to… She struggled to breathe normally. Maybe she wouldn't wear the dress for Christmas, after all. Maybe she wouldn't wear it ever again.

A few minutes later she was ready for bed, her teeth brushed with her finger and a bit of toothpaste. She wondered if she'd get any sleep. Doubtful, considering how everything in the room served to remind her of Luc—and the passion they'd shared…almost shared. It had to be Luc's not-so-subtle way of tormenting her.

The worst part came when she slipped between his sheets and rested her head on his pillow. His spicy scent clung to the pillowcase, filling her lungs with every breath and arousing emotions she'd sooner forget. She clenched her fists. He'd done this on purpose. He wanted to drive her insane. Well, it wouldn't work.

Three hours later, and on the verge of true madness, she started to drift off to sleep. An urgent banging put paid to that. Totally disoriented, it took her several seconds to realize the pounding came not from outside her bedroom but from outside the apartment. Grabbing her robe, she thrust her arms into it as she dashed for the door. For endless moments she fumbled with the lock and by the time she'd reached the hallway, Luc raced just ahead of her. Wearing the pajama bottoms she'd left out for him, he opened the front door, running a hand through his hair.

"What—" he began.

To Grace's horror, she saw a pair of policemen standing there, Mrs. Bumgartle right behind them, a self-righteous expression on her face.

"Arrest him," Mrs Bumgartle demanded, pointing an accusing finger at Luc. "Arrest them both! Those... those...those babynappers!"

For a long moment, no one moved. Then Luc asked, "What's the problem, Officer?"

"Mr. Salvatore? I'm Officer Hatcher. We met two days ago at your office."

"I remember," Luc replied evenly. "Is there a problem?"

"Babynapper!" Mrs. Bumgartle proclaimed from behind the policeman's broad shoulders. "He said the baby was his niece—that she was his brother's child. But all his brothers visited tonight and she wasn't theirs. And he—" she pointed a finger at Luc with dramatic emphasis "—warned them that they couldn't afford to have the police called in again."

Officer Hatcher glanced from Luc to a clearly nervous Grace. "Perhaps I better come in and straighten this out. Carl," he addressed his partner, "escort Mrs. Bumgartle to her apartment and take a statement."

After a momentary hesitation, Luc stepped back to allow the policeman access. Though he didn't say anything, Grace saw the muscle leaping in his jaw and the dark, furious glitter of his eyes. Why, oh why, she wondered with a sinking heart, did it have to be Hatcher who responded to the call?

"There's nothing to straighten out," Luc insisted, leading the way to the living room. "I explained before that we were baby-sitting my niece and that's precisely what we're doing."

Hatcher pulled a notepad out of his pocket and flipped through the pages. "According to my notes, you said you were baby-sitting for a few hours. It's now been almost two days. Would you care to explain the discrepancy?''

Luc glanced briefly at Grace, then said, ''I believe I mentioned that my sister-in-law's mother is ill. My brother and his wife were going to fly to Italy with the baby, but decided at the last minute to leave Toni with us.'' He caught Grace's hand in his and pulled her close. ''Is that a problem?''

Officer Hatcher began adding to his notes. ''You have something from the parents stating this?''

''No,'' Luc admitted. ''I didn't realize that would be necessary.''

The policeman's gaze sharpened. ''A medical release form? A birth certificate? Anything?''

Luc shook his head. ''They should be back soon.''

Hatcher glanced at his notes again and froze. ''How old is your niece, Mr. Salvatore? What's her birthdate?''

Grace started, staring up at Luc in a panic. His arm tightened around her, crushing her to his side. ''She's three months,'' Luc said stiffly. ''I'm...I'm not sure of the exact date of her birth.''

''And when did her sex change from male to female?'' Hatcher asked with unmistakable sarcasm. He had them and he knew it.

Luc swore beneath his breath.

''You didn't know she was a girl, did you?'' The patrolman's mouth twisted in a parody of a smile. ''Is she even your niece?''

''I didn't know she was a girl until we changed her diaper,'' Luc was forced to concede. ''Carina called her Toni, and since Salvatores have a history of producing boys, I assumed...'' He shrugged, then stated forcefully, ''But she *is* my niece.''

Officer Hatcher checked his notes again. ''The baby's

name is Antonia Donati...Salvatore? Or was that a lie, too?''

Luc closed his eyes, releasing a long, drawn-out sigh. ''Carina and my brother aren't married. Yet. I expect that to change very soon.''

''Let me get this straight.'' The officer's words fell, cold and hard as chipped ice. ''You said the parents left the baby in your care and would be back in a few hours. That was a lie. You said the child was your nephew. That was a lie. And you said the baby's parents were married. Another lie. You don't have any legal authority to care for this baby whatsoever, do you?''

Luc's fists clenched at his sides. ''Look. Carina, the baby's mother, left Toni with my brother because of a family emergency. That much is true. And she needed someone to care for Toni during her absence. That is also the truth. Since my brother Pietro is the baby's father, he was the natural choice. The only problem was, Pietro didn't know about Toni until Carina arrived at my office.''

Understanding dawned. ''Which explains the argument in the lobby.''

''Yes. My brother went after Carina to try and stop her. Thanks to your intervention, he wasn't in time.''

Grace winced. ''Luc, it won't help to antagonize him,'' she murmured.

''I don't care,'' he snapped. ''If the police hadn't been so quick to let Carina go, we wouldn't be in our current predicament. Not that it matters. When Pietro does catch up with her, they'll marry and return for Toni. Until then, my fiancée and I are taking care of the baby. She's perfectly safe and in good hands.''

''That's not for me to decide.''

Luc stiffened. ''What the hell does that mean?''

"Easy," Grace murmured, laying a restraining hand on Luc's arm.

"No!" He shook free of her hold. "I want to know what he means."

Hatcher eyed them sternly. "I mean that what happens to the baby is up to social services, not me. Legally, she's been abandoned."

"No, she hasn't!" Luc bit out. "The mother left her child with the father."

"Mr. Salvatore, I don't intend to argue with you about this. I'm taking the baby into custody. If you resist, I'll arrest you."

Before Luc could respond, Grace asked, "What will happen to Toni?"

Hatcher explained while writing. "The law requires we have her transported by ambulance to the local hospital. She'll be examined there and kept overnight at the child-protection center. In the morning they'll put her in a temporary foster home while an emergency-response worker investigates the case." He spoke by rote, his demeanor cool and dispassionate, repeating an explanation he'd obviously given before.

"How do we get her back?" Grace questioned.

He hesitated, glancing up. For the first time, his guard relaxed slightly. "To be honest, I'm not sure you can. The best chance you have is to get in touch with the legal guardian—presumably the mother—and obtain a signed custody statement and a medical-permission slip. A copy of the birth certificate wouldn't hurt, either."

Grace gazed at Luc. "Can we do that?" she whispered.

He gave a brief nod. "Pietro can fax it to us."

"Even then, it's questionable whether the authorities will release her to you. Though—" Hatcher hesitated, eyeing Grace "—a *permanent* female presence in the home could possibly tip the scales in your favor." He snapped his notepad closed and pocketed it. "Take me to the baby."

There was nothing they could do after that. Luc went into the spare bedroom and packed a diaper bag with several days' worth of clothes, diapers and baby paraphernalia. Fighting back tears, Grace carefully bundled up Toni for the trip into the frigid night air. The entire time, Officer Hatcher stood in the doorway, watching their every move.

"Wait." She stopped Luc before he could close the diaper bag. Handing him the baby, she grabbed a floppy-eared rabbit from the pet net and thrust it in among the clothes he'd packed. "What about a bottle and a spare can of formula?" she asked the policeman.

"Can't hurt."

"It'll only take a minute." She glanced at Luc. He held Toni, his face expressionless, but she could sense his impotent fury. "Officer Hatcher, would you mind helping me?" She sent Hatcher a pleading look, hoping against hope that he'd give Luc the few moments of privacy he needed to say goodbye to Toni.

After a brief hesitation, the policeman nodded. "Two minutes. No more."

Chattering nonsense while she prepared a bottle, Grace prayed that Luc wouldn't do anything foolish. To her relief, he appeared in the doorway just as she'd finished mixing the formula. Without a word, he handed the officer the baby and the diaper bag.

"Here's my business card," Luc said. "My home phone number's on the back. I'll expect the emergency-response worker's call first thing in the morning." It wasn't a request.

Hatcher inclined his head. "I suggest you get those papers together and fast. You haven't a prayer otherwise."

And with that he left, Toni gently cradled in his arms.

The minute the door closed behind him, Luc slammed his fist against the wall, knocking a hole in the plaster. Grace came up behind, not sure approaching him at this time was the wisest course of action. "It's all right," she murmured. "We'll get her back."

He turned on her, his eyes wild with fury, dark color streaking across his angled cheekbones. "I won't let it happen again, Grace. I won't let them split up my family again."

Again. She stared at him in alarm. "What do you mean, again?" He didn't answer. Instead, he headed for the guest room, forcing her to run to keep up with him. "Luc?"

He crossed to the empty crib, spinning the colorful mobile with a surprisingly gentle hand. Removing Toni's crumpled pink blanket, he folded it and tossed it across the headboard. He'd cut himself hitting the wall; a streak of blood oozed from his bruised and scraped knuckles. If it bothered him, he gave no indication.

"I was fourteen when Pietro was born," he began. "I guess you'd call my brother an afterthought, though Mom and Dad were delighted by the addition. He'd make it an even half dozen, they'd say. The first time I saw him, I thought he was the ugliest creature ever created. I called him 'monkey face.'"

Grace curled up in the rocker near the crib and watched him with concern. She'd stumbled across something—she didn't quite know what—but at a guess it had a great deal to do with his feelings for Toni. "Pietro's looks have improved with age," she said lightly.

To her surprise a brief grin creased his face. "Yeah. They did." The grin faded. "Mom died when he was only a couple of months old."

"Oh, no," Grace cried softly.

He swatted at the mobile again, sending the cartoon characters careening in a drunken circle. "I'm not sure whether it was the stress of Pietro's birth—she was in her forties by the time she had him—or the pneumonia that killed her. Who knows? Maybe it was a combination of the two. Not that it matters now."

"Where was Dom?"

"Dad was in Italy on business. We had trouble contacting him." His voice deepened, the sound raspy with emotion. "Mom had all that information, but she went so fast she didn't have time to tell us how..."

She left the rocker and crossed to his side. "What happened?" she asked, slipping her arms around his waist and resting her cheek against his broad back. His skin felt warm and smooth beneath her face.

He didn't push her away. Instead, he drew a deep breath. "Same as tonight. The police arrived to take us into foster care until Dad could come for us. I fought them. I mean, physically fought them."

He sounded so cold and remote, so removed from his memories. But she knew it was a false impression. She could hear the harsh sound of his breathing, feel his tension beneath her hands. "Why did you fight?" she asked.

"Family unity was drummed into us from the cradle. My mother's last request was that I keep everyone together until Dad returned. But the police wanted to separate us. I couldn't let them do that."

"You did your best, Luc," she said urgently. "You

were so young. Too young to care for an infant, to supervise four rambunctious boys.''

His hands fisted on the bars of the crib. ''I was in charge. It was my duty to keep us all together until Dad came home. I tried. Heaven knows, I tried. But I didn't succeed. They took my brothers. Alessandro, the twins, Rocco and Pietro. They needed three policemen to hold me down while they got them all out of the house.'' He closed his eyes, swallowing hard. ''We were dispersed to various foster homes. Three weeks later Dad returned.''

''He didn't blame you?'' she asked in alarm.

''Never. But I knew I'd failed. I won't fail again. I swear, I'll do anything—*anything*—to regain custody of Toni until Carina and Pietro get back.''

''What are you planning?'' she asked uneasily.

He turned in her arms, gazing down at her, his eyes dark with a passionate intensity. ''You and I,'' he informed her in a hard, determined voice, ''are now officially married.''

''You *can't* be serious,'' she exclaimed, taking a quick step back.

His hands dropped to her shoulders, holding her in place. ''I'm dead serious. Hatcher said having a permanent female presence in the house might tip the scales in our favor, and that's just what I intend to have.''

''But what about Will...William?''

''What about him?'' he demanded.

There was a recklessness about Luc that worried her, and her gaze slid nervously from his. Perhaps this wasn't the best time to mention her supposed fiancé. ''I'll...discuss it with him.''

''Yeah. You do that. In the meantime, I want as much of your stuff over here as we can carry. When Miss

Emergency Response Worker arrives on my doorstep, I want her to find a happily married couple—his-and-hers hairbrushes on the dresser, our toothbrushes sharing a tube of toothpaste and my shoes playing footsie with yours on the closet floor."

If only she had time to think, time to line up all the reasons why his plan wouldn't work. She pulled from his grasp and tightened the sash of her robe, thrusting her hair back from her face. "In case it escaped your notice, I haven't agreed to your request."

He turned on her. "Are you refusing your help?"

Was she? She frowned, eyeing the empty crib with a sick feeling in the pit of her stomach. With each passing hour, Luc drew her further and further into his personal problems. When Dom returned, could she face him honestly and say that she'd kept their agreement? But then, how could she leave Luc in such dire straits? How could she desert him?

"Do we have to claim we're married?" she asked. "The police think we're engaged. What happens if they compare notes?"

"Then we'll show them our marriage certificate."

She stared at Luc in shock. *"What?"*

"Tomorrow we apply for a license and have all the required testing done, just in case a temporary marriage is necessary."

"No! I won't do it."

He approached, towering over her, his face set in hard, determined lines. "Oh, yes, you will. I don't care what it takes. I'll give you whatever you want, but you will do this. If not for me, for Toni."

She faced him defiantly. "You have such a way with words."

He inhaled deeply, pain etching deep furrows across

his brow. "I'm sorry. I know I'm doing this all wrong. But... Please, Grace. I need you. I need your help. I can't let them take Toni away."

She closed her eyes, knowing she should turn him down flat. A strident voice of logic told her there wasn't a single valid reason for helping him, and every reason in the world for refusing. If she was smart, she'd listen to that voice. If she was smart...

"All right," she whispered. "I'll do it."

And then he kissed her, a kiss of such passion and heat that it was more than enough to still even the voice of logic.

THE PHONE WOKE her at the crack of dawn that morning. Grace crawled out of bed, every weary muscle in her body making her painfully aware that she'd hardly slept a wink after the police had left. Once again, she pulled on her robe and trudged toward the study.

"Pietro!" she heard Luc exclaim. "Where are you? *What! Épazzo!* What the *hell* are you doing back in Italy?"

"What's going on?" she asked, fighting back a yawn. "What's Pietro doing in Italy?"

Luc covered the mouthpiece. "Trying my patience." He spoke into the phone again. "Listen up, it's gotten serious here. The police came last night and took Toni."

She winced, able to hear Pietro's furious protests clear across the room. "Tell him we need a custody statement," she urged.

"Shut up and listen," Luc snapped.

She couldn't hide her hurt. "I was just trying to help."

"No, not you, Grace. Pietro. Come again? Never mind

what she's doing here at this hour. It's what you have to do that's important.''

Grace closed her eyes and groaned. Just when she'd thought matters couldn't get any worse, fate...or in this case Luc Salvatore...proved her wrong.

''You know that if it's within my powers I'll get Toni back, but we need a signed custody statement from Carina and a medical-permission slip. Can you get her to give them to you?''

Grace crossed to Luc's side. ''Don't forget the birth certificate,'' she reminded him.

''Right. And a copy of Toni's birth certificate. You fax me the documents as soon as possible, is that clear? Otherwise, they'll put your daughter in a foster home and you'll have a hell of a time getting custody again.''

Grace tugged at Luc's arm. He glanced down at her, exhaustion lining his face. Clearly, he hadn't slept, either. ''Tell him it'll be okay,'' she said. ''Tell him to take care of Carina and we'll take care of Toni. Reassure him.''

He nodded briefly. ''Don't worry, Pietro. You know I'll take care of everything. Just get home as soon as you can.'' After exchanging a few more words, he hung up. ''Get dressed,'' he ordered Grace briskly. ''If we're going to get Toni home tonight, we've got a list of chores a mile long to accomplish beforehand.''

First on his list turned out to be moving as many of her belongings as possible to his apartment. In no time, they'd practically stripped her place bare and filled up his car with personal possessions.

Jingling the car keys in his pocket, he stood by her front door. ''Ready?'' he asked, obviously impatient to get to the second item on his list—the marriage license.

''I'll be right out,'' she said, suddenly remembering

her answering machine. Who knew when she'd return to her apartment. She'd better check messages before she left. She didn't doubt there'd be at least one from her father.

To her dismay, there were three. Each one urged her to call home, that he had a surprise for her. Well, the surprise would have to wait until her situation returned to normal. Next on the tape was her ridiculous conversation with the fictitious William. Shooting a nervous glance over her shoulder, she fast-forwarded through the nonsensical spiel. To her horror, right after her monologue came a message from Luc.

''Well, well...'' he practically purred into the tape. ''How very interesting.''

She stared at the machine in confusion. What...? Then she remembered the call he'd made in the study—right on the heels of her own. Did his phone have one of those buttons that automatically redialed the last number called? She struggled to remember. She could check, but she was about ninety-percent positive there had been. Which meant that after she'd supposedly chatted with her ''fiancé,'' Luc had pushed the redial button and discovered that far from calling William, she'd phoned her own apartment.

She shut her eyes. No wonder he'd questioned the existence of any remaining roadblocks. With her disguise stripped away and his discovery that William didn't exist, he must have figured the road was perfectly clear—clear for seduction.

''Grace! Move it, will you?''

She jumped. How could she face him? What could she possibly say? ''Coming!'' she called.

She'd just have to muddle through the best she could. He must have left the message deliberately, so she'd know he knew. And now that she did…and he did… She groaned, covering her face. Maybe she could pretend she hadn't listened to the messages. She could give him her most innocent look and pray her eyes didn't go all cloudy or any such nonsense. Yes. That's what she'd do. Hadn't she gotten rather good at these sorts of fibs?

"What the hell is taking so long?" Luc strode into the room.

Oops.

His gaze moved from her answering machine to her bright red face and for the first time that day he grinned. "Something you forgot to tell me?"

"Not a thing," she declared, leaping to her feet. "Shall we go?"

He stood in front of her, his arms folded across his chest. "Not until you admit there is no William."

She lifted her chin. "Of course, there's a William." Whipping past him before he could stop her, she headed for the door. "I just don't happen to be engaged to him."

With a bark of laughter, Luc followed.

The next few hours passed in a mad dash. After setting the wheels in motion for a quickie wedding should the need arise, Luc purchased a wedding band for Grace, overriding her heated objections with callous determination.

"I don't have time to argue with you about this," he informed her impatiently, shoving the ring over her knuckle. "You've pretended to be engaged for the past eleven months. Now you're pretending to be married. What's the difference?"

She glared at him. "Give me a minute and I'll tell you."

"We don't have a minute. The emergency-response

worker assigned to our case is meeting us at the apartment at noon. That doesn't give us much time to get everything in place."

Realizing her arguments were fruitless in the face of such overwhelming resolve, she gave up and returned with Luc to his apartment. At the stroke of twelve she positioned the last of her personal possessions, and as if in response, the doorbell rang. Joining Luc at the door, they welcomed the social worker together.

Ms. Cartwright proved to be a very pleasant, no-nonsense careerwoman in her late thirties, and it took Luc precisely three minutes to totally charm her.

The first minute they exchanged names and business cards. Luc introduced Grace as his wife and thanked Ms. Cartwright for taking the time out of her busy schedule to visit with them.

The second minute, he fired a thousand questions about Toni's well-being at the startled woman.

The third minute, he relaxed, apologized for his abruptness and offered her one of his most stunning smiles. Grace had long ago realized that his smile could melt steel. Melting Ms. Cartwright was a cinch compared to that. Drawing her into the living room, he focused both that smile and his intense golden eyes on the hapless woman.

"You see," Luc explained, and there was no mistaking the rough sincerity in his voice, "Toni is family. You tell me what I have to do to get her back here until her parents return from Italy and I'll do it. Anything."

Ms. Cartwright visibly softened. "Please understand, Mr. Salvatore. We aren't trying to split your family apart. We just want what's best for the child."

He inclined his head in satisfaction. "Then we have the same goal. I think you'll find what's best is for Toni to be returned to her family. Let me show you around and then we'll discuss what needs to be done."

Ms. Cartwright inspected every inch of the apartment with a nerve-racking thoroughness. Eventually, she wandered into their temporary nursery. "Why, what a beautiful room you have here," she said, pausing in the doorway. "You did all this for your niece?"

"Not just for Toni," Luc claimed, shooting an openly smoldering look in Grace's direction. "I was hoping to give her cousins sometime soon."

Ms. Cartwright beamed, patting Grace's arm. "I can tell by that blush that you're a newlywed. Ben Hatcher referred to you as Mr. Salvatore's fiancée in his report. You must have married recently?"

"Very," Luc answered for Grace.

The social worker made a brief notation on her clipboard. "I'm glad to hear that. I rarely approve a home where the primary caretakers aren't married. And who would have the main responsibility for Toni during the day?"

"We both would," Luc said. "I've arranged to work out of the apartment until my brother and his wife return."

"Wife?" Ms. Cartwright frowned. "I understood that Ms. Donati was a single parent. In fact, I'm a little concerned that you first told the police that your brother and Ms. Donati were married, then later admitted that wasn't true."

A variety of emotions chased across Luc's face...frustration, anger and finally resignation. "To be honest, Ms. Cartwright, I would have said just about anything to keep Toni with her family," he confessed in a low voice. "I know it's a terrible admission, but my brother had entrusted Toni to my care and I didn't want to let him down."

"I understand your feelings, but I must insist on absolute honesty from now on." The social worker was serious. She tapped her pencil against the clipboard, and Grace knew without question there'd be no charming her into overlooking any future fibs. "Lying to the police, or to us for that matter, is a grave offense. If we uncover any further...discrepancies, you will not be permitted to care for your niece now or any time in the future. Are we clear on this?"

Grace thought she'd pass out at the woman's feet. She didn't dare look at Luc. Instead, she stood as still as possible, fighting to keep from toying nervously with her phony wedding band. How had she managed to get herself into this mess? Maybe she'd phone her father, after all. She needed a good, strong dose of his common sense and principles. One of his lectures wouldn't go amiss around about now, either.

Luc weathered the imminent crisis far better. He forked his fingers through his hair and then inclined his head. "We're clear," he said.

Ms. Cartwright didn't seem to notice anything wrong. She examined the pages attached to her clipboard and said, "I'm also concerned about the mother in this case."

"Carina is young and rather emotional," Luc offered, stepping into the breach once again. "She wasn't thinking straight when she left Toni with us. She'd just had a baby out of wedlock—something both her family and her religion frown on. And she'd just learned her mother was on death's door. The one smart thing she did was to come to my brother for help."

"But he left the baby, too."

"In my custody. I'm the eldest, and my brothers have always come to me when they needed help. Look, Ms. Cartwright. I'm positive they'll marry very soon and return to straighten all this out. If social services wants to investigate me to ensure I'm a fit temporary guardian for Toni, then fine. If they want to camp out on my doorstep in order to keep an eye on me, they're welcome. All I ask is that you let me take care of Toni until Carina and Pietro get back."

His impassioned speech clearly had an affect on Ms. Cartwright. "You make a very eloquent case for yourself, Mr. Salvatore," she said with a sigh.

"That was my intention."

She frowned as she considered the viability of his request. "Very well," she said. "I still have to do some routine investigation of your situation. It would help if you'd provide references, both financial and personal."

"Done. Will that take care of it?"

"Not quite. *If* you can get a letter of consent from the mother, a copy of the baby's birth certificate and a medical-permission slip in my hands by the end of the day, then I'll recommend that Toni be returned to you."

"Returned tonight?"

She smiled. "I'll do my best. If she is, a case manager will be assigned to check up on you. You realize that even when Ms. Donati returns this won't be over, don't you? In the eyes of the law, she abandoned her child. We take a very dim view of that."

"She'll have the support of the Salvatore family. And she'll have her husband's support."

"I hope, for her sake, you're right."

A few minutes later, Ms. Cartwright left and Luc grabbed Grace, wrapping his arms about her waist and twirling her around until the room spun in a dizzy arc.

''We did it!'' he announced jubilantly, setting her back on her feet. ''Didn't I tell you everything would work out?''

''Yes, you did,'' Grace murmured, clutching his shoulders.

But she wasn't quite as confident. Not only were their lies compounding by the hour, so was her commitment to Luc and the baby. How could she possibly face Dom and claim she'd kept her part of the bargain, when she'd become so involved in this situation with Toni.... Toni? What about Luc? She closed her eyes. If she was honest—and she had to concede that honesty was something in disastrously short supply these days—she'd admit she'd become very involved with Luc.

If she didn't get out of this situation soon, she'd lose everything... Baby Dream Toys, for one. But far worse, her heart.

CHAPTER EIGHT

The Great Lie
Day 340 and complications abound…

TONI ARRIVED SAFELY back at Luc's apartment by dinner time that evening and all Luc's brothers were there to celebrate her return. Dinner proved to be loud and rowdy, not that Toni seemed bothered by the noise and confusion. If anything, she reveled in it. Wearing a frilly pink dress and a matching bow, she charmed one uncle after another with her full repertoire of baby coos, babbles and toothless grins. It wasn't until the gathering started to break up that the trouble began.

"This is an interesting addition," Marc proclaimed loudly. He snatched Grace's hand and examined the wedding band decorating her finger. In ten seconds flat, Luc's brothers had her surrounded.

"Is it real?" Stef demanded.

"You didn't marry that Will-William guy, did you?" Alessandro questioned in a disapproving voice. "He's not good enough for you, Grace—not if he makes you dress like a bag lady."

Before Grace could answer, Luc cut through and snagged her elbow. "The wedding band is there because I put it on her finger," he announced, tucking her close to his side.

Dead silence met his explanation. Then Rocco asked, "But is it real?"

For a moment Grace thought Luc would lie. She poked her elbow in his side to discourage any such plan. "Don't you dare," she muttered. "I've had my fill of fibs."

He stared down at her, his eyes glittering with devilry. Shrugging, he admitted, "No. It's not real."

"Yet?" Marc suggested with a grin.

Luc ignored him. "The people at social services believe it is real. If anyone finds out otherwise, we'll lose Toni. So keep your mouths shut."

Stef's face was a study in confusion. "When did this marriage business start? I thought you guys were just pretending to be engaged."

"That's for the police. Get with it, bro," Alessandro said with an exasperated sigh. "Look..." He ticked off on his fingers. "They're boss and assistant at work, engaged for the police, married for the baby people and just good friends in front of us."

"You guys ever consider scorecards? This is getting confusing," Stef complained.

Alessandro lifted an eyebrow, his expression reminding Grace forcefully of Luc. "What I want to know is which category they fall into when they're alone with Toni."

"Maybe they don't fall into any category," Marc suggested with a mock leer in Grace's direction. "Maybe they fall into the nearest bed."

"That's enough," Luc said, a hint of anger sparking in his eyes.

"Yeah!" Rocco slugged Marc in the arm. "Watch your mouth."

"I'd rather watch Grace's."

"Oh, yeah? How are you going to do that with two black eyes?"

Marc's hands balled into fists. "You'll have to land a punch first—something you haven't been able to do since I was twelve."

"Then, it's about time I remedied that oversight!"

"Do it, Rocco," Stef cheered him on. "This I gotta see."

"I said, that's enough!" Luc glared from one to the other. "Get out of here, the lot of you. Toni's just been put to bed and I won't have you waking her up again. We get little enough sleep as it is."

"That answers that question," Marc said with a hoot. "Maybe you'd get more rest if you didn't spend your nights jumping Grace's—"

Luc silenced his brother with a single look. "Time to go. All of you, out of here," he said, maneuvering them from the room and out the front door. This time, they didn't make a sound as they left, though Marc thumbed his nose at Mrs. Bumgartle's door before anyone could restrain him.

Alone again with Luc, Grace glanced at him with a troubled expression. "Is it really wise to involve your brothers in this deception? I feel guilty enough, as it is."

"Really? Did you feel guilty pretending to be engaged to William?" he asked, crossing to stand in front of her.

She looked away, hot color creeping into her cheeks. "That was different."

He hooked her chin with his finger and forced her to look at him. "Was it? Why?"

"You know why. I wasn't trying to deceive the police or social services."

"No, only me." His watchful gaze sharpened. "You never did explain that."

She stepped away from him. To her relief, he let her go. "Didn't I?" she asked evasively.

"No. Care to take a stab at it now?"

"Not really."

"Afraid?" he mocked. "Shall I guess why you did it?"

"We've already played this game, Luc?" She spoke more sharply than she'd intended. "It didn't end well."

"Did I win? I can't seem to remember."

"I believe it was a draw."

"Then, I insist on a rematch."

Not since their deception began, had she felt this vulnerable. Her attraction to Luc grew with each passing moment they spent together, as did her craving for his touch, his kisses, his passion. How, after holding him at a distance for eleven long months, could she now be on the verge of surrendering?

Catching her by the elbows, he tugged her close. He looked so large and enticing. She rested her hands on his chest, feeling the hard muscles tauten beneath her fingertips. It took every ounce of determination not to let her hands roam, exploring what lay beneath his crisp white shirt.

She bowed her head, fighting her wayward urges. "Luc, don't," she whispered.

"I think you disguised your appearance and wore that engagement ring for protection."

"Protection?" She managed a light laugh. "That's nonsense."

He shook his head, eyeing her with a nerve-racking intensity. "No. I think I'm right. My guess is you had a bad experience with your last employer." His voice held a tender note that completely disarmed her. "Did he harass you? Is that why you went to such lengths to protect yourself—because you thought I might be like him? I can understand, sympathize even. But why let the pretence go on for so long, once you knew I wasn't like that?''

She felt like a worm. He'd gotten the wrong end of the stick entirely. How could she tell him that far from such a reasonable, sympathetic motivation, she'd gone to such lengths because of his father's request and her own greed. ''No! You're wrong, Luc. I swear it.''

He lifted an eyebrow, a teasing smile tugging at his mouth. ''After all the deception between us, I'm supposed to believe you?''

If he only knew! ''For your information, until I started working at Salvatore's I'd told a grand total of six lies in my entire life.''

He slid a hand along the nape of her neck, his fingers sinking into her hair. ''Then I'll assume you've been making up for lost time.''

She stirred within his hold. ''You promised not to touch me, remember?''

''I remember.'' His mouth hovered a breath away from hers. ''But it was a promise meant to be broken.''

His head came down and his kiss blocked all thought, all resistance. She slid her arms around his waist, desire racing like wildfire, threatening to flare out of control. He pressed her close, his thighs cradling hers, and she snuggled into his embrace, the feelings he aroused unlike any she'd ever experienced.

Drawing back slightly, he loosened the top few buttons of her blouse. Sweeping it from her shoulders, he exposed the long line of her neck and sloping curves of her breasts. He lowered his head, pressing a lingering kiss in the soft hollow of her throat.

"I want you, *mia amorata,*" he muttered, his breath fast and hot against her neck.

Her heart pounded beneath his hands and she shook her head, desperately clinging to the tiny bit of sanity remaining to her. Every instinct urged her to give in to his demands, but she couldn't cross that line, couldn't permit a physical relationship without the emotional commitment to go with it. "We can't. It wouldn't be right." But it felt right—exquisitely right.

"It would be wrong not to," he argued. "What's the problem? You've admitted there's no William. Your job is safe. You want me. And I want you."

His hands tightened on her hips, making the extent of his desire abundantly clear. She wasn't certain how much longer she could hold him off. She wasn't certain how much longer she *wanted* to hold him off. But she had to try. "Luc, this is crazy. We've known each other for almost a year and this has never happened. Think about it. We're under a lot of stress. We're forced to live together in very difficult circumstances. It's...it's an involuntary reaction or something."

He stared at her in disbelief. "An involuntary reaction? You're kidding, right?"

"I'm serious," she insisted. "It's the situation we're in, it's not because we really want...you know."

He laughed, the sound harsh and taunting. "Believe me when I say that I really want...you know. I ache for...you know. If I don't experience...you know soon, I might do something drastic—like bite the damned buttons right off your blouse."

"Luc!"

"You don't get it, do you? I want to kiss every inch of your body, starting with that luscious mouth of yours. I want to strip off your clothes and make long, sweet love to you. And I want to do it in every room of this apartment, starting right here and now. And once we've done that, I'll want to do it all over again. Does that give you some idea of how much I want...you know?''

She wondered if she looked as shocked as she felt. Nervously, she licked her lips and watched in fascination as Luc's eyes flared a brilliant gold. ''Where is this leading?'' she asked.

''Straight to bed,'' he answered without missing a beat.

''That's not what I mean, and you know it. Are you interested in marriage, or are we just talking about an affair?''

His hands tightened on her shoulders. ''You'd like an honest answer, I assume?''

''It would be refreshing.''

He hesitated, then said bluntly, ''I want to make love to you. That's as honest as I can be at this point.''

''I see.''

She looked away, hoping to hide her distress. He'd been very tactful. But the bottom line was, he wanted a mistress, not a wife. It wasn't as if she hadn't suspected as much. Still, she hadn't anticipated how badly the truth would hurt. Stepping from his hold, she pulled the front of her blouse closed. She didn't try to button it. Her hands were trembling too much to even try.

''Grace...''

''What about my job? I mean, affairs don't last forever. An ending is inevitable.''

''Whether we decide to become involved or not, I don't think we should work together any longer,'' he said carefully. ''There's an opening at management level. I'd planned to tell you about it at your year-end review. It would mean a promotion—more money, great potential for advancement.''

She could hardly take it all in. She'd never suspected he might want to promote her. Nor could she deny how tempted she was by his offer. Too tempted. She had to remember Baby Dream Toys. Only, why had remembering become such a struggle? Wrapping her arms around her waist, she said, ''This is too much, too soon. I need time. I'd rather not do anything I'll later regret while we're still taking care of Toni.''

''You want to wait until Pietro and Carina return, is that it?''

''Yes.''

''That won't be for another week. Not until Thanksgiving.''

Her head jerked up and she stared at him. ''What!''

''I'm sorry. I should have told you sooner.'' He watched her with a hooded expression. ''I guess I had other things on my mind. Pietro called right before my brothers arrived. They're still in Italy with Carina's family, while her mother recuperates. He says Carina's talking to him now, but he hasn't convinced her to marry him yet.''

''But seven more days! When does Dom get back?'' she asked in a panic.

''He's due in the week after Thanksgiving.''

That cut it close. Too close. She needed time to think, to get her priorities straight. Whether he realized it or not, Luc was asking her to sacrifice everything she'd worked so hard to attain. And for what? A brief affair. A few weeks or months of passion. How could she agree to that? Her answer should be obvious. And it would be, if it weren't for one small detail. She wanted him every bit as much as he wanted her.

"Grace?"

"I need time," she informed him. She fought to cloak herself in the calm, collected air she'd spent eleven long months cultivating. It was more of a struggle than she would have thought possible. Where had her control gone? Her detachment? "Once our lives get back to normal, I'll give you my answer."

"By Thanksgiving?"

After a brief hesitation, she nodded. "By Thanksgiving."

"And between now and then?"

The look she cast him was direct. "You're not to touch me. Not a kiss. Not so much as a hug. I don't intend to be seduced into a decision."

She could tell he wasn't pleased. "And if I don't agree?"

"Then you can explain to social services why your wife doesn't live with you." Not waiting for his reaction to her threat—not allowing herself time to change her mind and tumble back into his arms—she practically ran from the room.

THE NEXT FIVE DAYS proved to be the longest of Grace's life. Now, a mere forty-eight hours from their Thanksgiving deadline, the final days of her tenure at Salvatore's crept ever closer, as did the day of Dom's return. True to his word, Luc didn't lay a finger on her, which stretched both their frustration levels to the limits. As a result, she didn't know whether to thank him for keeping his promise or hit him. But since she'd been the one to set the rules, she was stuck with them.

How she wished she'd had the chance to talk to her father—to get his help and advice. But they'd been out of touch for the past couple of weeks, and though she'd left messages, they kept missing each other.

The doorbell rang. ''Luc!'' Grace called, struggling to pin the diaper around Toni—a determinedly wiggly Toni. ''Get the door. It's probably the case manager. Can you answer it?''

''What?''

''The doorbell!''

''I'll get it.''

Grace sighed, snapping and buttoning as quickly as she could. ''You don't give your uncle this much trouble when *he* changes you. I think it's very unfair of you to fight me, since I'm the one who just filled you up with a nice, warm bottle.''

Toni responded with a string of bubbles and a determined pumping of limbs. Just as Grace finished, she heard the front door crash shut. An instant later, Luc raced into the room. One look warned her it was bad news.

''Quick!'' he said, snatching Toni off the changing table and dumping her into a laundry basket of clean baby clothes that was sitting on the bed. ''Come with me. Hurry.''

''You can't put Toni in there! Luc! What's wrong? What's happening?''

He didn't answer, simply clutched the basket and dashed toward his bedroom. Grace gave chase. The doorbell rang again, a strident, urgent sound. Flinging open his louvered closet doors, Luc swept shoes to one side and set the laundry basket on the floor. Toni gurgled happily. Propelling Grace in beside the basket, he slammed the door.

''Stay there,'' he ordered. ''Don't move and don't make any noise.''

"Luc!" She thrust the door open and poked her head out. *"What is going on?"*

"In case you weren't aware of it, when you open your mouth and speak, you make noise. You've got to be *quiet!*" The doorbell rang again, short, multiple, staccato rings. Kissing her swiftly, Luc pushed her toward the back of the huge closet. "My dad's here. Now keep it down." He closed the door.

Grace opened the door. "Dom's here?" she asked in a panicked whisper. "He's not due back for another week."

"I don't have time for this," he said through gritted teeth. "Dad can't find out about Toni until Pietro and Carina are married or he'll disown the lot of them. Which means you two have to stay hidden."

"I understand that. But why here? Why not the guest room?"

He ran an impatient hand through his hair. "This is the safest place in the house. He hasn't been in my bedroom since the time he walked in without knocking and caught the cleaning lady making my bed. So you should be fine *if* you keep quiet." He slammed the door shut.

She opened it, staring at him in bewilderment. "What was wrong with the cleaning lady making your bed?"

He spared her a brief grin. "She was naked at the time." The doorbell was ringing nonstop now. "Grace, for crying out loud! Open this door again and I'll haul you out there, introduce you as my wife and tell him Toni is yours!"

Without another word, she slammed the door shut. To her disbelief, Toni had fallen asleep. How could Toni possibly nap through all the confusion? Grace wondered in amazement. Babies were such strange, little creatures.

She heard the front door crash again. Had Dom left already? Did she dare sneak out and see?

Infuriated Italian burst from the direction of the living room. Well, that answered that question. Unable to resist, she pressed her ear to the louvered slats. Dom was still speaking...or yelling...in Italian.

"I told you I was sorry," she heard Luc's deep voice reply in English. He sounded remarkably calm. "Why didn't you let us know you were coming?"

"I wished to surprise you for Thanksgiving. I called the office. They said you were working from your apartment. Why is this?"

"It seemed like a good idea at the time," came the dry reply.

There was a long silence, and Grace could almost see Dom mull over Luc's response. "You have a woman here, am I right?" he demanded. "That is why you slam the door in my face. Where have you hidden her?"

Grace shrank back, tripped, and tumbled to the floor next to the laundry basket. She gripped her fingers together and prayed they hadn't heard her—praying even harder that Toni wouldn't wake up and bellow in annoyance.

"Actually, I have two," came Luc's cool response. "A blonde and a brunette."

Grace held her breath, waiting for Dom's reaction—waiting for him to explode or come and ferret her from her hiding place. An instant later she heard his bark of laughter. "*Due.* That is a good one. I almost believe you."

"You want to check the bedroom? I have them hiding in there."

It was all Grace could do to keep from shrieking. Was he crazy? Luc's question seemed to hang in the air for endless minutes. Then Dom sighed. "I apologized for that little incident," he grumbled. "The young lady forgave me, even if you did not. I wish to change the subject. Where is Grace? I asked for her at the office and they said she was out as well."

"I gave her the afternoon off. She's been working very hard lately."

"She is a good girl. I am very fond of her."

"There's certainly more to her than meets the eye."

Dom chuckled. "I think your words are more true than you realize."

"Don't count on it," came Luc's risky reply. "But enough about business. How was your trip to Italy? We've missed you."

As their voices grew fainter, dropping to a gentle rumble, Grace curled up next to the laundry basket. That had been close. If Dom had walked in and discovered her… She shuddered. It would have meant the end of her plan to open Baby Dream Toys.

Not that it didn't anyway.

She dropped her chin to her knees and sighed. One thing she did know—she couldn't avoid Dom forever. What would she say when they met? She couldn't very well pretend this year had gone off without a hitch. She'd have to be honest with him, tell him what she'd been up to the past ten or eleven days.

If he chose to renege on their deal, she wouldn't argue. After all, she'd been the one to break their agreement. Remembering Luc's passionate kisses with a wistful longing, she was forced to admit she'd broken the agreement more than just a time or two. Once in possession of all the facts, Dom would be within his rights to refuse to set her up in business. Well, she could live with that.

But what about Luc…? She bit her lip. She didn't doubt he'd find out the real reason for her disguise, discover that her motives had been less than pure. It was inevitable that Dom would tell Luc the truth. How would he react when he found out? She closed her eyes, stifling a groan. She knew how he'd react. Those gorgeous golden eyes of his would ice up. Her job as his assistant would be over. Her management-position job offer would vanish like dust in a high wind. And their affair would end before it ever began. Just as it should.

She fought back a sob, smothering the sound against her knees. Time to face facts. Because the fact was that at some point she'd fallen hopelessly, helplessly in love with Luc Salvatore. And as much as she should care about the loss of Baby Dream Toys, she cared more about losing Luc.

Sitting there on the closet floor—alone and hurting—she faced the death of all her dreams. And no matter how hard she tried, she couldn't prevent a scalding tear from drifting down her cheek.

LUC SURREPTITIOUSLY checked his watch as he escorted Dom to the door. ''It's great having you home, Dad. Thanks for dropping by.''

''It is very good to be home. I decided to return early so I could have the whole family over for Thanksgiving dinner.'' He paused in the entranceway. ''Would this be convenient?''

''Terrific. Just terrific.'' Luc opened the door.

A young woman dressed in a business suit, with wire-rimmed glasses perched on the end of her nose, stood there, poised to knock. ''Oh, my goodness,'' she exclaimed. ''You startled me.'' Recovering swiftly, she held out her hand. "Hello. I'm Miss Carstairs," she announced. "I'm your—"

"My masseuse!" Luc greeted her loudly. Grabbing her hand, he yanked her into the apartment. "At last!"

"No! I—"

Dom chuckled. "A blonde, a brunette and now a redhead." He wagged his finger at Luc. "I knew you were up to no good. One of these days, my boy…"

Luc wrapped an arm around the shocked social worker. "I never could put one over on you. Talk to you later, Dad, and welcome home." He slammed the door closed.

Miss Carstairs wriggled from his hold, stumbling back against the door. "Oh, my," she murmured, red-faced and breathless. She tucked a stray curl back into the tight knot on top of her head. "I am *not* the masseuse!"

Luc lifted an eyebrow. "You're not?"

"No! I'm Miss Carstairs, from social services. Are you Mr. Salvatore?"

"In the flesh. Pleased to meet you." He offered his hand.

She stared at his outstretched fingers as if they had fangs and a rattle. "I'm…I'm your case manager." She peered up at him suspiciously. "Are you sure you're Luc Salvatore? Mr. Luc Salvatore, whose wife is Mrs. Grace Salvatore?"

"That's right."

Perhaps he shouldn't have introduced her as his masseuse, but it was the only thing he could think of at the time. If he was smart, he'd get little Miss Carstairs on her way fast—before she discovered Grace and Toni hiding in the closet. Social services would have the baby out of his apartment like a shot if that happened.

"Listen, I'm sorry but Grace and Toni aren't in."

Dropping his hands to her shoulders, he peeled her off the door, opened it and glanced up and down the hallway. Dom was nowhere in sight. "How about coming back tomorrow?" Planting his hand in the small of her back, he propelled her into the hall.

A loud baby bellow resounded through the apartment and Miss Carstairs's eyebrows flew up. "Your wife and Antonia are out? And what, may I ask, is that crying? It certainly sounds like a baby to me."

Before he could stop her, she charged back into the apartment, leaving him no choice but to give chase. Following the sound of a very cranky Toni, she hustled into his bedroom and hesitated in front of the closet. Shooting him a look of disbelief, she threw open the closet door.

Luc inhaled sharply, positive he'd never seen a more appealing sight in his life. Grace sat there on the floor, Toni clutched to her breast. Wispy golden curls framed her sleep-flushed face. She blinked up at them, her light green eyes soft and drowsy. Clearly, she'd just woken up.

"You make your wife and niece live in a closet?" Miss Carstairs demanded, turning on him. "Or do you just make them sleep in there."

"No, I don't make my wife and niece live in a closet," Luc stated forcefully. "Nor do they sleep there. Most days. My father... You see, Grace..." He shoved his hand through his hair and sighed in exasperation. "It's a long story."

Miss Carstairs folded her arms across her chest and tapped her foot. "I have all the time in the world."

Slipping Toni back into the laundry basket, Grace crawled out of the closet. Attempting to stand proved more difficult. Her knees buckled. Luc caught her. "My legs fell asleep,'' she murmured apologetically. ''How long was your father here?''

''Ninety long, impossible minutes,'' he replied, cradling her close until she could shake the pins and needles from her legs. He gazed down into her face and frowned. Cupping her chin, he ran his thumb across her cheekbone, a question in his eyes. ''*Cara?* Are you all right?'' he asked in a low voice.

A hint of color lit Grace's face. Could he tell she'd been crying? Lord, she hoped not. She shifted her attention to the social worker, offering a smile and a hand. ''Hi. I'm Grace…Salvatore.''

''Lillian Carstairs. May I ask if you and the baby often hide in your husband's closet?''

''It's the first time that I'm aware of,'' Luc answered for Grace. ''I can't vouch for any other closets, however. Have you hidden in any others?''

''Only one. When I was twelve.''

''Excuse me,'' Miss Carstairs interrupted. ''Let's just deal with this closet and this time. Why were you hiding in the closet?''

''So Dom—Luc's father—wouldn't find us,'' Grace answered.

Luc released a gusty sigh. ''My father doesn't know about Toni. For that matter, he doesn't know that Grace and I are married. We…eloped while he was still in Italy. And until I tell him…''

''Your wife and niece will be kept hidden away in the closet?'' the social worker suggested dryly.

''We'll use the bathroom next time,'' Grace offered. ''Would that be all right?''

''Perhaps it would be best if you told him the truth,'' Miss Carstairs said in no uncertain terms. ''I suppose that also explains the rather…unusual greeting at the door.''

A hint of amusement lightened Luc's expression. ''I'm sorry. I didn't want to introduce you to my father. He'd already assumed the worst as far as your presence was concerned, and I just went along with it. I apologize, if I offended you.''

Color spotted Miss Carstairs's cheeks and Grace could tell that the infamous Salvatore charm was working its magic once more. ''This is all highly irregular,'' the young woman muttered.

''How about if we start over,'' Luc suggested. ''Come on into the kitchen and have a cup of coffee, and then we'll show you around and answer any questions you might have. Coffee, Grace?''

''Sounds great,'' she agreed.

''And a bottle for Toni, I think.''

Grace pulled the basket from the closet and picked up Toni. Once again Luc would talk his way out of a sticky situation. How she wished she had his gift. It would certainly come in handy over the next few days.

She closed her eyes and buried her face against Toni's neck. Matters were becoming much too complicated. How much longer could she keep doing this—living a lie? Perhaps she'd better confess her subterfuge to Luc once Miss Carstairs left. She'd be as frank with him as she intended to be with Dom. But if she did, how would Luc react? Would he understand why she'd chosen to deceive him? Somehow, she suspected he wouldn't. At the very least, it would change their relationship, and she didn't think she was ready for that.

''Grace?'' Luc called to her. ''Are you coming?''

She lifted her head and took a deep breath. Maybe she'd have a hot cup of coffee and think about it for a while. There was no rush, right? She'd get a good night's sleep and reconsider her options tomorrow.

Though, somehow, she suspected matters wouldn't be any more clear-cut come morning.

CHAPTER NINE

The Great Lie
Day 346 and Grace's situation can't get any darker…or can it…?

AS SHE SUSPECTED, having a night to sleep on her problems brought Grace no nearer a solution. If anything, she awoke more confused than ever. She had several choices, none quite what she wanted. She buried her head in the pillow with a groan. Should she tell Luc about her deal with Dom? Should she accept his very tempting offer of a promotion, if she was unable to open Baby Dream Toys? Most important of all, should she agree to a temporary relationship and suffer the resulting consequences.

She didn't know. She just didn't know. What she wanted was Luc. But Luc didn't want her, at least not on a permanent basis. And facing that fact nearly ripped her apart.

Crawling out of bed to a brilliant, sunny morning, she discovered Luc already up and dressed in a business suit and tie.

"You're not going into the office, are you?" she asked, dismayed. She'd hoped to spend time with him—precious, fleeting time.

"I'm afraid so. Dad said he'd meet me there. I assume he'd like an update on our various business activities.

And since the only other option is to have him come here...'' He let the suggestion hang.

''No, that wouldn't work, would it,'' she agreed. ''What about Pietro and Carina?''

''I still expect them tomorrow for Thanksgiving. If they weren't going to make it, Pietro would have phoned. Will you stay here with Toni? If Dad asks, I'll say you're out sick.''

''More lies,'' she murmured, disheartened.

He frowned, then approached and pulled her into his arms. ''I know this is difficult for you. But we can straighten everything out when Pietro returns. How about once this is over, we confess our various sins? You and I will have a frank talk and put all our cards on the table.''

She smiled. ''I'd like that. And you're right, of course. I have a sin or two of my own to confess.''

''Somehow that doesn't surprise me.'' He dropped a kiss on her mouth. Then, as if unable to resist, he kissed her again, more deeply, with an underlying urgency. ''Grace...I know I'm breaking our agreement, but I can't help it. I want you.''

She nestled into his embrace, and suddenly everything crystallized in her mind. Through the long, endless night, she'd struggled to make a decision. To decide whether she'd fight for Luc's love or do the safe thing and walk away. But now, in the cold light of day, she knew what her answer would be. In that instant, held in his arms, all her doubts vanished.

For the first time since their escapade began, she was certain in both heart and mind. Once they'd settled their problems with Toni, she'd tell Luc the truth. Every bit of it. Then, it would be up to him how they proceeded. She knew he wasn't interested in a permanent relationship, and though it meant future heartache, she'd take the tiny slice of heaven he offered. Because she knew, deep in her heart, that she'd never love anyone as much as she loved Luc.

"I want you, too," she admitted. And though she wished she could tell him of her love, that she could coax similar words from him, she was willing to give it time. Maybe even a lifetime.

His eyes darkened. "Say that again."

"I want you," she repeated. "Very, very badly."

"You sure that isn't frustration speaking?" he asked, skepticism clear in his voice. "What about when Toni's out of our life and you've had time to reconsider? What will you say then?"

"The same."

She'd surprised him, and he studied her expression intently. "You're sure?"

"I'm positive," she said, and he couldn't mistake her sincerity.

"Just so you know, your timing *really* stinks," he told her with a short, impatient laugh. Pulling her more fully into his arms, he kissed her again, the embrace passionate and thorough. "As much as I want to carry you back to bed, I have to leave."

"Will you be gone all day?" she asked wistfully. "Can you break off early?"

"I hope so. I'll see if I can't return for lunch." And with a final kiss, he left.

She secured the door behind him and leaned her forehead against the cool wooden surface. Another day or two and her subterfuge would end. Pietro would return, Toni would be back with her parents, and she and Luc would clear up all the lies and deceptions between them. She could hang on for that long, couldn't she? Not that she had a choice. Straightening, she tightened the sash on her robe and padded toward the guest bedroom. Toni lay in her crib, watching the mobile spin lazily above her.

"Good morning," Grace said with a smile. "You're certainly in a happy mood this morning. Ready for breakfast? Or should we have our bath first." Toni kicked her feet and let out a shrill gurgle. "Breakfast, it is."

Lifting the baby out of the crib, Grace headed for the kitchen, when a peremptory knock sounded at the door. Later, she realized she should have peered through the spy hole first. But at the time, she didn't think twice. She opened the door.

Dom Salvatore stood there.

He looked at her, took a stumbling step backward, double-checked the number on the door and then looked at her once more. Slowly his gaze took in her sleep-ruffled hair—her sleep-ruffled *blond* hair, her bathrobe-covered nightie, and finally the baby Grace held clutched in her arms. His face crumpled.

"You are not wearing your glasses," he blurted.

"No," she confessed. "I'm not."

"And your hair..."

"I know. It's blond again." She touched the tangled curls self-consciously, then stepped back. "Why don't you come in."

He looked appalled, and for an instant she thought he'd burst into tears. Then he slowly followed her into the apartment. "All my plans...ruined," he moaned.

"It's not so bad," she attempted to reassure him, wondering desperately which story to tell. Did she mention Pietro and Carina? Did she claim Toni as her own? Lord, how she wished Luc was here to help.

Dom shook his head, muttering in Italian. Finally, he implored, "How could this happen?"

Oh, Lord. How should she answer? She had to pick a story and fast, and salvage what she could of this mess. She bit down on her lip, forced to face facts with a vengeance. It was too late to save herself, but... She straightened her shoulders. She could still help Pietro and Carina.

To her relief, Toni came to the rescue. Reacting to the heightened emotions, her face screwed into a frown and she began to cry. "Oh, dear," Grace said, "I think we'd better get busy with that bottle."

"Please wait." For a long minute Dom stared at Toni, uncertainty clouding his face. Grace could see his quandary, his delight at the possibility of a grandchild warring with his outrage at the circumstances behind that grandchild's conception. Then his hands inched out and he took the wailing baby into his arms. He jiggled Toni gently and when she stopped crying, he beamed. "And who have we here?"

"This is your granddaughter, Antonia," Grace said simply.

A look of wonder dawned on his face. "A granddaughter," he murmured in astonishment. "But...this is marvelous. How old is she?"

Grace's gaze slipped away from his. "Three months."

He gaped at Grace. "Three..." He burst into volatile Italian, stabbing the air with his free hand. She didn't understand a single word he spoke, but she knew exactly what he said. In order for her to have given birth to Toni, she would have had to tumble into Luc's bed her first day on the job. At long last, he drew breath. "*Three months!*" he exclaimed.

What possible explanation could she give that would

appease him? "The disguise didn't work," she said, her face burning with humiliation.

"This I have figured out for myself!"

To her relief, Toni once again came to her rescue. Wriggling in her grandfather's arms she began to fuss. "She's hungry," Grace said. "I need to feed her." Leading the way into the kitchen, she popped a bottle into the microwave. "Would you like a cup of coffee?"

"That would be very kind of you." He sat down at the kitchen table, holding Toni on his lap. "Tell me, Grace. What happened?"

She cleared her throat, pouring the fragrant brew into a cup. "Well... It's a long story." To her relief, the microwave beeped, providing her with a few extra seconds to gather her thoughts. "Would you like to give Toni her bottle?"

"I'd be honored." He cradled his granddaughter in the crook of his arm and Toni stared up at him with wide, curious eyes. Dom offered her the nipple and without hesitation she took it, wrapping her tiny fingers around Dom's and sucking contentedly. He glanced at Grace with a bittersweet smile. "She is the image of my own Anna. Thank you for naming her after her grandmother. It touches me deeply."

"She's a good baby," Grace said gently, unwilling to take credit for something that had nothing to do with her.

"A beautiful baby. You have done a wonderful job, my dear." Then he fixed her with a stern gaze. "And now, you will tell me your story, please. You say the disguise did not work? Not even for a single day?"

"Not really." She poured a second cup of coffee and took a sip. "Luc's not an easy man to fool."

Dom clicked his tongue. ''But a girl with such an impeccable background. Could you not resist him?''

''He's hard to resist,'' she confessed.

''But still...'' He seemed to be searching for a reasonable explanation. ''I thought starting your own business was important to you. I thought that, if nothing else, such an agreement would keep you from my son's arms.'' He shook his head and released a deep, heartfelt sigh. ''You must love Luciano very much, to give up your dream.''

To her dismay, tears welled in her eyes. ''Starting Baby Dream Toys meant more to me than anything. I wanted to keep our agreement. I really did. Please believe that I tried. I wore the disguise and pretended to be engaged. But, Luc... He... I...'' Her throat closed over and helplessly, she bowed her head.

''I am sorry, my dear. I did not mean to upset you.'' He stroked Toni's head with a gentle hand. Then, he looked up, pinning her with a reluctant, though stern gaze. ''I must tell you I am very disappointed in you both. It is my deepest hope that you and Luc have taken proper responsibility for your unthinking actions. As much as this grandchild means to me, as much as my son means to me, I would throw you out of the family if I thought you had not.'' He paused, waiting for her response.

Grace swallowed, realizing she was treading on very shaky ground. ''You'd throw us out of the family if we hadn't...what?'' she asked hesitantly.

''Married, of course! You are wed, yes?''

A footstep sounded behind her. And then, ''Of course, we're married, Dad,'' Luc announced from the doorway.

Grace spun around, her eyes widening in horror. Without any question, he'd overheard every word of their conversation. And he was *furious*. His eyes glittered with harsh gold lights and he stalked into the kitchen, reminding her of an angry panther she'd once seen pacing his cage at the zoo, roaring his frustration to the heavens. She tensed, waiting for Luc's roar.

"What are you doing here, Dad?" To her surprise, he spoke in a deceptively mild voice. But one glimpse of his set features warned her that, though he wouldn't lose his temper in front of his father, he wouldn't be so restrained when he got her alone. "I thought we agreed to meet at the office."

"So we did," Dom agreed, not seeming to notice anything amiss. He set the bottle on the table and lifted Toni to his shoulder, patting her back. "It occurred to me we might drive into work together." He fixed his calm, dark gaze on Luc. "You forgot to tell me something yesterday, yes?"

Luc shrugged, pouring himself a cup of coffee. "As I recall, I did mention I had a blonde and brunette hiding in my bedroom."

"I thought you made a joke," Dom dismissed contemptuously. "You know this. Why did you not tell me the truth? You marry, have a child, and do not bother to tell your own father?" He added something in Italian, hurt clear in his lilting voice.

Luc hesitated, then asked, "If I had told you, what would you have done?"

"I would have come home," came the prompt response.

"There's your answer. The doctors wanted you to retire. You know you wouldn't have, if you'd returned early from Italy."

"Bah! Doctors. What do they know? I am strong as a horse."

"A sixty-five-year-old horse with a heart condition."

Dom stirred uncomfortably. "I wish to talk about Grace and this situation we now find ourselves in, not about my health. You uncovered the truth about her, I am right?"

Luc leaned back against the counter and sipped his coffee. For a split second his gaze locked with hers. She froze, held in place by the icy fury she read there. "Uncovered the truth about her disguise and the fake engagement? Yes. I uncovered that much." But not about his father's bribe. Grace caught the omission. Not about his starting her up in business.

And Luc's expression warned he wouldn't easily forgive that exclusion.

Betraying his nervousness, Dom ran a hand along his jaw. "You...ah...you are not upset with me?"

"Should I be?"

Dom stiffened. "Is this why you did not tell me about Antonia? You were angered that we deceived you?"

Luc's expression softened. "*No, Papa.* I wouldn't do that. I've explained why I didn't notify you. You needed to get away from Salvatore Enterprises. This past year has allowed you time to recuperate and me time to take control of the business."

"Then, it was good I hired Grace. She has helped you focus on your work."

Grace winced, waiting for Luc's tenuous control of his temper finally to snap. "You didn't need to involve someone else," Luc bit out, slamming his coffee mug to the counter. "You should have trusted me to take care of the work situation without interfering."

"Perhaps." Dom shrugged, not in the least intimidated by his son's wrath. "But I wished to insure you would have a full year to concentrate on work and not be subjected to...irresistible temptations.'' He glanced at Grace and smiled apologetically. ''This will not be a problem anymore, eh? Once a Salvatore falls in love and marries, it is for life. The eyes, they become blind to every other woman.''

It was all Grace could do not to weep. How she wanted that to be true. But as much as she might wish it otherwise, Luc hadn't fallen in love with her, merely in lust. And that minor detail ensured a broken heart at the end of their affair. Assuming they even had an affair. In the meantime, she couldn't continue to stand there quietly as though condoning any further lies. Rinsing her coffee cup at the sink, she crossed to where Dom sat.

''Would you excuse us?'' she murmured, scooping Toni into her arms. ''I think it's time we got dressed.''

Dom stood. ''I am happy I returned for Thanksgiving,'' he said, enfolding her in a tender embrace and kissing her cheeks. ''I have come home to find much to be grateful for.''

Unable to think of a single response, Grace offered a watery smile. Turning to leave the room, she shot Luc a swift, beseeching look, praying he'd understand her silent plea. Perhaps agreeing to Dom's plan had been wrong, but it had been the offer of a lifetime—too good to refuse. Would Luc understand that? Would he at least be willing to listen to her explanation?

Twenty minutes later Grace returned with Toni, in time to bid Dom farewell. She stood next to Luc and smiled calmly, striving to appear the perfect wife. The minute his father disappeared down the hallway, Luc turned on her.

''Every damned word out of your mouth has been a lie, hasn't it?'' he snarled, kicking the door shut. It bounced back ajar, but he ignored it, stalking after her.

"Not every word." She backed toward the living room, clutching Toni to her breast like a shield. Realizing she couldn't continue to hide behind a baby, she spread a blanket on the floor and set Toni on it. Then she turned to face Luc. "Besides," she said, refusing to be intimidated by his fury. "What about all *your* lies?"

"I lied to protect the baby," he was quick to defend. "They were necessary lies."

She lifted her chin. "They're still lies. As far as protecting the baby... Haven't I done everything possible to help you since Toni arrived? Haven't I lied to the police and to the social-service people, in order to cover for Pietro and Carina? And for what? For you! What more do you want from me? I even lied to your father. And that cost me the chance to start my own business."

Her words brought home the cold, hard facts and she stared at him with anguished eyes, the full extent of her predicament finally sinking in. "My own business," she whispered. To her horror, she burst into tears. She looked around helplessly, trying to remember where the tissues were kept.

"Here."

He held out a handkerchief and she took it gratefully, struggling to stem the flood of tears. "I'm sorry," she managed to say. "It must be the stress."

Luc thrust his hands into his trouser pockets, a muscle leaping in his jaw. "Explain it to me. The deal you had with Dad."

She waved the damp hanky. "You already know most of it."

He paced in front of her. "I sure as hell didn't know you were in cahoots with my father."

"That's the only fact you didn't have. You knew about the disguise, the fake engagement..."

He nailed her with a disbelieving look. ''And my *father* put you up to it?''

Reluctantly, she nodded. ''He seemed to think it was the only way he could retire. All your employees kept falling in love with you and making a mess of the office situation. He thought I'd be different.''

''Why?''

She shrugged. ''He thought I'd be more levelheaded, that with the disguise and the engagement ring, you'd keep your distance—and because of his offer, I'd keep mine.''

''Ah, yes. The offer.'' A cynical note colored his words. ''A business of your own, wasn't it?''

''Yes,'' she confirmed. ''When we met during the young-entrepreneur's contest, Dom realized I was desperate to open my own store and offered a deal. If I'd work for you for one year—keep our relationship strictly professional, no personal involvement—he'd finance Baby Dream Toys.''

''Desperate?'' He seized on the word, his eyes narrowing. ''Why were you so desperate to start your own business?''

The question hung between them. ''Because of my mother,'' she said at last.

He stilled, watching her closely. ''Your mother?''

Grace bowed her head. ''We were going to start the business together. We dreamed about it, planned it. She used to make the most beautiful stuffed animals. She'd call them her 'baby dreams.' That's where the name for the store came from.''

''What happened, *cara?*'' he asked gently.

''She died right before the contest.'' Grace's voice broke and she buried her hands in her face. ''I wanted to open the store so much, to name it in her honor. It was wrong to deceive you, I know that. But at the time...all I could think of..." She shook her head, fighting for control.

"Why didn't you tell me?" he demanded. "When all the other deceptions were uncovered, why didn't you come clean? Didn't you think I'd understand?"

She crumpled his handkerchief in her fist. "You had all these wonderful, generous excuses for why I'd deceived you. But they weren't true. I knew when you found out my motivation was greed, you'd hate me. I'm sorry," she said, choking on the words.

He groaned, the sound low and rough. "*Cara,* don't. Don't cry. Of course I don't hate you." Crossing to her side, he swept her into his arms. Gently, he pushed her hair from her face and forced her to look at him. "Dad was right about one thing. If it hadn't been for that damned engagement ring, I wouldn't have been able to keep my hands off you."

He kissed her with an urgency she couldn't mistake, sweeping her into a firestorm of desperate need. She didn't resist. The thought never entered her mind. She loved Luc and she wanted him. If all he could give her were these few minutes, she'd seize them with both hands. "Luc, please..." she whispered.

He studied her expression intently. "Are you sure?" he asked. At her nod, he eased back and dropped his suit jacket to the floor. Next came his tie. Yanking the knot loose, he stripped off the red silk and tossed it to one side. It ribboned through the air, catching on a lampshade.

Eager to help, Grace applied herself to the buttons of his shirt, wanting to feel the hair-roughened skin beneath her fingers. "You never told me why you came back this morning," she said, dropping a string of kisses along his jaw. A minute later the shirt winged through the air, joining his jacket on the floor.

"Distracted. Forgot my damned briefcase."

He unfastened his belt and whipped it out of the loops. At the harsh sound of his zipper, Grace froze. She stared at Luc, seeing the passion that marked his high-boned face. His breathing was fast and irregular, his chest rising and falling as if he'd just run a marathon. Sensing her hesitation, he didn't touch her, simply waited, giving her the opportunity to retreat.

Never had she thought to find herself in such a position, where she'd feel such an urgent need for a man, be filled with such an all-consuming love, be so ready to forsake the teachings of a lifetime. And yet that was precisely what she intended to do. All doubts gone, she reached out and stroked the taut, muscular ridges of his chest, exploring at will from shoulder to abdomen. As her hand drifted lower, she hesitated, reluctant to traverse into uncharted territory.

"Your turn," he muttered, grasping the bottom of her sweater and pulling it over her head.

She emerged breathless and flustered. But the minute she looked at Luc, the minute she saw the intense yearning flare to life in his golden eyes, all doubt vanished. His hands slipped beneath the straps of her bra and he slid the narrow bands from her shoulders. When he released the hooks, the scrap of lace joined his tie on the lampshade.

For a long time they stood without touching, absorbed in a visual examination. Then Luc reached out and gently cupped her breasts and Grace's knees buckled. He caught her in his arms and kissed her—fast, hot, desperate kisses. Shedding his trousers, he peeled off her stretch pants with a speed that left her gasping.

"Maybe we should go to the bedroom," Grace suggested, tumbling back into his arms.

"The bedroom. Right." He toppled her onto the couch and followed her down. "Too far."

His mouth closed over hers again and his hands began a thorough, intimate exploration, each delicious caress driving her closer and closer to some sweet crisis, the intense pleasure almost painful.

"Luc," she said with a gasp, squeezing her eyes closed. "I can't take much more."

"Grace?"

Luc's voice seemed to float to her from a long distance. "What, Luc?"

He nuzzled her cheek. "I didn't say anything."

"I thought you said Grace."

"Only before meals."

"I'm too hungry to eat," she muttered, winding her arms around his waist and pressing her mouth to the strong line of his neck.

"Grace?"

She frowned, slowly opening her eyes. "What?"

Luc nibbled her lips. "What?"

"I mean, what do you want?"

He chuckled, the sound low and intimate. "You know what I want."

"No. I mean, why did you call my name?"

He pulled back slightly. "I told you. I didn't."

"Grace?"

They both stiffened, staring at each other in dawning horror. "Get off me, quick!" she whispered urgently, shoving at his chest.

Luc didn't move. "What—"

"Grace!" An appalled masculine voice spoke from the doorway to the living room.

"Oh, criminey!" No longer trying to escape, she buried her head in Luc's chest, attempting to disappear behind his broad shoulders.

Luc glanced down at her, then over his shoulder at the man and woman hovering just inside the living room. "Who the hell are you?" he demanded. "And what are you doing in my apartment?"

"Dear Lord!" The man continued to stare in shock. "I'm... I'm Reverend—"

"I'm Miss Caruthers with child protective services," the woman interrupted, pushing past the reverend and stepping boldly forward. She brandished her clipboard like a sword. "I'm your case manager."

"No. You're not," Luc contradicted. "Miss Carstairs is our case manager."

"Not anymore. I've taken over. Her report was so strange—closets and laundry baskets and elopements and so forth—"

"Elopements?" the minister cut in. "Did you say elopements?"

Miss Caruthers nodded emphatically. "Elopements. Poor Miss Carstairs has made such a muddle of everything, they've taken her off the case." She pointed an accusing finger in Luc's direction. "And it's all your fault."

Luc glanced first at Grace, then back at the intruders. "Turn around," he snapped. "And no peeking."

Hesitantly, they complied and Luc yanked Grace to her feet. Scooping a handful of clothes off the carpet, he tossed a pair of slacks in her direction and pulled on his shirt. Not wasting a single second, she thrust her foot into the pant legs.

"You want to tell me how you got in here?" Luc demanded.

"The door was open," the reverend replied, in an apologetic voice. His head swiveled toward the clothes-strewn lamp and quickly jerked away again. "Would you mind telling me what elopement this woman is talking about? And what baby?"

Grace grabbed Luc's arm, as if to physically restrain him. "Don't say it..." she whimpered—to no avail.

"My elopement," Luc announced, snagging her bra off the lampshade and tossing it to her. "And Grace's elopement."

"You're *married?*" the reverend gasped, spinning around. His eyes practically popped out of his head and he whirled away again. "Oh, good heavens."

"Yes, we're married," Luc confirmed.

"No, no!" Grace denied, dressing with a speed she'd never before attempted. "You don't understand. Just give me a minute to explain!"

Miss Caruthers began scribbling madly and Toni, fed up with being neglected, began to cry. Grace gave serious consideration to crying, as well.

The minister's gaze seemed drawn to Toni like a magnet. "You have a *baby?*" he whispered in disbelief.

"No!" Grace shouted.

"Maybe!" Luc shouted louder. "It depends on who you are." He looked at Grace. "Where's Stefano's scorecard? I'm getting confused. Which story do we tell the minister?"

"There isn't a minister on our damned scorecard!" she practically shrieked.

"Grace!" the minister exclaimed, clearly shocked.

She shut her eyes. "I'm...I'm sorry." Peeking at Luc, she said, "Did I ever mention that my father is a Methodist minister?"

''No,'' he replied dryly. ''I don't believe you did. Let me guess. This is him, right?''

''Bingo.''

''I should warn you that if you aren't married, there will be dire repercussions,'' Miss Caruthers announced.

''May we turn around now?'' Reverend Barnes requested.

''Sure. Why not,'' Luc agreed. He glanced at Grace. ''Your sweater's on backward.''

She folded her arms across her chest. ''It's a new fashion statement. It's called 'caught in the act.'''

''You two,'' Miss Caruthers informed them, ''are in deep trouble. I can guarantee there will be serious consequences if we discover you've been lying to us. Now are you or are you not married?''

Luc sighed, then forced a smile to his lips. ''Now, Miss Caruthers,'' he began.

The social worker stumbled backward. ''Get away from me, you...you...devil!'' She looked at Grace. ''This is what happened to Miss Carstairs, isn't it? We knew something was wrong when she let her hair down and started to wear makeup.''

Grace touched her own loose curls self-consciously. ''Yes, he seems to have that effect on women.''

Miss Carstairs drew herself up. ''Well, not me! He's not going to use his charms on me.'' She peered at Luc hopefully. ''You weren't going to try your charms, were you?''

Reluctantly, Luc shook his head. ''No. I guess not. I believe my charming days are over.''

The social worker struggled to hide her disappointment. ''We'll see what Mrs. Cuthbert has to say about all this. She's my superior. And I guarantee she won't be pleased!'' Spinning around, she scurried from the room. A minute later, the front door slammed.

With deep dread, Grace glanced at her father. ''I bet you're wondering what's going on,'' she said with a hesitant smile.

CHAPTER TEN

The Great Lie
Day 346 continues to darken—but all is not lost...

"I THINK WHAT'S GOING on here is painfully obvious," Reverend Barnes said, with more than a touch of irony.

"Yes...well..." Grace could feel the bright color returning to her cheeks and she scrambled for something innocuous to say. Something to help ease them into the coming conversation—or confrontation. "Gee, Dad. Your being here sure is a surprise."

"For both of us. I did try and call."

She stirred uncomfortably. "We kept missing each other."

"Yes, we did. Now I see why." He glanced around the room and Grace knew he'd misinterpreted the reason her possessions were so liberally scattered about. "You haven't been at your apartment recently, have you?"

"No," she replied, deciding a lengthy explanation wouldn't help the situation any. "How did you know I was here?"

"When I couldn't reach you at home, I stopped by your office. A very helpful security guard gave me this address, once I'd convinced him I was your father."

"Edward," Grace said with a sigh.

"I believe that was his name. Now. I think introductions are in order, don't you?'' He looked pointedly at Luc, who stepped forward.

''Luc Salvatore, Reverend Barnes,'' he said, holding out his hand. ''It's a pleasure to meet you.''

''Under other circumstances, I might agree with you,'' the minister replied, shaking hands.

''I'm sorry about that,'' Luc said, though his gaze remained direct and unrepentant. ''If the door had been shut properly, we would have all been saved some embarrassment.''

Reverend Barnes chose not to comment. ''You're Grace's employer, aren't you?'' he asked instead.

''Yes, she's been with me for almost a year.''

''And is she also your wife?''

Luc shook his head. ''No. Not yet.''

''You're certain? There seemed to be some doubt a few minutes ago.''

''I'm positive.''

''We're not married, Dad,'' Grace informed him quietly, though Luc's use of the word ''yet'' had thrown her. He couldn't possibly mean what she thought he meant by that, could he?

Her father glanced at her, a concerned frown lining his brow. ''Considering what was going on here a few minutes ago, I'm not sure whether to be relieved or dismayed. What about the baby? Whose is it?''

''Toni is my niece,'' Luc said. ''Grace is staying with me to help with baby-sitting duties. And for the record, our relationship has been regrettably innocent until today.''

''Thank heavens,'' Reverend Barnes murmured, his relief palpable.

Before Grace could manage to insert a single word,

Luc added, "You should also know that we applied for a marriage license last week."

Grace closed her eyes and groaned.

Reverend Barnes glanced from one to the other. "You're engaged?"

Grace glared at Luc, who merely smiled. Oh, he was clever, all right. He'd phrased his announcement very carefully and in such a way that she couldn't very well deny an engagement, much as she'd like to. What did she say now? That he hadn't actually proposed? That to the best of her recollection their engagement had come about through barked orders, demands and a certain amount of coercion. That she'd only agreed to marry Luc if push came to shove. If push came to shove? This wasn't a shove. It ranked more like a bulldozing.

"Yes," she muttered with ill-concealed resentment, "I agreed to marry him."

Her father's eyes narrowed. She knew that look. Many a wayward parishioner had seen it right before they'd broken down and confessed all their sins. "I'm beginning to realize there's a whole lot about this situation that I don't know," he said. "Nor am I sure I want to know. In fact, I'm positive I don't want to know." He studied the two of them for a brief instant, and Grace didn't doubt that he could read the guilt in their faces. At least, he'd be able to read her guilt. Luc managed to look slightly more enigmatic. "I'd like to make a suggestion if I may..." Reverend Barnes announced in a determined voice.

"You want me to make an honest women out of her, is that it?" Luc guessed.

"Yes, I do. Assuming you love my daughter." He clasped his hands together, the gesture betraying a certain level of nervousness. "Well, do you?"

After a brief hesitation, Luc nodded. ''Yes, I love her.''

Satisfied, Reverend Barnes relaxed and turned to Grace, his gaze less severe. ''I know you're ready, willing and able to marry this man. You wouldn't have allowed...er...matters to progress so far, if you weren't in love with him. Am I right?''

What could she say to that? ''Yes, Dad,'' she whispered.

''Then, it's settled. I suggest you two marry, and marry now. After what I just witnessed, I don't think that will be any too soon. I suspect it may actually be somewhat too late.''

Luc didn't even try to hide his satisfaction. And Grace knew why he looked so pleased. By marrying quickly, they had a chance of keeping Toni. ''You'll marry us right away?'' he asked.

''If you have the license and the blood test, I have the authority. All you need is a witness.'' He looked at Grace. ''A dress wouldn't go amiss, either.''

''A white dress,'' Luc stated. ''The one you have hanging in the back of the closet should do.''

''Luc, may I speak with you in the bedroom, please?'' she requested through gritted teeth. ''Dad, you'll excuse us? I think we need to talk this over before leaping to any hasty decisions.''

Her father nodded and Grace caught hold of Luc's hand, tugging him toward the guest bedroom. The door had barely closed behind them before her hurt and anger spilled out. ''How dare you lie to my father! And...and how dare you agree to marry me!''

''What the hell was I supposed to say? Tell him no, I don't want to marry your innocent, little girl—I just want to make mad, passionate love to her?''

"At least that would have been honest!"

"No, it wouldn't have been. I've changed my mind about an affair, Grace. I want to marry you."

She stared at him in disbelief. "You really will do anything to keep that baby."

He didn't deny it, not that she would have listened if he had. She turned away and wrapped her arms around her waist.

"*Cara...*" He came up behind, his hands dropping to her shoulders. "I know what I'm asking is unfair."

"Not to mention unreasonable, untenable and unethical."

"That, too. But would it be so bad?"

Jerking free of his grasp, she whirled around. "Be honest for once, Luc. Why are you doing this? Do you really want to marry me, or is this whole charade just to protect Toni?"

"Would you believe me if I said it was for you?"

She shook her head, tears filling her eyes. "No," she whispered. "How could I, after the extremes you've gone to, to keep Toni out of the hands of the authorities. You've told so many different stories, tried to con so many people, how do I know this isn't just one more lie to get what you want?"

A muscle leapt in his jaw, and his hands clenched at his sides. "You could try trusting me."

The words hung between them and Grace shut her eyes, wanting with all her heart to trust him, to believe he loved her, to allow herself to grasp with both hands the joyous possibility that they had a future together. But she'd just spent the past year clinging to a dream that would never materialize. She couldn't do that again. Because this time it wouldn't just be her hopes that were crushed, it would be her heart, as well. A tear escaped from the corner of her eye.

"Grace, please. Don't cry." He reached out to brush away her tear, but she evaded his touch. "Trust me. It'll all work out, I promise."

"You told me that once before and look where it got us." She searched his face with tear-washed eyes. "I told you I'd have an affair with you. We don't have to go to such extremes. You don't have to marry me." It was almost a plea.

"Yes," he contradicted, savagely. "I do. We will marry, Grace, even if I have to drag you to the altar."

"Because of Toni." It wasn't a question.

"If that's the only way to convince you to marry me, then, yes. Because of Toni."

So, now she had a choice. She could go through with the marriage or she could say no, and it would all be over. She could walk out the door, tell her father the truth and end her involvement with Luc. She never had to see him again if she didn't want to. Never see him again. Never be touched by him again. Never share another kiss, another laugh. Never be held in his arms or know true love again.

And Toni would be turned over to the authorities.

"Marry me, Grace," he urged. "I swear you won't regret it."

"I already regret it." She bowed her head, knowing she couldn't desert Toni, any more than she could explain the true situation to her father. Not when a single yes promised to give her what she wanted most in the world. "Okay, I'll marry you," she said, wiping her cheek with the back of her hand. "But it's going to be a marriage of convenience. I won't be your wife in anything but name. I won't live with you, I won't work for you and I won't share your bed. After a few months we'll have the marriage annulled."

"You can't be serious!"

"I'm very serious," she flashed back. "I was wrong to agree to Dom's plan. I admit it. But no one was supposed to be hurt. Well, people did get hurt, and I won't make that mistake again. I'll do this one last thing for Toni's sake, and because I'm too much of a coward to tell my father the truth. But once Carina and Pietro return, it ends."

"I'm not going to argue with you. But understand this..." He caught her by the shoulders, refusing to let go. "Today your father will marry us. And there won't be an annulment. After a few weeks or a month, once you've realized that an annulment is out of the question, we'll marry again in my church."

She shook her head. "No!"

He ignored her. "I have a couple of errands to run. It won't take more than an hour. I'll call Alessandro and ask him to be our witness."

"You're going to invite your family?"

"Just my brother. Dad already thinks we're married, and I don't think you want the rest of the rabble here." He lifted an eyebrow. "Do you?"

"I...I guess not."

"Get dressed, Grace. I won't be long." Then he swept her into his arms and kissed her, a gentle, lingering kiss that promised to make everything right again.

A kiss she didn't dare trust.

THE HOUR BEFORE her wedding passed with frightening speed. After checking to be sure her father didn't mind watching Toni, she prepared for the ceremony. Pinning her hair in a sophisticated pleat, she applied cosmetics and perfume with a light hand. Finally, she pulled the dress Luc had requested she wear from the closet.

It was a deceptively simple design, a mere slip of a dress, short-sleeved with a scooped neckline, made special by a matching bolero jacket. She lingered in front of the mirror, undecided whether or not to wear her pearl necklace and earrings with it.

A light knock sounded on the door. "Grace?" Luc called, stepping into the room. He stopped short at the sight of her. "Grace..." He whispered her name in a rough, deep voice. "You're beautiful, *mia amorata.*"

She slowly turned from the mirror and faced him, struggling to hide her nervousness. He looked rather fine, himself, she conceded. He'd dressed in a black suit and snow white dress shirt. Gold cuff links glittered at his wrists and a gold tie tack anchored his red silk tie in place.

"Is Alessandro here?" she asked.

"Yes. It's almost time to start the ceremony." He approached, a jeweler's box in his hand. "But first I have something I'd like you to wear. It belonged to my mother, a gift to her from my father—also on their wedding day."

"Luc—"

He shook his head, holding out the long, narrow box. "You can't refuse. I won't allow it."

Reluctantly, she took the gift and opened it. She gasped. A dainty opal choker lay on a bed of black velvet. Vivid green and blue sparks mingled with almost every color in the rainbow and blazed outward from the center of each gem. "Fire opals?" she whispered.

"Yes. They were my mother's birthstone. Let me help you put them on." He lifted the choker from the box and slipped it around her neck. Then he bent down and pressed his lips to the sloping curve of her shoulder.

"Thank you," she said in a muffled voice. "You shouldn't have."

"I have something else." With a wicked grin, he reached in his pocket and pulled out a ruffled blue garter, dangling the scrap of silk and lace from his finger. "The opals are something old. This is both new and blue. Would you like me to put this on, as well?"

She couldn't help smiling. "I can manage, thanks."

"Which just leaves something borrowed." His hand dipped into his pocket once again. "I didn't know if these would suit your taste, so they're on loan until you decide whether or not you want them." In his palm nestled a pair of opal earrings, fire opals that perfectly matched the choker.

She shook her head, taking an unthinking step backward. "Oh, Luc… It's too much."

He shrugged. "Then, we can return them after the ceremony."

"Why are you doing this?" she asked anxiously, clasping her hands in front of her. "It isn't like this will be a real marriage."

She instantly realized she'd said the wrong thing. His expression closed over, growing cool and remote. "Put the earrings on," he requested in a clipped voice. "And the garter, too."

Not wanting to argue with him, after all the trouble he'd gone to, she accepted his gifts. Turning her back to him, she slipped on the garter, then the earrings. "I'm ready," she finally said, and faced him.

He took her hand in his. "Let's go."

She stared at their joined fingers. Was he afraid she'd cut and run if he didn't hang on to her? Given half the chance, she just might. She looked up at him, searching his face for a hint of his innermost thoughts. He returned her look, his golden eyes glittering with determination. But love? If he felt it, it wasn't apparent. Defeated, she dropped her gaze and walked with him into the living room.

Her father waited in front of the picture windows. When he saw her, an expression of pride and tenderness leapt to his face. He crossed to her side and Luc released her arm, stepping back.

''You look beautiful,'' Reverend Barnes murmured. Gathering her close, he whispered, ''Are you certain, Grace? This is what you truly want?''

''Yes, Dad, it is,'' she responded quietly. ''I want it with all my heart.''

''Then I'm happy.'' He held her tight for an extra moment before setting her free.

Alessandro stood close by, Toni in his arms. As soon as Reverend Barnes returned to his stance by the windows, Alessandro took his place and dropped a kiss on Grace's cheek. ''Welcome to the family,'' he said with a warm smile.

''Thank you.''

Luc picked up a huge bouquet of pure white tea roses and handed them to her without a word. More moved than she could possibly express, she didn't resist when he cupped her elbow and drew her to stand in front of her father.

''Shall we begin?'' Reverend Barnes asked, giving Grace a final searching look.

She nodded, careful not to allow her doubts to show. ''I'm ready,'' she said.

''Very well, we'll begin.'' He settled his bifocals on the end of his nose. ''Dearly beloved—''

The banging at the door drowned out his words. With a murmured excuse, Alessandro practically ran to throw it open. "What are you guys doing here?" he demanded in exaggerated surprise.

Rocco shoved past his brother. "You told us to haul tail over here or we'd live to regret it. What's going on?" Stef and Marc piled in after him.

"Yeah. What's going on?" they chorused.

The three stopped dead in the entrance to the living room, their mouths dropping open. Marc recovered first. "You're getting married?"

"Without inviting us?" Stef followed up.

Luc glared at Alessandro, his look promising retribution. "Yes, I'm getting married. If you want to witness it, stand next to Alessandro and be quiet."

"Give me Toni," Marc told Alessandro.

"No, I want to hold her," Rocco said.

"*I'm* holding her."

Luc thrust a hand through his hair. "I want you four to *shut up* or you're out of here!" He took a deep breath, then said, "Please continue, Reverend Barnes. I'm sorry for the interruption."

"Go ahead, Dad," Grace urged.

The minister glanced uncertainly at the four Salvatore brothers. "All right. Now, where was I? Oh, yes. Dearly beloved, we're gathered here today to join this man and woman in the state of holy matrimony, a state not to be entered into lightly." He focused a stern gaze on Luc and Grace, then his brow wrinkled in concern. "Why didn't you invite your brothers?"

Luc gritted his teeth. "Because they don't know how to behave in public. Proceed. Please."

Toni let out a loud wail. "Uh-oh," Alessandro interrupted. "Can we take five for a diaper change?"

"No!"

"Luc, be reasonable," Grace murmured. "Go ahead, Alessandro. Marc, mix up a bottle—just in case."

Luc turned on her. "You know full well that if you fill up the one end it comes out the other," he argued. "Marc, no bottle."

"Never mind, Marc," Grace said, exasperated. "*I'll* get the bottle."

Five minutes later, they gathered once again in the living room. Toni was cradled in Rocco's arms, cooing happily. Marc held the bottle, ready to insert it at the first squawk. Luc's face had settled into grim lines.

"Are we set?" he asked the room at large. "Any other comments, criticisms or concerns?" No one said a word. He nodded in satisfaction. "Then, we can begin."

Reverend Barnes cleared his throat. "Let's see… Dearly beloved—"

"We did that part already," Luc bit out. "We're currently in a state we shouldn't enter lightly."

"Amen to that," Reverend Barnes muttered.

Grace tightened her hold on Luc's arms. "Dad. *Please!*"

"Perhaps if we skipped to the crucial bits?" Luc suggested.

Reverend Barnes glanced uncertainly at Grace. "You don't object?"

"No, Dad. I don't."

"Very well. I must say, this is highly unusual, but if you both agree, I guess it's all right. Let's see… Oh, right. Do you, Luciano Salvatore, promise to love, honor and cherish this woman?"

"I do."

"And do you, Grace Barnes, promise to love, honor and obey—"

"Dad!"

"Don't interrupt your father, Grace."

She turned on Luc. "I will *not* promise to obey. It's archaic. If you get to cherish, so do I."

The doorbell rang—a long, strident, insistent ring. Luc muttered beneath his breath in Italian. Grace closed her eyes and sighed.

"I'll get it," Alessandro offered brightly.

A minute later, Dom hustled into the room. "What is going on?" he demanded. "Why have I not been told there is to be a wedding?" He regarded Luc and Grace with a hurt expression. "And why did you tell me you were married, when you were not?"

Luc sighed. "You know why."

Dom nodded grimly. "Because I would have thrown you out of the family if I had known you had a baby with Grace without benefit of a wedding ring. I still might."

"What?" Reverend Barnes stared at them in shock. His gaze slid to Toni, kicking and gurgling in Rocco's arms. "She's...she's your baby, Grace?"

"No!" She covered her face with her hands. "Dad, could you finish the ceremony? Please? I promise I'll explain everything then."

"I think you'd better explain everything now."

A loud, determined banging resounded through the apartment, and Stef ran to the door. Luc threw his hands into the air. "That's it. Who the hell's left to barge in here? Wait a minute. What about the police? They haven't shown up yet. In fact, they're the only ones who haven't."

"I came in their place," a tall, stunning brunette announced from the doorway, Stef at her side. "Cynthia Cuthbert, social services." She smiled at the horrified gathering, her gaze shifting slowly to Luc and Grace. "Hello, Luc. It's been a long time."

If the identity of their latest visitor came as a surprise, Luc didn't show it. "Not long enough," he said dryly. "Hello, Cynthia."

Marc elbowed Stef. "Cynthia? *The* Cynthia? The woman Luc couldn't charm?"

"*The* Cynthia," his twin confirmed gloomily.

The social worker glided across the room. "You must be Grace," she said, offering her hand. She lifted an eyebrow. "Am I interrupting something?"

"You know damned well you are!" Luc spoke up.

"If this little event has been staged for Antonia's benefit, I'm afraid you're too late. The jig is up." She planted her hands on her hips and fixed Luc with an annoyed glare. "I must say, I'm not at all happy with you. You've positively ruined my caseworkers. They're as giddy as schoolgirls. Am I the only woman in the world you haven't charmed the pants off of?"

"You're the second." He pointed at Grace. "And she's the third. Though it's not for want of trying, I might add."

"Don't feel bad," Cynthia told him sympathetically. "I'm sure you did your best." She glanced at her watch. "I'm afraid I have to get down to business now. I've come for Antonia."

Luc folded his arms across his chest and shook his head. "Not a chance." His brothers instantly formed a protective circle around the baby. "In one minute Grace and I will be married."

The social worker shrugged. "That won't matter. You lied, Luc. You told the department the two of you were already married. Ms. Cartwright warned you of the consequences, if you told any more lies, and you ignored her warning."

"Don't treat me like a child, Cynthia," Luc practically snarled. "We both know the department can make exceptions. I want you to make one now."

A smile of genuine amusement touched her perfect features. "You always did have a way with words. Tell me why I should make an exception for you. Because we were once…friends?"

"That's one reason. You also know my family. You know we'll take care of Toni, that she's safe with us."

"Um…excuse me," Reverend Barnes interrupted. "I'm very confused. Exactly whose baby is this, and why are you trying to take her away?"

"This I would like to know, too," Dom chimed in, folding his arms across his chest.

"She's *my* daughter," a voice spoke from behind them. "And no one's going to take her away. Not if I have anything to say about it."

Everyone turned. "Pietro!" Grace exclaimed in delight. "You're back."

"Back…" He held out Carina's hand. A diamond-encrusted wedding band decorated her third finger. "And married. Everyone, my wife, Carina Donati…Salvatore."

"Antonia is Pietro's?" Dom questioned in confusion. "*Per dio!* Am I told nothing anymore?"

Spying her daughter, Carina wrenched her hand free of Pietro's and darted across the room, snatching the baby from Rocco's arms. "Toni!" she cried, bursting into noisy sobs, Italian endearments falling as fast as her tears. She hugged her baby close, dropping frantic kisses on Toni's tuft of black hair. Pietro crossed to her side and peered down at his daughter, an expression of wonder dawning on his face.

"She's beautiful," he whispered, reaching out a tentative finger to touch a round, pink cheek. "Everything was so hectic before I didn't really notice." He looked up and grinned. "I have a daughter," he announced in a proud voice.

It took close to an hour to straighten everything out. To Grace's secret amusement, Pietro proved to be the one Salvatore capable of charming the uncharmable Cynthia. By the time she left, he'd managed to straighten out most of their problems and had set up an appointment to settle any final questions.

Grace stood quietly by her father, grateful for the supportive arm he'd wrapped around her. She watched the happy reunion with a calm facade she hoped concealed her inner turmoil. *Luc didn't need to marry her now.* And though the knowledge came as a relief, it also caused the most agonizing pain. But that pain was nothing, compared to what it would have been if they'd gone through with the wedding and the subsequent divorce.

It was time to face facts. Their marriage wouldn't have worked, not when Luc didn't love her. And no matter what he said, he didn't love her. Not enough, anyway. If she left now, she could leave with some dignity. A few minutes longer and she'd break down. She glanced up at her father. "I guess there's no more reason for the wedding," she told him quietly.

He covered her hand with his. "I'm sorry, Grace."

She blinked back tears. Obviously, he understood far more than she'd realized. Was her love for Luc so apparent? "Let's go, Dad."

"You're not going anywhere." Luc moved to stand in front of her, blocking her escape.

"Luc, don't," she pleaded. "Toni is safe now. You don't have to sacrifice yourself. There's no point."

"You're right. There is no point. Except this." He took her hand in his. "I want to marry you, *cara mia.* For real. Now. And it won't be a marriage of convenience. I love you, Grace. I want a forever kind of marriage with you, the kind with vows to love, honor and cherish...."

"Not obey?" she asked in a shaken voice.

He nodded in satisfaction. "Fine. And obey."

"Actually," Reverend Barnes interrupted, "I was planning to add just one more vow to all that. Love, honor, cherish and never tell another lie. Seems more appropriate that way, don't you think?"

"Done," Luc agreed. "Grace?"

She didn't dare believe. "Why, Luc? Yesterday you wanted an affair. It wasn't until Miss Caruthers found out we weren't married that you changed your mind."

He shook his head, his golden eyes dark and stormy. "Something else happened."

"What?"

"Your father walked in." He cupped her face in his hands, speaking softly, for her ears alone. "Making love to you was beautiful beyond compare. When he walked in the door, it became sordid. I could see it in your face. You were ashamed. And I realized I'd turned something beautiful, something you should remember with joy for the rest of your life, into something shabby. In that moment, I realized I didn't want an affair with you. Affairs end. And I don't want what we have to end. I don't want you just for my lover. I want you for my wife. I want a forever with you."

Tears shimmered in her eyes. "I love you, Luc."

"*Bellissima mia,*" he murmured. "Haven't I told you

how much I love you? You're the only woman I see anymore. You've made me blind to all others. Awake or asleep, I see only your face, hear only your voice. The air I breathe is filled with your scent.'' He held out his hand. ''Will you marry me?''

''Try and stop me,'' she said with a huge smile, and slipped her fingers in his.

Luc turned to Reverend Barnes. ''From the top, Reverend. And this time...don't skip a single word.''

And he didn't.

Leigh Michaels has always loved happy endings. Even when she was a child, if a book's conclusion didn't please her, she'd make up her own. And, though she always wanted to write fiction, she very sensibly planned to earn her living as a newspaper reporter. That career didn't work out, however, and she found herself writing for Mills & Boon® instead—in the kind of happy ending only a romance novelist could dream up!

Leigh likes to hear from readers; you can write to her at PO Box 935, Ottumwa, Iowa, 52501-0935 USA.

DREAMS TO KEEP

by

LEIGH MICHAELS

CHAPTER ONE

CHELSEA leaned over the draughtsman's table and pointed a pencil at the drawing he was working on, 'Jim, are you certain I put a closet in there?' she asked.

The draughtsman raised an eyebrow. 'I only follow directions, Chelsea,' he said mildly. 'I don't imagine closets. That's your department.' He finished the line that completed the closet wall and tossed his pencil down. 'What's the matter, anyway? You aren't a little nervous this morning, are you?'

'Of course not,' Chelsea jeered. 'Why would I be nervous?' Why indeed, she thought. Just down the hall, the three senior partners of the architectural firm were meeting. When they came out of that room, there would be one more partner, to fill the vacancy left by Martin Burns' sudden death three months ago. And that new partner, if she was lucky, would be Chelsea Ryan.

'Do you really think you'll get the job, Chelsea?' Jim picked up the pencil again.

'Why shouldn't I? I have as much experience as any of the other applicants. I'm a better architect than most of them, and I'm a woman, which is an image this practice could stand.'

'No fooling? You're really a woman?' Jim looked up in mock astonishment. His eyes swept over her, from auburn hair arranged in a neat and professional knot at the back of her neck to the apricot-coloured dress and delicate gold jewellery. 'By golly, you are a woman. Why didn't I ever notice?'

'Because you weren't looking before, I suppose,' Chelsea retorted. 'After all, you've only dated my roommate for a year now.'

Jim was suddenly serious. 'Just don't count on getting the job, Chelsea. The senior partners around here have never been known for liberal thinking, and they aren't apt to start now. There has never been a female partner of Shelby Harris and Associates, and you may not be the first.'

'Oh, come on, Jim, Carl Shelby himself complimented that last design of mine—the Wharton house. He called it an architectural gem.'

'And it is. Mostly because I drew it.' He preened himself playfully. 'But you're still designing houses, Chelsea.'

'What's the matter with that? I like to do houses.'

He spoke slowly, as if explaining to a kindergarten. 'The partners think that since you're a woman, that's the only thing you can be trusted with. And because none of them like residential work, they will keep palming it off on you just as long as you'll take it. Especially now that Martin's gone.'

Chelsea frowned thoughtfully. 'You may be right, Jim.'

'Of course I am. I am never wrong. I'm betting that they'll give the partnership to Owl Eyes here.' He tugged open a bottom desk drawer and pulled out a pile of sketches. The top one was a caricature of an earnest young man with horn-rimmed spectacles and a pointed nose, perched on the branch of a tree.

'You promised that you'd take those things home, Jim,' Chelsea accused.

'I forgot.' He flipped through the sheets. 'Or maybe they'll pick this one. What did you call him?'

'Granite Man,' Chelsea said automatically. 'Jim if you get caught with these . . .'

'I won't get caught.'

'That's easy for you to say. It's my name on the corner of them, and it will be my job if Carl Shelby ever sees the one of himself.' She picked up the top sketch, with her initials printed neatly in the corner, as was characteristic of all of her drawings. Granite Man stared stonily back at her from the side of Mount Rushmore, where she had neatly inserted him between the sculptured heads of Theodore Roosevelt and Abraham Lincoln.

'What's his real name?' Jim pursued. 'I've forgotten.'

'Nick Stanton. Didn't you meet him when he came for his interview? He's the original cold fish. There would be no bending the rules with him around, that's certain.'

'And Chelsea does like to bend the rules. That's probably why you won't get the partnership. That and your age. And the red hair.'

'It's auburn. Besides, what does the colour of my hair have to do with it?'

Jim shrugged. 'Little things often do. You know Carl Shelby has a million prejudices, and that Frank Harris goes along with anything Shelby wants.'

'Well, Burke Marshall doesn't.'

'Wow. One out of three, and you were always Burke's favourite. It's no majority, Chelsea.'

'Why did it have to be Martin who died? He was the easiest of them all to work with,' Chelsea said thoughtfully.

Jim grinned. 'Sure, because he was always too busy to worry about what you were doing, so you did things the way you wanted. Working for Martin was like having no boss at all.'

'He and Burke always backed me up.'

'Of course they did. But that's not the kind of behaviour that wins you a popularity contest, Chelsea. Harris and Shelby don't think anyone under fifty has learned enough about life to be rewarded with a partnership.'

'Well, that leaves out about half of their applicants. Including Granite Man.' Chelsea slid the sketch to the bottom of the stack.

'I'll take those home, just as soon as you finish the set,' Jim offered cheekily. 'I want to see what you can do with Eileen.'

Chelsea stared at him for a long moment. 'If I draw Eileen, will you promise to get these things out of the office?'

'Boy Scout's Honour.'

'Then give me a sheet of paper.'

Her pencil hovered over the sheet for several seconds, as Chelsea thought about Eileen, who was the newest of the secretaries. Then the needle-sharp point began to move. Chelsea didn't know where the caricatures came from; they just seemed to flow from her pencil, leaving her as surprised as any observer.

Jim laughed as he watched Eileen take shape on the paper, the buxom blonde in a tight sweater and painfully high heels, bending seductively over the copy machine while Carl Shelby himself stared down her neckline.

'There,' Chelsea said and tossed her pencil down.

'I'm surprised you didn't put Frank Harris in there too. He certainly spends enough time studying Eileen's architecture.' Jim leered.

Chelsea shrugged. 'I hadn't noticed.' She pushed the sketch across the drawing board. 'Now you have enough blackmail material on me for a lifetime. And that's the last piece you're going to get, too.'

'You didn't sign it,' he objected.

Chelsea sketched her interconnected initials on the corner of Eileen's short skirt and handed it back to Jim.

'I'm going to paper a wall with these someday,' he announced. 'After you're famous, of course.'

From the doorway Chelsea's secretary spoke disapprovingly. 'Miss Ryan, your new clients are here.'

Chelsea glanced at her delicate wristwatch. 'I forgot all about them, Marie.'

Jim scrambled the caricatures together and slid them into the bottom drawer. 'I'll have the drawings of the Emerson house for you this afternoon, Chelsea.'

'That will be fine, Jim,' She followed Marie down the hall.

Without looking up from her typewriter, the secretary said, 'I showed them into your office and brought them coffee, Miss Ryan.'

'Thank you, Marie,' Chelsea said gently. It was unfortunate for Marie, she thought, that she had inherited Chelsea as a boss when Martin Burns died. Marie didn't approve of the cut of Chelsea's clothes, or her informal office manners, or the style of her hair. In fact, there was almost nothing about Chelsea that Marie approved at all.

The couple waiting in Chelsea's office were in their mid-fifties. Mr Sullivan's face was ruddy and his suit expensive but not well fitted. Mrs Sullivan's hair was elaborately coiffed in a style totally unsuited to her face.

Chelsea felt a familiar sinking sensation in the pit of her stomach, and turned on the charm. 'Good morning,' she said warmly, 'I'm sorry to keep you waiting.'

Mr Sullivan got reluctantly to his feet to take her outstretched hand. 'Is it going to be much longer before Mr Ryan gets here?' he demanded. 'I'm a busy man.'

It wasn't the first time a client had assumed that she was another secretary; far too many of them thought that no woman—especially a young very petite redhead—could possibly be an architect. 'I am Chelsea Ryan,' she said gently.

Mrs Sullivan looked offended. 'Oh, no. There must be some mistake.'

If there is, Chelsea thought wryly, my parents would probably like to hear about it.

'Our friends' house was designed by C. J. Ryan,' Mrs Sullivan said. 'I saw the name on the blueprints.'

'And who were the friends, Mrs Sullivan?' When she heard the name, Chelsea smiled in brief satisfaction. That was one of her best houses. If the Sullivans wanted something like that . . .

But there was a standard answer for clients who wanted a male architect, and arguing with them about her qualifications, no matter how superior, wasn't the way to convince them. Chelsea reached for the notepad and pen which Marie had left ready on the corner of her desk and sat down in a comfortable chair. 'I'm sure if you'd prefer having a man design your house that any of our other staff architects would be happy to help you,' she said, her low voice musical. 'Unfortunately, they are all busy at the moment, and I'm afraid your trip would be wasted. So—since you're already here—why don't you tell me about the house you have in mind, and then I can pass that along to whichever of our staff you choose.'

And he, she thought rebelliously, will take one look at it and say, 'Oh, go ahead, Chelsea, design it yourself. I'll put my name on it if it will make the client happy, but I get so bored with houses.' Yes, she thought, Jim was right. She was a member of this staff because no one else liked to do the residential work. Fortunately for her, she did like it.

She thought for a moment she had lost them. Mrs Sullivan's lips were tightly compressed, and Chelsea wouldn't have been surprised if she had insisted on seeing another architect that very minute. Then Mr Sullivan stirred restlessly and said to his wife, 'Doris, I took the day off for this, you know, I hate to waste the time.'

Chelsea didn't wait for the argument to start. 'Are there just the two of you?' she inquired gently.

Mrs Sullivan nodded reluctantly. 'Our children have all moved away.'

'Tell me about yourselves,' Chelsea urged. 'Your jobs and your hobbies, the kind of entertaining you do—all that sort of thing.'

She listened for what seemed an hour, asking a question here and there, jotting down facts and ideas in the pidgin shorthand that made sense only to her. 'That brings us to the kitchen, Mrs Sullivan,' she said finally. 'Do you prefer a large one with plenty of room for projects, or a small, efficient one that is easier to keep clean?'

Mrs Sullivan looked at her with hard-won respect in her eyes. 'You really do know about houses, don't you?'

Chelsea nodded. 'I've designed hundreds. They're my favourite things to do.'

Marie tapped on the door and came in to hand Chelsea a note. She unfolded it and her heart started to pound. Burke Marshall, her favourite of the senior partners, had invited her to lunch at his club. Could she be ready in twenty minutes?

She nodded her answer to Marie, who went out as noiselessy as she had come in. But Chelsea's heart was still racing. Having lunch with any or all of the senior partners was nothing unusual, but today . . . It must mean that the decision had been made.

She pulled her mind back to the Sullivans, glancing over her notes to see if all of her questions had been answered, and clipped the sheets to the sketch they'd brought of their land. 'I'll go look at your lot this week,' she promised. 'As soon as I've seen it, I can put together some tentative drawings. I'll call you when they're ready.'

'Will you need me any more?' Mr Sullivan asked grumpily. 'I can't take too much time off. This house is for Doris, anyway. I couldn't care less where I live.'

'We have a whole chain of retail stores,' Mrs Sullivan said proudly. 'They keep Charles very busy.'

Discount outlets, no doubt, Chelsea told herself. Then, sternly, she reminded herself that the Sullivans deserved the best she could do for them. If it turned out that they wanted a one-room tar-paper shack, it would at least be the best tar-paper shack Chelsea Ryan could design.

'As a matter of fact, we will need you, Mr Sullivan,' she said quietly. 'But perhaps we can meet in the evening so that it doesn't inconvenience you.'

He finally unbent. 'That would be very thoughtful, Miss Ryan. Doris has always wanted to live out where there are some honest-to-goodness trees,' he added a little stiffly. 'We've had that piece of land for years, but it's only now that we can build on it. And she's going to have the house she wants. She's waited long enough for it, that's sure.'

'And you'll have the very best house we can build, Mr Sullivan,' she assured him.

There was no more talk of a male architect. Chelsea walked down the hall with them, listening to the last few afterthoughts from Mrs Sullivan.

'I'm sure you'll think of more ideas,' Chelsea said gravely. 'Why don't you jot them down and drop them in the mail? I like having clients who are absorbed in designing their own homes. They're much happier with the results, you see.'

Mrs Sullivan glanced at the engraved business card that Chelsea handed her, and agreed, Chelsea turned from the door with a sigh of relief.

Burke Marshall was standing behind her, 'That was neatly done, Chelsea,' he applauded, 'With one quick suggestion you made her feel vitally important, and you forestalled the hundred 'phone calls she would otherwise have made to tell you "just one more thing".'

'It's absolutely true, too. I do prefer clients who really get absorbed in the planning.' She tipped her head to one side to study Burke, tall, distinguished, and white-haired, still slim despite his sixty years. 'Are you ready to go, Burke? I'm starving.'

'Don't you need a hat or something?'

'I'll be just a minute.' In her office again, Chelsea

adjusted her sunglasses, tipped the brim of her wide straw hat at the proper angle, and touched up her lipstick. 'This is your big day, Chelsea Ryan,' she told herself softly. 'The day you've been aiming for since college. A partnership well before you're thirty years old—who would ever have expected that?' She smiled at the excited woman in the mirror and practised a look of interested calm. She would look like that when Burke gave her the news, and he'd be amazed that she was so collected. It was fun to tease Burke; he'd been like an uncle since they'd met at her college, where he had been a guest lecturer. It had been her own qualifications that had won her the job with Shelby Harris, but Burke had been the one who gave her the chance to prove herself. And now it was Burke who had lobbied for her to get the partnership . . . She should be taking him out to lunch, she thought, instead of the other way around.

Burke's club was a pillar of downtown St Louis society, and from the top-floor restaurant the view was breathtaking. Chelsea looked out over the city to the river and the sweep of gleaming stainless steel that formed the Gateway Arch, towering over the skyline. What a daring proposal it had been, back in the forties when it was designed, she thought, and wondered if she would have had the nerve to submit such an audacious design for a riverfront memorial.

'Shrimp cocktail and a chef's salad,' she told the waiter, and Burke frowned.

'Nothing more than that? You can't work all afternoon on lettuce,' he complained. 'You forget that the chef serves it in a mixing bowl,' Chelsea reminded. 'How's Helen?'

Burke shook his head. 'It's been several weeks since you saw her, hasn't it?'

'Yes. I've been awfully busy since Martin died, but that's no excuse for neglecting Helen.' She felt a twinge of guilt; Burke's wife was one of her favourite people, and since she had contracted a crippling disease, Helen seldom left the house, Chelsea tried to stop by at least once a week, but the press of work that Martin Burns had left undone was still forcing her to spend long days in the office.

'Her doctor says her spine is getting worse, and that she'll be confined to a wheelchair in another six months or so.'

'Oh, no, Burke.'

Burke nodded sadly. 'We've known it was coming, of course. She's been in more pain lately. At any rate, Chelsea, it's time to start designing our new house—one that Helen can run from the wheelchair.'

Chelsea was thinking about Hillhaven, the big old Victorian mansion that Burke and Helen had remodelled so patiently, with love in every door frame and light switch. 'There are so many obstacles for people with physical handicaps.'

'Especially in that house. There are thresholds in every doorway, Chelsea. Helen won't even be able to get from room to room without help.'

'Being dependent on someone else would kill her, Burke.' Chelsea's mind was already busy designing a new house. Spacious enough for a wheelchair, yet compact enough to avoid fatiguing Helen . . .

'Will you do it? She's not wild about the idea just yet—I don't think she's entirely accepted the fact that the doctor knows what he's talking about. But if you had some sketches tucked away to show her just as soon as she is ready to discuss it . . .'

'Sure, Burke. I'll run something up.'

'It's going to be so hard on her,' Burke went on. 'Since she first became ill, she has managed by having the housekeeper come in a couple of days a week. It's important to her to continue being self-sufficient.'

Chelsea nodded and thoughtfully dipped a jumbo shrimp into the spicy sauce. 'If she can't run her own home anymore, she isn't going to want to fight that disease.'

'That's what scares me,' Burke said. Suddenly he looked old.

'And in that kitchen, she can't even cook from a wheelchair.' Chelsea's mind was churning. There are some new books out on designing for the handicapped, she was thinking. 'I'll see what I can come up with.'

'Nothing too elaborate at first,' Burke warned. 'I don't want her to think we've been scheming behind her back.'

'Even if we have,' Chelsea said demurely.

Burke smiled at that. 'I hope that Helen will bring it up to you herself. She loves that house, and I don't want to push her into giving it up.'

Chelsea finished her shrimp and pushed the glass aside. 'I don't suppose we could just re-model?'

Burke considered and shook his head. 'I don't see how. And let's face it, Chelsea, we bought that house thirty years ago when we thought there would be kids in every bedroom. We certainly don't need a fifteen-room Victorian mansion now.'

Chelsea shrugged. 'Needing and wanting are two different things. If I had a dollar for every client who wants a house she doesn't need . . .'

Burke laughed. 'I see your point.'

'And when I try to design the house she needs, she gets upset and finds an architect who will sell her what she wants.'

'Helen is just going to have to be practical.'

'Well, surely there's a house that she can't help but fall in love with.'

'Good girl. And stop by to see her, too. She gets lonely.' He studied her thoughtfully over the rim of his glass. 'It's just work that's been keeping you away? I thought perhaps it was a new boyfriend.'

'Nothing so original, I'm afraid.' Chelsea swirled

the ice cubes in her glass and said, with her heart in her throat, 'Burke . . . how did the meeting go this morning?'

He set his cup down with a clatter. 'I'm sorry, Chelsea. I was so concerned about the new house that I forgot.' His eyes were dark. 'They made the decision, and . . .'

If it was me, Chelsea thought with sudden frozen logic, he would have said WE decided.

'I'm sorry, Chelsea. Carl and Frank think we need someone with more experience, with a broader record in public buildings, and . . .'.

'And not a woman,' Chelsea said bitterly. 'Burke, I've got the experience. And they certainly know my work. I've done plenty of it since Martin died, finishing up all his projects.'

'I know, Chelsea. You've been valuable; no one else could have stepped into Martin's shoes. We all know what a mess you inherited when he died.'

'Then how could they pass over one of their own staff to bring in an outsider?'

'Because he's one of the best-known new lights in architecture, that's why,' Burke said.

'If he's so damned good, why is he willing to move? Why does he even want a partnership? He could start his own firm.'

'Any architect would be please to join Shelby Harris. It has a national reputation, Chelsea.'

'If the partners aren't careful, Shelby Harris will be nationally known as a bigoted, discriminatory . . .'

Burke looked shocked. 'Are you saying that you might sue the firm?'

'Why shouldn't I?' Then Chelsea relented. 'No, I won't sue. I know what would happen. I'd lose, and the whole cause would be set back ten years.'

'You would lose,' Burke agreed. 'Your credentials are good, but Nick Stanton's are so outstanding that nobody could argue with the decision.'

'Stanton? They hired Granite Man?' Chelsea's tone was unbelieving.

'The entire stack of applications couldn't have beaten him if they were put together.' Then Burke said, unbelievingly, 'What did you call him?'

'Nothing important, Burke.' She bit her lip. 'You know that it's going to very hard for me to work with him. After Martin, it will be hard to have any new boss. But answering to Nick Stanton . . .'

'That's why I brought you to lunch—to talk to you before the official announcement is made. I was afraid you'd blow up in public if it took you by surprise.'

'I probably would have,' Chelsea admitted. 'When is it going to be announced, Burke?'

'Immediately, Carl called Nick this morning, and he'll start to work Monday.'

'That's prompt. Hasn't he got anything better to do than wait around for a 'phone call?'

Burke didn't answer. A fleeting look of pain crossed his face, and he said, 'You aren't going to like this, either. Helen and I are having a cocktail party this weekend to introduce him to the whole staff.'

'Traitor,' Chelsea muttered.

'I have to work with him, too, Chelsea. And even though I was promoting you for the position, I have nothing against Nick. He will add fantastic strength to the firm. So I volunteered.'

'Can Helen handle it?'

Burke shrugged. 'It will be catered. There's nothing to handle, really.'

'In that case, I won't offer to help. Let's see, what plans can I make for next weekend? I haven't been up to Norah Springs to visit my parents in a while.'

'Don't you dare,' Burke threatened. 'You have to show up at that party, Chelsea.'

'What will you do if I don't? Spank me?' Her big green eyes widened in mock fright.

'I'd be tempted, it's imperative that you swallow

this resentment, Chelsea. If you just look at it as a learning experience . . .'

'Oh, I've learned from it already. I've learned that if I want to be a partner, I'd better start checking out some different firms. Shelby Harris won't be it, that's sure.'

'Are you certain that you want to move? You have more prestige on the staff at Shelby Harris than you would as a partner anywhere else in St Louis. It's small, but there isn't a better-known firm in the whole state.'

'That's true,' Chelsea admitted grudgingly. The mere mention of Shelby Harris at a gathering of architects was enough to bring respectful silence.

'And if you insist on moving, remember that you won't get much of a reference from Nick if you can't work with the team. So dump the resentment and bite your tongue and be nice to the man, Chelsea. You might discover that he isn't so bad after all.'

'I'm not holding my breath,' Chelsea announced. 'He's got an annoying little trick of looking at a set of plans and dismissing them as if they were no better than an infant's scribble.'

'He's a good architect, Chelsea.'

'I'm not questioning his skill. But he pulled that trick on me while he was here interviewing. I had the drawings for the Wharton house on my desk and you'd have thought he'd never seen anything so dreadful.'

'Did he say anything?'

'He didn't have to. He just turned up his nose as if the drawings smelled bad.'

Burke tried to hide a smile. 'And what did you do?'

'As soon as he walked out, I put them in the wastebasket,' Chelsea admitted reluctantly.

'The set I saw was beautiful.'

'That was the second try,' Chelsea muttered. 'Carl Shelby liked them too.'

He sobered again. 'Chelsea, if you can just pretend that he's a human being . . . Think what you can learn from the man. And he can't be all that hard to work for.'

'I'm not betting—but what choice do I have? I'll try, Burke. I will really try.'

Her chef's salad suddenly didn't taste very good. Chelsea made a pretence of eating, but she was relieved when Burke finally pushed his coffee cup aside and said, 'Shall we walk back to the office?'

She had kept the afternoon free of appointments so she could visit the sites of the several houses that were being built to her design around the city. Instead, she shut her office door, flung her hat and handbag into a chair, and strode over to stand by the window, her clenched hand pressed against her mouth, fighting back the tears that threatened to flow.

She had wanted that job so badly, had planned and schemed and played office politics. And they gave it to someone else. It hurt with a deep stab that nearly took her breath away. But what also hurt was the discovery that she had allowed herself to count on getting the partnership, on being one of the four people who made the policy for the firm. All the time she had been telling herself that it was a wonderful opportunity, that if she was lucky she might be selected, she had really been thinking that it was a sure thing. Now she had to readjust her whole attitude.

And instead of moving into that walnut-panelled office down the hall, she would have to walk by it and know that Nick Stanton was there instead.

He was a fantastic architect. Burke was right about that. Chelsea had seen his designs, had read the articles he submitted to the professional journals. It wasn't his talent she despised, but the man himself. He was cold and silent and supercilious and arrogant. Granite Man, she thought. There couldn't have been a better name for him.

There was a perfunctory knock and then the door opened. Chelsea wheeled around to see Jim, a set of drawings rolled up in his hand, come in.

He stopped, surprised, when he saw her. 'I thought you were going out to the sites today,' he said.

'I changed my mind. Is that my new house?'

Jim unrolled the finished work on the drawing board. 'And your rough sketches,' he said, handing her the originals. 'The elevations are all there, too.'

'Good.' She stared at the sketch of the front elevation, the house low and rambling, its wide roof overhanging the inviting front door, the big oak tree framing the view. They'd have to be careful of that tree during construction; it was one of the best features of the lot the clients had chosen, and she was not going to allow its removal. She made a mental note to talk to the contractor. 'It's a pretty house, isn't it, Jim?'

'How professional you are,' he mocked. 'With all of the terms that apply, you choose "pretty".'

'It's true,' Chelsea defended herself. 'And that's the way the clients will think of it.'

'You amaze me, Chelsea. But if it works . . .' Jim shrugged. 'Tell Judy I'll pick her up at seven.'

'Why don't you tell her yourself? You have a telephone.' Then Chelsea regretted the sharpness of her tone.

Jim just raised an eyebrow. 'The grapevine must be right. Rumour has it that you didn't get the job.'

Chelsea turned back to the window, staring out towards the wide Mississippi. She almost wanted to go jump into the water, to let the river carry her down to New Orleans. 'It's right,' she said. Dejection dripped from her voice.

'It isn't the end of the world, you know.'

'It certainly feels like it, Jim.' Her voice suddenly rose vehemently. 'I hope Nick Stanton makes such a mess of things that he's tarred and feathered before the year's out.'

Jim watched her thoughtfully for a few minutes. Then he said, 'Actually you should be praying he makes it big.'

Chelsea wheeled around. 'Why on earth?'

'Because the partners have already taken one enormous step forward by choosing him at all. He's still in his thirties, you know. And if he does well, they might be encouraged to go one step farther and give a woman a chance.'

She considered it and shook her head. 'It's going to be years before there's another vacancy in the partnership.'

'Maybe not. Nobody anticipated this one. Just watch your step, Chelsea. Something tells me that Nick Stanton isn't the kind of enemy you want to have. I'll bet he plays rough. A whole lot rougher than you can.'

CHAPTER TWO

'AREN'T you going to get dressed soon?' Judy Martin stood in the doorway between hall and living room, her hair in electric rollers, wearing a silky slip and almost nothing else.

Chelsea didn't even look up from the drawing board that was tucked into a corner of the living room. She checked a figure in the book and erased a line on her paper, wishing that she had brought home an electric eraser from the office. This new house for the Marshalls was giving her fits—she had drawn every line at least three times.

'It's only a cocktail party, Judy,' she said finally. 'You aren't dressing for dinner at the White House, you know.'

'Sometimes you infuriate me, Chelsea.' Judy put her hands on her hips. 'It's very important that I make a good impression on all those people. I'd hate to make a fool of myself by falling into the punchbowl or something.'

'There won't be a punchbowl.' Chelsea didn't sound interested. She sketched a corner of Helen Marshall's prospective new kitchen on a scrap of paper and finally looked up. 'You will not get drunk. You will not drop a glob of taco dip on to Carl Shelby's fifty-dollar tie. You will not look gauche. This is no different from the company Christmas party, for heaven's sake. You enjoyed that.'

'But it is different.' Judy sounded terrified. 'The senior partners weren't at the Christmas party. I don't know if I can handle meeting all of them at once. I mean, Shelby and Harris and Marshall!'

'You've talked to Burke dozens of times on the

'phone. Besides, all you have to do is sip a drink and bat those big blue eyes and gush, "How very interesting!" once in a while, Carl will be charmed.'

Judy didn't sound convinced. 'Will you at least come along with us?'

'I'll be there, Judy. I don't dare skip it, but I don't plan to go any earlier than I have to.'

'I don't want to walk in by myself.'

'You're going with Jim,' Chelsea pointed out. 'You won't be alone a minute.'

'But men don't understand!' Judy wailed. 'He'll just go off and get a drink and stand in a corner and talk buildings and . . .'

'And you're going to rip yourself into a small pile of shreds if you don't stop.' Chelsea put her pencil down. 'All right, if it will make you feel better. But I'm staying for dinner with Burke and Helen, so I'll take my own car. I will follow you out there and walk in with you. Is that good enough?'

Judy nodded. 'I'm sorry to be such a baby,' she said. 'It's just that elegant parties really throw me.'

'Only because you aren't used to them.' Judy looked about three years old, Chelsea thought. She was a perfectly competent young woman ninety per cent of the time, but she felt inferior to the people at Shelby Harris because they had more education. Sometimes Chelsea wanted to scream at Judy that she was worth three of them.

'Besides,' Chelsea added, 'nobody ever called Helen Marshall's parties elegant. They are, of course, but everybody has such a good time that they forget to notice.'

'It's easy for you. You know everybody.'

'Well, if you want something to make you feel better, think about Nick Stanton. He's meeting everyone for the first time.'

'Poor man.' Judy was plucking rollers from her hair. 'Jim will be here in half an hour.'

'Listen, there will be no one at that party that I want to impress badly enough to spend half an hour making myself beautiful.'

'Not even your new boss?'

'Especially not him.'

'That's what's really aggravating,' Judy scolded, back to her normal tone of voice. 'You take five minutes in the shower and another five getting dressed and everyone will tell you how lovely you are. I've spent all afternoon trying to look good and nobody will even notice.'

'Jim will.' Or I'll kill him right on the spot, Chelsea decided.

'That doesn't count. Jim has to notice; it's his obligation.' She went back into her bedroom, but her voice floated out to Chelsea. 'Are you sure my blue dress will be all right?'

'It's wonderful.' Chelsea stacked her books on the stool beside the drawing board and started for her own bedroom. Once Judy was in this frame of mind, there would be no work done. Besides, despite what she had told Judy, Chelsea had already decided that she was going to look her best for this party. She was not going to wear her heart on her sleeve; the whole staff might already know that she was disappointed because she hadn't been offered the partnership, but she would not give them the satisfaction of confirming it.

So she put on the new kelly green dress that her mother had sent her last week. It wasn't the sort of thing that Chelsea would have bought for herself, but the sequin trim brought out the sparkle in her big green eyes, and the artistically uneven hem showed off perfect legs. It was a slinky dress, and it looked marvellous on her. She tucked the auburn curls up into a twist, leaving wisps and tendrils soft around her heart-shaped face, and took special pains with her make-up. Transluscent skin that leaned towards freckles was such a pain, Chelsea thought. She had to be so careful not to get sunburn that it took much of the fun out of summer.

Cars were already clogging the driveway and lining the quiet street in front of Hillhaven when Chelsea parked her Mercedes convertible behind Jim's battered compact car. The house was tucked into one of the old residential neighbourhoods of west St Louis, where wrought-iron gates closed off the streets to keep the casual sightseer out. There had probably been more traffic in this cul-de-sac today than in the last month.

Jim looked impatient as he helped Judy out of the car. She must have been fussing about her fears throughout the drive, Chelsea knew.

Much more of that nonsense, Judy, my girl, she thought, and you may be surprised to find Jim escorting someone who does feel at ease at the office parties. And you'll be sitting at home.

She climbed the brick steps slowly, listening to the leaves that rustled on the huge old oaks beside the double front doors. The trees were still the warm yellow-green of spring. It was May, and nature again held out the promise of warmth and growth and renewal.

Jim rang the bell. Then he looked down at Chelsea and said, 'Are you nervous, too?'

'I am never nervous,' she lied bravely.

Jim hooted, but before he could answer, Burke opened the door. 'Hello, Chelsea,' he said cheerfully. 'Jim. And . . . Judy, isn't it?'

Judy looked as if she was going to shrivel up under Burke's friendly gaze.

'They're all in the drawing room,' Burke gestured towards the long French doors. A burst of laughter came from the room, and Chelsea lifted an eyebrow with an inquiring look.

'Your Mr Stanton must be the life of the party,' she said sweetly, hanging back to talk to him as Jim and Judy crossed the hall.

Burke shook a finger at her. 'Now, Chelsea,' he warned.

'Oh, I'm trying to pretend that he's human,' she added. 'Just as you requested. But it requires such a dreadful amount of concentration, you see.' She drifted into the drawing room without waiting for Burke's answer.

The room must have been forty feet long, but the proportions were so perfect that it looked comfortable and intimate. Chelsea never walked into that drawing room without hesitating an instant by the door to recognise the perfection of Helen's decorating scheme, too—the heavy Aubusson carpet laid atop a hardwood floor that was polished to a mirror gleam, the furniture scattered in casual conversational groupings, the green plants. Today, with the easy warmth of summer flowing throught the open windows, the fireplace was hidden by an elaborate needlepoint screen that mimicked the design in the carpet.

I do love Hillhaven, Chelsea thought idly. I wonder, if Burke and Helen are going to sell it, if they would make me a deal.

'Chelsea!' A low, musical voice pulled her across the room to the high-backed chair where Helen sat.

Burke was right, Chelsea thought with her first clear view of Helen Marshall. Lines of pain were written deeper than ever before into that lovely patrician face, and though she was smiling, there were faint shadows etched below her eyes. Chelsea drew a quick breath of horror. Helen's physical condition was deteriorating quickly.

Helen raised a thin hand to take Chelsea's. 'My dear, you look so lovely today,' she said. 'I want you to meet Nicholas Stanton, dear, Nick, this is Chelsea Ryan. She's a staff architect at Shelby Harris, and a particular favourite of my husband's.'

Nick Stanton hadn't warmed up a bit, Chelsea thought as she looked up at him. His deep blue eyes were just as cold, his face under the even tan just as hard, as when he had come to the office for his interview.

'We've met,' she said coolly, and offered her hand.

He shifted his glass from right hand to left after a split-second hesitation, and clasped Chelsea's fingers briefly.

If she had been trying to make a good impression on him, she would have been insulted by the mockery of a handshake. It was a good thing that she didn't really care what Nick Stanton's opinion was of her, Chelsea thought.

'Yes,' he was saying. 'I understand that Burke and Miss Ryan are . . . very close.'

Chelsea saw red. So he thought that Burke had tried to get her that partnership just because she was his protegé, did he? Well, she was going to remove that idea from his mind if she had to batter his head against the fireplace wall to do it.

'Burke is a wonderful man,' she said. 'He has given me more than I could have ever expected.'

'I've heard that,' Nick said silkily.

'I mean attention,' Chelsea stormed. 'And knowledge. Not jobs, Mr Stanton, whatever you think.'

'Chelsea is a wonderful architect, Nick,' Helen put in. 'She planned all the re-modelling we've done to Hillhaven.'

Nick raised his glass, sipped, looked at Chelsea over the rim. 'I have no doubts whatsoever about her professional standards,' he said.

Chelsea stared at him for a full minute. 'If you'll excuse me, Helen,' she said. 'I'm sure there are people standing in line to meet Mr Stanton. I'd hate to keep him from his adoring public.'

Her mind was whirling as she turned away. Obviously it was going to be open warfare between them; it was the one thing she hadn't expected. She hadn't dreamed that Granite Man would give a damn what she thought about him; once he had the partnership, why should he care? And after all, it wasn't as if Burke's partiality to her had even a breath of favouritism about it. She was darned good at her job, and everyone in the office knew it.

Well, if Mr Great Architect Nicholas Stanton wanted to make a fight of it, she swore, he'd discover that Chelsea Ryan could scrap just as hard as he could.

Burke handed her a glass of champagne. Chelsea sipped it, and since she didn't want to answer the question she saw in his eyes, she said, 'Helen looks tired today.'

'She is,' he admitted. 'She's always tired now. She's such a good sport, but it wears her out just to move around.'

Chelsea's eyes rested thoughtfully on Helen across the room. She hadn't moved; she sat gracefully in that high-backed chair receiving her guests and apologising now and then for not rising to greet them. Most of them probably hadn't noticed the fatigue that Chelsea saw in every line of the woman's body. They didn't even realise that she wasn't the old Helen, the one who could dance the night away and who never, never sat still. Chelsea's eyes filled with tears as she watched the gallant performance.

Then she looked away from Helen and her eyes locked with Nick Stanton's. Was it mockery that flashed in those deep blue eyes, she wondered, as he watched her and Burke standing there? But there was no time to analyse it; with a tiny shrug that looked like disgust he turned away and spoke to Carl Shelby.

'Your Mr Stanton doesn't like me any more than I like him,' she said.

'You don't even know each other yet.' Burke sounded irritable.

'And I have no desire to study the subject, either.'

He ignored the interruption. 'You'll have a chance to get acquainted a little later.' He set his empty glass on to the tray of a passing waiter, reached for a full one, and started to move away.

'Burke!' Chelsea's voice rose. 'What does that mean?'

But Burke just saluted Chelsea with the champagne glass and went to answer the doorbell.

There was an uncomfortable twisting sensation in the pit of Chelsea's stomach. Whatever Burke had meant, she was certain that she wasn't going to like it, Chelsea thought.

She stayed off to the side of the room, her glass of champagne going flat long before she had finished it. She had discovered years ago that the most fun to be had at a cocktail party was to stay in a corner and watch the rest of the crowd. More could be learned about a person by his conduct with a drink in his hand than in any other way, Chelsea was convinced.

Eileen, for instance. The buxom blonde had arrived alone this evening, but she was surrounded by most of the young, unattached men, and a few of the married ones as well. It was no wonder that the men were hovering, Chelsea thought. Eileen's ivory silk blouse was so tight that if she took a deep breath it would probably rip, and the neckline was enticingly low.

'I'm going to take Jim home and kill him,' Judy muttered into Chelsea's ear, and sat down on the loveseat beside her. She looked sulky, and it took Chelsea just a moment to discover why. She saw that Jim, too, was on the outskirts of the crowd that surrounded Eileen.

'Don't bother. Haven't you noticed that she isn't

paying any attention to the boys? Her mind is on bigger game.' As she watched, Eileen cast a longing look towards Nick Stanton.

'The new partner? Handsome dude, isn't he?'

Chelsea shrugged. 'If you like statues.' She finished her champagne and set the glass down on the marble-topped table beside the loveseat. A waiter replaced it with a full glass so smoothly that Chelsea didn't have a chance to tell him she didn't want any more.

'I think he is gorgeous,' Judy announced. 'I always did go for guys with black hair and blue eyes. Do you know if he's attached?'

'Who cares? Are you worried that Eileen might be wasting her time? I'm sure she'd appreciate your concern.'

Judy ignored her. 'He also has two brothers. A shame they aren't in St Louis, too. If they look like him, the three of them could take the town by storm.'

'Judy, I could have nightmares thinking about Nick Stanton in triplicate. Don't do this to me.'

Judy was still staring at Nick Stanton. 'If Jim ever finishes ogling Eileen, he's taking me out to dinner. But I'll probably starve before he notices.'

'That leaves you a choice,' Chelsea said coolly. 'You can sit here and be resentful about it, or you can go tell him that you're ready to leave.'

Judy looked horrified. 'I wouldn't dare. I wonder if I could get another glass of champagne.'

Chelsea shrugged. 'Have mine.' She handed her untouched glass to Judy.

'If you're sure you don't want it.' Judy didn't wait for an answer. She sipped the wine and looked around with a sigh. 'This is a gigantic house. I bet it's beautiful at Christmas.'

Chelsea half-closed her eyes and remembered the holidays she had spent with Burke and Helen. When Helen felt up to it, Christmas at Hillhaven was a dream world. Every year there was a different decorating theme, but always the big tree stood in the bay window in the drawing room, agleam with the precious ornaments that Helen had brought back from all over the world. The last few years, though, had been quieter.

'Do all their kids come home at Christmas?'

'They don't have any.'

Judy sipped her champagne, her face registering astonishment. 'This enormous house and no family?'

'They didn't exactly plan it that way.' Chelsea said. She felt a little defensive about Burke and Helen, as if they needed protection, which was silly. 'Helen wanted about eight kids, and Burke wanted whatever Helen did. It just didn't work out.'

'Too bad. It must take a fortune to keep this place running. Do architects make that kind of money?'

'Some of them do. Burke doesn't have to; Helen's father was a millionaire.'

'Nice for him. I wonder where the waiter went.' Judy set her empty glass down with a sigh.

'Where all good waiters go when cocktail parties are over. Back into a closet somewhere, I expect.' And not a bit too soon for her friend, Chelsea thought. With relief, she watched Jim and Judy leave a few minutes later. If Judy had indulged in one more glass of champagne, she'd probably have told Eileen exactly what she thought.

The crowd thinned out rapidly then. Chelsea was standing in the hall at the bottom of the elaborate stairway when the last of them left. Her hand unconsciously caressed the satin smoothness of the walnut woodwork as she watched Burke at the door, saying goodbye to his guests. Then she felt the weight of a stare and turned to see Nick Stanton leaning against the drawing room door, his arms folded across his chest and those big dark blue eyes focused coldly on her.

If those eyes belonged to a woman, Chelsea thought

resentfully, she'd be burned as a witch. They were framed with a wealth of black eyelashes, for starters, and they had an odd slant that combined with the dark slash of eyebrows to make him look positively evil. Right now his gaze was ice cold, and Chelsea had all she could do to keep from shivering as he continued to regard her unblinkingly.

'You seem to like this house, Miss Ryan,' he said coolly. 'Or do you make a habit of checking out the finish on everyone's woodwork?'

Chelsea looked at her hand, resting on the carved newel post, as if surprised to find it there. 'I adore old houses,' she said. 'And if I have a personal stake in this one, it would be no surprise.'

'So I understand.' His voice was perfectly smooth, but there was a slur underneath it that made Chelsea indignant.

'I drew the remodelling plans as a special project for Burke while I was still in college,' she said, and wondered why she was bothering to explain.

Nick raised an eyebrow. Who cares? it seemed to say.

'And an excellent job she did,' Burke had closed the door. Now he crossed the hall and drew Chelsea's hand comfortably into the crook of his arm. 'It was a warren of little dark rooms before—typically Victorian, you know, Nick. I would have been delighted to go out to the suburbs and build, but Chelsea and Helen got their heads together and outnumbered me.' He chuckled fondly and patted Chelsea's hand.

The little black-gowned maid from the caterer's service came down the hall. 'Dinner is served, Madame,' she told Chelsea.

Nick's eyebrows drew together in a sharp frown. 'I'll see if Helen is ready,' he said in a voice that was deceptively soft. His eyes snapped.

'I'll go, Nick,' Burke said. 'It takes a bit of practise to be able to help her. You two go on into the dining room—-we don't stand on ceremony at Hillhaven anymore.'

Chelsea's fingers tapped gently on the carved newel post as she looked up at Nick. 'You're staying for dinner?'

'I was invited.' He offered his arm. 'May I escort you, Miss Ryan?' he said, and the tone was an insult.

'The dining room is three steps away. I think I can manage to stagger that far without the support of your strong arm,' Chelsea snapped. I'm going to kill Burke for this, she thought. He could at least have warned me.

And you could at least have suspected it, dummy, she thought. The guest of honour at a cocktail party would obviously be invited to dinner. Dad always told me my hard head would get me into trouble even if my red hair didn't, she reflected.

'Interesting that the maid thought you were the hostess,' Nick mused. 'Are you planning to be the lady of the house someday?'

'For God's sake, the girl made a mistake,' Chelsea said tartly. 'She was hired for the party; she can't possibly know any of us. And if you're implying that I'm here all the time, I'm not. I haven't seen Helen in weeks.'

He nodded thoughtfully, but somehow Chelsea felt that her explanation had bounced off him without leaving a dent in his convictions.

Helen appeared in the doorway, her hand on Burke's arm. 'After sitting so long, I need help getting out of my chair,' she said, smiling. 'It's the price one pays for getting older.'

The sheer bravery of the woman took Chelsea's breath away. She was obviously in pain, but never would Helen admit that there was anything seriously wrong with her. 'I don't want sympathy,' she had told Chelsea once, in a rare confiding moment. 'I don't want people hovering over me, and watching out for what they say. I hate being an object of pity.'

And she never would be, Chelsea thought. When her time came, Helen Marshall would die as she had lived—proudly and self-sufficiently. And the world would be a worse place without her.

'Chelsea,' Helen said softly, 'there's a bottle of capsules on the table beside my bed. If you would bring me one . . .'

'Of course.' Chelsea ran up the stairs and stopped in the doorway of Helen's room. The pink and gold furnishings were the same as they had always been, except that where Helen's four-poster had stood was now a hospital bed, the electric variety that adjusted to any position. It was a jarring note in the princess-pretty room, and Chelsea went back downstairs in a sombre mood.

Nick was waiting impatiently to hold her chair. She dropped the capsule into Helen's hand and walked around the table to her own chair. 'It's so rare to find a gentleman these days,' Chelsea said with a sultry smile as Nick sat down beside her. And you aren't one, the tone of her voice added.

'Don't bait me, Miss Ryan,' he said so softly that she didn't think either Burke or Helen heard. 'You might not like the results.'

'Why, Mr Stanton,' she replied, and hated herself for sounding like a bad imitation of a Southern belle, 'can't a girl pay a man a compliment these days?'

'Knock it off,' Burke commanded. 'If I hear another Mister or Miss at this dinner table tonight I will send you both to your rooms.'

'Yes, Burke,' Chelsea said demurely and picked up her spoon.

So they were polite all through dinner, but underneath the courtesy was a vicious wit. And as she sipped clear consommé and nibbled at stuffed veal and crisp fresh vegetables and excellent hot rolls, Chelsea wondered why the venom was so hard to restrain. She knew why she didn't like Nick Stanton. But Nick had the job he wanted; why should he be angry at her?

Helen pleaded exhaustion, looking as if the pain of admitting that she could not brave out another hour of polite conversation hurt her even worse than her spine did. Burke helped her up the stairs, while Nick and Chelsea waited silently in the drawing room with the coffee tray for his return.

Chelsea hoped that he would take the hint and leave soon. She wanted to talk to Burke about the plans that were already underway for the new house. But Nick seemed to be very comfortable. He leaned back in his chair, looked up at the excellent oil portrait of Helen that hung above the fireplace, and said, 'What exactly did you do to this house?'

'Is that polite conversation or do you really want to know?' Chelsea refilled her delicate china cup from the huge silver pot.

He sat up slowly. 'If I didn't want to know, why would I ask?'

Chelsea shrugged. 'I'd guess that you merely want to criticise my architectural style. But I really don't care what you think. You see,' she added gently, 'I don't attempt to read a man's mind unless I'm interested in him.'

He looked her over with insulting thoroughness and then said, 'Of course, with Burke in the palm of your hand you wouldn't need to be interested in anyone else.'

'If you're implying that Burke's interest in me has had anything to do with my career . . .'

'I don't imply things, Miss Ryan,' he said with sardonic emphasis on the title. 'I come straight out and say them. I'm amazed that you aren't trying to fix an interest with me. Obviously Burke wasn't quite powerful enough, and yet you seem very loyal to him.'

Chelsea sat up very straight. 'It has nothing to do with . . .'

He cut her off neatly. 'Or are you after bigger game? Carl Shelby himself perhaps? Or Frank Harris?' Before Chelsea had regained her breath, Nick had changed the subject. 'You must have had quite a time replacing that cast plaster ceiling. It can't have been that way before, if this room was originally several small ones.'

'Don't remind me,' Burke said heartily from the door. 'We searched for months for an artisan who could do that work. Helen's poured a fortune into the place over the years, you know. You should see the pictures.'

Chelsea set her cup down firmly. 'Burke, it's been lovely——' Her voice sounded hollow to her own ears, and on Nick's face was the first smile she had ever seen there. 'But I'm tired. I'll see you at the office Monday—I have some plans to show you.' She retrieved her handbag and then stood on tiptoe to kiss Burke's cheek lightly.

Nick rose lazily. 'I'll walk you to your car. I should be on my way too, Burke.'

Outside the range of Hillhaven's lights, Chelsea turned on him fiercely. 'You needn't protect me, you know. I can walk to my car by myself.'

'Who said I was protecting you? As a matter of fact, I feel sorry for the attacker who takes you on.'

'You knew I wanted to talk to Burke privately . . .'

'I certainly did. And it didn't take a great deal of imagination to know what you were going to talk about. I simply refused to be a part of it.'

'What do you mean?' Chelsea stopped suddenly, in the middle of the street. 'You refused to be a part of what?'

He laughed sardonically. 'For all I know, you'll drive around the block and go back in. I can hardly stop you.'

Chelsea's head was spinning. 'And why shouldn't I go back to talk to Burke?' She stopped beside her car and took her keys from her handbag.

'A Mercedes,' he mused. 'I should have know.'

'It was a gift,' she flared, sensitive to the accusation in his tone.

'I didn't think that you earned it. Unless it was for services rendered.' He leaned against the fender, his arms folded. 'Did Burke use his own money to buy it, or did he charge it to Helen? You have a lot of nerve to steal from the woman you're deceiving.'

Her throat was so tight she could hardly breathe. Stupid, she thought. Everything he had said all evening led to that single conclusion; it had been staring at her and she had missed it. 'I am not having an affair with Burke Marshall,' she said. Her voice was taut.

'About those plans you intend to show Burke on Monday,' Nick added pleasantly. 'I'd like to see them first.'

'Those plans have nothing to do with the office,' Chelsea snapped, and bit her tongue.

Nick smiled. 'Somehow I expected that,' he murmured.

Chelsea opened the car door. 'If you would have the decency to get off my car, I'd like to go home.'

He didn't seem to hear. 'I am the boss now, Chelsea,' he warned.

'What does it matter to you whether I'm having an affair?' she asked, her curiosity raging despite her best efforts to keep quiet. 'Even if it was true, which it isn't . . .'

He interrupted. 'Because as long as people like you are licenced to practise architecture, it cheapens the rest of us who have worked like hell to get to where we are. I didn't earn my licence in a bedroom, and I resent women who do.'

She slammed the car door, rolled the window down,

and said, 'Don't take it personally, Mr Stanton.' The motor roared to life.

He moved unhurriedly away from the fender and leaned in the window. 'I take women like you very personally, Chelsea. You'd better get used to it.'

CHAPTER THREE

AND why should it matter to me? That was the question that tormented Chelsea throughout the weekend. It was still bothering her on Monday morning as she drank her second cup of coffee, standing at the kitchen counter in their little apartment.

If Nick Stanton chose to believe that Burke's interest in her was more than fatherly, that was his problem. There was no point in trying to convince him; any effort on her part would look as if she was guilty. Besides, it wouldn't take long for him to realise that she had talent, despite what he thought. Which brought her back to the original question: Why did it matter what Nick Stanton thought?

Judy came out of her bedroom, sleepy-eyed, still wearing her oversized nightshirt. She yawned and reached for a mug. 'The first week of working the evening shift is a drag,' she moaned. 'No social life and no sleep. Are you going to work already?'

'I left a lot of things hanging on Friday.'

'Trying to impress the new partner by going in early?' Judy guessed shrewdly.

'No? I told you what I think of him.'

'And what he thinks of you.' Judy dropped into a chair at the table and looked Chelsea over. 'I think it's funny. The idea of you and Burke as a twosome is laughable.'

'Too bad Nick doesn't see the humour.'

'I know what you should do. Invite him over for dinner.'

'I don't want to spend any more time with that . . . that cannibal than I absolutely must. Why should I see him on my own time?'

'Because if he saw where you live he'd know that this isn't any love nest of Burke Marshall's. That's why.'

Chelsea had to laugh. She looked around at the small kitchen. 'I've been meaning to talk to you. Don't you think we could afford to move?'

Judy shook her head. 'You can. I can't. Besides, there's a little reverse snob appeal in living here.'

'But it's more than half-an-hour from downtown.' Chelsea looked at her watch and hastily swallowed her coffee. 'Which means I'd better be going.'

'Hey, let's have lunch sometime this week, all right? Otherwise we won't see each other at all. I don't plan to be up at this hour every morning, you know, when I work till midnight.'

'Call me at the office.' Chelsea rinsed her cup.

Judy grinned. 'Which days do you reserve for Burke? I wouldn't want to interfere.'

Chelsea turned, the dripping mug in her hand, and threatened, 'You start on me and I'll move out.'

Which wouldn't be a bad idea at all, she thought as she threaded the Mercedes through heavy morning traffic on the Daniel Boone Expressway. She and Judy had shared an apartment for nearly five years. Before that there had been a succession of roommates since she had left home. Chelsea had never lived by herself, and it was beginning to look like an inviting idea. She could afford a nicer apartment now, which was more than she could have said five years before. And the cheap, boxy construction of their present home was beginning to wear on her artistic soul. She longed for some outstanding feature, something that would make her home different from the others.

Like Hillhaven, she thought, and then reluctantly put the idea aside. Even if Helen agreed to move, even if the house was sold, even if Chelsea could scrape up the mortgage payments, the maintenance and upkeep would impoverish her. She'd forgotten just how large a fortune Helen Marshall had poured into that house. No, Hillhaven was just a dream.

The man at the parking ramp waved as she took the time-punched ticket from the machine, and Chelsea smiled back, an every-morning routine. They ought to have a lottery with these tickets, she thought. Paying the bill in a parking ramp day after day was a dreary experience. But if the ticket number might be the lucky one to win a prize it would at least add a bit of excitement to the routine.

She crossed the skywalk and took the lift to the Shelby Harris floor. As she passed the closed walnut door of Nick Stanton's new office, she had to fight off an impulse to childishly stick out her tongue at the engraved nameplate. She didn't; she smiled ruefully at herself and walked on down the hall to her own office.

The office suite was quiet, the time of day when Chelsea did her best work. She got out the folder full of notes about the Sullivan's house, and started to work. She hadn't seen the site yet; that would be a project for this afternoon. She made it a habit never to begin to visualise a house until she had seen where it would stand. But in the meantime she could list the Sullivan's requirements and make sure her notes to herself were clear. A big workshop for Charles, a craft and hobby room for Doris—Chelsea wondered briefly just what sort of crafts she did. She probably crocheted rugs out of plastic bags, Chelsea thought dryly, and then brought herself back with a snap to the work at hand.

When Marie came in, Chelsea gave her a list of clients to contact. It was unusual for her to have so many projects on her desk at the same time; it seemed that half of St Louis was suddenly ready to build, and they all wanted Chelsea Ryan designs. Even Martin's clients seemed to be content to have Chelsea working for them instead. It was flattering, she thought, but she wondered what would happen if all twelve projects reached the construction stage at the same time. She'd be running all over greater St Louis every day trying to keep up with contractors.

She picked up the set of preliminary sketches for another house and started for Jim's office. Thank heaven for a draughtsman who knew what he was doing, she thought. Having Jim around had saved her hours of tedious drawing when it was time to turn the rough schematics into detailed floor plans.

'Hello, Jimmy-boy,' she sang out as she breezed into his office. 'Do I have a project for you. You're going to love this one.'

Nick Stanton turned from the draughting table and looked her over coolly from head to toe. 'I can hardly wait,' he drawled.

Chelsea couldn't help it; she went beetroot red and then pale as a ghost. 'Have they demoted you to draughtsman already?' she asked sweetly. 'I never dreamed the partners would catch on to you so quickly.'

'Your . . . friend . . .' The word was heavy with insinuation '. . . called in sick today. I was looking for the template I need when I ran across his unusual hobby.'

For the first time Chelsea saw what was scattered over the tabletop. In his right hand Nick held a sheet of draughting paper on which she could see the outline of Mount Rushmore, complete with four President's faces, and Nick's.

Chelsea started to feel a little ill. Dammit, she thought, Jim had promised to get those things out of the office.

'He had quite a lot of talent,' Nick said, holding up a sketch of Chelsea as an angel, halo slightly askew and eyes mischievous. 'This one is particularly appropriate. He might find a job as a political cartoonist after he gets fired here.'

'Jim didn't draw them.' Her voice was faint. There

was no point in pretending innocence, anyway. Everyone in the office would recognise Chelsea's style.

'I beg your pardon?' He sat down on the high-backed stool at the draughting table.

'Jim didn't draw them. I did.'

Nick's left eyebrow raised. It made him look like the Devil incarnate, bargaining for her soul. Except right now there was no bargaining to be done. Chelsea could see few options. 'Protecting Jim? Is he another of your lovers?'

'Jim is a friend and nothing more.'

'I doubt Burke would be convinced,' he drawled. 'You are really taking a risk for Jim, you know, Chelsea. If Burke finds out . . .'

'I'm telling the truth. My initials are on those sketches. See?'

He made a show of looking. 'Sorry, I don't see anything that marks them as yours.'

'I don't exactly advertise that I drew them!' Chelsea snapped. Reluctantly she walked towards him, holding out her hand for one of the drawings.

He didn't seem to see her. He held the drawing up to the light and inspected it. When Chelsea tried to snatch it out of his hand, Nick held it even higher and gave her a chiding look. 'Now, now,' he said. 'It won't do you any good to tear it up.' Leaning against the draughting stool as he was, he was still inches taller than she. Never before had Chelsea so regretted her lack of height.

'I didn't intend to destroy it. I was going to show you my initials.'

'Proud of your work?' he asked, and his eyes narrowed.

'Why shouldn't I be? You obviously think they're good, or you wouldn't be so angry.'

'And of course you're protecting your friend.'

'It's not fair to let him be blamed. I'm responsible.'

'So show me,' he said softly.

Chelsea looked thoughtfully from his face to the sketch. She would have to reach as high as she could just to put a finger on the paper. 'Give it to me.'

He shook his head. 'No way will I let you have this. Come here.'

It was a momentary battle of wills as their eyes locked. Chelsea gave in first and reluctantly stepped closer. By the time she could put her finger on the tiny monogram she had sketched into Abe Lincoln's beard, she was so close to Nick that she could feel his breath warm against her cheek. She felt trapped.

'So they are really yours. What's the matter? You aren't nervous, are you Chelsea?' he asked. His voice was very soft, but she wasn't fooled. Underneath the gentleness was a thread of steel.

'My name, as far as you are concerned, is Miss Ryan,' she said. Her voice shook just a tiny bit, and he smiled.

'Not any more,' he said softly. 'I'm tired of that game. Let's start a new one. I'm sure we have all sorts of things in common.' His fingertip traced the line of her chin.

'No, thanks.' Chelsea started to edge away from him, but his hand shot out and caught her elbow, holding her next to him in what was almost an embrace.

'It might be a lot of fun. But of course if you don't want to play——' His long slim hand fanned the sketches out on the drawing board and selected the one of Carl Shelby peering down Eileen's neckline. 'Carl might be very interested in seeing this one of him.'

'So show it to him.' Chelsea was damned if she'd submit to blackmail.

'You don't seem to understand the consequences,' Nick observed.

'If you don't give up these tactics, I'll file a complaint against you for sexual harrassment. And we'll see who comes out ahead.'

'I will,' he said. He didn't sound interested. 'I'm the fair-haired boy around here at the moment.'

'I shouldn't expect it to last long,' Chelsea snapped.

'Oh, I don't know.' His blue eyes, which had been icy, warmed. 'Do you think of every man in sexual terms, Chelsea? Or should I be flattered that you find me more attractive than most?' His fingertips slid gently down the silky sleeve to her delicate wrist.

'Attraction has nothing to do with it. Take your hand off me, you lecher! I don't care if you're the boss. I don't have to put up with this kind of nonsense!'

He ignored her request. 'Come to that, you could steam up a few windows yourself,' he said thoughtfully. 'Well, I'll give you a few days to think it over. It would be a shame to push you into a choice like that.'

'I don't play by those kind of rules,' Chelsea snapped. She pulled away from him.

He shrugged and turned away, pushing the caricatures into a careful stack. 'It seems to me you wrote the rules,' he said pleasantly.

'I'm a damn good architect, Mr Stanton,' she said. Her voice was trembling with anger.

'So you keep telling me. You have one chance to prove it. In the meantime, don't worry about your drawings. I'll keep them very, very safe.' He looked up then, his eyes brilliant. 'That's a promise, Chelsea.'

Marie cradled her telephone and handed Chelsea her appointment book. 'I contacted every one of those clients,' she said. 'It must be some sort of record to get them all in a single morning.'

Chelsea flipped through the book. 'I'll be stuck in the office for the next two weeks,' she complained. 'Any calls?'

'Just your mother. And there is a full staff meeting at one.'

'I was going out to the sites this afternoon,' Chelsea

muttered. Oh, well, overtime was part of the business, and she was certainly putting in her share. She just hoped that she could get to the Sullivan's lot before dark. 'Order me a sandwich from the deli downstairs, would you, Marie? I'll work through lunch.'

She dialled her parents' number and sketched a perspective drawing of a dressing room as she listened to the mysterious clickings and buzzings while her call worked its way upstate. Chelsea was no fool, but the intricacies of the telephone system defeated her. How a string of eleven digits could make a phone ring in a specific kitchen two hundred miles away was something she had never understood.

Her mother was cheerful. 'Hello, darling. Your father asked me to call you.'

'Oh?' Chelsea teased. 'Does that mean you didn't want to talk to me?' She began to shade in her drawing.

'Don't be difficult, dear. After all, telephones work both ways, and you could come home for a weekend now and then. Of course, I'm not trying to make you feel guilty.' But Sara Ryan's tone was light.

'It's been hectic around here for three months.'

'That's why Josh asked me to call. He'd like to take you to dinner Wednesday, and he wanted to be certain you could come.'

'I'll check my calendar,' Chelsea said in her best sophisticated tone. Then she started to laugh. 'I'd break any date I had to have dinner with Dad, and he knows it. What's the occasion?'

There was a long moment of silence. Then her mother said gently. 'It's your birthday, Chelsea.'

'I'd forgotten.'

'Chelsea? Are you certain you're feeling all right?'

'I think it's just that I'm getting a little older, Mom. Birthdays aren't as much fun these days.'

'It took me that way, too,' Sara said pensively.

'Why don't you come with him? We can celebrate

together.' Would she dare to ask for a day off right now, with all the work that was piled up on her desk? Nick Stanton would have fun with that request.

'Josh is coming on business.'

'Oh, now we get the truth. I'm not his very best girlfriend after all.'

Sara didn't bother to answer that one. 'I'd be bored to tears while he's in court.'

'Bring your easel and you can sit down on the riverbank and paint the Arch, or something.'

'That's hardly my style. Next time I'll come along and we'll go shopping—we'll buy you some new clothes.'

'I have a closetful now.'

Chelsea could almost see her mother's careless shrug. So what? she seemed to be saying. Sara Ryan had once been a clothing buyer for one of the big chain stores, and she had never got rid of the urge to dress Chelsea like a doll. Her taste was marvellous, too, but Chelsea suffered pangs of guilt every time Sara went on a shopping spree. She'd seen her mother shop, and she knew first hand that Sara never looked at a price tag.

'Thanks for the new green dress, by the way.'

'I'd almost forgotten sending you that one. Silly of me, isn't it?' Sara didn't sound worried. 'By the way, one of your old classmates called last week. He wanted to invite you to a barbecue the last weekend of May. A lot of your old friends will be back to visit.' Sara's tone was just a touch plaintive.

'I'll try to get up to Norah Springs soon, Mom.' It had been a long time since she'd been home. 'It depends on how many of these houses get off the drawing board and into construction. If my clients don't make some decisions soon, I'll still have a dozen projects next fall.'

'Surely it isn't necessary to work all the time,' Sara scolded.

'Right now it's a very good idea. I have a new boss, by the way.'

'Oh, Chelsea! You didn't get the partnership?'

''Fraid not, Mom. A woman in the higher echelons was just a little more than the partners could stand right now.'

'I was so certain you'd get it.'

'So was I,' Chelsea admitted. 'I'd better get back to work, Mom.'

'Is he nice?'

'Who? The new boss?' Nick Stanton's unsmiling face seemed to appear before her eyes, and Chelsea shuddered. 'No. See you later, Mom.'

She cradled the 'phone with a pang of loneliness. Chelsea was that rare person who had come to adulthood as a true good friend of both her parents. Given the choice, she was delighted to spend time with them. But since she had moved to St Louis, her time at home was rare.

It was an option, though. If life at Shelby Harris became unbearable . . . 'No, Chelsea,' she told herself firmly. 'Be honest. It's Nick Stanton that might become unbearable. And you could always go back to Norah Springs and open a practice of your own.'

Her parents would be delighted. For a moment, Chelsea sat there at the drawing board, staring out across the bustle of downtown St Louis and hearing instead the calm quiet of Norah Springs. Then her backbone straightened, and her little pointed chin set firmly. She was damned if Nick Stanton would drive her out of this firm and this city, and this job she had worked so hard to get. She would fight him, and she would win.

The staff meeting droned on until Chelsea was ready to scream. It was the one time of the week when all the partners and staff architects met to compare notes, and usually she was eager to find out what the other divisions of the practice were doing. But when her own desk was piled high, Chelsea's enthusiasm for discussion was lacking.

Plus, she had to admit, it wasn't pleasant to find herself sitting across the conference table from Nick, who was jotting occasional notes to himself on a legal pad and who seemed to spend most of his time looking through Chelsea.

She summarised the progress of her own projects and tried not to notice Nick's pen skimming down the legal pad as she talked. Was he ignoring her completely, she wondered, or were all those notes referring to her houses? If so, she was in trouble already, she thought grimly.

'Is that everything?' Carl Shelby asked finally. At the nods from around the table, Chelsea started to push her chair back. But Carl didn't stop talking. 'There is a new competition beginning this week, that I want to talk to you all about.'

Chelsea tried to hide her sigh and pulled her chair back to the table. At this rate she might as well sleep in the office tonight, she thought glumly.

'You all know the Jonas Building, of course. To refresh your memories, it was the downtown anchor of the department store chain. It was built at the turn of the century, and it was one of the biggest buildings in the city for years.'

'Eight stories, granite and brick construction, cast iron façade and columns,' Nick added quietly. He hadn't looked up from the notebook. 'Not a particularly important building.'

Chelsea happened to be looking at one of the apprentice architects at the time, and she nearly choked with laughter at the expression on his face. He looked as startled as if Nick had suddenly pulled a rabbit out of a hat. Calm down, she wanted to tell him. If Carl Shelby knew about a contest, all the partners did. Nick would have had plenty of time to do his research. It didn't mean that he knew every obscure building in St Louis!

'It's worth saving, none the less,' Frank Harris said, looking a little offended. 'Most of the cast iron architecture in the city has been destroyed. And it was one of our most important industries.'

'Of course it's worth saving. If it's properly done.' Nick's words were conciliating, but his tone didn't give an inch.

'The store has been closed about five years. With business shifting to the suburbs, it didn't pay the company to keep it open. They nearly tore it down a couple of years ago. Some of you probably remember.'

Chelsea did. Groups of people interested in preserving the city's past had picketed the store's headquarters till the management gave in.

'Then they tried to sell it, and had no luck with that,' Carl continued. 'Now the company is sponsoring a contest for the best plans to re-model the building. Their idea is shops on the lower floors and condos on the top.'

Nick was doodling now, Chelsea saw. 'Office space?' he asked.

Shelby shook his head. 'No offices—their marketing research says there is no demand in the downtown area at present.' He leaned forward and said in a confiding tone, 'I don't mind telling you all I want this firm to win that competition. We'll submit one entry from this office, and we'll win the prize, because Shelby Harris is the best in the business. I have the details, specs, and blueprints in my office for all of you who want to take it on.'

He pushed his chair back from the table. 'Don't waste any time, though,' he warned. 'They're in a hurry for this, and the deadline is not far off. If there is nothing else to discuss, we'll meet again next week.'

Chelsea tried to vanish silently, but Burke stopped

her by the door. 'Didn't you say you have something to show me?' he asked.

She could feel Nick's gaze on the nape of her neck. 'I'd rather talk about it after office hours, Burke.' The designs for the new house were strictly free-lance; they had nothing to do with the firm, and so they were none of Nick's business. And she knew that Burke would rather no one else knew about them, either, at least till Helen had given her blessing.

He looked puzzled, but agreed. 'Then I'll buy you a drink after work.'

'Sorry, Burke. I don't know where I'll be at quitting time. I'm on my way out to the sites now.'

'All right. Perhaps tomorrow then. By the way, a neighbour of ours down the block wants to renovate his house. It's quite similar to Hillhaven—I told him about your work.'

Chelsea groaned. 'That's all I need right now, Burke—another project!'

'Well, he'll give you a call anyway.'

Chelsea started for her office, but Nick caught her in the hall. 'I'll meet you in my office in ten minutes,' he said. 'Bring all the designs you're working on at the moment.'

Chelsea looked up at him coldly. 'I've planned my afternoon, Mr Stanton. I have two houses to stake out and a new lot to look over. I have no time to discuss my work.'

'Make time,' he recommended, and turned away.

'It would be easier to move you than it is to bring all my designs. If you want to see them, you can come to my office,' she snapped.

He didn't appear to have heard, and Chelsea went back to her own office feeling grim. Norah Springs and a little office next to her father's law pracitce was sounding better and better, she thought resentfully.

She was just putting on her hat when Nick walked

in. 'Knocking is still considered good manners,' she snapped.

'Sorry. I didn't stop to think about what I might find here,' he said cheerfully and sat down on the corner of her desk, arms folded. 'You're absolutely right.'

Somehow she didn't feel as if she'd won anything. 'If you'll excuse me, I really haven't time to go over all my current projects this afternoon.'

'I believe you said that before,' he said. 'Go ahead, if you must leave. I'll just look at them by myself.' He leaned over the drawing board and unrolled a set of blueprints.

Chelsea sighed and put her hat back in the closet. She couldn't just leave him there with her precious drawings; he might do anything. 'That's the Emerson house,' she said.

Nick looked up with a glint in his eyes. 'I can read,' he said gently.

'You amaze me. Anything you want to know?'

'No. I think it's all here.' He scanned the blueprints with a practised eye and laid them aside.

'I'm staking that one out this afternoon,' she said. 'Unless, of course, you want to do it over?'

'No, thanks. Houses really aren't my line.'

'They don't seem to appeal to anyone around this practice, except me,' Chelsea muttered. 'Martin liked them, but no one else does.'

'And you inherited his unfinished work.'

'Yes, and all of his clients have been very pleased, too,' she snapped.

He didn't answer. He just loosened his tie, pulled a stool up to the drawing board, and started to work. In half an hour he had inspected every drawing, every preliminary sketch, every construction document, right down to the casual notes for the Sullivan house. As he laid those aside, he leaned back against the drawing board, tapped his pencil thoughtfully against the edge, and studied her with a speculative gleam in his eyes. 'I don't see anything for Burke,' he commented.

'And you won't either,' Chelsea retorted, before she had a chance to think how foolish an answer it was.

'That means that I was right—your plans didn't have anything to do with architecture. I must say it doesn't surprise me. What does amaze me is that you had the sense to keep it out of the office today. You may be learning after all, Chelsea.'

She didn't bother to answer that one. 'If you've finished, I'd like to go stake out those houses so the contractors can start this week.'

'Let me get my jacket.'

'Why do you need your . . . Hey, I don't want your help.'

Nick's eyebrows raised. 'Who asked if you wanted help? I'm just doing a little field research—catching up with the projects that are under my direction.'

'Don't you have any of your own to work on?'

'Not yet,' he said pleasantly. 'I didn't bring a single commission with me. So you can count on me for any assistance you need. I'll be right at your elbow all the time, at least till my own practice builds up again.'

'I'm not an apprentice, you know. I'm a fully licenced architect and I can practise without anyone supervising me.'

'I know you can,' he said. 'But you aren't going to. Make up your mind to having me hanging around.'

'Why don't you just fire me outright, Nick?'

'Oh, I wouldn't do that,' he said. 'But I'm going to make sure you have plenty of opportunities to trip yourself up. The first mistake you make will be your last one at Shelby Harris, Chelsea.'

CHAPTER FOUR

THE roar of the Mercedes engine echoed in the parking ramp, and Chelsea sat for several seconds with her foot on the brake. She looked over at Nick finally and said, 'Are you certain you don't have anything you'd rather do this afternoon than help me stake out houses?'

'Can't think of a thing,' he said cheerfully. She sighed and put the car into gear.

The parking lot attendant turned his radio down when he saw the Mercedes coming. He leaned out of the window, popping his bubble gum in time to the music, to take the ticket and money out of Chelsea's hand. 'There you go, darlin',' he said cheerfully as he dropped the change into her palm.

'Darling?' Nick asked. 'Not him, too?'

Chelsea put her sunglasses on and tossed the change into her purse. 'Just how many affairs do you think I can manage at one time, anyway?' she asked tartly. 'I'm not Superwoman, and he calls everybody darling.' To get rid of some of her frustrations, she stepped on the accelerator a little harder than she otherwise would have, sending the Mercedes flying out on to the street.

Nick's head snapped back against the headrest. 'I hope you're insured for my whiplash,' he said.

'That's the risk you take when you force your company on me.'

'I'm just doing my job as your supervisor. And by the way, every plan that goes out of your office from now on must have my signature on it.'

Chelsea was so angry that she let the Mercedes drift across into the oncoming lane, and only pulled it back when another driver's horn blared.

'Do you plan to still have this car by the end of the

day?' Nick asked. 'If so, would you kindly pay attention to your driving?'

She ignored that. 'After my apprenticeship was over, Martin never again asked to see a line of my work. If I got into trouble, I took it to him, but . . .'

'Remember?' he interrupted. 'I'm not Martin.'

'In the four years I've been at Shelby Harris I have worked on a couple of hundred houses. I am damned if I'm going to . . .'

'Look on it as an opportunity to instruct me,' Nick said calmly. 'Just think how much I can learn from watching you work.'

She would have thrown something at him, but there was nothing close at hand. So Chelsea bit her lip and guided the car on to the expressway.

'Would you like to tell me about these projects?'

'No,' Chelsea said sweetly. 'You saw the blueprints. What else do you want?'

'What kind of house are you planning for the Sullivans?'

'How should I know? I haven't seen the lot, yet. We're going there first, by the way.'

'Let's drive by the Jonas Building on the way.'

She looked over at him curiously and then switched on the turn signal. 'Why don't you hire a chauffeur?'

'Because you're handy.'

She slowed the Mercedes to a crawl as they drove past the massive old building. 'You can almost see the buggies driving by on the granite streets, can't you?' she remarked.

'It certainly looks as if it hasn't had a facelift in eighty years,' Nick agreed absently. He was running a practised eye over the fluted cast iron columns that set off the first floor display windows.

Chelsea turned the corner. 'Look, there are french doors on the second floor,' she remarked. 'I don't remember those, and I've driven by that store a million times.'

'At least there's plenty of light to work with—all that cast iron framing is good for something.'

'Seen enough?'

'For right now. What's it like inside?'

'Nick, I haven't been in that store in twenty years, and I think then we were shopping for a teddy bear. There's a big central open area that goes all the way to the ceiling—with skylights, I think. I can't remember anything else. Are you going to submit a plan?'

He shrugged. 'Now tell me what you're going to design for the Sullivans,' he suggested. 'You have the site plans. Surely you have some ideas.'

'Oh, we aren't going to talk about the Jonas Building?' She took the Mercedes up the freeway ramp with a roar, and Nick winced..

'Site plans don't always tell the whole truth, you know,' she pointed out. 'And I make it a practise never to visualise a house until I see the land. It doesn't start to take shape in my mind till then.'

He didn't answer. 'While we're out, how about showing me some of the sights?'

'Are you going tourist on me? To your right in a few minutes you will have Forest Park, home of the zoo, the art museum and the municipal opera. That's about the size of the sights in this part of town.'

'You lack enthusiasm as a guide. Is it me, or don't you appreciate the attractions of your home town?'

'It isn't my home town. But I like the zoo and the opera just fine, and I get positively sentimental about the art museum.'

'Why? Did you meet Burke there?'

'No. But it would be a good enough reason.' They were silent until the Mercedes left the freeway and dropped down into the city again. 'There's a street map in the glovebox,' Chelsea said. 'Would you look for the turnoff, please?'

He hunted for the map. 'What would you do

without me?' he asked cheerfully.

'Pull off to the side and find it myself, thank you.'

'You really prefer to work alone, don't you Chelsea?'

'Yes. Design by committee usually results in trash. That's why I stick to houses; there is only room for me to work on them.'

'Was that supposed to give me a message?'

'It certainly was,' she said pleasantly.

There was a silence as Nick watched street signs. 'That was it, back there.'

'You could have warned me.' Chelsea wheeled the Mercedes into a driveway and backed out, heedless of oncoming traffic.

'Watch out for the . . .' He bit his tongue, and said, 'Are you going to work on the contest project?'

'I thought we weren't going to talk about the Jonas Building. Anyway, why would I want to?'

'Because it's a challenge.'

'I have plenty of challenges already. That big block-square barn holds no attraction for me. Even if I'd work on it, by the time Carl Shelby got done with my proposal, it wouldn't bear any resemblance to what I started with. Carl and I don't agree on much when it comes to architecture.'

'You and Burke obviously do,' he remarked.

'Burke's a little different.'

'He certainly seems to be. Especially where you're concerned.'

Chelsea didn't answer. She propped the site plan against the steering wheel and let the Mercedes creep up to the curb in front of the Sullivan's lot. 'That's the deepest ravine I've seen in years,' she said. 'If Doris Sullivan wants to live out in the wild, she certainly picked a good spot.' She shut the engine off, kicked off her shoes, and reached into the back seat for her pumps.

'It's going to take a lot of fill,' Nick said.

Chelsea looked up in surprise, but she couldn't tell whether he was serious. 'Why?'

'Because you can't build on air, that's why.'

She tied the shoe-strings thoughtfully. 'You are ioking, aren't you? Or did you skip residential architecture altogether?' She didn't wait for an answer.

She wandered over the lot, studying it from the bottom of the ravine, from the top, from the lawn of the house next door. She stood there for a long time, eyes closed, visualising what the Sullivan's house should be. It was going to be tough, she thought. The house would have to be multi-level because of the site, and that was hardly ideal for a couple the age of the Sullivans.

Well, that isn't my problem, Chelsea decided. If they want to build in a ravine, they'll have to accept the drawbacks.

'What are you doing?' Nick asked.

She opened her eyes and gave him an exasperated stare. 'Look, you can force me to turn in all of my plans for your approval—whatever that's worth—but you can't make me share them before they're written down, for heaven's sake. Just leave me alone, would you?'

He did, wandering over the steep hillside with his hands deep in his pockets. He'd left his jacket in the car, and his blue shirt was a spot of distinctive colour among the yellow-green of spring. He stooped to pick up a branch, and Chelsea told herself firmly to stop watching Nick and concentrate on the house plans. She was beginning to see it now; a small but spacious house half buried in the side of the ravine . . .

'What are you doing?' The question was repeated, but this time it was a friendly voice at her elbow.

Chelsea looked down to find a freckled, chubby-cheeked little girl, her blonde hair tied up in pigtails, beside her. She was probably four years old, Chelsea thought.

'I'm just looking at the land. We're going to build a house down there this summer.'

The child looked delighted. 'A whole new house?'

Chelsea laughed. 'Brand new.'

A warm little hand was tucked confidingly into hers. 'What's it going to look like?'

'I don't know yet. That's what I'm thinking about now.'

The child turned that over in her mind for a moment. 'Do you have any little girls like me?'

'What? Oh, the house isn't for me, honey. I'm the architect, but I won't be living here.'

'Oh.' The child's face dropped, and Chelsea almost felt guilty that she wasn't the new owner.

You're losing your touch, Chelsea, she told herself. A four-year-old smiles at you, and you become a marshmallow.

They were on the way to the next site before Nick said, 'I see you found a friend back there.'

Chelsea shrugged. 'She thought I was going to be her new neighbour.'

'You charm them from the cradle to the grave, don't you?' he asked, with admiration in his voice. 'So tell me. What is the Sullivan's house going to look like?'

'What makes you think that I know?' Chelsea countered.

'Because you'd have stood there all night if necessary, till you saw it. As soon as you did, you relaxed.'

It bothered her, that he had read her mood so easily. Obviously he'd been watching her more closely than she had thought.

'Tell you what,' she offered suddenly. 'I'll make you a little bet.'

'I'm listening.'

'What if you design the Sullivan's house, too, and we show both plans to a neutral party?If yours is better than mine, I'll submit everything I draw from now on for your approval without a whimper. But if mine is better, then I can go back to working on my own—no interference.'

Nick shrugged. 'You're on. You won't win, of course. It's not a very sensible bet to make, you know.'

'What have I got to lose?' Chelsea countered.

He smiled, and drawled, 'You might be surprised.'

The Mississippi River washed gently against the old brick levee, and across the warm night air came whispers of Dixieland jazz. Chelsea's high-heeled sandal tapped impatiently on the gangway as she and her father boarded the riverboat restaurant, and Josh Ryan laughed. 'Chelsea, you'll fall overboard if you keep that up,' he warned.

'I can't help it. My feet just won't stay still when I hear Dixieland.'

He had turned to the hostess on the main deck. 'We have reservations for Ryan.'

'The first dinner seating,' the hostess commented. 'You're right on time, Mr Ryan. Your table is ready on the steak deck, to your right, if you'd like to go on in. And welcome aboard!'

'Daddy,' Chelsea protested. 'You know how much I like the lounge. Can't we go listen to the music?'

'After dinner,' he said firmly. 'Chelsea, have a heart. I've been in court all day, and I'm starving.'

Chelsea relented. He held her chair and then dropped into one across from her. For the first time she realised how tired he looked. 'How is the case going?'

He shook his head. 'It's over. But sometimes I wish appeals courts had never been invented.'

'Especially when you won the original case, right?'

A reluctant grin reached his eyes. 'Exactly. I'm representing George Bradley again.'

'My favourite tycoon?'

'Is there another one? We won the case hands down at the first trial, but who knows what the court will say this time? The appeals could drag on for years.' He stared moodily into his water glass. 'But let's find a happier subject for your birthday dinner, all right?'

Above them, the steam whistle blew, and the riverboat glided into motion on its way downriver for the dinner cruise. Chelsea looked out at the darkening shoreline. 'This is my very favourite place to eat, you know.'

'I know. Darn your mother—she had to raise you to be a romantic just like her.'

'And you had nothing to do with it, I know,' Chelsea teased gently.

'Who, me?' He sounded astonished. 'All I did was propose to her on the art museum lawn at midnight. Fillet or prime rib, Chelsea?'

'Oh, the rib, of course. Rare.'

'And champagne, to make up for missing the lounge?'

Chelsea laughed. 'The champagne doesn't have the same atmosphere. Now if they delivered it with a Dixieland . . .'

'Listen closely and you can hear the one in the lounge,' he recommended. 'How does it feel to be twenty-seven?'

She grimaced. 'Not as good as nineteen, but since I don't have an option, I'll just have to get used to it.'

He gave their order to the waiter. 'Your mother said the partnership fell through.'

'Ouch. I thought you said something about happy topics.' Chelsea handed her menu over.

'So instead of being the boss, you have a new one.'

'That's right. Tell me, can a good architect make a living in Norah Springs these days?'

'That bad, hmmm?'

'Oh, Nick Stanton is excellent, especially on big projects—office buildings, that sort of thing. He's done a couple of beautiful skyscrapers. But he's impossible to work with. He's somehow got the idea that . . .' She had second thoughts about telling her father about Nick's crazy suspicions about Burke, and stopped there. 'You've had personality clashes sometimes, haven't you, Dad? I mean, two people can both be perfectly reasonable, but they still can't get along together.' Not that Nick Stanton is reasonable, she thought, but the principle applies.

'It happens. I've had a lot of cases through the years that could have been settled amicably if the people hadn't hated each other to begin with. Are you serious about coming home?'

'I don't know just now. It depends on how bad it gets at Shelby Harris. I can't imagine getting rich by building two houses a year in Norah Springs. And to do that I'd have to get the commissions on all the new construction!'

Josh shrugged. 'You did a good job with Bradley's house. He told me that they're always getting comments about it.'

Chelsea sipped the champagne the waiter poured for her and murmured. 'Probably a lot of remarks about him going clear to St Louis for a high-falutin' architect.'

'Well, some of that too,' her father admitted. 'It would make a good advertisement for you, though, if you decide to hang out a shingle. And then there is our house, of course— though some people think we're prejudiced when we tell them how much we love it.'

'Building the Bradley house was fun,' Chelsea mused. 'Working within strict limits is a challenge, but it was delightful to have no budget restraints for once.' She smiled, reminiscently.

'In any case, you don't need to worry about the money, dear. If you come back to Norah Springs, your mother and I will see that you don't starve.'

'I would probably need some help,' Chelsea

admitted. 'But Dad, you know that I want to be independent. I don't like to take money from you and Mom. It's bad enough that she sends me clothes every other week.'

'I don't understand why you're so sensitive about it. You're our only child, Chelsea, and there is no point in you scrimping and saving on your own and then paying inheritance tax when we're gone.'

She shook a finger at him. 'Dad, you're far too young to be thinking about things like inheritance tax.'

'An attorney who doesn't think of things like that is a fool.'

'I don't care if you write your darn will, but don't talk to me about it, all right?' She sat back in her chair and stared at him, her chin defiant. If it wasn't for the streak of white hair at each temple, Josh Ryan could pass for forty. And he took excellent care of himself. In winter it was handball and swimming, in summer tennis and golf. He was still as trim in dinner clothes as he had appeared in his wedding pictures; he said it gave him an advantage in the courtroom to look better than his opponents. 'If there ever was a candidate to reach the age of a hundred, it's you, Dad. So stop trying to make me feel sorry for you.'

'You win. But I'd like to point out, Chelsea, that I didn't hear anything about independence when we bought that sporty little car of yours.'

'That was a gift, Dad. It was completely different.'

'If you say so, Chelsea.' He raised his glass. 'To my lovely daughter, who makes twenty-seven look wonderful.'

'Thank, Dad.' She was a little misty-eyed as they touched glasses, and she was thoughtful as she sipped the tangy wine. Her father was a darling, and if things didn't get better she might take him up on that offer If she could just have that little office rent-free for a few months, she was certain that she could make it work.

She looked up from her glass, and her eye was caught by a dark-haired man at a table across the room. He was alone, and he looked like . . .

'Oh, my God,' she said as Nick raised his glass in an ironic salute. What awful luck had brought him here, on this evening-long cruise, she wondered?

Her father had bent over to rummage in his attaché case. 'What did you say?'

'Oh—nothing.'

He didn't push the subject. Instead he set a box before her. It was small and nearly square, wrapped in silver paper, with a matching bow that—before it had been crushed in the attaché case—had been huge and elegant. 'Sorry about the ribbon,' he said. 'That's just a little something from your mother.'

Chelsea eyed the box with foreboding. 'I've had some experience with Mom's idea of a little something,' she said, and pleaded silently, please don't make me open it here. Not with Nick sitting over there watching.

'Go ahead,' her father invited. 'Rip it open. I don't even know what it is, but she told me it was something you'd really like. Just a little nonsense thing.'

Chelsea closed her eyes for a second and sent a silent prayer skyward. Please let Mother have exercised some sense this time, she thought. It wasn't that her mother's gifts were ever in bad taste. They were always elegant and lovely and well-chosen. It was just that they were also horribly expensive. If only this time Sara really had sent a nonsense gift!—something that she wouldn't mind unwrapping in front of Nick Stanton . . .

Think positive, Chelsea, she told herself. At least it's a smaller box than last year's, so it can't be another bronze sculpture.

She unwrapped the box gingerly, as if expecting it to bite her. The name of the store did nothing to soothe her anxiety, for it was Sara's favourite jewellery store. Chelsea pulled open the box and took out a tissue wrapped bundle.

'A coffee mug?' she asked as the tissue slid away from the handle. But her instant of relief passed as she took the rest of the paper off. The mug was heavy in her hand, and she didn't have to look at the small, distinctive green label, or the equally obvious facets in the glass to know she was holding a piece of hand-blown, hand-cut crystal.

'A Waterford crystal mug?' she asked. 'What in the world does she expect me to drink out of a crystal mug?'

Josh shrugged. 'Champagne, I suppose. Would you care for some more?'

'No, thanks, I wouldn't dare put hot coffee in it,' Chelsea mused, and wrapped it carefully again.

'That must be why your mother said it was a silly thing.'

'Only Mom would consider a piece of hand-cut crystal a gag gift.'

'Though come to think of it, I don't know why it wouldn't work for coffee. In fact, it would be kind of pretty.'

'I'll think about it.' Chelsea laid it carefully back in the box, and just then the waiter served their meal. She was very careful not to look over towards Nick's table again; she didn't want to see the expression on his face. With her luck, he'd turn out to be a connoisseur of Waterford crystal.

The whole upper deck was devoted to the lounge, where most passengers spent the majority of the cruise. The Dixieland band was playing 'St Louis Blues' as Chelsea found her way to a table in the open section on the forward deck. 'This should be just right,' she said as Josh pulled out her chair. 'It's far enough from the music so that it isn't deafening.'

The cool river air brushed her face and made her glad of the lacy shawl that lay about her shoulders over the pastel lilac dress. The deck was dimly lit, with lamps on each table casting a dull glow. When viewed from the shore, Chelsea knew, the riverboat was rimmed with brilliant lights and looked almost as if there was a carnival on the river. But on board, the atmosphere was dim and intimate, a retreat for lovers.

She sipped her pina colada and thought about it. Here she was, on a riverboat meant for lovers, with her father. Birthdays were a time for taking stock, and perhaps at twenty-seven it was time for her to do that. 'Perhaps I'm ready for a change,' she mused.

'Coming home, and setting up your own practice?'

Chelsea nodded. 'That's one possibility. I was thinking about moving, too. Even if I stay here in the city, I mean. Judy is a good friend, but . . .'

Josh swirled his drink and set it down. 'Do you want a place of your own, or do you have another roommate lined up?'

She smiled, and her face lighted. 'A man, do you mean?'

'It has crossed my mind,' Josh said gently.

'Would you be upset?' she asked curiously.

He shrugged. 'Depends on the man. But I imagine you would be careful with your choice.'

'I should hope so. There really isn't anybody in my life right now. Does that disappoint you, Daddy?'

'Me? Disappointed that my daughter might be a spinster?' Mock horror dripped from the word.

'Only because I haven't found anybody like you. Mom was lucky, you know. You both were.' Her voice was pensive. Then, suddenly, she smiled and patted his hand. 'When I find a man like you, Dad, then you can walk me down the aisle.'

'That's gratifying. Misguided, perhaps, but gratifying. Let's take a turn around the deck.

'Why is it misguided to look for someone like you?' she questioned as they stood at the back rail, watching the huge paddle revolve as the boat made its wide sweeping turn and began to churn its way back upriver.

'Because you don't need a man just like me. And if you could find one, you'd discover that you didn't really want him, either. You're not like your mother, dear. Her dream man——' he bowed—'is not yours.'

Chelsea laughed. 'So what should I be looking for?'

He looked down at her, and Chelsea could feel the gentleness of his smile. 'Only you can know that, Chelsea. And if you don't find it—well, there are worse things than being alone. Some of the divorces I've worked on are enough to sour anyone to the state of matrimony. My God, those people should have never married.'

Chelsea turned to look out over the river. 'Maybe they thought they loved each other.'

'And maybe they seized on what looked like the last opportunity to get married, too. Don't do that, Chelsea,' he said and his voice was stern. 'Don't marry at all unless you are sure you want him, and not just that wedding ring.'

She laughed. 'I'll keep that in mind. But if it doesn't work, I'm sure you'd give me a cut rate on a divorce.'

'Chelsea, I'm going to shake you!' he threatened. 'That's exactly the attitude that worries me about young people getting married today—they walk to the altar thinking that if it doesn't work they'll just get a divorce. A lot of your school friends are already on marriage number two, and . . .'

Chelsea interrupted, suddenly serious. 'You don't have to preach to me, Dad.'

'Sorry.' He grinned sheepishly. 'I was, wasn't I?'

She nodded gently. 'If I can't find the same thing in marriage that you and Mom have, then I'd rather be alone.'

'Friendship. That's it in a word, you know. Your mother and I are best friends.'

'Then that's what I'll look for. Thanks, Dad.' She put her arm around his waist and they stood there for a long time, staring out over the river. Finally Josh patted her shoulder and said, 'I'm going after another drink. Want one?'

'No, thanks. One of those frothy things is my limit.' Chelsea's voice was dreamy as she looked out into the midnight blue.

'Then would you mind keeping an eye on my briefcase? I hate to carry it around.'

'Why didn't you just leave it at the hotel?'

'I am not a fool, Chelsea. Clothes and toothbrushes are replaceable, valuable papers are not. At least not by tomorrow morning. And I didn't have time to check it into the vault.'

'I thought you were finished in court today.'

'I was. I didn't say it contained court documents.'

'Oh. I thought George Bradley had retired. Is he working on another deal?'

'Sometimes, Chelsea, you are too darn telepathic for your own good,' he scolded and went off towards the bar.

She shook her head, smiling. Her father had neither confirmed her suspicion nor denied it, and he wouldn't. No wonder the old fox was such a good attorney, she thought.

'All alone in the dark?' A voice came out of the darkness, and Nick Stanton followed.

Chelsea turned her back to him. She'd actually forgotten that he was on board, she thought, and wished that she had trailed down the promenade to the bar with her father.

'This isn't a safe place to be alone,' he continued.

'Obviously,' she said, over her shoulder. 'Especially as long as there are wolves like you on board.'

'I'll stay around to protect you,' he said, and came over to the rail. 'I'm amazed that your companion would leave you up here.'

'He just went down for a drink.'

'Champagne and a gift at dinner, and then he leaves you alone on deck? It isn't very polite of him.'

'You needn't stick around. In fact, please get lost, Nick.' She stared out over the dark water.

'I thought perhaps you'd like to introduce me.' His voice was caressingly soft, and his fingers brushed the delicate skin on her shoulder as he tucked the shawl closer about her.

Chelsea's spine straightened and she took a step away from him. 'Now why would I want to do that? And just what do I have to thank for the honour of finding you aboard?'

'Dinner cruises are such a good idea, aren't they?' he mused. 'Especially when one is trying to hide out. It makes it much less of a risk than the average restaurant, where people keep coming and going. At the ordinary restaurant, you might even run into—Burke, or someone. And that would be very embarrassing. Or are you using this one to cover up your relationship with Burke?'

So he thought that her father was yet another lover. She'd never met anyone who was so suspicious. Well, Chelsea wasn't about to straighten him out; someday soon Nicholas Stanton was bound to make a fool of himself, and she would do nothing to prevent that happy day from arriving quickly.

'You were very discreet, to make the reservation in your own name. But it was not so discreet to mention it to your secretary this afternoon.' He took a step closer and raised a hand to her cheek, brushing back the tendrils of auburn hair that had been teased loose by the breeze.

'So you decided to come along.'

'It wasn't entirely because of you. I've been told that you haven't really seen St Louis till you view it from a riverboat.'

'That's true,' she said reluctantly, and then warmed

to the subject, hoping to distract him. 'From the water, you can see it the way the old settlers did, and almost ignore the new skyline.'

He didn't seem interested. 'I have to grant you better taste with this one,' he said thoughtfully. 'A whole lot younger than Burke; probably a great deal more fun. Just what do you stand to gain from him? Or is it just toys like the crystal mug?'

'I don't know why you think it's any of your business.'

Nick moved suddenly, putting a hand on the rail on each side of her, and Chelsea found herself trapped. 'Do you like pretty things, Chelsea?' he asked. 'You should. You are a pretty thing yourself.' His mouth was so close to hers that she could almost feel the shape of his words.

She turned suddenly away from him, clenching her hands on the rail to keep from hitting him. 'Go away, Nick.'

'Till later,' he said, and his hands were warm on her bare shoulders, sliding intimately under the shawl. 'That's a promise, Chelsea.'

He left so silently that she wasn't even sure for a time whether he was still there. When she finally looked around, a shudder of relief hit her as she realised that he was gone. A couple of minutes later her father came down the promenade.

'Sorry, dear, the bar was busy. I see we're almost home.'

Chelsea hadn't noticed. She looked up then at the sheen of moonlight on the stainless steel of the Gateway Arch, at the gleam of lights along the riverfront, at the dark bulk of the arched bridge that stretched across the Mississippi. She heard, dimly, the Dixieland band start to play 'Won't You Come Home, Bill Bailey?'

Home, she thought. Was going home the answer?

'Want me to keep that office open for a while, Chelsea?' her father asked. 'Just in case you want it?'

'You're a little telepathic yourself, you know,' she said. It would be so easy. She'd have to work at building up a practice, but it would be so nice not to have to fight . . .

Then that stubborn little jaw set. No matter how hard he tried, Nick Stanton was not going to drive her out. He might succeed in getting her fired, but he could not make her run.

'No, Dad,' she said, and her voice was steady. 'Rent it. I won't need it.'

CHAPTER FIVE

She was filling the crystal mug from the coffee machine in the employee's lounge the next morning when Nick came in. She saw, out of the corner of her eye, that his mouth tightened when he spotted the mug, and was insanely glad, deep inside, that she had given in to frivolous instinct and brought it to work.

'Good morning,' she said brightly, and tried to brush past him in the doorway. Confuse the enemy! that was her new strategy.

But he settled himself against the jamb and said, 'You're very cheerful this morning. Cruises must do you good.'

'Innuendo doesn't suit you,' she said, shaking her head sadly. 'You're much better with the direct approach.'

He just raised an eyebrow. 'Let me get my coffee and I'll be in to help you this morning.'

'With help like you, I could be six months doing this week's work,' Chelsea retorted.

She was at her drawing board, working on the preliminary sketches of the Sullivan house, when there was a tap on her door. She grimaced and scrambled the drawings into a drawer. The last thing she wanted was for Nick to see those sketches. After they were out of sight, she called, 'Come in.'

It was Jim, and he was pale. 'Chelsea—those caricatures. They're gone.'

'I know.'

He took a deep breath. 'You took them? Thank heaven. I know I promised to take them home, and I really meant to, but I forgot, and . . .'

'I don't have them. I simply know where they are, and it would take a bit of burglary to get them back. Nick Stanton has them.'

Jim's face darkened. 'We're done, Chelsea.'

'I don't know about you. He's using them to blackmail me.'

He just shook his head.

Chelsea picked up her pencil again. 'By the way, Jim, he'll be designing a house in the next week or so. The Sullivan house—but he may not call it that. It sits down in a ravine. When you get the drawings . . .'

Jim looked puzzled for an instant.

'Just make sure I get a look at them, and I'll forgive you for leaving those caricatures lying around.'

His face brightened. 'You've got it, Chelsea. Shall I make copies?'

'No, that's taking a risk. I only need to see them.'

A tap sounded at the door and Nick came in without waiting for permission.

'Here you go, Jim,' Chelsea said, and pushed a stack of meaningless drawings across the board to him with a look that spoke volumes. 'Thanks for waiting.'

He left in a hurry. Nick stood behind her for a few minutes, sipping his coffee and looking over her shoulder as she translated rough sketches into schematics that the clients would see. Finally Chelsea couldn't stand it any more. She tossed her pencil down and turned to him. 'If you want to do this house, help yourself. Or else get out of here and let me do it.'

He shook his head sadly. 'Don't you welcome the chance to teach me?'

'There isn't anything you want to learn from me.'

'Perhaps not in the office,' he said smoothly, and laughed as Chelsea's face flooded with colour. Then he bent over the drawing board. 'Where is the Sullivan house? I thought you'd be hard at work on it.'

'I'm certainly not going to let you see it till I'm finished.'

'Are you so uncertain of yourself?'

'Not at all. I just don't want you to steal my ideas.' She thought about those first sketches, of a three-level house snuggled into the side of the hill, and felt a quiet glow of pride. It was a good house. No matter what Nick did, he'd have trouble beating that design.

He made no comment. 'Let's get to work on the Jonas Building today.'

Chelsea's mouth dropped open. 'Not I,' she said with feeling.

'Why not?'

'I told you three days ago that I wasn't interested in that contest. Besides, I'm over my head with work now. I must have at least a dozen projects on the board, four under construction, and two that I haven't even thought about.'

'Then let's get busy and clean all these things up.' He loosened his tie and unbuttoned the collar of his silk shirt.

'I wish it was that easy.'

He speculated, 'You must be intrigued by the condos. Have you looked at the specs? There is plenty of space for about fifty units.'

'If it was just the condos, I might be interested,' Chelsea admitted.

'I went over to look at the building yesterday. With those lovely high ceilings it's a natural for conversion. And that centre bay you were telling me about would be ideal for indoor balconies.'

She shook her head. 'It sounds as if you've fallen in love with the building, after all.'

'Not necessarily. I still don't think it's a particularly valuable piece of architecture, but it's sturdy, and I still want to win that contest.' He stretched out on the couch and propped his feet up on the arm.

'Why are you lying on my couch?'

Nick shrugged. 'I offered to go to work, but it seems that you'd rather argue. I thought I might as well be comfortable while we discussed it.'

'I suppose you're hoping that Burke will walk in.'

He looked intrigued. 'It had never crossed my mind. Does he?'

'Never without knocking,' Chelsea snapped.

'Pity,' Nick murmured.

'And as for the Jonas Building,' she said, feeling the conversation slipping from her grasp, 'you needn't fear any competition from me. It sounds as if you have plenty of ideas already, and I'm certainly not going to fight you for the honours.'

'I'm not afraid of your competition. But it won't be easy for me. After all, I am the new kid in town.'

'And everybody still thinks you're wonderful. You shouldn't have any trouble getting the project all to yourself. No one on this staff is foolish enough to tangle with you.'

'Except you, Chelsea,' he said softly.

A flood of colour swept over her face. She said stubbornly, 'All you have to do is announce that you're going after it.'

'Maybe I don't want it by myself. I don't know enough yet about how this firm works.'

She looked up in mock amazement, her big eyes innocent. 'My God, there is something that Nicholas Stanton doesn't know?'

'Once in a while,' he said dryly. 'How about it? Do you want to do the condos?'

'Work with you on the Jonas Building?'

He nodded. 'Equal partners.'

Chelsea stared at him for a long time, eyes narrowed. Just what was he up to now, she wondered. 'Sorry, I'm too busy.'

'Would you rather I made it an order?'

'Why do you want me?'

'Because you know things about the city and the

firm that I don't. And you've done far more renovation work than I have.'

'So you're going to pick my brain.' She sipped her coffee thoughtfully and set the crystal mug safely on the corner of the desk. 'More likely you just want someone to share the blame if another firm brings in the winning design.'

'You'll get equal credit if we win.'

Chelsea was no fool. She knew what her name on a winning contest design could mean for her career, even if she was listed only as an assistant to Nicholas Stanton.

He let her think about it for a moment. Then he pulled up a stool. 'Where do I start? Construction specs? Do you have some blank forms?'

'That's the most boring part of a house. You're really serious, aren't you?'

'Never more so. You're going to help with this renovation, whether you want to or not. So you might as well work up some enthusiasm for the project.'

'How open-minded of you.' She thoughtfully tapped her triangle against the edge of the drawing board.

'Let's put it this way. If you decide not to work on the project, I have a lovely Christmas gift for Carl Shelby to hang in his office. And he won't have to wait till Christmas to get it.'

'What if I work with you? Will you give me those drawings back?' she asked shrewdly.

For a moment she thought he hadn't heard. Then he said, quietly, 'Sure. I'll give them back. In return for some real co-operation, of course.'

'I'll think about it,' she said. She pulled a set of drawings out of the cabinet and thrust them into his hands. 'Since you volunteered to help, you can start with these electrical plans while I'm thinking.'

'What's there to think about? Have I left you a

choice?' But he didn't push for an answer. He cleared a space on her desk and started to work.

Chelsea sat there for a few minutes, her pencil idle, staring out over the city. Her head was spinning. It was an invitation she had never expected. All his reasons sounded valid, and yet she didn't trust him an inch. Nick Stanton shouldn't need anyone's help on a project like the Jonas Building. So why was he asking for hers?

She sighed, put a needle-sharp point on her pencil, and started to work.

Marie came in a couple of hours later, and Chelsea straightened her spine, sighed at the stiffness in her muscles, and flexed her fingers. Two hours of uninterrupted concentration had done wonders for the work remaining to be done. She glanced over at Nick, still sitting at her desk, and felt a spark of amazement. He'd been so quiet that she'd forgotten he was even there.

'Mr Shelby wants to see you, Miss Ryan,' Marie said softly. 'He has a client with him.'

'If you don't mind, Nick?' Chelsea said, with more than a hint of irony in her voice.

He looked up and smiled. 'I don't mind a bit. It won't bother my work if you see a client here.'

'That wasn't quite what I meant. Would you please leave?'

He leaned back in her desk chair and studied her, not missing a detail. 'No, thanks,' he said pleasantly and turned to a new drawing.

Marie was back by then, ushering in Carl Shelby and an enormous bear of a man who made the senior partner look something like a tugboat guiding an ocean liner.

Chelsea gave up on dislodging Nick. 'Mr Bradley!' she said, with genuine delight. 'I'm glad to see you again.'

George Bradley stretched out a big hand and engulfed hers. 'Well, if it isn't little Chelsea Ryan,' he boomed. 'Your daddy told me you were prettier than ever, but I figured he was just opinionated.'

Chelsea couldn't help herself; she darted a look at Nick. He raised an eyebrow as if to say, Another victim, Chelsea?

'And this is Nick Stanton, our newest partner,' Shelby twittered, and George Bradley turned that wide grin on Nick. 'So you're the young man who's been changing the looks of public buildings all over Missouri,' he said.

'I have been doing my fair share of them,' Nick admitted.

Marie handed George a cup of coffee. He settled himself comfortably on the small couch beside Chelsea, his large hand making the plastic cup look like a toy, and said, 'That's why I'm here, young man. I like the looks of your buildings. Well, most of them, that is. Once in a while you go a bit too far. At any rate, I want one of those buildings for Norah Springs. The old home town, you understand how it is. I want the best.'

Chelsea could have screamed. If George Bradley wanted to build anything in Norah Springs, why hadn't he come to her first? To turn her town over to Nick Stanton . . .!

Nick cut neatly across the stream of chatter. 'Just what sort of building are you wanting, Mr Bradley?'

'Civic centre. Auditorium, place for the theatre club to have its shows. I'm sure you know the sort of thing.'

'Yes, indeed, Mr Bradley.' Nick's voice was smooth.

George Bradley looked fondly down at Chelsea and patted her shoulder. 'And I want this lady in on it, too. Chelsea knows just how much Norah Springs will stand for. She'll keep you in line, young man. Good taste, that's what we're after.'

Chelsea nearly laughed at the look on Nick's face, at the idea that any of his buildings could be considered not in good taste. But it was absolutely true, she told herself. Norah Springs wasn't quite ready for the kind of thing Nick had built in St Louis and Jefferson City.

Nick quickly recovered his poise. 'I'm sure we can design a civic centre that Norah Springs can be proud of, Mr Bradley.'

'That's great. Our board meets ten days from now—over Memorial Day weekend, as a matter of fact. Any chance you two could come up then? Look over the site, talk to the board, that kind of thing?'

My mother had something to do with this, Chelsea thought. Who else would arrange a meeting like that on a holiday weekend but a mother who wanted to have her daughter home for a few days?

'What about you, Chelsea?' Nick questioned. 'I have plans, but I can change them.'

'Of course. I can go that weekend.'

'Good!' George Bradley boomed. 'I'll make sure there's a reservation for you at the hotel, Mr Stanton. Of course Chelsea won't need to worry about a place to stay.' He grinned and patted her shoulder again. 'This little lady built my house a couple of years ago, you know. Did a fine job, too. A right fine job.' He hoisted himself to his feet. 'Look out for her, Mr Stanton. She has a way of getting what she wants.'

He was still booming when he and Shelby reached the lobby. Chelsea closed the office door behind them.

'Where the hell is Norah Springs?' Nick asked.

'About a hundred miles north of here. It's small, but definitely not the boondocks.'

'And he knows your father? Wonderful connections you have, don't you, Chelsea?'

'A few here and there,' she said, and wondered

which shade of red his face would turn the first time he was introduced to her father. It was an entertaining speculation.

'And you'll be staying at Mr Bradley's new house, that he's so proud of.'

Chelsea allowed herself a smile. 'Are you jealous that he doesn't have a room for you?'

'Not at all. I prefer my privacy. Especially when the alternative is watching—shall we say, inappropriate behaviour?'

Chelsea coloured, and said angrily, 'For your information, George Bradley has been married for fifty years and has a half-dozen grandchildren.'

'Well, Burke doesn't have the grandchildren, but otherwise . . .'

'I am tired of you saying nasty things about Burke!' Chelsea's temper flared, and she was beyond the point of wanting to control it. 'He adores Helen, and so does everyone else who knows her. No one wants to hurt that woman!'

'Want to or not, you seem to be doing a good job of it,' he said soberly. He picked up the documents he had been working on and left the room.

Chelsea slammed her fist down on the drawing board and the pencils jumped. 'And good riddance to you, Mr Stanton,' she snapped.

It was very late when she raised her head from the drawing board, and her spine was cramped from sitting so long in that unnatural position. Dusk had come while she worked. A couple of blocks to the south, the harsh lights of Busch Stadium glowed, and inside the round arena she could see the seething crowd watching a baseball game. 'It's nice that someone has time for recreation,' she thought. Yes, a weekend at home, even if it involved some work, would be good for her.

She sighed and turned back to the drawings.

There was a tap at her door, and Nick looked in.

'What do you want?' Chelsea asked wearily.

'Something to eat.'

'I don't hide a smorgasbord in my desk drawer. Eileen keeps sugar cookies in her file cabinet, and Carl has a fully-stocked bar, but . . .'

'I was thinking in terms of a complete meal, at a restaurant.'

'Try Angelo's downstairs. I can recommend the manicotti.' She turned back to her drawing.

He hesitated a split second. 'Want to keep me company?'

'Must I?'

'No, but you've been here twelve hours today. And you didn't have lunch.' He pulled the knot of his tie and settled his shirt collar.

'You're wrong about that. Marie brought me a sandwich.'

'After working that long without a break, you can't be doing anything constructive for your clients.'

'I should have known it was the clients you were worried about.'

'Isn't that the whole point? Come on, Chelsea, stop arguing. You know you're hungry.'

She looked at the drawing, which swam before her eyes, and then the spicy aroma of manicotti seemed to float through the office, tickling her nose. 'All right.'

It was late enough that the crowd at Angelo's was beginning to thin, but the restaurant was never quiet. The *maitre d'* led them to a table tucked away in a corner, and Nick sat down with a sigh. 'They specialise in privacy, don't they?'

'Yes. All the executives bring their secretaries here for intimate little lunches.' Then she flushed red. If he says anything more about Burke, she thought . . .

Nick didn't seem to hear. 'I'd forgotten how much work it is to do the specs for a house,' he said, and rubbed his eyes.

'Nobody likes houses. I don't understand, Nick. I know they're hard work and the fee isn't nearly as large as in the bigger projects, but there is so much joy in creating space for a family, on a budget they can afford. And then watching the house go up, and the family move in . . .' She shook her head. 'I can't describe the feeling.'

'Wouldn't you get the same thrill from the condos in the Jonas Building?'

'No. There is no individuality in condos—all the units are alike.'

'If they turn out that way in the Jonas Building,' he said, 'you will have only yourself to blame.'

She stared at him for a full minute. 'I hadn't considered that possibility.'

'See? That's why I'm the partner and you're the lowly staffer.'

Chelsea shook her head. 'I doubt that it would be practical.'

'I'm really amazed that you aren't excited by that building. You seem fascinated by other old places.'

'Old houses,' Chelsea corrected firmly. 'I love to renovate and remodel them.'

'Like Hillhaven.'

She couldn't find a trace of sarcasm in his voice then, and so she nodded slowly. 'It's a pretty house. There are hundreds of them out there, structurally sound but deteriorated. Have you been down to Laclede's Landing, right by the riverfront?'

'Not yet.'

'If you'd been looking when you went to the riverboat the other night, you could have seen part of it. That whole nine-block area is coming back to life, after years of standing empty and desolate and falling down. I'd like to do for the houses of St Louis what has been done for the Landing. There are so many old treasures.'

'Which do you like better—old houses or new?'

Chelsea considered, and the waiter put a steaming plate in front of her. She breathed deeply of the sharp tomato scent and said, 'That's hard. The challenge of renovation, against the sheer freedom of starting out with an empty lot—I don't know. What about you?'

'It isn't houses at all for me, you know. So I don't care much which kind, as long as I don't get stuck with too many of them.'

Chelsea shook her head. 'I couldn't disagree with you more. I like the variety in single-family houses. Besides, I don't think I could stay interested in one project for months or years at a stretch. I like change.'

There was a brief silence, as if Nick was debating with himself about whether to answer. Then he said, 'Have you ever designed a place for yourself?'

'Half a dozen times.'

'Have you built it yet?'

'No. I'm still living in a little cardboard box out on the west edge of town.'

He laughed at that. 'And the shoemaker's kids go barefoot, too.'

'That's right. Why invest in a house? I may not live here for long.'

'Why not? You could always sell it.'

'I'm not sure the house I want would be saleable. I want to burrow underground, you see. Not many people get turned on by that.'

'I never would have suspected you of being a hermit. Building a cave and crawling away to hide in it—for shame, Chelsea.'

'I'm not a hermit,' she denied. 'The house I want will be built around an atrium covered by a glass bubble. Even underground, it will have more light than the average house, and it will be quieter and more private.'

'I can hear you now, on the 'phone to the police. "Officer, someone is bubble-peeking!" ' Nick mocked gently.

Chelsea stood her ground. 'With the earth berm and a flagstone floor in the atrium, it will just about heat itself with passive solar. And . . .'

'You're going to have trouble getting it past the zoning board.'

'I know.' She cut another slice of bread off the crusty loaf. 'That's probably the biggest reason for not building it now. Why must zoning laws be twenty years behind technology?'

Nick shrugged. 'Because now and then they're right and technology is wrong, I suppose. It makes it unnecessarily hard on us. Are you serious about not staying in St Louis?'

She was instantly suspicious. 'Why do you want to know?'

Nick shrugged. 'You're the one who brought up the subject, Chelsea.'

'I'll probably be at Shelby Harris till I'm old and grey,' she said.

'Unless something happens to prevent it,' he agreed.

Chelsea moved the last bit of manicotti around on her plate and thought about throwing it at him. Calm down, she told herself. He's right; you're the one who said you might not stay. Be smart, and change the subject. 'I might look into building a dome home,' she said finally.

'What kind? Geodesic? Plastic? Concrete?'

'Foam, I think. The kind they're building out on the West Coast. There's a seminar offered next autumn in Los Angeles, and I'd like to go and find out how they'd work around here.'

'Sounds good. Let me see the details, and we'll try to work it out.'

Chelsea sighed. She'd forgotten that he'd have to approve any travelling she did from now on. 'Yes, Boss,' she said, keeping her tone as even as possible.

Nick's eyebrows went up, but he didn't comment. 'Want something for dessert?'

'No, I'm ready to go back to work.'

He signalled the waiter for the bill. 'How about some fresh air first?'

'If you call it fresh.' Chelsea reached for her purse. 'What's my share of that?'

'Your share is precisely nothing. I invited you.'

'Nick, I wouldn't have come if I hadn't intended to pay for my own meal.'

'Do you think I don't know that?' Nick pushed his chair back. 'If it makes you feel better, the next one is on you.'

'I don't like owing you anything,' Chelsea told him frankly.

It was the first time she had heard him really laugh. He tucked her hand into his arm as soon as they reached the street. 'Tell me about Norah Springs and George Bradley. Sounds as if they're having an affair, doesn't it?'

'Just as long as you don't think I'm sleeping with him,' Chelsea muttered. 'George is the premiere citizen of the Springs. Small-town boy made good in the city, that sort of thing. Just don't be fooled by that country-boy talk of his, because he's no fool. A couple of years ago he retired, sold his manufacturing business here in St Louis, and went back to the old home town.'

'And built a big new house . . .' he prompted.

'Ballroom, music room—the whole caboodle, George's wife likes to think she's musical, so there is always a string quartet playing when she throws a dinner party. She's trying to bring culture to the Springs.'

'So it's really her idea?'

'Oh, I don't think so. Norah Springs was quietly cultured long before Elsie Bradley took it over. By the way, be sure to take a dinner jacket.'

'You're joking.'

'No. It's required at Elsie Bradley's table. Which

reminds me, I'll have to get something. She's seen every dress I own.'

'Does Norah Springs need a civic centre?'

Chelsea nodded. 'Oh, yes. And the acoustics had better be as good as anything in St Louis, or you'll have trouble.'

Nick looked down at her quizzically. 'Don't you mean, we'll have trouble?'

'This one is strictly your department, Nick,' she said. 'Remember? I'm only going along to keep you straight on what fits into Norah Springs.'

'What makes you the expert? Building Bradley's house?'

'And a few other things. I grew up in Norah Springs.'

'I see method in the madness. What happens if I go beserk and design something totally inappropriate?'

Chelsea smiled sweetly. 'If you are nice to me in the meantime, I'll rescue you from the tar and feathers. Otherwise . . .'

Nick tightened his grip on her hand and started across the street.

'Don't you think we'd better go back? The only thing down this way is the parking ramp.'

'I know. I'm sending you home.' He turned in at the entrance.

'I wanted to work a while.'

'So come in early tomorrow. In the meantime, go home and read a good book. That's an order.'

He spotted the Mercedes right away in the almost empty floor, and he put her firmly into the driver's seat. She rolled down the window to protest, and he leaned on the door, arms folded. 'My car's up a level if you'd like me to follow you home—make sure you get there safely.'

'I'm a grown woman, Nick. I can drive myself across town.'

'After riding with you, I'm not so sure,' he muttered.

For a moment, there in the dim light, she thought she saw something flare in his eyes. Was he going to kiss her? she thought a little breathlessly.

But he just said, 'I'll see you tomorrow,' and stepped back from the car. He was still standing there when the Mercedes coasted down the ramp and out to the street.

CHAPTER SIX

'DON'T sweat it,' Jim said, his voice low but stern. 'You have that bet won hands down.'

Chelsea shook her head. 'Something is wrong. I can feel it.' She leaned against the corridor wall, a Shelby Harris portfolio containing her drawings of the Sullivan house in her hand. She was waiting for Nick, and she was getting uncomfortably warm in the belted raincoat.

'Oh, don't go getting female intuition on me,' Jim begged. 'I can't take it. You saw Nick's design. It was . . .'

'It's competent,' Chelsea interrupted.

Jim nodded. 'That's about the best word for it. And yours is original, it fits the site . . .'

Chelsea wasn't listening. 'I didn't expect Nick to design something that is merely competent.'

'Come on, Chelsea. He's a whizz at office buildings and factories, but he doesn't do houses. He's competing out of his own territory. Besides, you know you have it won. Don't be such a worrier.'

Chelsea smiled reluctantly. Her design was better; she knew that it was not prejudice. 'I just won't be comfortable till he admits that I've beaten him,' she admitted.

'Well, the professor will do that for you soon enough,' Jim consoled. He waved a casual hand and vanished down the hall. He was doing that a lot since Nick Stanton had joined the firm, Chelsea thought; he seemed to possess some sort of radar that warned him whenever Nick was coming around a corner.

And Jim was right again, Chelsea realised as Nick's office door opened. He was elegantly tailored today in light grey, a dark blue shirt setting off the even tan of his skin. The portfolio he carried was identical to the one in Chelsea's hand, and she looked at it with a sudden flash of confidence. Nick had made a mistake when he took her on in her own speciality, and he was going to pay for that mistake.

He set the portfolio down and pulled a trenchcoat on. 'Of all the days it has to choose to rain,' he said with a note of disgust in his voice. 'Are you ready? The professor will be waiting for us.'

'I'm not only ready, I'm eager to hear what he has to say,' Chelsea said and started down the hall. 'I hope you aren't too disappointed at the results.'

Nick's eyebrows arched. 'A little over-confident, aren't you?' he asked softly, falling into step beside her.

'I have reason to be,' Chelsea murmured.

He didn't seem to hear. 'Besides, I happen to think you're the one who will be disappointed.'

'Now who's sounding overconfident?' she warned. 'Let's take the Mercedes.'

'Only if you promise not to drive,' Nick countered.

'It's my car,' she snapped as they entered the parking garage.

'And it's one of the miracles of the modern world that it's still in one piece.' He reached for the keys, and after a moment's hesitation, Chelsea handed them over. Let him have his moment of glory, she thought. Her victory would soon knock him out of the water.

He whistled as they drove through the light summer rain, keeping rhythm with the windshield wipers. He sounded cheerful and not at all concerned about the outcome of this bet. Then he broke off abruptly to say, 'Nice car. I'm sure you enjoy the distinction of being one of the privileged few.'

'I like it,' Chelsea said, just a little warily.

'It's a pretty toy. But aren't you afraid to get it wet?'

'A car is a car, Nick. How would I keep it dry, for heaven's sake?'

He didn't answer. 'Who gave it to you? Burke, or was it the gentleman from the riverboat?'

'Perhaps it was neither of them.'

It didn't seem to bother him. 'In fact, possibly you don't even remember.' He wheeled the car into the driveway beside the professor's house and turned to her with a smile. 'What do you say, Chelsea? Shall we save the professor some time—do you want to concede now and get it over with?'

Chelsea saw red. 'I certainly do not,' she snapped. 'If you think you can bluff me, Nick Stanton, you're crazy!'

He shrugged. 'Come along, then.'

The professor was one of the grand old men of architecture in the city. They had spent a whole afternoon in Chelsea's office arguing before finally settling on him as the arbiter of the contest. No one in the firm would do, especially not Carl Shelby or Frank Harris, Chelsea had said. Neither of them would see any humour in the competition, to begin with, she argued, and besides, Nick would have an unfair advantage. She'd just as soon the partners didn't even know about this little spree, until after she'd won it, Chelsea thought. Then she'd make sure there was a splash!

Nick had solemnly agreed to her demands, but then added that he would not trust any male under the age of seventy because then Chelsea would have an advantage. It was the closest she had ever come to throwing something at him.

The professor was waiting for them at the door. He was stooped with age now, but his eyes were still bright, and he smiled under the droopy moustache that was his trademark. 'So we have a contest,' he said as he hung up their wet coats. 'Come in, come in. There isn't enough excitement in buildings these days? You need to make your own contests?'

'This is a little different than most,' Nick said. 'This is to settle a bet.'

The professor's eyes gleamed. 'I see,' he said in his soft voice, and Chelsea wondered just what he thought was going on. It made her a little uneasy, as if the professor thought he was dealing with a couple of lovers!

'Let's see the plans,' he said. 'You go set them up in the next room. Just prop them up anywhere, and let me know when you're ready. Shall I get you something to drink, Miss Ryan? How about a beer, Nick?'

Nick shook his head. 'Not during working hours. Thanks anyway, Professor.'

The old man looked disappointed. 'Then I'll bring some iced tea.'

'That would be fine,' Nick said. 'Give us five minutes to set these things up, Professor.'

Chelsea said, her teeth gritted, 'You didn't tell me you were on a first-name basis with him.'

Nick shrugged and tried to look innocent.

Chelsea glared at him and went on into the living room. She was setting up her display when Nick brought his portfolio in, and she concentrated very hard on getting her drawings at just the right angle. The front elevation was the most important, the view as the house would appear from the street. She fussed with it, getting it to stand up just right.

Nick opened his portfolio, took out a series of mounted drawings, and lined them up on the couch. He was very casual about the whole thing. Then he sat down across the room and observed Chelsea.

'If you're so confident, why are you nervous?' he asked finally.

She tossed her head, making the auburn waves bounce on her shoulders, and came to sit down. 'I happen to think the presentation of the plans is sometimes just as important as the plans themselves.'

'Not with the professor. He isn't going to be fooled by any tricks like that.'

'Tricks!' Chelsea sputtered. 'If you're going to talk

about tricks——' She turned her back on him indignantly, and her eyes fell for the first time on his design. 'Oh, my God . . .' she breathed.

The house seemed to hang from the side of the ravine, as airy as a spider's web. The steel of its framework gave it strength, yet the glass walls left it looking as delicate as a fairy castle.

'Do you like it?' Nick asked politely.

She turned on him with the fury of a wounded tiger. 'That's not the house Jim . . .' she stumbled and stopped.

'Cheated, did you?' he asked. 'I thought you would.'

'I did not cheat!' Chelsea wailed. 'I designed my house just as I would have if it hadn't been a bet. I only wanted . . .'

'You only wanted an advance peek at the competition. And I simply made sure you got it. It just didn't happen to be my final design, that's all.'

'This is nothing like the first one,' Chelsea said, with all the dignity she could muster.

Nick grinned. 'So who says only a woman can change her mind?'

The professor came in with a tray. He handed out the glasses and looked speculatively at Chelsea, who had put one hand on her throbbing head.

'It looks as if we won't even have to bother you, Professor,' Nick said smoothly. 'The lady has conceded.'

Chelsea sat up. 'The lady has conceded nothing,' she said, her voice a little shrill. 'I was surprised, that's all.'

The professor tried to hide a smile. Then he walked over to the couch and looked at the two sets of drawings. He studied them both, then he tapped Nick's. 'This one surprised you, little one?' he asked, his eyes intent on Chelsea.

She nodded reluctantly.

'It's a surprising house,' the professor continued. He sipped his iced tea and continued to look from one to the other. 'Using the techniques of a skyscraper to build a residence—it's very interesting, Nick.'

'Thank you, Professor,' Nick said modestly. Chelsea could have cheerfully dumped her iced tea over his head.

'Now, from what you have told me about the clients, and from what I know of the neighbourhood . . .' There was a long pause. 'For sheer beauty and grace, this one.' He thumped a finger loudly against Nick's drawing.

Nick relaxed and turned a self-satisfied smile to her. 'Are you ready to concede now, Chelsea?' he asked softly.

'Don't hurry me, young man,' the professor snapped. 'For the practical needs of the client, this one.' He waved the front elevation of Chelsea's house under Nick's nose.

Chelsea would have given a great deal at that moment to have had a camera. The look of utter disbelief that spread across Nick's face should have been preserved for future ages, she thought; it was so very well done.

'And the winner?' Nick asked. His voice was a little hoarse.

The professor smiled, an expression of singular sweetness. 'I declare it a draw,' he said softly. 'I suggest you learn to work together, instead of competing, and let the vision and the practicality go hand in hand. Then you will go far.'

It had something of the note of a benediction about it. There was nothing else left to say, and they packed up the drawings in silence.

Chelsea drove back to the office. There was not a word spoken all the way.

Jim saw her come in and met her at the door of her office. 'Well?' he asked eagerly.

Chelsea silenced him with a finger to her lips. Once inside the room, she hung up her wet coat and flung herself down on the couch. 'I didn't win,' she said.

Jim looked stunned. 'The professor has lost his touch,' he declared.

Chelsea shook her head and told him what had happened. 'The house you drew for Nick wasn't the real one. He gave it to you because he knew you'd show it to me, and he drew the real one himself. I don't know why I didn't expect that.'

'It makes sense,' Jim admitted. 'That guy is the most suspicious character I've ever met.'

'Are you just figuring that out?' Chelsea asked tartly. She stood up. 'Well, I'd better get the plans ready to show the Sullivans this evening.' She opened the portfolio.

'It's beautiful,' Jim breathed as he caught sight of the top drawing.

'If you think this is nice you should see Nick's,' Chelsea told him. Then she looked down at the drawings she held, and stopped dead. 'He took the wrong portfolio out of the car,' she said. 'We both had Shelby Harris portfolios—and he was in such a hurry he grabbed the wrong one.'

'What are you going to do, Chelsea?' Jim asked with avid interest. 'Tear them up?'

'Destroy anything this beautiful?' She was concentrating on Nick's drawings as she spoke, and in the back of her mind the professor's words rang out. They could have both beauty and practicality, he had said . . .

'Out, Jim,' she ordered, and shut the door tight behind him.

The next morning, bright and early, she tapped on Nick's office door, the crystal mug of coffee in her hand. He sounded grumpy, she thought, when he called, 'Come in, if you must.'

'Good morning,' Chelsea announced from the threshhold.

Nick's eyebrows drew together. 'Oh, it's you.'

'I thought you'd be delighted to see me. After yesterday, you know, I don't have to consult you about anything I'm working on.'

'That's not quite what happened.'

'Well, let's not argue about details, shall we? I just came to tell you that the Sullivans were very intrigued by the preliminary house plans. They took them home to show her brother, the contractor. I hate to work with that man,' she added thoughtfully. 'Rumour has it that he once read a book on how to build a house, and now he thinks he's an authority.'

'Will you stop babbling?'

'Must you be irritable? I thought you'd like to know that it went well.'

Nick sat down in the big leather chair behind his desk. 'You're only here so you can enjoy my defeat.'

'Actually, I thought you'd like to see the plans.'

'I looked them over thoroughly yesterday, thank you.'

'That was yesterday,' Chelsea said gently. 'It took hours of hard work to make my practical and efficient interior fit into your beautiful and graceful exterior, but . . .'

Nick rocked his chair back, and put his feet up on the corner of his desk. His eyebrows were still fierce. 'You redesigned it? Combined the drawings?'

'The best features of both,' Chelsea said modestly.

He grunted. 'That's a matter of judgment, and I don't always trust yours.'

'I realise that. When it comes time to do the actual blueprints we will probably fight over every line. But as the professor said, your drawings didn't really address the needs of the client.'

'I'll argue that, too. How long has it been since the professor designed a house?'

'Come on, Nick. You and I together couldn't catch up with him by the time we're sixty.' Chelsea walked over to the wide windows that faced out over the river.

How was it possible, she wondered vaguely, that Nick's office, just down the hall from hers, had a much better view?

He had moved so silently that she had not heard him, and she was startled when he spoke, for he was standing right behind her. 'You and I together,' he quoted gravely. 'How about it, Chelsea?'

She stood there frozen for a moment, wondering why her pulse was fluttering so.

'Shall we be partners on the Jonas Building, too?' There was a brief pause. 'Wrangling over every decision will make us both better architects, you know.'

Professional partners. Chelsea's heart rate slowed a little. She turned around, and had to look a long way up to meet his eyes.

He was holding out his hand, and she put hers into it. 'Partners,' she said, a little breathlessly.

His hand was warm. Chelsea let her fingers slip out of his grasp. 'I'd better get back to work,' she said.

He didn't try to prevent her from leaving. 'Let's start on the Jonas Building this afternoon,' he said. He sat down at his desk and pulled a stack of papers across the blotter.

All they had agreed to was to work together, Chelsea scolded herself as she walked back to her own office. So why should she feel that she had made some sort of vow?

'I've already explained why I want to take the Mercedes to Norah Springs,' Chelsea argued. 'It's already packed, for one thing——'

'So is my car,' Nick interrupted.

'And I want to get the engine tuned while I'm home.'

His eyebrows went sky-high. 'On a holiday weekend?'

'Obviously, you don't know Norah Springs.'

'I can't wait to learn,' Nick said sourly.

'So I'll follow you over to your apartment, and we'll transfer your luggage into the Mercedes and . . .'

'Does it have air bags?'

'No. Why?'

'If you're driving, I want all the protection I can get.'

Chelsea put her hands on her hips. 'I'll have you know, Nick Stanton, that in more than ten years of driving I have never so much as scratched a fender!' She realised abruptly that he was paying more attention to the way her beige trouser suit clung to her curves than to what she was saying. 'It's three o'clock, Nick. If we're going to be in Norah Springs by the time the holiday traffic picks up, we'd better leave soon.'

He grinned. 'You're so cute when you're mad. All right, you win.'

Chelsea was speechless. Nick picked up his briefcase and stopped at the door. 'Are you coming?' he asked. 'Or have you decided to turn into a statue?'

He didn't wait for an answer. Instead, he paused beside his secretary's desk. 'Miss Ryan and I are off for the weekend,' he said.

Chelsea recovered her voice by the time he had tossed his briefcase into the Mercedes. 'You didn't need to make it sound like a rendezvous!' she snapped.

'Did I?'

'You know quite well you did. You probably planned it that way.'

He had the grace to look ashamed of himself, then abruptly he grinned. 'If the typing pool is going to start rumours anyway, we might as well enjoy ourselves this weekend,' he suggested.

'I'm not dumb enough to have an affair with you,' Chelsea snapped.

Nick looked hurt. 'It sounded like a lot of fun to me.'

'I'm sure it did. And it would probably be even more fun when you could fire me next week.'

'Why would I want to do that? You're actually quite good at what you do.'

'I suppose it should be some comfort that you've finally noticed!' She put the car into gear.

She followed him to his apartment and waited patiently as he transferred a leather suitcase to the Mercedes. By the time everything was arranged, and he settled himself in the passenger seat, Chelsea had cooled off somewhat.

Nick fastened his seatbelt, tested it with a jerk, and leaned back with a sigh. 'Well, I've done all I can do to protect myself. The rest is up to my guardian angel.'

The Mercedes' tyres squealed on the pavement.

Nick winced and added, 'I don't quite understand, you know.'

'Understand what?'

'Why you turned me down. Frankly, Chelsea, Burke is getting old professionally. His name doesn't carry the same weight that it used to in the field. I think you'd be wise to look around for a new patron.'

'I have never needed a patron, as you so politely put it. I think of Burke as—as an uncle. Nothing more.'

'Strange family you have,' Nick commented. 'By the way, that truck is a little larger than the car, I'd appreciate it if you wouldn't challenge him for his half of the highway.'

Chelsea bit her tongue. The look she gave him should have shrivelled him up to a crisp.

Nick didn't seem to notice. 'Are we taking the River Road?'

'It's the most scenic.'

'Also the most curvy, narrow and dangerous,' he pointed out.

'If you're so afraid of travelling——'

'I'm not. It's just your driving that panics me.'

Chelsea slammed on the brakes and pulled the car to a stop on the verge of the road. 'So why don't you drive, instead?' she said coldly. 'That way I can enjoy my favourite route up to Norah Springs in peace!'

'Sounds good to me.' He unfastened his safety belt and walked around the car. Chelsea settled herself with a flounce in the passenger seat and stared out the window, determined to pay no attention to him for the two-hour drive.

The effort was doomed to failure. Nick talked gently on subject after subject, sometimes answering himself where called for, until Chelsea gave in.

'Does it bother you to spend three days in Norah Springs?' she asked finally. 'You said you had plans for the weekend.'

Nick shrugged. 'It was nothing important. There will be other weekends.'

Chelsea thought about that for a moment. 'She must be very understanding,' she said finally.

Nick grinned. 'What makes you think it was a woman?' he asked innocently, but there was a smile in his voice.

There had to be a woman, she mused. They probably threw themselves in piles at Nick's feet. Just because Chelsea didn't find him appealing didn't mean that other women weren't intrigued by that boyish charm.

There must be a woman, and yet the office grapevine didn't seem to know anything about his private life.

Chelsea was startled when she sighted the big sign announcing Norah Springs. 'We can't be here yet,' she announced, and checked her watch to find that two hours had indeed passed.

'I wondered if you were ever coming back out of your episode of deep thought.'

She ignored him. 'Take a left at the first intersection,' she instructed.

'Is that the way to the hotel?'

'No. It's downtown. But you'll probably need the car tonight, so you can drop me off first.'

'Is George providing you with transportation?' Nick asked. He didn't sound interested.

'I shouldn't need any, Should I?' Chelsea retorted.

Nick shrugged. 'I suppose not, if all the events are at his house.' He made the turn on to a winding, quiet street. Most of the houses were set well back from the street on large, landscaped lots. 'Nice neighbourhood.'

'There's the house I grew up in.' Chelsea waved a careless hand.

Nick slowed the Mercedes to look at the blue and white split-level. 'Not what I would have expected,' he said.

'Unlike you, I wasn't born an architect,' she said coolly. 'Turn right up here.'

This street was newer, and wilder. The lots were more as nature had intended, and the houses were larger and farther apart. Most of them looked as if they had grown right there on the site. 'The one on your left is George Bradley's,' Chelsea pointed out.

The Mercedes slowed to a crawl as Nick studied the cedar-shingled exterior of the house. 'Where do I park?' he asked.

'At the house across the street. I'm staying with my parents.'

The car swerved a little as he turned to look at her. 'But you pointed out that split-level . . .'

'I said I grew up there, not that Mom and Dad still lived there. You assume an awful lot, don't you, Nick? No one ever said I was staying at the Bradley's either.'

It was the first time she'd ever seen him at a loss for words. He pulled the Mercedes up in the circular drive beside the Ryan's forest green house.

'Chelsea!' Sara came across the drive just as Chelsea opened her car door. 'Oh, darling, it's so good to have you home!'

'Believe me, it feels wonderful from this side too,' Chelsea murmured. 'Mom, this is Nick Stanton, my new boss. Sara Ryan, who has the singular honour of being my mother.'

'Nick, do come in for coffee.' Sara urged Chelsea towards the house. 'We can unload all the luggage later.'

'I'm only home for the weekend, Mom. I brought one tote bag—that's all.'

'More's the pity,' Sara murmured. 'Well, we'll just do the best we can. Let's have coffee on the gallery.'

'The gallery?' Nick asked.

'Yes. It's my favourite room. I couldn't express it very well when I tried to tell Chelsea what I wanted, but she seemed to read my mind.' Sara led the way into the great family room that stretched the length of the house, looking out over the tangled growth on the hill. Today the long windows stood open and the May breeze teased the leaves of the green plants that formed the only curtains. Nick walked across the room and stood staring thoughtfully out across the hillside and the fenced-in swimming pool that lay below the house.

Sara poured coffee. 'Cream and sugar, Nick?'

He shook his head. 'Neither, thanks.' He waved a hand out to the view. 'It's nice, Chelsea.'

'Should I take that as a compliment?'

One eybrow arched. 'Take it however you like. It was meant to be one.'

'Chelsea, come get your cup,' her mother ordered. 'Nick, you must be an unusual person. I can think of only a couple of others who have been allowed to drive Chelsea's car.' She smiled.

Mother, don't do this to me, Chelsea pleaded silently. Please don't get started with stories about when your darling was little. I can't take it.

'Where's Dad?' Chelsea asked, hoping to get her mother's attention refocused.

'Oh, he'll be home soon,' Sara went on. 'A late appointment—they always happen when he most wants to get out of the office early. I hope you can join us for dinner, Nick. Josh is going to grill steaks.'

Nick's eyes met Chelsea's, and a gleam of humour sprang to life in those blue depths. 'I'd love to, Mrs Ryan.'

'If the Bradleys are expecting you, I can just give them a call. Of course, Elise has probably already spotted the car. She always knows everything that happens over here.'

Nick looked a bit puzzled. 'I'm staying at the hotel, Mrs Ryan, not with the Bradley's.'

Sara looked up, startled. 'Do you know, I'd forgotten that they built that enormous house with only one bedroom. Chelsea, I'm ashamed of you for letting them do it.'

'That makes two of us,' Nick murmured. 'Why only one bedroom?'

'I built exactly what they wanted. George told me,' Chelsea explained patiently, 'that he'd had all the overnight guests anyone should be expected to put up with in a lifetime, and he wasn't ever going to have another one. From now on, all his guests have to go home after dinner.'

Sara sniffed. 'So there they are, those two old people with their elaborate house, and not even a place to tuck a baby grandchild away for the night.'

Chelsea laughed. 'That doesn't upset George a bit. And an afternoon with his grandchildren would probably drive even you wild, Mom.'

'But to send your own children to a hotel!'

'He owns the hotel, Mom.'

'I don't care, Chelsea. It's still inhuman. And how they think they'll ever sell that huge house . . .' Sara shook her head.

'George doesn't intend to. He'll laugh from heaven—or wherever—while the kids try to get rid of it.'

Sara ignored the interruption. 'But speaking of the hotel, Nick, it makes no sense for you to be all the way downtown when you can stay right here with Chelsea.'

A wicked sparkle flared in Nick's eyes. 'With Chelsea?' he murmured.

Chelsea said, keeping her composure as well as she could, 'Mom always keeps the guest room ready.' And just wait till I get a chance to talk to her about this, Chelsea resolved.

'I'd be honoured,' Nick said.

'That's taken care of, then. Why don't you two bring in your luggage and get settled? There are just a few things I need to finish about dinner.' She paused in the doorway. 'Chelsea, there are some new things hanging in your closet. I thought a new dress might come in handy for the weekend.'

'Mother . . .' But Sara was gone. Chelsea shook her head.

Nick was unloading the car when she caught up with him.

'My mother likes to manage things,' Chelsea said, and picked up her briefcase.

'I can see that,' he said gravely.

'If she wasn't right all the time, it would be infuriating.'

A horn beeped and Chelsea looked up as a sporty bright red car turned into the driveway. She set the briefcase down and waved.

Josh Ryan unfolded himself from the driver's seat. 'Chelsea! How's my darlin' today?'

'Just fine, Daddy,' she said demurely, and looked up at Nick, whose face had gone white. The taste of revenge was sweet indeed, she told herself. The look on Nick's face almost made up for all the nasty things he'd said to her all week.

Almost, she added. She owed him a few surprises yet.

CHAPTER SEVEN

BUT nothing could keep Nick silent for long. By the time the steaks were cooking, he and Josh were on the best of terms out on the patio beside the pool, and Chelsea, drinking dry sherry on the gallery with her mother, could have screamed.

It just wasn't fair, she thought, half-listening as her mother chatted on. Then she realised that Sara had stopped talking, and looked up. 'What, Mother?'

'What is wrong with you, Chelsea? I don't believe you've heard a word I've said.'

'Sorry, Mom. I'm really tired these days. Overwork, I suppose.'

Sara's face reflected instant concern. 'You need a vacation, dear. Why don't you stay for a couple of weeks and rest?'

Chelsea shook her head. 'Perhaps later in the summer. But right now there is just too much work to do.'

'Well, at least don't work too hard this weekend. All you have to do, after all, is go to Bradley's cocktail party on Sunday and listen to all the plans for the civic centre.'

'Nick will want to look at the site, and . . .' Chelsea was suddenly so tired she could scarcely hold her head up.

'So let him,' Sara ordered. 'That doesn't mean you have to go with him.'

'Why did you invite him to stay, Mom?'

'I'm surprised at you, Chelsea. It was the only polite thing to do.' She looked at her daughter with a speculative gleam in her eyes. 'He seems to be a very nice man.'

'Most men set out to charm you, Mom. There's something about you that they want to impress.'

Sara patted her daughter's hand. 'It's sweet of you to say that. And it might even have been true twenty years ago, dear.'

'It doesn't mean that they're all really charming underneath, though. And Nick certainly isn't.'

'I still think he's delightful. The barbecue is tomorrow, by the way. It's out at the country club.'

'The civic centre thing? I thought you said it was Sunday.'

Sara looked at her with aggravation in her eyes. 'You really are tired, aren't you, Chelsea? The barbecue for your old classmates, I mean. You are going, aren't you?'

Chelsea groaned. 'I don't suppose I have a choice, do I?'

'I thought you'd like to see them.'

'There isn't much we have in common any more, Mom. Most of them are married with a couple of kids, and here I am——'

Sara softened. 'There's nothing wrong with being unmarried at your age, Chelsea. The right man will come along, you'll see. And as for children—well, there is plenty of time.'

'It isn't that, Mom. It's just that it isn't very comfortable being alone in a group of couples.'

'Well, you and Nick can go play golf tomorrow and then to the barbecue.'

Chelsea turned from the portable bar where she was refilling her sherry glass. 'Why would I want to take Nick along?'

'He is your guest, Chelsea.'

'No, Mom. He's YOUR guest. I didn't invite him to stay here.'

There was a momentary silence, and then Josh called from downstairs, 'Are you two coming down, or will Nick and I have to eat all this food by ourselves?'

'Don't you dare, Dad. I'm starving!' Chelsea called back. 'Mom, Nick is my boss. He is not my friend, or my boyfriend, or anything else, and he's never likely to be.'

'Did I say he should be?'

'Besides, I've known him three weeks longer than you have, and believe me, you don't know what he's really like. Trust me, all right?'

'Shall I hide the family silver?' Sara asked drily. She didn't wait for an answer, just picked up her glass and led the way down to the patio.

Nick held Sara's chair, and said, 'Josh tells me you did the portrait of Chelsea. The one in the gallery, with the daisies in her hand.'

Sara glanced up with a smile. 'Oh, yes. I think she was four years old.'

'She couldn't have been much older than that,' Nick observed.

'If anyone says anything about my chubby cheeks, I will leave the table,' Chelsea announced.

'That was from my short-lived photographic career,' Sara continued. 'But I never could master the mechanics of a camera, so I had to go back to oils.'

'You're an artist, then?'

'Quite a combination, aren't we?' Josh volunteered as he put Chelsea's steak down in front of her. 'Chelsea's an artist, too, you know. Have you seen any of her sketches, Nick?'

Chelsea swallowed hard, but Nick merely grinned wickedly at her and said, 'I've had the pleasure, Josh.'

'Yes, she's her mother's child, of course. I like to think that the taste for maths and logic came from me, but at any rate, Chelsea couldn't have turned out as anything but an architect.'

'Dad, please,' Chelsea sighed. 'Can we talk about something else?'

'Don't be so modest,' Nick said innocently. 'You're a fascinating topic of conversation, Chelsea.'

'Dad, do you suppose the garage could fit the Mercedes in for a tune-up tomorrow?' she asked, desperate to change the subject. 'The engine has been running a bit rough.'

'I didn't notice anything wrong with it today,' Nick disagreed. 'In fact, I've never driven a car that handled so well.'

Chelsea looked down at her plate and waited. She knew what was coming next.

'Chelsea let you drive the Mercedes?' Josh asked. 'She's never even let me drive that car, and I'm the one who paid for it.'

Nick's eyes, glowing with laughter, met Chelsea's across the table. I hope he's happy now that he knows where the car came from, she thought. 'The only people who drive my car are the male chauvinist pigs who won't take no for an answer,' she said acidly.

Nick smiled. 'Congratulations, Chelsea. You have finally discovered the essence of my character. I am never discouraged by a refusal.'

She stared at the bit of steak on the end of her fork, and put it down. Suddenly she wasn't hungry any more.

Chelsea watched as Nick carefully teed up a golf ball on the ninth hole. 'This is a nice course,' he said as he stepped back to take an experimental swing.

Chelsea waited till he had made his drive, and watched the ball as it bounced off the edge of a sand trap and on towards the green. 'And you are a lucky golfer,' she grumbled as they walked towards the women's tee. She set up her shot, uncomfortably aware that Nick's bright eyes weren't missing a detail of the tailored white shorts she was wearing. If I have to spend much more time around this man, she thought, I'm going to reduce my wardrobe to trench coats and tent dresses.

'Why? Just because you're six shots down doesn't

mean I'm lucky,' Nick protested. 'Perhaps I'm just a better golfer.'

'You aren't even using your own clubs, for heaven's sake,' Chelsea protested.

'Doesn't that illustrate my point?'

'And you're just a bit conceited, too.'

'Who, me?' Nick asked innocently. 'Why do you leave your clubs here, by the way? St Louis has golf courses too, you know.'

'When do I ever get a chance to use them?'

'That's true,' he mused. 'Most of your leisure time must be tied up with Burke, and he hardly seems the type for golf.'

His bland assumption made her so furious that her swing was jerky, and her ball sailed off into the little pond at the bottom of the hill, landing with a splash that seemed to echo over the course. Chelsea stood there for a moment and looked down the slope. Then, maintaining her dignity with all the control at her command, she turned to face him. 'I'll concede the hole,' she said coolly.

'Very well,' Nick said equably. 'That's the same as conceding the game, you know. Too bad I was cautious about using your father's clubs. I might have won something from you.'

'It wouldn't have been much,' Chelsea snapped.

'Why? Aren't you sure enough of yourself to bet?' Nick put her club back in the bag strapped to the golf cart. 'Care to try another nine holes?'

'No, thanks.'

'Afraid I'll beat you again?'

'All that match proved was that you're a better heckler than I am, Nick.'

He looked wounded. 'I never heckle,' he said. 'Unless, of course, there's something worth winning at the end of the match. It looks to me as if you're sadly out of practice.'

'That was my first round of the year, yes.'

'Let's take your clubs back with us. Maybe we can do something about that.'

'I think they'll be fine right here.' She smiled at the boy who came out of the pro shop to take care of the cart and bags. 'I think the crowd has started to gather down by the pool. I understand that you may be uncomfortable, Nick. If you don't want to be dragged into it, that's fine with me. After all, you don't know any of the people, and . . .'

'I know you,' he offered.

'Well, it can't be a comfortable evening for you . . .'

'How sweet of you to worry about my comfort, Chelsea,' he said, and before she could dodge he'd put an arm around her waist, pulling her close to his side. 'I couldn't be rude and walk out on you when you've gone to such trouble to make me comfortable this weekend.'

Chelsea was still trying to find an answer to that when they reached the bottom of the little knoll. A knot of people had already gathered around the umbrella-shaded tables, and the scent of roasting pork drifted down from the barbecue pit.

'Besides, I never miss a meal if I can help it,' Nick continued, 'and since you're paying for this one——'

'I no longer owe you,' Chelsea snapped. She tried to pull away from his possessive arm, but he merely tightened his grip and smiled.

'Surely you don't mind being a security blanket, of a sort?' he asked. 'You're right, I don't know anyone but you. And I wouldn't want to get lost.'

Chelsea thought briefly about telling him where to go, but just then a cry went up from the tables. 'Chelsea! Where have you been, you scamp? You haven't been to a reunion in years!'

'We haven't had one in years,' she parried, as she was swallowed up by the group. Nick let his arm drop casually, and Chelsea breathed a quick sigh of relief, but then she found her hand captured in his in a grip that promised not to loosen all evening.

'And who's this?' one of the girls asked.

'I'm Nick Stanton,' he said with that easy smile. 'Chelsea brought me home on approval.'

Chelsea's teeth clenched. I'm going to make him regret that remark if it's the last thing I do, she swore.

It seemed hours later that she finally found herself alone. Dinner was long over, and the women had gathered under the umbrellas to gossip while the men clustered around the keg of beer at the far end of the terrace. Chelsea found her eyes resting on Nick's white shirt, clearly visible even in the dusk. She watched the muscles play under the close-fitting material, and then told herself not to be silly.

'Mooning over him? You'll get over it, once you've been married a couple of years.' The young woman who sat down next to her waved a hand towards the men.

'Hi, Janice. No, as a matter of fact, I'm not planning to be married at all.'

'That's smart. Next time I'm going to do the same.'

'Next time?' Chelsea asked idly.

Janice nodded. 'I'm on my second now. He's the one right by the beer keg. He's always right next to the keg, or the bar, or whatever's handy.'

'Do I know him?'

'No, but you know my first husband. He's over there too. That been a long time, though—six years and two kids ago.'

Chelsea propped her chin on her hand. The two men near the keg suddenly gave a roar of laughter. 'They seem to get alone fine.'

'Oh, they do. They play golf together every Sunday morning,' Janice said. Her voice was bitter. 'All I say is, don't trust 'em. Especially the handsome ones. And that one of yours is handsome as the very devil.'

It wasn't quite the way Chelsea would have stated it, but she couldn't help feeling that Janice's comparison was apt. Nick not only looked like the devil's first cousin, he was just as unpredictable. 'He isn't mine, actually. He's only my boss.'

Janice nodded sagely. 'Married, right? They all are.'

Chelsea was taken aback for a moment. Then she said slowly, 'Even if he was, it wouldn't make any difference to me. We're here this weekend to work, that's all.'

Nick leaned over the back of her chair and said, 'Want to go for a moonlight swim, Chels?'

'No, thanks. It's too soon after I ate.'

He shrugged. 'All right.' He planted a swift kiss on the nape of her neck and was gone.

Janice raised a knowing eyebrow. 'Your boss, hmmm? And you're here to work? Sure, Chelsea.'

I'm going to kill him, Chelsea thought. As slowly and as painfully as possible.

The sun was hot on Chelsea's bare back as she lay beside the pool. It was Sunday afternoon, and she was drowsing as she let the suntan oil begin to work.

Her mother fussed as she stood beside the lounger. 'Chelsea, you're going to roast out here,' she warned. 'And then you'll look awful in that new dress I got you.'

'Mother,' Chelsea said indistinctly, 'I will lie here no more than fifteen minutes. And I'm basted like a turkey; I can't possibly burn.'

'Well, be sure you move into the shade before you ruin that lovely skin.' Sara fussed with the spaghetti strap at the neckline of Chelsea's swimsuit. 'Don't you want this untied, honey? It will leave a line in your tan.'

'Mom, you're a dreamer to think that fifteen minutes of sun will give me a tan. Just go to your party and have a good time.'

'I hate to leave you, Chelsea. If it wasn't that the bride's father is one of Josh's best clients, we wouldn't feel so obligated to go to this reception. But . . .'

'Please go, Mother.' Chelsea closed her eyes.

'Well, I'll ask Nick to keep an eye on you and make sure you don't go to sleep out here.'

'I've sunbathed for twenty years without Nick's help, Mom. I think I can get through the day.'

'Nevertheless, it's a good precaution. You'll probably be over at the Bradley's by the time we get home, so we'll see you there for cocktails this evening, dear.'

'Goodbye, Mom.'

She heard the door slam and the engine of her father's car start, and sighed with relief. Her mother had the best of intentions, but sometimes she could drive Chelsea crazy. And it didn't help that for the last two days Sara had been telling her what a wonderful person Nick was.

What was really infuriating, Chelsea thought, was that he had been charming every moment that Josh and Sara were in view. It was only when they weren't around that the cynical side of him showed.

She lay there in the warmth and thought about Nick and what she'd like to tell him. What was there about that man, she wondered, that could arouse her to anger so quickly? Why could she not just ignore him? But the words she was planning to say kept getting all tangled together in her mind. And Nick kept coming into her head, with that easy smile and those expressive eyebrows, seeming to read her thoughts . . .

She stirred, hazily aware that she had slept. Oh, my God, she thought, I'll be burned so badly I won't be able to move. But the back of her neck, when she laid an experimental hand on it, was cool and supple. She looked up at the umbrella that stood over her, sheltering her from the blazing sun.

'So you're finally awake. I thought you'd never rejoin the conscious world, so I pulled the umbrella over.'

She looked over at the lounge drawn up next to hers. It was still in the sun, and Nick lay there in swimming trunks with an old copy of ARCHITECTURAL DIGEST in his hand.

'Don't you ever stop working?' she complained, and started to sit up before she remembered that her mother had untied her neck strap after all. Chelsea caught the top of her swimsuit just as it started to slide.

'Pity,' Nick mused, his gaze resting on the brief bikini top.

Chelsea's deep embarrassed blush seemed to start at her toes and spread over every inch of delicate skin.

'It must be very uncomfortable, being a redhead,' he mused. 'That luscious complexion doesn't let you keep any secrets.'

Chelsea was re-tying the straps and trying to ignore his watchful eyes.

'It's sweet of you to concern yourself about me, by the way,' he said, and tossed the magazine aside. 'Actually, I don't consider this work. I wondered once if I was a workaholic, but since I don't enjoy anything else as much as I like my job, I decided I must not be.' He looked at her, bright-eyed. 'But why do you ask? Do you have some other form of entertainment in mind?'

'Only swimming,' Chelsea retorted. She plunged into the pool and was halfway across when he broke the surface of the water right beside her.

He shook the water out of his and said, 'Want to play hide and seek? You can be IT.'

'In a pool this size? There's nowhere to hide.'

'That's why I want to play.' He grinned. 'You could at least say thank you. I saved you a nasty burn.'

'Thanks.' Chelsea started for the side of the pool.

'That wasn't quite the sort of appreciation I had in mind.' He came after her, his powerful stroke making her look helpless in the water.

'Oh? What did you mean?' Chelsea asked warily, treading water and trying to stay away from him.

'This might do,' he said softly. Then, suddenly, his arms were around her, her body was held firmly against his, and the warmth of his skin scorched her. 'Just a nice kiss,' he whispered.

'One kiss?' Chelsea was feeling slightly breathless. You're a little old for games in the swimming pool, she told herself, and then thought, what harm can it do? Play along, Chelsea—one kiss and then you can laugh the whole thing off. Fight him, and he'll keep bothering you.

He nodded solemnly, and then there was no more choice, for his mouth was warm and firm on hers. The combination of sensual stimuli—the burning pressure of his kiss, the slickness of the cool water as it lapped against her body, the heat of his skin and the tautness of his muscles under her hands—made her almost dizzy.

She was helpless in his arms, and the warmth of his skin seemed to burn through the nylon wisps of her swimsuit. I might as well be naked, she thought with the last thread of sense, and gave herself up to the pleasure of his embrace.

His hands were restless, exploring her body, stroking the delicate skin. His fingers struggled briefly with the wet ties of her bikini top, and then her breasts were free as the swimsuit floated away.

Chelsea gasped, and stretched out a hand to retrieve the flimsy top. But Nick silenced her with a kiss and captured her reaching fingers in his. 'No,' he breathed against her lips. 'Don't be shy, Chelsea. Don't hide from me.'

She swallowed hard as his hand gently cupped her breast, his thumb toying with the taut nipple. The sensation that shot through her was like an electric shock.

My God, what are you doing, Chelsea? The

question echoed through her mind, and she felt for a moment as if she had screamed it. She didn't even like this man, and yet she was allowing him to kiss her, and touch her, and play with her . . .

In sudden panic she pulled away and struck out for the edge of the pool.

Nick was only seconds behind her, pulling himself from the water before she had even collected her thoughts. Before she had taken two steps towards the house, he reached out for her. Her breasts were crushed against his chest and his hands rested on the curve of her hips as he held her close against him. 'I have to agree,' he said softly, and his lips brushed her wet cheek. 'The pool is fine for playing, but when it comes to serious lovemaking . . .'

Chelsea could barely breathe. 'You heel,' she spluttered. 'You low-down, rotten scum! Let me go!'

Nick tightened his grip. 'What's happened, Chelsea?' he asked, his voice taut. 'You were with me every step of the way. You wanted me just as much as I want you.'

'That's not true,' she denied hotly.

He raised a doubting eyebrow. 'Shall we test the theory?' he asked, and bent his head to kiss her again.

Chelsea tried to wriggle out of his arms, and succeeded only in arousing him further. 'You adorable, changeable little redhead,' he said. 'How I look forward to taming you!'

She gathered every ounce of strength she possessed and shoved him away. He lost his balance on the brink of the pool and tumbled in. Chelsea didn't stay to savour her triumph; she fled towards the house.

Confusion and relief were warring in her head as she reached her room and closed the door gratefully behind her. She sank on to the bench in front of her dressing table and stared at herself in the mirror.

'What is the matter with you, Chelsea Ryan?' she asked aloud.

'Damned if I know,' came a tart voice from the door.

She wheeled around, flinging up an arm to cover her bare breasts. 'Get out of here! Can't you even act like a gentleman?'

Nick leaned insolently against the door jamb. 'I was just informed that I'm a heel,' he told her. 'So I don't feel obligated to follow the gentleman's code.' He held up the dripping top of her swimsuit. 'I thought you might like to have this back, by the way.'

'Give it to me.'

'Why don't you come and get it?' he invited.

She stared at him for a long moment. The brief dark blue trunks hid little of his long tanned body as he stood there, the dark mat of hair on his chest still beaded with water. He was silently and defiantly male as he leaned against the door, arms folded, the scrap of green nylon dangling from his hand.

'Burke must be quite a guy,' he speculated. 'Or else, if I'm right about him, you're afraid to try your luck with a real man. I don't understand you, Chelsea. I have just as much power in the firm as Burke does. And I'm much younger and a whole lot more fun in bed.'

'You have a lot of confidence in yourself, don't you?' she jibed.

'I'd be delighted to let you form your own opinion,' Nick said silkily.

'I have no intention of finding out what you're like in bed. Ever.'

'You'd better be careful about making sweeping statements like that, Chelsea,' Nick mused. 'It tempts a man so.'

'Give me my swimsuit and go away,' Chelsea ordered.

Nick held up the swimsuit top and inspected it. 'I don't think I'll give it back after all,' he mused. 'Just a little souvenir of Norah Springs . . . You wouldn't deny me that much, would you? I'll treasure it forever.' He tucked the scrap of fabric into the band of his trunks as if it was a scalp, waved a gentle hand, and vanished down the hall.

'I think it would be wonderful if the new civic centre had a bell tower.'

'A bell tower? Whatever are you thinking of, Elise?'

'I've seen them,' Elise Bradley defended her idea. 'They're lovely, really they are, with the bells pealing out over the city. It's a wonderful memorial.'

Chelsea tried to suppress a shudder, and said a silent prayer of thanks that George Bradley, and not Elise, was the one donating the civic centre to Norah Springs.

'So if you want a bell tower in your memory, leave the money in your will,' the other woman said bluntly. 'Bells on the civic centre! The idea, Elise!'

Chelsea finished her martini and set the glass aside. This had not been a good idea, she thought moodily; George should have had better sense than to turn the design of his civic centre over to a committee. If they actually incorporated all the suggestions that she had heard tonight, the place would look like a Rube Goldberg invention. And if they didn't, there would be a war in Norah Springs.

There was no point in her even being at the party anyway, she thought crossly. It would be Nick's project from start to finish; why should she even be involved in it? After the events of this afternoon, she would certainly have no influence on Nick.

But Chelsea was still caught in the crossfire. She smiled at another member of George's committee, and listened politely to yet another set of ideas, nodding once in a while. Then she looked up and found Nick's eyes resting on her from across the room. She felt suddenly very exposed in the backless black dress, and she turned away quickly and said something to the committee member that had nothing to do with his question.

Damn Nick Stanton anyway, she thought defiantly as she sipped another martini. All he had to do was look at her and she was uncomfortably aware that he knew precisely what she looked like without that basic black dress. She'd have worn something less revealing, except that her mother would have been disappointed if Chelsea had turned down the new dress. And, to tell the truth, she admitted, it wouldn't have made any difference what she was wearing. Nick would still have looked through it, as he was doing right now, making her feel absolutely naked in the middle of a crowd.

'You look as if a breath of fresh air would do you good.' The committee member had moved off and Nick appeared beside her.

'I don't want fresh air.'

'But I do.' His hand rested gently on the small of her back, seeming to burn an imprint on the bare skin. 'So let's go have a professional chat.'

'Strictly professional?'

'Cross my heart.'

'Well, I don't believe you. I think I'll stay right here.'

Nick shrugged. 'Have it your way. Do you know how beautiful you are tonight, by the way?'

'Yes. My mother told me.'

'Mothers don't count,' he said softly.

'I thought this was going to be a professional chat.'

'It would have been if you'd come outside. But since you decided to stay here . . .'

'You're going to tease me.' Chelsea tried to keep her voice steady.

'Oh, I'm not teasing. I believe every word I'm saying. You deserve to be told how beautiful you are out on the patio, in the moonlight, by your lover . . .'

'If I get desperate, I'll let you know.'

'You do that, darling,' he suggested, and his voice was a sensual caress. 'I'll be there.'

'Don't hold your breath, Nick.'

'Let me know when you change your mind, Chelsea.' He brushed a gentle finger down one tendril of auburn hair, and somehow the simple gesture became charged with sexuality. 'Remember that I never give up. I'll just keep rewriting the rules till you find a set you like, and eventually, you'll give in. You know it as well as I do.'

CHAPTER EIGHT

THE city sparkled under the afternoon sun, but Chelsea could almost see the heat waves bearing down on the concrete ten storeys below her office window. And some seventh sense deep inside her could feel the vibrations of the building as the cooling system struggled to keep the inside temperature down.

It is so early in the summer for it to be so hot, she thought moodily as she pushed the weight of her auburn hair up off her neck. Even air conditioning can't really fight the heat. She thought longingly of Norah Springs, of the shaded gallery, and a tall glass of freshly-squeezed lemonade . . . or the cool water in the pool . . .

She pushed her chair back from the desk with a motion so violent that it almost tipped over. Her face was flaming with the very memory of that pool as she strode across the room and stared out over the city.

'You're trying to hide, Chelsea,' she told herself glumly.

It had been three days since she and Nick had come back from Norah Springs, three days packed with hard work as they struggled with designs for the Jonas Building. The long, lazy weekend might have never been. She was just as overworked and exhausted now as she had been before the brief vacation.

Nick was a slave-driver, she thought, and then conceded that she too had been pushing hard on the project. She was in a hurry to have it done; there were too many other things to do . . .

'That's not true,' she told herself slowly. There was always other work waiting, but that wasn't why she was devoting so many hours to the Jonas Building.

She was pushing herself because she wanted to do her best work for Nick, to impress him with her ability.

What was happening to her? She was so confused that she didn't even know what she wanted any more. She did know that she wanted more from life than this unending race from project to project. She was tired of working from early morning till late at night, and then returning to an apartment where the only evidence of another human being was Judy's clothes scattered over the furniture. There was not so much as a goldfish that depended on her, that cared what happened to Chelsea Ryan.

There had to be more to life than that. Surely somewhere in the world was a person with whom she could share her life. There was such a thing as lasting, romantic marriage—her parents had found it, and Burke and Helen Marshall. Surely, somewhere, there was a man for her.

And you're least likely to find him when you're looking so hard, she scolded herself. It would be better by far to be alone than to be trapped in a loveless marriage, to be like Janice at the reunion who was married for the second time and already looking for a way out. No, that was far from what Chelsea wanted.

'You need a real vacation,' she told herself. Three days in Norah Springs had left her with only a taste of peace and quiet and relaxation, not enough to do any good. Perhaps if she could get away from everything for a while, she could regain her sense of humour. Away from the office, and the work piled high . . . away from Nick . . .

Was Nick what she wanted? The question seemed to echo deep in her mind. 'Don't be silly,' she told herself firmly, but the question wouldn't go away. What had happened to her there in the pool was unlike anything Chelsea had ever felt before. She had been no prude, even in high school, but never had she allowed herself to be so abandoned, so . . . She put her hands to her hot cheeks, and tried not to think about Nick.

Nick——! The weekend might have never happened to him, either, from the way he had behaved since their return. He was polite, but preoccupied, and Chelsea was confused. He'd almost ignored her for the last few days. Had she, after all, only imagined those stunningly sensual moments in the pool?

'Well, I know I didn't imagine that threat at the cocktail party,' she told herself aloud. He had told her in no uncertain terms that he would continue to make passes at her until she gave in. But he hadn't. In the last three days he'd done nothing that wasn't exactly what she would expect from an employer . . .

And she was disappointed.

Chelsea's eyes widened in shock as the realisation hit her, and she groped for support, her hand clenching on the back of her chair. She dropped weakly into it.

She was disappointed that he had become the perfect gentleman. She had been enjoying the innuendo, the subtle teasing, the sensual byplay . . .

He had set a trap for her, and she had almost fallen into it, she realised. Anger swept over her. The sudden change in his behaviour had kept her off balance, made her wonder if she really did want him after all. And he had planned it that way, had schemed and plotted and probably enjoyed watching her confusion. He was waiting for her to come back and beg him to pay attention to her again!

Well, he would pay for that insolence, she was determined. And as she thought about it, a little smile crossed her face, and the big green eyes sparkled. She drew a wicked little sketch on a bit of scatch paper—Nick, wearing an explorer's pith helmet, sitting in a big iron pot, up to his neck in steaming water.

She shredded the drawing and hid it at the bottom of her wastebasket, and made a promise to herself. If

Nick Stanton thought he was going to have it all his own way, he would soon find out differently.

'May I come in, Chelsea?'

'Hi, Burke.' She looked up from the drawing board, feeling almost disappointed to see him. Surely sometime today Nick had to show up. She didn't want to go in search of him; it would fit much better into her plans if he came to her.

'Do you have the house plans here?' Burke closed her office door behind him. 'Helen and I were talking about it last night.'

Chelsea reached into the bottom drawer of her desk. 'They're pretty rough so far,' she warned, and handed him the roll of paper. 'How is Helen feeling?'

'Fair, these days. She misses you, by the way.'

Chelsea groaned. 'I know, Burke. I promise, I'll get out to see her this weekend.'

'Sorry. I didn't mean to make you feel guilty, Chelsea. Helen knows you're busy.' He spread the drawings out on the board.

'Do you have a site in mind?' Chelsea asked, leaning over his shoulder to help hold the drawings down.

'It will have to be almost perfectly level, won't it?'

'Not really. The design is adaptable. Is she seriously thinking about giving up Hillhaven now?'

He nodded. 'It's increasingly harder for her to move around. Helen's no fool.'

Chelsea bit her lip. 'How long does she have?' she asked quietly. 'Before she can't walk at all, I mean.'

There was a tap at the door, and Nick put his head in just as Burke said, 'I think the doctors were generous when they said six months, Chelsea She's getting weaker by the day.'

'Sorry to interrupt this important conference,' Nick said. His tone was cheery, but his eyes snapped as they rested on Chelsea, who was still leaning over Burke's shoulder 'Will you be able to see me a little later?'

'Come back in half an hour,' Chelsea said.

Nick didn't take the hint. He came across the room. 'New project, Burke?'

'Just a . . .'

Chelsea firmly cut across the sentence. 'Nothing important, Nick.' Her quelling look silenced Burke, and she rolled the plans up again so that Nick couldn't get a look at them.

He looked through her. 'I'll see you in thrity minutes, Chelsea.'

The door hadn't completely closed behind him when Burke leaned back in his chair, tented his fingers together, and said, 'What's up, Chelsea? Why didn't you want Nick to see the house plans?'

'Because the house doesn't have anything to do with the office, that's why. It's strictly a free-lance project, and it's none of his business.'

Burke looked thoughtful, but he didn't push the matter.

Chelsea didn't give him a chance to ask more questions. She spread the plans out again and picked up a pencil. 'I just took a guess on size. I don't imagine Helen will be entertaining as much.'

'That's a safe bet.' He studied the drawings. 'The kitchen looks really strange.'

'I know. But it follows the best advice available. They took a bunch of architecture students at one of the universities and put them in wheelchairs for a week. It drove them crazy, but at the end of the week they had come up with the handicap-free kitchen. This is it, with a few modifications of my own.'

'Hmmm. Want to bring these over this weekend and talk to Helen?'

'You can take them with you if you like.'

'I'd rather you came over.' Burke let the drawings curl up into a loose roll. 'You can do a better sales job than I could.'

'Burke . . .' Chelsea's voice was hesitant. 'If Helen is going downhill so rapidly . . .'

'What, Chelsea?'

'Can we even have the house built in time?'

'We can hurry it along, and by the time she's confined to the wheelchair . . .'

'That wasn't what I meant, Burke.' Chelsea's voice was gentle. 'This is a progressive disease, and it isn't just crippling. It's a killer.'

He sighed heavily. 'I know. It may just be another worry to her, and pointless in the end. But it might also give her a new interest, something to look forward to. I think Helen has to make the choice.'

'You're right, of course.' Chelsea put the drawings away. 'I'll come this weekend.'

'How was your holiday? I've barely seen you since you came back.'

'Norah Springs was wonderful. Since then, we've been working on the Jonas Building. It's soaking up all my time.'

'That's what I heard. Stanton and Ryan, together again.'

Chelsea's heart did a strange little flip-flop.

'You really ought to stop fighting with the man, you know, Chelsea. Everybody who has seen the Sullivan house agrees that you do better work together than either of you can alone.'

'I know.' Her tone was sarcastic. 'It's one of the seven wonders of the world.'

This time Nick didn't bother to tap on the door. When he came in, Chelsea lost her temper. 'Dammit, Nick, would you learn to knock?' she snapped.

'I did make an appointment,' he pointed out. But his expression dared her to remember another time, and another door, and Chelsea fought to keep herself from blushing at the memory of sitting in her bedroom in half a swimsuit with Nick lounging in the doorway and enjoying the view. She found herself wondering just what he had done with the top of her bikini.

Burke stood up. 'I'll leave you to your work. See you this weekend, then, Chelsea.'

'Saturday afternoon?'

'That would be fine.'

Nick waited till the door had clicked shut. 'So you're making dates. I always thought the chief advantage of affairs was that you never had to plan ahead.' He frowned. 'Or is it the other way round?'

'Do you really care?'

'No. I'm sure you understand all the fine details, and that's all that is necessary.'

'Then shall we get to work?'

'Certainly. What in the hell is this?' He was leaning over her drawing board.

'It's a bathroom. You've probably drawn a few in your day.'

'Not like this one. It looks more like a massage parlour. Where are the specs?'

'Oh, come on, Nick. I'm not even finished designing it yet and you want specifications?'

'You have them somewhere or you couldn't draw the darn thing.' He snapped his fingers. 'Hand them over, Chelsea.'

Reluctantly, she did. He scanned the pamphlet and looked up in shock. 'You're putting in contoured bathtubs? What's wrong with the old kind, for heaven's sake?'

'From you, of all people, I expected a little creativity,' Chelsea snapped. 'A standard bathtub is dangerous and uncomfortable.'

'Also cheap,' Nick pointed out.

'Which the condos in the Jonas Building are certainly not going to be, so why not put in a safe tub? Five hundred dollars more for a comfortable one . . .'

'Per tub?'

'Yes,' she admitted.

'Times a hundred bathrooms makes fifty thousand dollars. We could build another whole unit for that.'

'We could not. And we don't need a hundred, anyway. I'm standing firm, Nick. I'm tired of building bathrooms for the convenience of the plumber, instead of the owner. The tub is contoured for proper support of the spine . . .'

Nick grunted. 'You take a lot of bubble baths, don't you?'

'Yes.' Chelsea refused to be disturbed. 'And so do a lot of other people. Taking a bath should be a sensual experience.'

He grinned suddenly. 'In that case, let's put in bathtubs built for two!'

Chelsea fought the blush, and lost. 'Whirlpools are standard in those tubs. That's included in the price.'

'I'm charmed.' He didn't sound it. 'While we're talking about surprises in store for the new owner, I'm sure you have done something to the all-American shower.'

'Nothing.'

He quirked an eyebrow. 'A bit discriminatory, aren't you?'

Chelsea gave in. 'All right. But all I did was add an extra shower head, lower, so you don't have to get your hair wet if you don't want. And . . .'

'Where do you plan to cut back expenses to balance these extravagances?'

Chelsea lost her temper. 'Obviously you've never shared a bathroom in a modern apartment block or you wouldn't call six extra square feet an extravagance!'

'Does Burke take up a lot of room?' he asked interestedly.

Chelsea bit her tongue, clenched her fists, counted to ten, and still wanted to hit him. Then she remembered the plans she had made earlier in the afternoon, and slowly she relaxed her grip and smiled, a sweet, charitable smile. 'You asked me to design the condos,' she reminded him. 'If you've changed your mind . . .'

'Oh, of course not. You're the expert, after all.' He walked slowly across the room towards her, and stopped just inches away. His voice was a slow caress as he said, 'I'd love to have you teach me all you know about . . . everything. Tell me, Chelsea, have you changed your mind?'

'Are you asking me about the condos or the affair?' she asked tartly.

'Affair?' he asked innocently. 'I'm sorry to disappoint you, Chelsea, but I never discuss intimate matters like that in the office. If you'd like to have dinner with me tonight, though . . .'

She didn't look up at him; she was afraid if she did he would see the gleam of amusement in her eyes. So she kept her gaze demurely downcast and said, letting just a wisp of uncertainty creep through, 'Perhaps we should get this all straightened out, Nick. The Sullivans are coming in at six to talk about their house plans, but after that we could go somewhere quiet. What about Top of the Tower? Shall I call for reservations?'

He looked suspicious. 'Are we suitably dressed?'

'As long as you wear a jacket they'll let you in. But if you'd like to change clothes, you can pick me up at home on your way.' She raised innocent green eyes to his.

'I don't trust you as far as I can throw you, Chelsea Ryan. I'll make the reservations.'

'Why, Mr Stanton, I'm shocked that you'd say such a thing to a lady.'

'As a matter of fact,' he smiled suddenly, 'I wouldn't. But then, you aren't a lady. What about the rest of the condos? Is there anything else we need to argue about?'

* * *

The Top of the Tower was the best-known restaurant in the city, located in one of the classic old hotels. Strictly speaking, the restaurant was not the top, because the penthouses were above it, and at ten stories, it scarcely qualified as a tower. But the name had stuck.

And, what was far more important to Chelsea, the place had a reputation for serving the best food at the most prohibitive price in the entire state. It was the ideal opening gun in her campaign to get even with Nick Stanton.

She adjusted the spaghetti strap of her midnight blue dinner dress and looked down at Judy, who was curled up on the couch, with a frown.

'Sorry about the summer cold,' Judy said, and sneezed. 'Believe me, it doesn't fit into my plans any better than it does yours. I just hope I can shake it before the weekend. I don't want to meet Jim's aunt and uncle with a red nose and watery eyes.'

'They'll love you,' Chelsea said automatically. 'But make sure you disappear into your room by the time we get back.'

'Oh, I will. I think you're crazy, Chels, and I want nothing to do with this escapade. I'm actually sorry I didn't go to work.' She watched Chelsea step into the highest-heeled shoes in her closet. 'Make sure you take your charge card.'

'Why on earth should I?'

'Because if your plans go wrong and you get stuck with the bill, it would take years to wash enough dishes to pay it off,' Judy warned.

'I'll just call you to rescue me.'

'Don't bother. I don't get paid till tomorrow, and right now I don't have a dime.' Judy scooped up her blanket and box of tissues. 'I shall now retire until after Sir Galahad has swept you off.'

'I think you have the wrong knight.'

'Perhaps, but I know you do. You are going to regret this stunt.'

Chelsea shrugged. 'I might. But Nick Stanton certainly will, and that's perfectly good enough for me.'

'Why don't you stay home and we'll mix up an oatmeal facial and catch up on the gossip? I haven't talked to you since I went on the afternoon shift.'

Chelsea just shook her head. 'No. I'm determined to do this.'

The doorbell rang just as Judy disappeared down the hall into her bedroom, and Chelsea took a deep breath and crossed the living room to answer it.

You're going to get along with him tonight if it kills you, Chelsea, she reminded herself firmly. At least till the end of the evening. And then——!

She flirted with him throughout dinner. At first she felt self-conscious and a tiny bit guilty, but after a few moments of wary surprise, Nick seemed happy enough to play along. Chelsea ate her steak and lobster with delighted unconcern for what the bill would total. To Nick's credit, he didn't seemed worried either. He merely kept her wine glass filled and the conversation going on one light topic after another.

The only time it got serious was when Chelsea brought up the Sullivans. 'I didn't think they were going to accept the house,' she said. 'There was a moment when Doris was explaining why none of their friends liked it, and I thought she was going to turn it down altogether.'

Nick shrugged. 'They're pretty conventional people. And you have to admit that's a very unconventional house.'

Chelsea dug the last bite of meat out of her lobster tail. 'But it's so beautiful.'

He shook his head. 'To people like the Sullivans, it isn't a matter of beauty. That house is simply outside their ability to understand.'

'To say nothing of the difficulty with her brother. I told you that man thought he was an expert. I still can't believe he told them they ought to stick to a ranch-style for the resale value!' She shook her head in disbelief.

'You did a marvellous job convincing them to go ahead, Chelsea.'

'I'm certain they'll love it, once it's built.'

'Perhaps. But even if they change their minds, we'll still build that house, Chelsea.'

The easy assumption that their partnership would continue caught at Chelsea's throat.

'Someone else will appreciate it,' Nick went on, 'probably far more than the Sullivans are capable of.'

'They are going to love it,' Chelsea said firmly. 'But let's stop being serious, Nick. This is a night for fun.'

'My thinking exactly.' He reached for her hand. 'Are you ready to go?'

Chelsea felt just a little breathless. 'Before dessert? The pineapple torte here is wonderful.'

'I have no doubt it is.' He was smiling, just a little, and for a moment Chelsea wondered uneasily if she ought to call the whole thing off. But the waiter brought the dessert trolley by just then, so she told herself firmly that nothing was wrong; she was still in perfect control of the situation. She toyed with her dessert for a long time before finally pushing the plate aside. 'It's late, Nick.'

'You finally noticed?' But there was an undercurrent of amusement in his voice.

'Coffee at my apartment?' she asked, trying to sound casual.

Nick didn't even look at her. 'If you like.' He paid the bill with no more than a glance, which disappointed Chelsea, and spent a great deal of time draping her shawl just right around her shoulders. By the time they reached his car, she was feeling uneasy again. The brush of his hands up her bare back had been far from casual.

The night sky was like velvet as it lay over the city.

Nick took the indirect route back to her apartment, through Forest Park, Chelsea let her head rest against the back of the seat and watched dreamily as they passed the lagoons and fountains left from the turn-of-the-century world's fair. If she half-closed her eyes, she thought, she could almost see the ladies with their long skirts and parasols and hear the bustle of the crowd as they waited to ride the enormous observation wheel.

She was almost reluctant to have the ride end, and her heart was pounding as she climbed the stairs with Nick beside her. When he took the key from her fingers to unlock the apartment door, she was trembling.

Now, she thought. Now all you have to do is let him make a fool of himself, and then laugh at him. And then Nick Stanton will never bother you again . . .

When she would have turned on a light, he caught her hand and pulled her tight against him. 'It's pleasant to be the seduced instead of the seducer, Chelsea,' he murmured, his voice a sensuous whisper. He found her lips in the darkness, and took his time about kissing her, gently at first, and then with a growing hunger.

This was the weak spot of her plan, she knew, but she had gambled everything on being able to resist the awesome magnetic pull of his charm. Besides, she thought, what had happened in the pool that day had been the exception. It had been coincidence, and it couldn't happen again.

She was quickly disillusioned. She could not hold out against him; she simply didn't have enough strength. Her body was instinctively answering his demands, wanting him, begging for more. Then panic took hold of her mind, screaming at her to break away from him, to release herself from his arms no matter what the cost.

She tore herself away from him, gasping for breath

and feeling as if she had ripped herself in two. She reached for the nearest support, bracing her hands on a small table to hold herself upright. If he touches me, she thought, I will be finished.

'Are you having a few last doubts?' Nick asked softly. 'If you'd like, Chelsea, we could always have another contest. That might help you make up your mind.'

'Contest?' she asked breathlessly. It was the only word that seemed to make sense to her whirling brain.

'Yes. If I win, you go to bed with me. If you win—but you wouldn't, would you, darling?' His voice was as intimate as a touch could have been. 'Even if you had to lose on purpose, you would lose. Because this is what you want——'

Her hand found the switch on the table lamp. Fury burned in her veins now, and she turned on him like a wildcat. 'You really think you're something special, don't you, Nicholas Stanton?'

Nick's body tensed, and Chelsea's anger gave way to raw fear. Thank God, she thought, that Judy was in the next room . . .

With an effort, he relaxed, and reached out to touch her cheek. Chelsea shivered under the gentle fingers. If he tries to kiss me again, she thought, I can't say no. It's crazy, but I couldn't refuse him anything right now.

The telephone rang almost under her hand, and she picked it up. Before she could say anything, a tense, frantic voice said, 'Chelsea?'

She said, slowly, 'Burke? What is it?'

'Helen's ill. I'm at the hospital—they say she's had a stroke, Chelsea. She asked for you.'

'Which hospital?'

He told her. 'She may not make it through the night.'

'I'll be right there, Burke.' She put the phone down and stood there for an instant, her fingers still clenched on it.

'It's always Burke, isn't it? It will always be Burke.' Nick's voice was quiet. 'I wish I understood why, Chelsea.'

She turned slowly. 'Well, this time it isn't Burke. It's Helen, and she may be dying.'

He stared at her for a long moment. Then his mouth twisted. 'So the mistress is going to join the deathwatch. Six months, I believe Burke said this afternoon. Perhaps you won't have to wait so long after all, Chelsea.' He turned on his heel. 'I'll be leaving now. I wouldn't want to delay you.'

'Nick, it isn't that . . .' Chelsea's voice trailed off. What point was there in trying to explain?

And at any rate, he was already gone.

Chelsea was late to work the next morning, and she felt like yesterday's leftovers after a night at the hospital. But at least Helen had hung on through the long hours, and it looked much more positive in the light of day.

Marie was looking particularly testy; she didn't even say good morning before telling Chelsea that Mr Stanton wanted to see her immediately.

Chelsea glanced at her watch and made a face. 'If I'm already two hours late, it can't hurt to have a cup of coffee, can it?' she asked, trying to sound unconcerned.

Marie gave her a sour look and turned back to her typewriter.

Chelsea took her time, straightening her hair, picking up the designs that she had been working on the previous afternoon. After all, she thought, that might be all Nick was looking for—but she wasn't convinced.

His secretary tapped on the heavy door and announced her. Chelsea followed the girl in, doing her best to look airily unconcerned.

Nick didn't bother to stand. He waved a hand

towards a chair and Chelsea sat down, straightening her white linen skirt.

'I brought the condo designs,' she said.

'Cut it out, Chelsea. You know damned well that you're not here to discuss condos.'

'Oh? Then what did you want to talk about?'

'Just what sort of game were you playing last night?'

Chelsea parried, 'I thought you never talked about things like that in the office.'

His eyes smouldered. 'That was yesterday, Chelsea, and now I want an answer. Were you planning to seduce me to cover up your affair with Burke, or just to see how big a fool I'd make of myself?'

She arched her foot and studied the curve of her instep in the high-heeled, strappy sandal. Then she looked up at him and said softly, 'I certainly had no plans to go to bed with you, Nick.'

He raised an eyebrow. 'And I played right into your hand, didn't I?' he said softly.

'It was rather amusing,' she agreed. Her voice was brittle.

'And yet, you weren't exactly untouched, my dear. Just how much longer do you think you'd have held out, if it hadn't been for Burke's call?'

About another thirty seconds, came the answer from the back of Chelsea's mind. She shrugged and tried to look unconcerned.

'How is Helen this morning, by the way?'

'Better. She's paralysed on one side—that may go away or it may last.'

'But she'll live.'

'Yes.'

'So you and Burke will have to wait after all. And I don't think you want to kick up a scandal right now.'

'What are you suggesting, Nick?' she asked coolly.

'That we have a little fun together in the meantime.'

'An affair?'

'That seems to be the standard terminology.'

'Why?' Chelsea asked baldly.

'I've grown fond of Helen in the last few weeks,' Nick said. His tone was casual, conversational. 'I'd like to do my part to make sure she dies in peace. If I'm in the picture, she certainly isn't going to be suspecting Burke.'

'How self-sacrificing of you.' Chelsea's voice was sweetly sarcastic.

'Oh, I think it will be worth my while. And I am still attracted to you.'

'Whoopee.'

'I know. Foolish of me, isn't it?'

'Are you certain you can afford me? I'm rather expensive.'

'Yes, I found that out last night. I think I can manage the price for a while.'

Chelsea held her temper with an effort. 'What if I don't . . . co-operate?'

'Carl Shelby will get a set of caricatures to hang on his office wall.'

She'd forgotten that he still had the drawings. Her throat was tight; it hurt to breathe.

'Funny,' Nick mused. 'I had them in the car last night. I was going to give them back to you.'

'We did have a bargain. The Jonas Building condos for the drawings. Remember?' Chelsea kept her voice steady with an effort.

'Of course I remember. But after last night, all deals are off.'

'You must be very desperate, Nick.' Chelsea stood up. 'I'm not interested. Do what you want with the drawings. Even if Shelby fires me, at least I'll be rid of you. But I warn you, Nick—don't bring Burke into it, or hurt Helen.'

She closed the door very quietly behind her and stood in the outer office for a moment. She wanted to run down the hall, or to burst into tears. But the secretary was there, and a client, reading a magazine as she waited. Lovely woman, Chelsea thought absently. Nick would like working with her; she was just his type. Dark and exotic, slim and elegant and probably very tall . . .

Nick's secretary looked up at Chelsea and then reached for the intercom button on her desk. 'Mr Stanton?' she said quietly. 'Mrs Stanton is here. Shall I show her in?'

CHAPTER NINE

CHELSEA'S first instinct was self-preservation. She ducked down the hall and was out of sight by the time Nick's office door opened. But she heard him say, 'Vanessa!' and the tone of his voice brought hot tears to her eyes.

What man wouldn't be delighted to have Vanessa Stanton waiting for him, she thought drearily. The woman was gorgeous—exquisite features, designer clothes . . .

And Nick was a lying, two-timing cheat! The fury that spread through her like a fever burned away the tears. He had a lot of nerve to accuse her of having an affair with Burke, when Nick himself was cheating on his wife.

But he didn't actually do anything immoral, Chelsea's conscience argued. She thought about that, and then shook her head. That didn't excuse Nick's behaviour, she told herself firmly. At the very least, he had been perfectly willing to start an affair with her, and in Chelsea's estimation, it added up to the same thing.

For that matter, she told herself forlornly, there probably were any number of other women in Nick's past. Stupid, she thought, to have imagined that there was something special about the chemistry between the two of them. Utterly stupid.

She had known perfectly well that women found Nick attractive. And vice-versa, too, she told herself cynically. So why was she so surprised that he had a wife?

But the grapevine hadn't known. She would swear that no one in the office knew he was married . . .

So the plans he'd given up for that holiday weekend

had included his wife. And when he couldn't spend the time with Vanessa, he had turned to Chelsea.

Her cheeks were burning by the time she reached the relative safety of her office. She closed the door firmly behind her and leaned against it with a sigh of relief. She wanted to barricade the furniture against the door and stay there, hidden in her burrow, forever. It would be easier if she never had to see him again . . .

'But you do have to face him,' she told herself firmly. 'And if you walk around the office looking like this, it will take about two minutes for the entire staff to know what happened.' The thought made her shudder. They no doubt knew about Vanessa already, and Chelsea would be just another titbit. The phony concern, the gossip behind her back—she could almost hear the vicious whispers now.

'Did you hear about Chelsea? She thought—the poor dear actually thought that Nick Stanton was serious about her. You should have SEEN her when she met his wife! . . .'

It would go on and on, passing from secretary to secretary, from department to department, until it would be impossible for Chelsea to hold up her head at Shelby Harris.

'I'll go home,' she said. Home to Norah Springs, and Mother, and that little office waiting for me . . .

But that would be no better. She might not have to listen to the gossip, but running away would not stop it. It might even fuel the fires of speculation.

'It must have been pretty serious if she ran away when his wife found out about them. I wonder if Nick paid her off. I wonder . . . I wonder . . .'

Chelsea shuddered. The gossip would be bad enough, but such an act would be professional suicide. She couldn't afford to leave Shelby Harris without giving notice and without any kind of reference. It would be hard enough to set up a practice in Norah Springs even if she had the firm's blessing and the recommendation of the partners. But the way it was, she would get no help at all to set up her own practice.

'I'm stuck,' Chelsea told herself fatalistically. 'I'm going to have to stay here and face it.'

No wonder all the experts preached that romance didn't belong in the office. The pain was too great for everyone when it didn't work out.

Of course, a little honesty would have helped, she thought. If Nick had just told her the truth, she would never have got into this mess. Then she jeered at herself. Silly, to expect honesty from a man who was determined to seduce her. If she hadn't been so innocent, she'd have suspected all along that he was married.

'You learned your lesson cheaply,' she told herself, keeping her voice firm. 'It didn't cost you anything but a lot of pride. So take the medicine and hide your hurt, and tomorrow will look brighter.'

It sounded good. She wondered unhappily if she could carry it out.

Her nerves were raw. She had managed to do a great deal of work in a couple of hours, but her hands were shaking and her concentration was gone. When Jim tapped on her door, Chelsea wanted to scream at him to stay out.

'Chelsea? I hate to question you, but . . .'

'What is it, Jim?'

He bit his lip. 'I know you're the architect and I'm only the draughtsman, but on these re-modelling plans that you gave me this morning . . .'

Get to the point, Jim, she wanted to yell. But she held on to the shreds of her sanity.

'Look at this, Chelsea. You knocked out a load-bearing wall, and you haven't reinforced it. The house will collapse if you actually do that.'

'Where?' He was right; she could scarcely believe herself that she had been so careless. 'Thanks, Jim.

I'm glad you spotted that.' Before it got to Nick, she thought. Nick would not have found the mistake humorous—or forgivable.

'Anytime. Hey, are you all right? You look really strange.'

'I'm sure some fresh air would do me good.' She finished off her cold coffee and set the crystal mug aside. 'I think I'll go out on the sites today.'

'Maybe it's just too much coffee. You've probably drunk a gallon of the stuff today.'

'Perhaps I have.' Chelsea didn't care.

'Have something to eat. That will help.'

She was, she found to her surprise, actually a little hungry. No sleep last night, no breakfast this morning . . . No wonder she felt so awful. 'I'll do that, Jim. Thanks for caring.'

'Sure, Chelsea.' He sounded a little surprised.

Watch your step, she warned herself, and left a note on Marie's desk to tell her that she'd be out for the afternoon. She was silently thankful that the woman had gone to lunch; Marie seldom missed anything.

One mistake like that one getting past Jim and on to Nick, and Chelsea wouldn't need to worry about serving out her notice. She'd be fired on the spot, she thought morosely as she followed her favourite waiter to one of the secluded booths that were so popular at Angelo's. Nick would probably be delighted to have an excuse to get rid of her.

And then I'd go back to Norah Springs with one more strike against me, she thought. She moodily nibbled on a breadstick, grateful for the secluded corner where no one in the restaurant could see her. Chelsea didn't think she could maintain her poise if any of the girls from the office happened to come in and join her.

She'd try to eat something, and then she'd go out to the sites. It had been a week since she'd checked on them, and an afternoon of fresh air, warmth, and solitude would do her good. Then when she had checked on all of her projects, she'd stop to see Helen at the hospital, and go home to catch up on her sleep.

That was why she had reacted so strongly to Vanessa Stanton, she told herself. It had nothing to do with Nick, at all, it was simply hunger and lack of sleep. Feeling a little better about herself, she munched another breadstick.

'It's a cute place, Nicky, but the calories . . .' The low-pitched, sexy voice from the next booth caught Chelsea's attention. 'I didn't know you were into Italian food.'

'One of my colleagues recommended it.'

Nicky? Chelsea thought. The waiter put a plate of fettucini before her, and she stared at it silently. So she was a colleague now, was she? What else did you expect, Chelsea? she asked herself sarcastically. He wouldn't be likely to say, I brought a girl from the office here and tried to seduce her.

Nick continued, his voice clipped, 'It wouldn't hurt you to put on a few pounds, Vanessa.'

'The camera sees every ounce, Nick. I can't model if I'm fat.'

'You? That would be a joke if we weren't talking about a life being at stake here.'

'Oh, come on, Nick! It's not alive, it's hardly even a lump of protoplasm yet. Would you come down out of the pulpit now? You told me yourself two years ago that you thought I'd make a terrible mother.'

'That's absolutely true.' Nick's voice was dry. 'I did say that.'

'Now all of a sudden you're saying I should keep the baby. Come on, Nick, be reasonable.'

'Abortion isn't a reasonable alternative, Vanessa.'

'So what am I supposed to do? If I go through with this pregnancy, I'll be out of work for nearly a year. By that time the style could change, and I might never be able to work again, Nick. A cover girl doesn't have a long career expectancy, you know, even without taking time off to have a baby.'

'I know.' Nick's voice was cold. 'But there are other people involved in this decision.'

'I don't see why. It's my body, and I want an abortion.'

Chelsea pushed the fettucini around on her plate and searched desperately for a way to avoid hearing this conversation. She couldn't just walk out; it was impossible to reach the entrance without Nick and Vanessa seeing her.

Vanessa said, 'You make sacrifices for your career, too, Nick. My God, you live in St Louis—that ought to be sacrifice enough for anyone.'

'The things you give up are entirely your choice, Vanessa. It's no one's business but yours if you stop eating pastry and chocolate bars. But it seems to me that the one doing all the serious sacrificing here is an innocent baby.'

'God, Nick, would you stop calling it a baby? You make it sound like I'm smothering some cute little bundle in a cradle!'

Chelsea gestured to the waiter. 'I'd like my bill, please,' she told him.

He looked horrified. 'But Miss! You have eaten nothing! Nothing!'

'I know. Just bring me the bill.' I can't take any more of this conversation, she thought.

Nick's quiet voice broke through her determination not to hear. 'I do have more than an abstract interest in this particular baby, Vanessa.'

Chelsea could take no more. She slid out of the booth and met her waiter halfway to the kitchen. 'Here,' she said, and thrust a twenty-dollar note into his hand. 'Keep the change. Is there a back entrance to this place?'

He looked down at the money in his hand, and Chelsea could almost see his brain working as he calculated the percentage of his tip. Then he looked up at her with a wink. 'Miss is avoiding someone?' he asked with a broad smile.

'Miss is certainly trying to,' Chelsea retorted.

'This way,' he said, gesturing confidentially, and turned to lead her through the kitchen.

Sorry, Angelo, she thought as she ducked her head to avoid the curious gazes of the aproned cooks, but I won't be coming back. I still love the food, but after today the atmosphere will never be the same.

The early heat wave had broken, and the day was as perfect as June could make it. The construction workers were making the most of the pleasant weather; most of them were stripped to the waist as they climbed like monkeys over the rapidly-growing framework of the house. The sharp scent of freshly-sawed wood, the piercing roar of the power tools, the rhythmic banging of the hammers tugged at Chelsea's senses as she parked the Mercedes at the curb and reached for her low heeled shoes.

Funny, she thought, how a house could look so big in the drawings, and then so very cramped when the site was staked out. But now, as the framework grew, the house would seem to expand again. It was one of the small joys that kept her fascinated with building houses.

The foreman saw her coming. 'Hi, Chelsea. Grab yourself a hard hat and come on in.'

She tucked the auburn waves of her hair up under the bright yellow plastic helmet and followed him in, ducking through the doorway. 'It's going fast,' she observed. She'd staked this house out only a few weeks ago.

He grinned and wiped a gloved hand across his brow to mop away the perspiration. 'We're in a hurry for the topping-off party.'

Chelsea's experienced eyes summed up the work. 'About another week to finish the framing, right?'

'Something like that. The owner's already talking change orders on the interior, by the way. He was out this morning with all kinds of grand ideas. I told him to call you.'

'What sort of changes?'

'Oh, the wife has decided she'd rather have casement windows. And the bathroom looked too small. I told him it was a bit late to do anything about that. That's the problem with amateurs, Chelsea.'

'I know. But what other kind of clients do I get?' She gave him a innocent smile. 'Everybody likes the houses I design so well that they never want to move again.'

The foreman groaned. 'Come on, Chelsea! We all know you're good, but that's spreading it on too thick.'

Chelsea shrugged. 'If no one else will say nice things about me, I'll have to do it myself.'

'Don't give me that garbage. I wasn't born yesterday. Hey, since you're here—will you interpret some drawings for me?'

It took the better part of an hour to straighten out all the details, and to answer all the questions that had popped up since her last visit. By the time she pulled the Mercedes back into traffic, Chelsea felt a little better. The concentration on the job she really loved, instead of on the office-bound paperwork that was so necessary, had brightened her outlook.

The next house was beautiful from the street. If it wasn't for the look of horrible emptiness conveyed by bare windows and scraps of wood scattered around the unfinished lawn, it would almost have looked complete. Only an electrician was at work, whistling out of tune as he installed light fixtures in the kitchen. Chelsea inspected the work, made a mental note to call the owner, and found the electrician taking a coffee break.

'We're ahead of schedule,' she said, leaning against the kitchen counter.

He nodded. 'Feels good for a change. Want a cup of coffee?'

Chelsea shook her head. 'Where are the rest of the guys today?'

'The contractor pulled them off here to start another job.'

Chelsea frowned. 'That's just great. When does he plan to finish this one?'

The electrician shrugged. 'You know how some of these big shots are sometimes. Unless they're running from job to job they don't think they're making any progress. He left some bills over there for you to approve.'

Chelsea looked at the bills, dog-eared and grimy from being moved around the construction site. She signed three of them, and left a note on the fourth that she'd be delighted to approve it except that the work it covered hadn't been done yet.

She still had trouble with contractors sometimes, she reflected. Some of them thought that because she was a woman they could get by with half-done jobs, or poor workmanship, or shoddy construction.

She wondered idly if Nick might have some suggestions for convincing the contractors that there were no short cuts with her. And then anger rose in her again as she remembered what Nick still thought of her, even after all this time—that she had won her present position by sleeping with Burke Marshall.

The contractors, Nick—all of them assumed that a woman architect had to be incompetent. It wasn't very smart of them, actually, to jump to that conclusion. After all, Chelsea had passed the same exams as any man to get her licence. In fact, she'd always thought her education was worth more than that of most of the men she'd gone to school with. She'd had to work ten times harder to convince her professors that she really wanted to be an architect, that she hadn't chosen the profession because—as the rare woman in the field—she could have a larger choice of men.

Men! They all thought alike, and Chelsea was tired of listening to them. Maybe we should start our own company, she thought. There were some good women carpenters around. A plumber here and there, an electrician ... A construction company composed entirely of women. Why not? They'd probably pay much better attention to details, she thought.

She glanced at her watch. Better stop playing with ideas and get to the hospital, she told herself. She hadn't talked to Burke all day.

But she found herself driving along the side streets instead, down the winding lanes of the suburb where the Sullivans had bought their land. There was nothing to be done there yet; she had talked them into continuing with the planning process, but until final plans were drawn and accepted there would be no work to be done at the site.

But Chelsea found herself parking the Mercedes at the corner of the lot anyway. She walked back over the hillside, kicking at the sticks and bits of debris that lay over the untended ground, visualising the house as it would appear. It would be fun to build that one, she thought.

The Sullivans were crazy if they didn't jump at the chance to build Nick's design. The sheer beauty of it brought a lump to Chelsea's throat as she thought about the house clinging to the steep hillside. But the Sullivans were conventional people, and they didn't see the sculptured beauty. They only saw that the house was different from everyone else's.

Funny, she thought, that at first they had wanted a male architect, and then when they got one, they didn't like his ideas.

Absently, Chelsea paced out the dimensions of the house. Right about here was where the kitchen would be, she thought, and stopped to stare out across the hillside at Doris Sullivan's view. She sat down on a little patch of grass under the sunlight that streamed through the trees, and relaxed. No one could find her here; no one knew where to look. There was great relief in knowing that no telephones could ring out here.

A songbird began to sing, and Chelsea tried to identify his call. But she couldn't place it. After years of city living, it was hard to remember the little she had learned in her childhood about birds. 'I hope Doris puts up a bird feeder at least,' she told herself idly. What a waste it would be, in surroundings like these, not to enjoy nature's bounty.

The scent of the earth and the new green grass tugged at her. Chelsea's fingers itched to dig into the warm soil, to pack it around fragile little plants and nurture them. 'You're just a country girl at heart,' she scolded herself lightly.

Then playful shrieks from the house next door drew her attention. Across the ravine, the little girl with the pigtails was playing with her puppy. They rolled over and over on the grass, then the child flung a stick and the dog, ears flying, romped after it.

I want that, Chelsea told herself suddenly. I want all that she represents—a husband, a home, a child . . .

It wasn't that she didn't like her job; she would never give it up. But it wasn't enough. Building houses for other people could never take the place of building a life for herself.

Sunlight poured down across the hillside in streaks and caught the child and the dog. They seemed to freeze into position in the pool of light for a long moment, then the dog barked and tore off across the lawn to greet a car as it pulled into the drive. The little girl followed, and when the car stopped, she flung herself into the arms of the man who stepped out.

'Daddy's home,' Chelsea murmured, and tears rose in her eyes.

And you, she scolded herself, are a sentimental fool, to let yourself be carried away by such nonsense. She rose briskly and brushed loose debris off her skirt. It was long past time to go to the hospital, and sitting here any longer could only lead her into dangerous thoughts.

Burke was in the lounge, his tie loose, his jacket tossed aside. His feet were propped up on a chair, and his eyes were closed. He looked every year of his age, today, Chelsea thought, and her heart ached for him. Helen was the dearest thing in his life, and he had no one to help him bear the pain.

He roused suddenly and smiled when he saw her. 'She's better, Chelsea.'

'I'm glad. Have you had some sleep?'

He avoided her eyes. 'Some. They've been letting me stay with her most of the time.'

'Well, I think it's time you got some genuine rest. I'll stay here for a few hours. You go home and sleep, and that's an order.'

'No. I'll be all right.' Burke stood up, yawning. 'It's time for me to go back in. She sleeps most of the time, but she likes to have a hand to hold.'

'Shall I come?'

'Will you? She'd love to see you.'

The intensive care unit was quiet, except for the machinery humming beside each patient. Helen's eyes were closed, but when Burke gently picked up her hand, careful not to disturb the intravenous lines, it seemed to Chelsea that Helen's fingers tightened ever so slightly around his.

It brought tears to Chelsea's eyes again. You have to quit this, she told herself impatiently, or you'll turn into a bowl of mush. I need some sleep, soon, or I'm going to be a zombie.

Burke settled himself in the chair next to the high

hospital bed. 'They make allowances for my age and infirmity,' he joked quietly. 'They usually don't put chairs in here because they don't encourage people to stay long.'

Chelsea folded her arms along the top rail of the bed and stared down at Helen. One corner of the woman's mouth seemed to have a tired droop to it. It was the side that had been affected by the stroke, Chelsea knew, and wondered just how bad the damage would turn out to be.

'Mr Marshall?' A white-uniformed nurse was at the door. 'There's a man here asking to see you. Mr Stanton, I believe he said.' She glanced at the clock and reached for the blood-pressure gauge. Chelsea moved out of her way.

'Nick. That's sweet of the boy,' Burke said. 'If you wouldn't mind, Chelsea—I'd rather just stay here. Would you tell him how much I appreciate his visit?'

Chelsea closed her eyes briefly and gathered all the arguments she could make. But the fact was, Burke was at his wife's bedside, and if he didn't want to leave, no one could force him. Besides, who knew what Nick might say? And if he said anything at all to Burke right now . . . Or if he'd brought Vanessa with him . . .

'I'll be right back,' she said.

Burke gave her a grateful smile. 'Take as long as you want.'

It will only take thirty seconds, Chelsea thought, to tell Nick Stanton what I think of him.

Nick was waiting in the corridor. He was alone, Chelsea saw with relief as she let the heavy door shut behind her.

'Burke asked me to thank you for coming,' she said coolly.

His dark blue eyes summed her up. 'So you're back, hovering beside the deathbed.'

'I told you this morning that with any luck, Helen won't die.'

'Now what makes you say that, I wonder? If you're trying to impress me, don't bother. Your charming devotion to a friend isn't quite convincing.'

'Really, Nick.' Chelsea kept her voice even with an effort. 'Just what would you do for entertainment if I wasn't here to vent your anger against?'

His eyes narrowed. 'Are friends allowed to visit?'

'No.'

'I'll send flowers.'

'Don't bother.' Then she tried to soften the statement. 'They're not allowed in the unit. As soon as she's moved to a room she can have them.'

'How did you manage to get in to see her?'

'Believe it or not, Helen thinks of me as a daughter.'

Nick started to laugh. 'How cosy!'

Chelsea saw red. He had a colossal nerve to say things like that to her, with Vanessa waiting for him in the lobby, or in the car, or at home . . . She held her temper with an effort. 'Let's not squabble in the hallway, for heaven's sake.'

'Where would you prefer to do it?'

'Nowhere at all.' She put a hand on the doorway. 'Goodbye, Nick.' It was quiet, and it felt very final. She hadn't told him how furious she was with him, Chelsea realised as she went back to Helen's room, but there would always be time for that.

Helen was awake and trying to swallow some clear broth when Chelsea returned to the little room.

'I'm making a mess of it,' she told Chelsea. The words were understandable, but muddled, and Helen closed her eyes tightly in frustration.

Chelsea thought, Don't give up, Helen. She squeezed the woman's hand and was rewarded by a brief half-smile and a renewed effort to eat. Admiration woke in her. With so many problems, Helen was continuing to fight. And she would overcome this, too.

The nurses finally overruled Burke and sent him

home to sleep. Chelsea stayed much later than she had planned, waiting for Helen to settle down for the night, and it was after midnight when she entered her own apartment.

Judy was pacing the floor. Her hair was in rollers and she was wearing the oversized nightshirt that was her favourite. 'Where have you been?' she demanded. 'I've nearly worn a hole in this carpet, waiting for you.'

Chelsea tossed her handbag on to the hall table. 'At the hospital.'

'Nick said he'd tried to reach you there.'

Chelsea shrugged. 'Perhaps I just didn't hear the page.'

'He wants you to call him, by the way.'

'Oh, he does? I wonder what the dear boy wants this time?' She flung herself down into a chair.

'Are you going to call him?'

'Perhaps.'

Judy just looked at her for a long time. 'Do you want to talk about it?'

'Not right now.'

'Just remember that I'll be gone this weekend. There's a package for you, by the way.' Judy went off down the hall to her bedroom.

Chelsea picked up the package, addressed in her mother's neat, careful hand. She cut the cord and out tumbled a yellow linen dress, tailored with tiny cap sleeves and a narrow belt. She found a note tucked into a fold.

'Stewart's was having a sale,' she read, 'and I thought this would look good on you. We loved having you at home, Chelsea. Come more often. And tell Nick that we enjoyed his visit too. Love, Mom.'

Chelsea shook out the dress and laid it aside. Darn her mother anyway, she thought. From a hundred miles away she could make Chelsea feel guilty. Tell Nick they'd enjoyed his visit, indeed! If she told Nick anything, it certainly wouldn't be that.

Why had Nick called? Chelsea sat there and stared at the telephone. Then, reluctantly, she picked it up. It was all her mother's fault, she thought glumly. Sara was the one who had raised Chelsea to always answer letters, write thank-you notes—and return telephone calls.

Nick's phone rang several times, and then a sleepy female voice answered.

She hadn't even thought about what she would do if Vanessa answered. It must have been only a couple of seconds, but to Chelsea it seemed forever before she heard herself ask, 'Is John there?'

'John?' Vanessa yawned, and then drawled, 'You've got the wrong number. And check it before you dial it again. Some of us are trying to sleep.'

'I'm sorry,' Chelsea said softly and cradled the phone. So Vanessa was in residence. Chelsea hadn't expected that. After the argument she had overheard at Angelo's, she would have thought Vanessa would be staying at a hotel.

They must have come to some agreement about the abortion, and Chelsea found herself wondering what it was. Had Vanessa yielded—with the great charm she undoubtedly possessed—and agreed to give Nick his child? Or had he reluctantly given in to that same charm and consented to allow the abortion?

'I wish I had Vanessa's choice,' Chelsea murmured, and then realised in shock what she had said. She sat down suddenly, hands pressed to her hot cheeks. If she had Vanessa's choice, it would be no choice at all.

'I would be delighted to have Nick's baby,' she said, and the words seemed to echo in the quiet room. 'How long,' she asked herself miserably, 'how long have I been in love with him?'

CHAPTER TEN

It was a long, lonely weekend. Judy and Jim left early Saturday morning for their visit to Jim's family, and Chelsea spent most of her time at the hospital. When she wasn't there, she was at home, sometimes listening to melancholy music on the stereo, sometimes mindlessly watching television, sometimes just sitting in the darkened rooms, thinking about Nick.

How had she let herself slip into this dreadful muddle? When had her loathing of some of his personal traits faded? When had respect for his skill as an architect evolved into love for the man?

If he'd only been honest with me, she thought, I wouldn't be in this spot. And then, with brutal truthfulness, she admitted that it wouldn't have mattered even if she'd known he was married. Knowing that he had a wife didn't relieve the awful longing in her heart. She still wanted him, whether or not Vanessa was in the way.

How had a man as intelligent as Nick allowed himself to get mixed up with Vanessa, anyway? She raged about that a little. The woman was heartbreakingly lovely, there was no doubt about that. But surely even someone who was infatuated with her beauty could see that there was no soul under that lovely shell, no warmth, no love.

'Come on, Chelsea,' she scolded herself, 'you're more than a bit prejudiced when it comes to the luscious Vanessa.' Perhaps Nick had truly loved the woman. Perhaps—she faced the most awful truth of all—perhaps he still did.

And with that thought dragging her down, she showered and dressed and went back to the hospital, to the only thing that could take her thoughts off Nick.

On Sunday morning they moved Helen to a side ward. The relief in the air was almost visible, and Burke and Chelsea did a quick dance step down the hall when they got the news. The nurses watched them indulgently.

'The therapist will come in tomorrow to start working with you, Mrs Marshall,' one of the nurses told Helen. 'We'll soon have you back on your feet.'

'Telling me that is something like the old joke, you know,' Helen answered weakly. 'The patient asks his doctor if he can dance after his injury heals, and the doctor says of course he can. And the patient says, "That's good, Doc, because I never could before!"' Her speech was improving, and her sense of humour with it. 'I haven't been so great at dancing lately, so I'll settle for ordinary walking.'

But the move wore her out, and she slept most of the day. Mid-afternoon she woke, watched Chelsea quietly for a while, and said, 'What's wrong, dear?'

Chelsea jumped. She had been lost in thought, expecting that Helen would sleep longer. She looked down at the newspaper that lay open on her knee. She'd started out to work the crossword puzzle, but there in the margin was a pencilled sketch of Nick's face. She folded it carefully inside the paper, and said quietly, 'I was just thinking about going back to Norah Springs.'

'A vacation? That would be nice, Chelsea. You need one.'

Chelsea shook her head. 'Not a vacation, Helen. To stay.'

There was utter silence in the room for a moment. Then Burke wheeled around from the window, where he'd been standing, and said, 'You're going to leave Shelby Harris?'

'I'm thinking about it.'

'Why, Chelsea?'

'And I want to try my own wings, Burke. Since I

didn't get the partnership, I think I'll go back to Norah Springs and set up my own practice.' She raised her chin a defiant half-inch.

'It's going to look as though you're a sore loser, Chelsea. You can't fool anyone with that story.'

Had he looked into her heart, Chelsea wondered uneasily.

'Everybody knows you've been deadly jealous of Nick since that partnership came open. Leaving now won't look good on your records, Chelsea.'

'Perhaps it won't,' she said quietly. 'But I really don't care what it looks like, Burke.'

Burke shook his head. 'You'll have to finish your commitments, Chelsea. The houses you still have on the drawing board, the civic centre up in Norah Springs . . .'

'I'll be right on top of that one,' Chelsea said sweetly.

Burke ignored the interruption. 'To say nothing of the Jonas Building.'

'If we win the contest.' Chelsea dismissed the Jonas Building with a wave of her hand.

'From what I've seen, I'd bet on you and Nick.'

She thought about her bet with Nick on the Sullivan house, and allowed herself a brief smile. 'It isn't wise to bet on rumour, Burke. Sometimes the advance sketches bear no resemblance to the finished product.'

'I have my sources,' Burke said stiffly.

'I know. But the deadline for submitting plans isn't till Tuesday. Something wonderful may come in at the last minute.'

'At any rate, whether you win the contest or not, you and Nick are a darned good team, Chelsea. Why do you want to break that up?'

She almost told him. But Burke, sympathetic soul that he was, tried so hard to make things better that he sometimes wasn't wise about his methods. Chelsea knew that if she told Burke why she was leaving, he would try to fix it all up. He'd probably call Nick in and talk to him, and try to straighten the whole mess out.

Chelsea shuddered. That would be the last unbearable straw. So long as Nick didn't know how hopelessly she had fallen in love with him, Chelsea could hold up her head. But if he ever found out——

She sidetracked that train of thought and tried a different approach with Burke. 'No matter when I leave, I'll have a dozen projects in the works,' she pointed out. 'There will never be a time when all my work is done.'

'That's true, but . . .'

'Are you suggesting, perhaps, that Nick isn't capable of taking over a few houses?' Her tone was sweetness itself.

As she had expected, Burke was instantly defensive. 'Of course not. He's the best there is. But——'

'Then I'll leave my work in good hands, won't I?'

A nurse tapped on the door and brought in an amber glass vase filled with yellow and white daisies. 'Mrs Marshall? One of your admirers discovered that you can have flowers now. My goodness, that young man is right on the ball.' She waved the flowers under Helen's nose, arranged them on the bedside table, and handed Chelsea the card with a flourish.

Chelsea tore the little envelope open. 'They're from Nick,' she announced.

'That's sweet of him,' Helen murmured and stretched out her good hand to caress a smooth petal. 'I wonder how he knew that daisies are my favourite.'

'He probably reads minds, along with all of his other superhuman traits,' Chelsea said.

Burke gave her a warning frown.

'If you're determined to move, Chelsea,' Helen said, 'at least we can relieve you of one project. I've decided I don't want to build the new house after all.'

'Helen, are you sure?' Burke asked. 'You haven't even seen the plans.'

She nodded. 'Yes, dear, I'm certain. I've loved Hillhaven for so many years that no other house would feel like home. How can I leave it now? We'll be able to manage, you'll see.'

It was what Chelsea had half-expected. 'Of course we can arrange it, Helen. That little den at the back of the house would work for your bedroom.'

'You don't mind, Chelsea?' Burke asked. 'I'm sorry about putting you to all the work.'

'It's no problem, really. It only took me a few hours, and it was good practice.'

'I'll pay you for the plans, of course.'

Chelsea came as close as she ever had to losing her temper with him. 'I don't want to hear another word about being paid, Burke,' she said sternly. 'I did it because I love you, and that's all the pay I need.'

Burke seemed chastened. 'Very well, Chelsea. If you insist.'

'That's the way it has to be. I think I'll go home now,' she said. 'I have to go to work tomorrow, you know, and I'm worn out.'

'Stop in anytime,' Helen said. 'But don't feel that you have to come, Chelsea. It sounds as if they'll be keeping me busy.'

Chelsea forced a smile. 'Just work hard at that therapy, and you'll be back at Hillhaven even before all your friends have a chance to visit you here.'

'Going home is a good goal,' Helen admitted. 'You aren't hurt about the house?'

'Heavens, no. I suspected that you might change your mind.' She dropped a quick kiss on Helen's cheek and waved goodbye to Burke.

Outside the door, she nearly fell over Nick, who was leaning against the corridor wall. 'So it was a house, and you did it for love,' he said softly. 'Is there anything you wouldn't do for Burke, my dear? For love, of course.'

'Don't you have anything better to do than eavesdrop outside hospital rooms, Nick?' she asked crossly. Why aren't you at home entertaining Vanessa, she wondered, and her heart ached.

'But I find out so many interesting things this way,' he pointed out, and dropped into step beside her as she started down the hall. 'And you even announced your devotion in front of Helen. Don't you feel a bit embarrassed about that?'

'Not in the least.' She looked at him defiantly. 'Why should I?'

'The scandal, of course. Just in case you change your mind about that little discussion we had, I'm still available,' he added. 'See you tomorrow, Chelsea.' He turned back towards Helen's room, leaving her standing, speechless, in the middle of the hall.

The apartment was dark; Judy was not yet home from her weekend trip. Chelsea hated the loneliness. How much her point of view had changed over the last few weeks, since that day when she had half-decided to look for an apartment of her own. Now she longed to have people around, to be kept too busy to think.

She put a frozen pizza in the oven and decided to spend the evening catching up on her professional journals. At least if she was absorbed in her reading, she couldn't be thinking about Nick.

She was still sitting at the dinette two hours later, but she had to admit the results had been mixed. She had turned a lot of pages, but she was glad she didn't have to take a test over the information she had absorbed.

Judy burst in, her dark eyes glowing, and seized Chelsea in a bearhug. 'Look!' she exclaimed, holding out her left hand. 'This is why Jim took me to visit his family!'

Jim had followed, a little more slowly, with Judy's luggage. 'I just wanted to have all of her attention when I proposed,' he told Chelsea modestly.

Chelsea dutifully admired the diamond ring. 'It's beautiful. When's the wedding?'

'Late summer.' Judy was bubbling over with happiness. 'Oh, Chelsea, I'm so happy!'

'I can see that,' Chelsea said gently.

Jim glanced at his watch. 'I'd better get home. See you at the office tomorrow, Chelsea.'

She retreated to her bedroom to let them have some privacy, and stood there in the dark staring out over the asphalt parking lot. One more thread that had held her to St Louis had been broken. She hadn't been looking forward to telling Judy that she was moving out of the city. Judy could not afford the big apartment without a roommate to split the expenses. But once Judy was married, Chelsea would have nothing to feel guilty about when she left.

When she returned to the living room, Judy had thrown herself down on the couch and was holding the new diamond up under the lamp, watching it fracture the light as she turned it back and forth.

'You look very happy,' Chelsea observed.

'Oh, darling, you have no idea! I've always wanted to marry Jim, but I thought I was just a pastime for him. When he proposed, he was so unsure of himself he was just like a little boy, and . . .' She paused. 'What's wrong, Chelsea?'

'Nothing. What could be wrong?'

Judy sat up straight. 'Is it Helen?'

'She's much better.'

'Then what . . . Oh. The apartment.' Judy bit her lip. 'I'm sorry. I just was so excited by my news that I didn't stop to think what it meant to you.'

'It isn't that, Judy. Really. I was trying to find a way to tell you that I'm leaving the city soon. Very soon, actually.'

'You're leaving St Louis? And the firm?'

'Yes. I'm going back to Norah Springs.'

'Back home? But why, Chelsea?'

Chelsea closed her eyes briefly. She could tell Judy the same story she'd been telling everyone else—but after the tears and laughter they had shared in the five years of their friendship, Judy deserved better than that. 'Because Nick Stanton is married.'

Judy started to laugh. 'And so is the governor of Missouri, but I don't see that influencing . . .' Her voice trailed off. 'You're actually serious, Chelsea!'

Tears burned in Chelsea's eyes. She tried to blink them away, and nodded. 'You were right, when you told me not to play games with him, that he'd hurt me. Well, I hurt myself, Judy.' She wiped the tears out of her eyes. 'Actually, it was pretty funny.'

'It really looks funny,' Judy said. Her voice was crisp.

'I took him to the Top of the Tower and ate lobster to show him that he couldn't afford me. That was a big joke. Next to Vanessa, I'm about as expensive as popcorn at the movies.'

'Vanessa? I didn't know anyone was actually named that.'

'She may not have been born with it, but it certainly fits. She's no amateur when it comes to spending money, that's certain.'

'Is she pretty?'

Chelsea pulled another tissue out of the box. 'Have you looked at the cover of VOGUE lately? That's the type. In fact, that's what she does for a living.'

'A model?' Judy whistled softly. 'She wasn't at that cocktail party. Nobody even said anything about her.'

'She is apparently a deep, dark secret. Nick's secretary didn't look surprised when Vanessa turned up in her office, so she must have known. But that woman doesn't confide in anyone. She even considers the time of day a secret.' She wiped her eyes again.

'None of the others knew, or it would have been all over the office.'

'How does one keep a Vanessa hidden? And why?'

'Apparently Nick didn't think it was anyone's business. Vanessa doesn't live here, anyway.'

Judy kicked off her shoes and curled up with her feet under her on the couch. 'If they're separated, Chelsea,' she began thoughtfully, 'there is such a thing as divorce, you know.'

'I know.' Chelsea's voice was miserable. 'I've thought about it. But Nick doesn't want to marry me, he just wants to have an affair.' She swallowed hard and pressed on. 'Even if he would divorce Vanessa for me . . .' She shook her head. 'I wouldn't want that. If he would leave her for me, then what happens to me next time he finds an attractive woman?'

'That's true. It's a risk.' Judy thought it over, and asked, 'Why doesn't she live here?'

'Her work is in New York, I suppose. One of the larger cities, at least. She certainly can't make much money modelling in St Louis.'

'Then why didn't he move there, instead of joining Shelby Harris? From what Jim says, Nick's good enough that he could work anywhere.'

'How should I know? I suppose he'd rather be one of the shining lights of architecture out here than to be lost in the crowd on the East Coast.'

Judy shrugged. 'It doesn't say too much for the marriage, does it? And if she isn't any more important to him than that . . .'

'She's recently become a lot more important, Judy.' Chelsea blotted tears off her cheeks, then pressed the tissue into a wad and threw it as hard as she could at the wastebasket. 'Vanessa is pregnant. And Nick isn't questioning whether the baby is his.'

'Oh, for heaven's sake, Chelsea. How can you be so calm about it?'

'This is calm?' Chelsea retorted. 'I'd like to bang my

head against that wall, but the landlord would make me pay for the damage.'

'Sorry, Chels.' Judy fought a yawn and lost. 'What a mess.'

'At any rate, that's why I'm going home. I don't dare stay here. I know what a rotten liar he is, and I still want him so badly that I . . . I can't trust myself.' Chelsea methodically began to shred the tissue box. 'I'm going to sit here a while, Judy. Go to bed if you want. You don't have to keep a watch on me; I'm not going to slash my wrists, or do anything crazy.'

'Good. Because no man is worth it.'

It brought a faint smile. 'Not even Jim?'

'No way,' Judy said firmly. 'No man is worth a slashed wrist, or even a banged head. You'll be all right.'

Chelsea's smile wavered. 'I have to be, don't I? I don't have any other choices left.'

Marie's good-morning smile was tinged with malice. Eileen's hello held a smug giggle. And the silence that fell in the employee lounge when Chelsea went in to get her first cup of coffee was too complete to be a coincidence. They knew about Vanessa, and they had drawn their own conclusions about Chelsea, too.

Oh, stop it, she told herself angrily, once she was barricaded in her own office. All those people may have their suspicions, but there is no evidence. On the other hand, if you go around here like a misunderstood Victorian heroine, everybody will know before lunch.

So she put on a cheery smile when she had to face any of them and spent the morning working on the Sullivan house. She'd met the main challenge of combining the best parts of her efficient and practical interior with Nick's dream-castle exterior before the Sullivans had even seen the rough drawings. Mostly it had been a matter of adjusting dimensions in one plan or the other. But now that it was time to finish the plans, there were an unbelievable number of details to fit in.

She was still struggling when Marie came in. 'I'm going to lunch, Miss Ryan. Do you want me to bring you something from the deli?'

She should go out, Chelsea knew. She should make an appearance to convince them that everything was normal. But why bother? Who cared what the office gossips thought? She wouldn't be around much longer to worry about it. Chelsea suddenly felt very tired. 'Please, Marie. Roast beef on rye with horseradish.'

She picked up the electric eraser again and took out the line she had just drawn in. Her idea of an adequate laundry room didn't want to fit anywhere in Nick's drawings. She picked up his floor plans again to see what he'd done with it.

She was working a lengthy maths problem on her calculator when there was a knock on her door. 'Come in,' she called absently, and didn't raise her eyes from the little machine. If I move that wall, she concluded, I can fit the laundry room in here . . .

'One roast beef on rye, with horseradish on the side, coming up.'

'Nick!' She sat absolutely still for a couple of seconds, trying to bank down the wave of joy that had instantly—embarrassingly—sparkled through her. By the time she raised her eyes to his, she was in control again. 'I didn't know you had become a messenger boy for Marie.'

He shrugged. 'I was standing in line at the deli when Marie said you were working through lunch again. I thought we could talk.' He set a brown bag down on her desk. 'I also brought you a salad, so you wouldn't miss out on your green vegetables today, and a carton of milk, because with all that other stuff you're asking for an ulcer.'

What does he want to talk about, she wondered warily.

'On rye, too, as if the sauce wasn't spicy enough,' he scolded.

'They make the best horseradish in the whole city. It's really very mild. Want to try some?'

'I'm having ham and cheese on white, Chelsea.'

'No spirit of adventure,' she sighed.

He raised an eyebrow a fraction, and his big blue eyes held a sudden gleam of humour. Chelsea thought her heart would break with longing, just looking at him.

'Is that a challenge?' he asked.

'Do you ever turn one down?'

'Rarely. Hand over the horseradish.'

She did. 'Is that why you keep asking me to have an affair with you? Because I'm a challenge?' She felt a little breathless.

He slanted a brief look at her and then smeared horseradish gingerly along the edge of his sandwich. 'You certainly are one,' he agreed.

'Hasn't anyone ever held out this long before?'

'Never. Hey, this stuff isn't half bad.'

'I told you.'

'Stop acting superior and drink your milk.'

'I want you to take a look at the Sullivan plans this afternoon. I think I have the problems solved, and we end up with the best of both designs.'

'Ha. That house was perfect just the way I drew it.'

'Without a laundry room? Don't clothes get dirty in your dream world, Nick?'

He looked chastened. 'So I overlooked something. Let's hit the Jonas Building plans this afternoon. They're due at the end of the week.'

Chelsea sighed. 'Must we?'

'What's the problem? Your condos are almost done.'

'Do you really think we're going to win this? We've put two weeks' work into it.'

'Nothing ventured, nothing gained, you know. Besides, how can we lose? Stanton and Ryan—it's an unbeatable combination.'

Chelsea bit her lip. His light-hearted comment seemed to catch at her throat. 'Why not Ryan and Stanton?' she asked, trying to deny the emotion that he'd roused merely by coupling their names. How silly can you be, Chelsea! she scolded herself.

He looked offended. 'That doesn't sound very liberated of you, Chelsea, wanting top billing. After all, I'm the senior partner.'

'You win.' You always win, Nick, she thought miserably. I can't keep fighting you much longer. 'Where do I start?'

The office was quiet, and not even Marie interrupted. Chelsea was making tracings of the condo floors, cleaning up her rough sketches so that Jim could do the final copies. She was beginning to regret the idealism that had made her design each of the condo units separately. If she had only fallen in with the usual procedure, she could have got by with drawing one floor and letting Jim duplicate it.

She'd almost forgotten Nick was even in the office until mid-afternoon, when he stretched, stood up, and said, 'Do you have any tapes lying around for that sound system?'

'In the bottom drawer of my desk.' She didn't even look up.

Cassette tapes rattled, and then Nick said, 'Vivaldi and Brahms with a sprinkling of hard rock and Dixieland jazz. You're a woman who can't make up her mind, aren't you?'

'No. I just enjoy variety.'

'Isn't that what I said?' The tape player clicked on and started to play a jazz number. Nick adjusted the volume and went back to his work.

For the rest of the afternoon they took turns choosing music, and the soothing strains seemed to speed the work along. The regular office noises subsided as Marie and the rest of the staff went home, and still Nick and Chelsea stayed, absorbed in the drawings. Chelsea's tracings were nearly completed when Nick said, 'Shall we break for dinner? I'll take you to Angelo's.'

'No.' Then, thinking that it hadn't been necessary to be quite so abrupt, Chelsea added, 'I'm almost finished.'

'Whatever you want.' He didn't seem upset, but Chelsea had to make a real effort to get her mind back on her work. She knew it would be foolish to go anywhere with him. Whether he behaved himself or not, she would only be hurt deeper by the memories of dinners when she hadn't yet known about Vanessa, when her love for him had been quietly growing. But another part of her would have gladly suffered any amount of pain to have that last evening with him.

It was growing late when Nick put in yet another Dixieland cassette, dropped the classical one they'd been listening to back in the drawer, and crossed the room to stand behind Chelsea. 'What I don't understand is this—if you like variety so well, why are you still saying no to me?' His hands rested lightly on her shoulders.

'Perhaps I just don't like people who pull rank on me,' she said. She was tired. She wanted only to go home.

'Come on. You never believed those threats, did you?'

'They sounded very realistic.' Chelsea rubbed a hand across the tight muscles at the nape of her neck.

'I would never have given those drawings to Carl. Besides, you could publish that cartoon in the local newspaper and he'd grit his teeth and smile, because he knows very well he can't afford to lose you.'

'I wouldn't like to test that idea.' Chelsea was staring at the paper on her drawing board. Her fingers were clenched on her pencil.

Nick unfolded her fingers and laid the pencil aside.

'Let's test this one, then, shall we?' He tipped her face up, his hand under her chin.

'You don't do things like this in the office,' she protested faintly.

'You drive all sense from my mind, Chelsea,' he said, very softly. His mouth was warm and firm and gentle, and the kiss teased at her senses. 'You taste like horseradish,' he murmured, against her lips, and kissed her again.

This is madness, she thought, and felt as if she were two people—the Chelsea who wanted to hold him close and kiss him with all the longing and love she possessed, but also the Chelsea who stood back and said, Remember Vanessa. Remember the baby . . .

She pulled away, feeling as if she was leaving her heart behind in his arms.

'Chelsea?' he questioned.

'Get away from me,' she ordered. Her voice was taut. 'Don't ever put a finger on me again, Nick Stanton. Do you hear me?'

'Loud and clear,' he agreed. He stalked back across the room to his drawings.

Her hands were shaking. She picked up her pencil, and then laid it aside. It's over, Chelsea, she thought. It's all over.

She sat there for a long time, making meaningless marks on a piece of scrap paper. She didn't want to leave, that was the problem, she realised. Even with the heavy atmosphere in the room just now, there was joy for her just in knowing that he was there, in seeing the sure movements of his pencil from across the room, in watching the set of his shoulders and the way he occasionally ran a hand back over the rumpled dark hair.

She wasn't even angry any more, just very sad. How dreadful it must be for him, she thought. Married to someone who didn't even want to live with him—and obviously caring very much about her. If he didn't love Vanessa, he would have left her; sentiment wasn't a part of Nick's character. In his own way, Chelsea realised, he was faithful to his wife. It didn't make the pain any easier to bear.

Finally she said, 'These are ready for Jim to start on in the morning, Nick. I'm going home.'

'Wait just a minute. Most of mine are finished, too. I just have to put the titles on this one.'

She watched as he labelled the main scale drawing in swift, sure strokes. The Jonas Building, Shelby Harris and Associates of St Louis, Missouri, she read over his shoulder. Below that, in smaller letters, he wrote Nicholas Stanton, Architect. Then for the first time his pen hesitated. 'Chelsea or C.J.?' he asked. 'You've signed your plans both ways.'

'Chelsea.' And she watched as he added her name directly under his. Not as a mere assistant, she saw through misty eyes, but as a partner.

For the first time, she found herself hoping, almost praying, that their design would win. For if it did, then their names would be linked together in the Jonas Building for all time. Future students of architecture would know that the Jonas renovation had been done by Stanton and Ryan.

It would be some kind of comfort, she thought, some sort of immortality for her love, to have their names remembered together, even if she never again saw this man she loved.

CHAPTER ELEVEN

'SHALL we have dinner at the club tonight, dear?' Sara Ryan brought the coffeepot over and refilled Chelsea's cup.

Dinner. I wish I'd had dinner with him that one last time, Chelsea thought. There wouldn't have been anything wrong with that. If only she had some real memories, not just these haunting dreams to keep hidden away forever in the back of her mind.

'Chelsea?' Her mother's tone was sharp.

'Dinner? Whatever you and Dad plan will be fine.'

Sara stared at her daughter, bit her lip, and sighed. Then she pulled a chair out across the table from Chelsea and sat down. 'Chelsea Jean Ryan,' she said, and her tone would have brought Marco Polo back from China. 'You have been home for almost two weeks now, and it's as if we're living with a ghost. What is the matter with you?'

'It's . . . overwork, I suppose, Mom.'

Sara gave a genteel little snort. 'I believed that for the first two days. But you've now had two weeks of relaxation and square meals. Instead of gaining weight and getting a tan, you're even thinner and paler than when you came. You obviously haven't slept in three days, Chelsea.'

'Do I look that good?' Chelsea wisecracked.

Sara frowned. 'It seems to me that you're suffering from depression.'

'Well, I'm not,' Chelsea said shortly. 'I'm just . . .' She didn't know how to go on.

'Waiting? For what?' Sara asked. 'Just when are you planning to start doing something?'

'I thought you wanted me to come home, Mother.'

'I do, Chelsea. I love having you here. But you are so obviously unhappy, dear. You're used to being busy. If you'd just make some plans for your future——'

'I have. I talked to Dad about renting that office in his building.'

'I know. But that was the night you came home, and you haven't been down there to look at it. You haven't the foggiest notion what you'll need to set up your practice.'

'What does it take to be an architect, Mom?' Chelsea asked, a bit cynically. 'A drawing board, a few sheets of paper, a couple of pencils and a client here and there.'

Sara ignored her. 'And you spend most of the day in your room. You haven't even enjoyed the pool.'

Chelsea flared, 'I don't want to lie beside the pool and think——' She stopped abruptly.

Sara let the silence lengthen. 'Think about what, Chelsea?' she asked gently. 'Why did you come home, honey? It was so sudden. Something is terribly wrong . . .'

You are so correct, Mom, Chelsea thought. What's wrong is that he's haunting me. Do you think I haven't tried to get him out of my mind? I can't even pick up a pencil, because when I do, it automatically draws his face. I can't lie out there beside the pool without remembering the first time he kissed me. I can't bear to think of a life without him, and so I don't even want to think at all. Can you understand that, Mother?

But she said nothing. She didn't want to explain it all, and so she chose to share none of it.

'I'll go look at the office, Mom.' Her voice was quiet and almost lifeless.

Sara sat there silently for a while, drinking her coffee. Finally she gave up, and Chelsea quietly went out to the gallery, to fling herself in a hammock and think some more.

Sara was right. Chelsea didn't blame her mother for being concerned. She knew quite well that she had been nothing more than a worry to both Josh and Sara for the last two weeks, with her moping about and her inattention to detail and her sleeplessness. She couldn't even carry on a conversation.

Perhaps she shouldn't have come home at all, she thought. Nick haunted this place, too, and her parents' concern was only leading Chelsea to a morbid suspicion that there might be something wrong with her mind.

At the very least, she should not have come home in the middle of the night like that. Sara suspected that something dreadful had happened, she knew, and she didn't know how to tell her mother that she had been running only from herself.

She and Nick had left the office together, after the Jonas Building drawings had been completed, and walked out to the parking ramp. That was all. He had said a curt goodnight as he left her unlocking the Mercedes, and he'd gone on to his car. Chelsea had held herself together till she was away from the ramp, but then the tears started to flow, the tears of hopelessness and sadness and heartbreak. She had gone back to the apartment, but it was empty, so she packed a few clothes, left a note for Judy, and started home to Norah Springs.

She would never forget the shock on her father's face when he had opened the door that night. It was the only thing that had brought laughter. She had asked him about the office, and then gone straight to bed, certain that the long drive, coming after the longer day, would bring welcome oblivion. But she had not slept.

Reluctantly, the next morning, she had called the office, hoping that Nick would not be there. She had her message all planned and rehearsed, but hearing his voice had thrown her into disarray. 'What is it,

Chelsea?' he had asked, and she had stammered out her answer.

'I'm not feeling well, Nick. I need a couple of weeks to rest, or I'm going to break down entirely.'

He had been silent for a long time, and Chelsea had finally summoned up all her courage and added, 'That wasn't entirely true, Nick. The truth is that I won't be coming back at all. I'll mail you my resignation.'

'Why, Chelsea?'

'Nick, I don't think my reasons are any of your concern.'

'Then you had damn well better think about it again,' he had said coldly. He had still been talking when she hung up on him. She had mailed the letter, which said only that she wasn't coming back and that she hoped the partners would understand why she couldn't give notice. She had dropped it in the mailbox on the corner, and washed her hands of St Louis, and Shelby Harris and Associates, and Nicholas Stanton, with relief.

And then she had gone home and dreamed of him, and awakened drenched with tears.

Perhaps her mother was right, she thought. If she forced herself to do something—anything at all—perhaps tomorrow there would be something she wanted to do. It was worth a try. There must be some activity that would require so much concentration that there would be no room left in her thoughts for Nick. Inaction certainly hadn't helped; perhaps action would.

The telephone rang, and her heart began to pound. When Sara came to the door, Chelsea was already shaking her head.

'It's Judy,' Sara said. She looked worried.

Chelsea pushed herself up out of the hammock. Stupid, she thought. Utterly silly to be frightened every time the phone rang. It could ring hundreds of times, and it would not be Nick.

'Hi, Judy.'

'Chelsea? Sara says you're wasting away to bare bones.'

Chelsea glanced over her shoulder to make sure her mother wasn't within hearing. 'You didn't tell her, did you?'

'About Nick? No, but I'm regretting that I promised not to tell her,' Judy countered. 'Silence certainly is doing you no good.'

'It's my business, Judy.'

'Well, that's absolutely correct. Justas long as you haven't wasted into a ghost by the time I get married. We moved the date up, by the way. Will you be a bridesmaid?'

'Sure.' Chelsea wished that she could work up some enthusiasm. 'Judy—is there any news?' She hated herself for even asking.

'About Nick, you mean? I shouldn't do this, but Jim said to tell you that he's been a real bear lately.'

'Did the Jonas drawings make the deadline?'

'Yes. And Jim packed up all of your personal things and brought them to the apartment. All except your mug.'

'My crystal one? What happened to it?'

'He said Nick lost an account the other day and he picked up your mug and threw it at the wall.'

'At least he didn't throw it at me,' Chelsea muttered.

'From what Jim saw, Nick would have liked to. There were too many pieces to pick up.'

'I ought to send him a bill. That was a birthday present, dammit. He had no right to break my crystal mug!'

'Go get him, tiger,' Judy applauded. 'At least there's some life in your voice now. When are you coming back?'

'Next week maybe, just long enough to pick up my things. I'll see you then.'

'All right. Jim and I will take you out for pizza.'

'Thanks, Judy.' Her voice was softer, and she was actually smiling when she cradled the phone.

Activity. That was the key. She felt as if the last two weeks had been a bad dream, and that she had just awakened. She refused to let Nick Stanton turn her into a recluse. 'I'm going to walk down to the office,' she called to her mother, and left the house without waiting for an answer.

The streets were quiet, the breeze whispering along the shaded lanes and tugging at the locks of Chelsea's hair, left to flow loose down her back. It was mid-June now, and summer had matured since she had come home. The leaves were huge and brilliant green on the maples. The sun lay hot on the asphalt streets, and children's laughter echoed across the lawns.

Chelsea turned towards the centre of town. She noticed a sign in an upstairs window that offered an apartment for rent. She supposed she would soon have to look for a place to live. Much as she loved her parents, it wasn't healthy to continue to stay with them. 'You're going to have to grow up someday, Chelsea,' she muttered, and turned down a side street to the quiet brick building that held her father's law practice.

His secretary was grey-haired, correct, utterly discreet, the perfect legal assistant. She looked Chelsea over with a raised eyebrow, and seemed to focus on her clothes. 'May I help you, Miss Ryan?' she asked.

The woman had always been able to make her feel inadequate, Chelsea thought. A spark of rebelliousness rose in her. What business of hers was it what Chelsea chose to wear? The faded old jeans were just right for climbing about in an empty building.

'I stopped to get the key for the office next door. And do you happen to have a tape measure? I forgot mine.'

The secretary fished the keys out of her desk. 'Mr

Ryan said some time ago that you'd be coming in,' she observed.

'And now I'm here,' Chelsea said sweetly. She held out her hand for the keyring.

'I'm afraid I haven't anything to measure with. This is a legal office, you see—not a construction company.'

Chelsea thanked her gravely and went back out to the sidewalk. As she let herself into the empty office, she told herself grimly, 'If I'm going to work next door to that woman, we are going to collide.'

The idea actually had some appeal. It was the first time in a week that she had felt any particular interest in anything.

The office smelled musty. It had been shut up for some time. Chelsea paced off the length of the reception room and wished that she had asked for paper and pencil. The secretary would probably have told her that she didn't have any to spare, Chelsea thought spitefully.

There were two small offices at the back, a tiny bathroom, and a hidden exit. 'Trust Dad,' she said. 'He would never have an office anywhere that didn't allow him to avoid the waiting clients on his way to the handball court!'

She would have liked to design this office complex. But it had been completed while she was still in college. Maybe someday I'll have my own, she thought. My own offices, with a sign above the door that reads Ryan and Stan . . .

She pulled herself up short, the ache in her throat almost choking her, and stood there gritting her teeth against the pain. Nick's name had come so automatically to her tongue that it frightened her. 'Chelsea Ryan and Associates,' she said firmly. Her voice seemed to echo in the empty room.

Well, for right now it would be Chelsea Ryan without associates. She would even have to be her own draughtsman at first, until the business started to build. That part of it she wouldn't like at all.

She paced off the rooms. She'd have to come back with a tape and get the exact dimensions before she could even look at furniture. A desk and chair would probably be all she needed, for right now. Her drawing board was still in St Louis, at the apartment. Some filing cabinets, perhaps. It would take little enough to get started.

'Chelsea?' her father called from the front door. 'Are you in here?'

'Sure, Dad.' She came out of the back office, brushing dust off her hands. 'Don't you believe in cleaning ladies?'

'Not for empty buildings.' The relief on his face when he saw her smile touched Chelsea's heart. 'Have lunch with me? I'll buy you a tenderloin and fries at the club.'

Chelsea smiled. It was the bribe he had always offered in her childhood. 'French fries are in violation of my diet, Dad. Besides, they won't let me in. I'm wearing jeans.'

'We can go to the grill. And I'll let you have a salad instead of the fries.'

If he says anything about eating my green vegetables, Chelsea thought, I'll start to cry. You are such a sentimental fool, she told herself sternly. You can't give up lettuce forever just because Nick once bought you a salad.

For the first time, she made a real effort to bury him in the back of her mind. Josh seemed to recognize her struggle, and he exerted himself to be charming. By the time they left the country club, Chelsea's sides ached from laughing, and she felt more like her old self than she had in weeks.

'I'll drive you home,' Josh offered.

'I can walk if you have something important to do.'

He shook his head. 'I'm just playing tennis this afternoon.'

'Oh. The truth is, you have to go home to change clothes anyway.'

'Something like that,' he agreed.

The sun roof was open on his sports car today, and the breeze tugged at Chelsea's hair. It felt good. She thought about taking the Mercedes out this afternoon, putting the top down, and then speeding along the country roads.

Or perhaps while new ambition was still bubbling, she should measure the office and go look at furniture. Tomorrow she might find herself in the dumps again.

No, she decided. She wasn't going to be in the dumps any more. She had wasted too many days now in mourning Nick Stanton. It would take a long time to get over him, she knew, but she didn't have to hide herself away from the world to grieve.

Her mother was on the gallery with Elise Bradley. They were drinking coffee, and between them on the table was a watercolour of a sailboat on a lake. It had been painted by Elise, Chelsea diagnosed the instant she saw it. Sara had never painted anything so awful in her life.

'Hello, dear,' her mother said. 'Nick called right after you left.'

Chelsea swallowed hard. 'Oh?' She nodded a greeting at Elise.

'The number is beside the kitchen phone. I told him you'd call him at the office as soon as you came in.'

'I wonder if it's about the civic centre,' Elise speculated. 'Or perhaps it's something else.' Her tone was sly. 'I must say, Chelsea, everybody expected when you came home that Nick would spend his weekends here at least.'

'Why should he?' Chelsea asked quietly.

Elise tittered. 'It was fairly obvious, my dear. The two of you made such a cute couple. Didn't they, Sara?'

'I'm afraid I didn't pay any attention.' Sara pushed a plate across the table. 'Have another cookie, Elise.'

'Oh, I shouldn't. But . . .'

'Have you talked to your kids lately?' Sara pressed on ruthlessly. 'Will they be home this summer?'

Thank God for mothers to come to the rescue, Chelsea thought, and went down the hall to her room. What could Nick want now, she wondered. He should have received her resignation letter ten days ago, and there had been nothing but silence ever since. She couldn't imagine why he would be calling now. But if it wasn't her resignation, what could it be?

She almost didn't make the phone call, but she knew that Sara would catch up with her later if she didn't. She was shaking as she listened to the clicks as her call traced through the electronic jungle to Nick's office. And her voice trembled as she asked for him.

But his secretary said he wasn't there. 'He didn't tell me where he was going, Miss Ryan. I think perhaps he's out on the construction sites.'

'Thanks. Tell him I called.' Chelsea put the phone down, feeling as if she had broken her last connection with him.

Then she tried to shake herself out of the mood. Time to do something daring, she thought, and put on a brief swimsuit. Someday she was going to have to face that swimming pool. It might as well be today.

The water lay still and cool under the blazing sun. Chelsea dived in and swam laps as fast as she could, trying to tire herself out. Exhaustion came far sooner than she had expected, and she sat breathing hard on the edge of the pool for a few minutes, trying to recover. 'You're out of shape, Chelsea Ryan,' she told herself glumly, and reached for her sunscreen lotion. Wasn't talking to oneself the first classic symptom of mental disorder?

'The shape still looks pretty good to me,' a husky voice said behind her.

Chelsea turned around and lost her balance. She had to grab at the edge of the pool to keep from falling in. She pushed her wet hair back off her forehead and whispered, 'Nick? Oh, my God, now I'm having hallucinations.'

But the man standing at the edge of the pool beside her didn't look like a delusion. Instead he looked tough, as handsome as ever, and very substantial indeed.

'You're not seeing things, Chelsea. I'm really here.'

'Why?' she whispered.

He smiled faintly. 'Because I'm the most junior of the senior partners, I suppose. I've been covering for you for two weeks, Chelsea, but . . .'

'Well, isn't that sweet of you.' Her voice dripped sarcasm. She ignored his outstretched hand and got to her feet by herself. She pulled on her towelling robe and lay down on the chaise, her eyes closed. 'I'm so grateful.'

'If you'd let me finish my sentence, Chelsea?'

She shrugged and kept her eyes closed.

'Nobody else in that office can do your job. Hell, any two of us couldn't keep up with your work.'

'I told you I was overworked and exhausted.'

'I even lost the Sullivans. They decided to buy stock blueprints from some service in California, and build an ordinary split-level.'

'Is that why you broke my crystal mug?' She glanced up and saw the surprise on his face. 'I still have sources, Nick.'

He was silent. Finally Chelsea said, 'I half-expected they'd do that.'

He sighed. 'I suppose I should have seen it coming. It's cheaper—at least it looks that way at the beginning. And old Charlie does keep a close eye on his dollar.'

'It wasn't the money, Nick. It was the house. We drew it for each other, not for the Sullivans.' Then, as she heard what she had said, Chelsea flushed and squirmed a little in her chair. 'I mean, we had our eyes on the competition, not on the what the clients wanted. Of course they didn't like it; it wasn't their kind of house.' She lay back with a sigh and looked up at him. 'I couldn't have held them either, Nick. Don't blame yourself.'

He rubbed a hand across the back of his neck. 'I could shoot myself for interfering. If I'd left you alone, you could have done something fantastic for them.'

'Did you come up here to tell me that?'

'No. I came up to ask you to come back to work. What do you want, Chelsea? What arrangements can we make?'

She closed her eyes and let the silence lengthen. Finally she said, her voice so weary that there was no room for emotion, 'I want to be left alone. I don't want to see you again, Nick.'

'Look, I'm sorry it had to be me. But I could hardly tell Carl Shelby, when he asked me to come, why I didn't think you'd listen to me. So please just pretend I'm someone else and listen to what I have to say.'

Pretend he was someone else? When every sensitive nerve ending knew exactly where he was, and how close to her, even when her eyes were closed? When her hands, with a mind of their own, wanted to reach out to him and pull him down beside her on the lounger?

'So sit down and say it,' she murmured.

'I'm a heel.' He pulled a lounge chair up opposite hers.

'You certainly are.'

'A rotten scum.'

'That, too.'

He ran a hand through his hair. 'A misguided fool.'

'Absolutely.'

'At least we now have something we agree on,' he said, with a half-humorous note in his voice. 'What do you need to make you come back to the firm, Chelsea? A raise? An assistant? Two assistants?'

'No. No. And no.'

He went on ruthlessly. 'A partnership?'

'They are desperate, aren't they?' she asked curiously. She didn't look at him.

'Ive been authorised to give you anything you want, Chelsea.'

Except the one thing I want most, and that one I can't have, she thought. 'No, Nick.'

'I need you to help design the civic centre for Norah Springs.'

'What is this, Nick? A sudden attack of humility? It doesn't sound like you. Take two aspirins—you'll feel better in the morning.'

There was a brief silence. 'There is one more thing you should know. We won the Jonas competition.'

She opened her eyes at that. 'I haven't seen it in the papers.'

'And you won't for a while. It isn't official yet; they just called me this morning.'

'Is that the real reason you came up here?'

'It's part of it,' he admitted. 'I need you, Chelsea. I can't do it without you.'

She shook her head. 'That's not true, Nick. Any competent builder can read those blueprints. You certainly can.'

'Could you carry it through, when you're half of a team?' He paused, and added quietly, 'If you don't come back, I will forfeit the contest.'

'On purpose?' She studied his face. 'No, you won't, Nick. It means too much to you.'

'You still won't come? Why Norah Springs, Chelsea?'

She looked around as if curious herself. 'I'm a country girl at heart. And I'm tired of the pace in the city, and the workload. Is that reason enough?'

'When you put it that way,' he admitted, 'I almost want to join you. Is your decision final?'

'Yes.' Goodbye, my love, she wanted to say.

He sighed and ran a hand through already rumpled hair. 'I imagine Burke will try to persuade you.'

'He's welcome to try. In case you're worried about how you stand with Carl Shelby, you can relax. Burke won't be able to convince me either.' Then she realised abruptly that there had not been even a hint of sarcasm in his voice.

'Helen sent you her love,' Nick added.

She sat up slowly. 'Don't tell me. You finally figured out that Burke and I are not having an affair.'

A half-smile tugged at the corner of his mouth. 'Burke convinced me.'

'How did he do it? I've tried for weeks.'

Nick said reluctantly, 'I finally confronted him about it. He laughed till I thought he was going to have a heart attack.'

'That's hardly flattering,' Chelsea mused. 'But I suppose if it worked, I should be thankful.'

'Even Burke thinks you should give me a second chance.'

'I trust Burke doesn't know all the details. Tell Carl that I really appreciate the offer, Nick.'

'They'd rather have you than your appreciation.'

She shook her head.

Nick sighed. 'I guess that's that. I brought these back.' He dropped an envelope in her lap.

She opened it, and the caricatures slid out on to the table. 'No more blackmail?'

'No. I want you to come back with me, but not that way.'

'That's generous.' She flipped through the pile. 'One is missing, Nick.' She could see it in her mind, the sketch of Mount Rushmore with Nick as one of the great stone faces.

'I didn't think you'd begrudge me that one, Chelsea.'

She swallowed hard. 'Keep it, if you like,' she said.

'But as long as we're talking about personal property—you still have the top of my swimsuit.' She fought against the blush that was rising in her cheeks.

'Sorry. That's a souvenir of a very special woman.'

'Nick, give it back. It . . .'

'Chelsea, let me finish. Please?'

She sighed and leaned back in her chair, her eyes closed. 'Help yourself.'

There was a catch in his voice as he said, 'Thanks for the invitation. I think I'll do that.' An instant later, she felt his weight on the side of her chair, and before she could struggle or even catch her breath, he was kissing her with a gentle fierceness that sent lightning flickering along every nerve.

She couldn't stop herself. If she had had a chance to prepare for the onslaught, she might have exercised iron self-control. But instead, her will power shattered under that sudden, demanding kiss. She found herself responding gladly to the pressure of his mouth, and eagerly accepting his caresses when he impatiently pushed aside the towelling robe.

'I knew I was right, Chelsea,' he whispered, as his mouth brushed her earlobe. 'We are magic together. There's a certain something between us . . .'

And her name was Vanessa. The thought echoed through Chelsea's mind. Then she braced both hands against his chest and pushed as hard as she could.

Nick was stunned. 'What's wrong, darling?'

'Don't call me that,' Chelsea said between clenched teeth. She struggled out of the chair and stood at the edge of the pool, her head up, staring at him with defiance. 'Get out of here, Nick,' she warned, 'or I will scream.' She was breathing hard.

'Why?' he demanded. 'Just answer that for me, Chelsea. How can you turn your back on what we share?'

'Oh, you poor innocent dear,' she mocked. 'And just what would we share, if I came back? An office every day? A bed every night—except when Vanessa comes to town?' Her voice rose sharply till she was almost screaming at him. 'And what am I supposed to do then, Nick? Pretend that I don't know you? Call you Mr Stanton and exchange social chit-chat at the office parties with your wife?'

'Oh, my God,' he said.

'You didn't expect Vanessa to show up, did you?'

'Vanessa's chief charm is her unpredictability,' he agreed. 'Nobody ever expects anything from Vanessa. That way they are seldom disappointed.'

'I don't know what kind of a marriage that is, but I want no part of it.'

He sat down in the lounge chair and linked his hands behind his head. 'Is that why you were so cold those last few days? Vanessa?'

She was stunned. 'Isn't that enough reason?'

'So Burke was right. He thought that you were attracted to me. But I was sure you couldn't forgive me for thinking that you'd slept your way into that job. Funny, that I could be so blind,' he mused.

'Absolutely hilarious,' Chelsea muttered.

'I didn't even realise what was happening to me. It was plain old jealousy, Chelsea. I didn't just want to sleep with you; I wanted all of you—heart and soul as well as body.'

Her whole body was throbbing with the rhythm of his words. 'Go to hell, Nick Stanton!'

'I'll give you back the swimsuit top when you marry me,' he said. His tone was conversational.

'Didn't you hear me, Nick?'

'I heard you. Being married to a redhead just might be hell on earth—but I'm willing to risk it. Because, you see, I love you, Chelsea.'

'I will not marry a man who divorces his wife for me, Nick. I'd be afraid that the next time a pretty face came along——'

'Vanessa is my sister-in-law,' he said quietly.

'He'd divorce me, too. My God, Nick, she's pregnant! What did you say?'

'Vanessa is my brother's wife,' he said, enunciating each word carefully. 'She's Mrs Stanton, all right. Mrs Nate Stanton.'

Chelsea sat down, hard, in her lounge chair.

Nick smiled at her equably. 'There's a Mrs Miles Stanton, too. She's my other brother's wife. Just because you are an only child doesn't mean everybody is, Chelsea.' His tone was fond.

Judy had told her that, she thought. She had said something at that long-ago cocktail party at Hillhaven about Nick being one of three brothers. Chelsea vaguely remembered making a flip comment about the difficulty of dealing with Nick Stanton in triplicate . . .

Nick smiled angelically at her and went on, 'And then of course there's my mother. I must warn you that as Mrs Stanton you'll be one-fourth of a remarkable group. But you'll be the only Chelsea. And you'll always be the only one I want.'

'Why did she . . .' Chelsea swallowed hard and started over. 'Why did she come to you? Vanessa, I mean—about the abortion?'

He raised an eyebrow.

'I heard you talking about it at Angelo's,' Chelsea admitted.

'I see. Do you know, if we could come up with a lightweight material that is truly soundproof we could sell the manufacturing rights and retire wealthy?'

'I don't care, Nick. Tell me about Vanessa.'

'She was trying out the idea on me before she broke it to Nate.'

'It isn't your baby?' Chelsea whispered.

He looked offended. 'You have obviously never met my big brother. The expression is not simply a matter of birth order, you see. He outweighs me by thirty pounds. I am not crazy enough to tangle with Nate, Chelsea. Certainly not over Vanessa.'

She was shivering, despite the heat. She ducked her head and put her hands to her hot cheeks.

Nick glanced at his watch and stood up. 'Well, if we have everything straightened out,' he said calmly, 'I'd better be on my way back to St Louis. Unless you plan to offer me a reason to stay.' His eyes were disturbingly warm.

'Dinner at the country club?' she whispered.

He shook his head firmly. 'Not good enough. You're a tease, Chelsea Ryan.'

She held out a hand, and he pulled her to her feet. 'Will you come back to work?' he asked, suddenly serious.

Chelsea nodded. 'I did want to come home, to be on my own, Nick. But I would never have left if it hadn't been for you. To be near you, but not with you—I couldn't bear that.' Her voice broke as she finished the confession.

He pulled her close, and for the first time Chelsea went into his arms willingly, tugging his head down, clasping her hands at the back of his neck. 'I love you, Nick,' she whispered as her lips met his.

They were both trembling by the time he loosened his hold. 'That will do for a reason to stay,' he said, and laughed shakily. 'As a matter of fact, just try to get rid of me now!'

She let her fingers wander through his disordered dark hair. His hands were warm on the curve of her waist, under the towelling robe. 'Chelsea—if you want to come back to Norah Springs . . .'

She shook her head. 'Wherever you are is good enough for me, Nick.'

'The Jonas Building will take a couple of years. It will give us a chance to build a reputation as a team, and then, if you want, we can move up here.'

'Could we?'

'Of course. We'll be working all over the country anyway. And this must be a great place to raise kids.'

He laughed delightedly as the hot colour swept over her face. 'Chelsea, you're going to have to stop doing that. When my brothers find out how easy it is to make you blush, they'll never let you have a moment of peace.'

'And build a house, Nick? Our house?'

'If you like. It will take at least a couple of years for us to agree on the drawings.'

She let that one pass. 'And we'll start our own firm, too. I can see it now, Ryan and Stanton . . .' She darted a playful look up at him.

He frowned. 'Stanton and Ryan,' he countered, and then kissed her. 'Or better yet, Stanton and Stanton. Then nobody will ever know who comes first. Not even us.'

'It will do,' Chelsea murmured, and put her head down on his shoulder.